Firewater
Pond

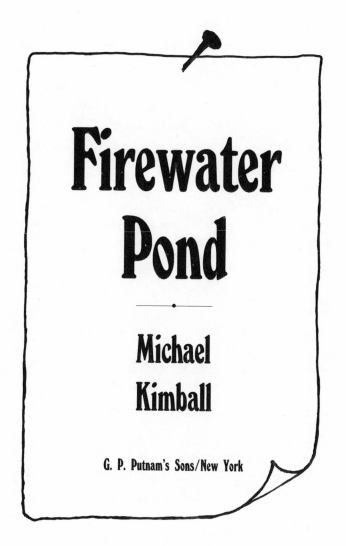

Firewater
Pond

Michael
Kimball

G. P. Putnam's Sons/New York

G. P. Putnam's Sons
Publishers Since 1838
200 Madison Avenue
New York, NY 10016

The author gratefully acknowledges permission from East/Memphis Music Corp. to reprint lyrics from "(Sittin' On) The Dock of the Bay." Words and music by Steve Cropper and Otis Redding, © 1968 & 1975 East/Memphis Music Corp.

Library of Congress Cataloging-in-Publication Data

Kimball, Michael.
  Firewater Pond.

  I. Title.
PS3561.I4163F5   1985   813'.54   85-12417
ISBN 0-399-13081-0

Printed in the United States of America
   2   3   4   5   6   7   8   9   10

To Harry and Lois
For Their Stories

Loving Thanks to my wife, Glenna, and children, Jesse and Sarah, for their support and sacrifices while I wrote my book; and for doing my chores

Special Thanks to my companions and comrades for their assistance and encouragement: Joan Bourassa, Ron Bourassa, Don Congdon, Glenna Kimball, Tabitha King, Bo Marks, Art Mayers, Ellis Percy, John Pierce, Terry Plunkett, Jean Riccardi, and Justin Smith; more thanks to George Fergusson for his computer help; Justin Smith and Ron Gaibl for talking me through the white water; Tom and Debby Rainey for the loan of their air conditioner; and Ace Mechanic Arthur Cooley for fixing my cars

My Deepest Appreciation to Steve King for his generosity and Good Spirit in everything he's done for me, including

Introducing me and my book to my editor Alan Williams and my agent Howard Morhaim, both of whom I also Warmly Thank for taking me on

Contents

"Honour is a luxury for aristocrats, but it is a necessity for hall porters."
—G. K. Chesterton

"Everythin' happens cuzza somethin' else."
—Harvey Duckoff

Part
One

1

Fried Egg Man

Carl Mason was a fried egg man—always had been. So much so that he saw—subconsciously—fried eggs everywhere: daisies in a vase, the light globe on his bedroom ceiling, even his wife's breasts sometimes gave him that fried egg feeling. Today it was the sun, burning through a white early morning sky. Carl turned from the window and stoked the woodstove with a couple of split birch logs, humming. He opened the draft. He took his breakfast plate out of the cabinet and set it on the woodstove to heat, then went to the counter and plugged in the electric coffeepot (Shirley always filled it with ground coffee and water before she went to bed at night). He readied two pieces of white bread in the toaster. He went to the electric range in the middle of the kitchen and turned the front burner on, taking care to set the dial between the E and the D of the words MEDIUM LOW (favoring the E). Precision frying: A man's day was shaped by the quality of his eggs. He put a wide, cast-iron frying pan on the front burner and dropped a wad of butter in to melt.

The kitchen brightened. Sunlight swept across the linoleum and warmed his heels. He turned as he waited for the frying pan to heat and gazed out the window at the band of his pond, flickering in the sunlight. It was a small pond, old and probably overused through the years. But it was gorgeous—craterlike on three sides—bordered by a tall, steep, pine-topped ridge on the right, and by long, dark, evergreen hills on the left and across. Only Carl's side of the pond was lowland, and that was a gently sloping, tree-dotted three acres of family campground. And every square foot of it—plus the ridgeland on the right and the long hill on the left—more than two hundred acres—belonged to him. His humming turned syllabic: "Dum, dum, dum, da-da-da dumm, dumm . . ."

Butter pooled in the frying pan. He spread it around with a spatula. Then he waltzed to the counter and pushed his toast down, grabbing a coffee mug out of the cupboard in the same motion. He set the mug on the woodstove to heat, then returned to the range by way of the refrigerator with two jumbo brown eggs in his hand. He cracked his first egg on the rim of the frying pan and opened the egg low inside the pan, lifting his wrists with a pianist's grace so that the eggmass eased out onto the hot cast-iron and spread into a perfect, whitening, yoke-centered disk. The coffee perked merrily; its smell filled the kitchen. Carl sang softly: "Oh what a beautiful morning . . ."

He cracked the second egg and deftly laid it beside the first. ". . .Oh what a beautiful day. . . ." He noticed a tiny, wedge-shaped piece of shell floating on the perimeter of his second egg and tried to snare it with a corner of his spatula, but it eluded him. He tried to press the shell piece against the pan and muscle it out of his egg, but the unwhitened gel followed his spatula and encircled his first egg. "Shit," he said softly. He slid the spatula under the first egg to free it from the second, but the second clung to the first and ripped so that its gel ran through the rip and spread to the edges of the frying pan, sizzling. The toast popped. "Balls," Carl said. He set both eggs back down and cut around the first, freeing it from the clutches of the second. Then he flipped the first and set it gently on a bare section of the pan: a near perfect fried egg. His second egg was showing signs of trouble, though. It was paper-thin and crisping around the edges; he decided he'd have to flip it, despite its un-cooked center. He slid the spatula underneath and lifted it, but, as he feared, the middle was too runny. It gathered and started rolling off the spatula. He tried to flip it quickly, to drop the egg in its rightful place, but he wasn't fast enough. The egg curled and dropped, gray and leering, onto the first, spilling its yoke over the top. "Jesus Christ!" Carl yelled, spinning away from the stove, flinging beads of egg yoke around the kitchen.

And that's when he spotted something outside the window, something wrong in his campground. He went to the window and peered out across the Camp Road to the pavilion area. "What the hell?" he said. He opened the door and hollered, "Hey!" He grabbed his blue baseball cap off the wall and ran outside. "Hey!" he hollered.

2

The End of Sex

Luthor Ellis was cracking up and didn't know it—didn't suspect a thing. One idea, as always, followed another, each complete from beginning to end. But—and this alone might have clued him—for once his ideas were bearing fruit. He was, as he put it, consummatin'. In fact he was downright purposeful—one might even say artistic—so much so that the big black man mentally signed each new work in a bold, blood-red scrawl: Nighthawk.

Of course his weird behavior had been more evident to his wife Trudy. She had skeptically watched him quit drinking—pour half a fifth of bourbon down the privy hole and swear off the firewater, as he called it, cold turkey. And worse, he had sworn off sex. "I am man. I am woman," he had told her. "I need no squaw."

He began spending his days up on the ridge above the pond, practicing with a bow and arrows he had bought at K-Mart. "This land will again be ours one day," he said to her, "as it once was."

Even their three children saw the change: Dad went around these days in only a torn bedsheet or a towel drawn around him in a loincloth. He buried the TV; buried all his clothes with the cassette player, so that the yard around their cabin began to look like sacred ground, ornamented with small mounds of earth and cryptic markers everywhere. He told the children countless tales of his grandfather, Running Bird, stories they knew from the start were fabricated. (Luthor's grandfather had indeed been a quarter Passamquoddy named Benedict Arnold Ellis after Maine's most famous Revolutionary War hero. He had worked all his life in a northern paper mill and died in his thirties of liver poisoning—too much firewater.)

Trudy fled with the children in the middle of one night when she awoke and found Luthor (he never slept) painting lipstick stripes across his cheeks.

"Me Nighthawk," he said into the mirror with glazed eyes.

"You're fucked up," she replied softly, and left.

He carried out the last of his magazine collection the next morning—eight years of *White Slaves*—and threw them onto the enormous pile he had made in the pavilion area, just above the pond.

It was a pornographile's dream heaped there in the dirt, page corners lapping capriciously in the slight morning breeze. Beneath the *White Slaves*, for starters, was a complete collection—thirteen years—of *Black Mamas*; and beneath them, in the bowels of the mound, were thousands of the over-the-counter variety of male magazines—*Playboy, Penthouse, Gent, Duke, Sir, Club, Hustler*—while spilling down the sides were thousands more of the behind-the-counter variety—small glossy numbers like *Black Bitches in Bondage, Rex and the Princess, Rex in the Girls' Reformatory, Rex at the Roller Derby, Rex and the Vet's Assistant*. Every perversion was covered.

Luthor Ellis had been a drunk and a poor, lustful soul who never did a day's work after Vietnam, who let his wife clean the houses of young white social climbers in town to supplement his disability checks and her own ADC payments—who never consummated a thing.

But Luthor Ellis was dying, near permanently gone this morning. And the man that stood there in his place, tall and righteous, soaking the base of that great pyramid of pornography with gasoline, this noble black man clad only in a Holiday Inn loincloth, was being reborn: *Nighthawk*.

"Hey!" It was Carl Mason, the campground owner and landlord, a man from another world, another time, and he was coming fast. "What the hell are you doing?" he said, kicking at the discarded gasoline can to gauge its emptiness.

Nighthawk ignored him. He dropped slowly to his knees, gathered two sticks from beside the pyre, and began methodically rubbing them together—one vertically pressed against an old pine shingle, the other bowing against it.

"No fires in the pavilion area," Mason said. "You know that." At first he had not realized what Nighthawk was intending to torch. That it was a mountain of magazines was of course obvious, but it wasn't until he came face to face with *Babysitter's Delight* and *Nursing Pixies* that he fully understood.

He grabbed Nighthawk's arm with both hands and felt a fearsome machine, hard and driving. He drew back. "Stop it," he warned—much as one would warn a slinking Doberman. "These magazines are Camp Property."

He turned away then and whistled through two fingers—Bowery Boys style. "Harvey!" he called.

Then to man: "I mean it now, Ellis." But the Nighthawk crazed black man kept stoking. So Carl took a different tack: "Okay, look, here's my offer—a week's free rent for the magazines . . . and a case of beer . . . all right, two cases then."

Across the Camp Road a trailer door banged open and Harvey Duckoff leaped over his half cinderblock porch step, running full tilt to his boss, holding his red pajama bottoms up as he ran.

Carl glanced at him, at his pale bony chest, his matted brown hair, his droopy bee-colored eyes, his flap ears that attached like flags to the sides of his head—glowing red now as the boy came with his back to the low morning sun. Carl was glad the boy wasn't his own.

"Yo, Mr. Mason, what's up?" he panted.

"Yeah, Harvey, save these magazines before he torches 'em all. Make another pile over there."

As Harvey grabbed a handful of magazines, Carl turned again to Luthor Ellis. He implored with upturned palms: "Look, Ellis, you've got a fortune here, for crissakes. Don't burn 'em." But Nighthawk wasn't listening. So Carl lumbered up to the top of the mound and began chucking armloads of magazines down onto the safe pile. He was tough, a plug of a man—compact and strong as a boar. But as he worked, the gasoline fumes snaked into his lungs and brain, and he began feeling airy and queer.

Below him Nighthawk squatted, furiously bowing the sticks in short, blurred strokes like a wild African fiddler. A quiver of arrows plumed in pulsating reds, yellows, and blues danced on his back, and gleaming beads of sweat rolled off his nose and broke onto his hands as he worked. Carl thought of diamonds, of *National Geographic*, and hurled another armload of pornography into the air. Then he noticed a thread of smoke rise from the sticks. "Jesus Christ," he whispered. He clutched an armload of magazines to his body and rolled down the pile, and picked himself up and swaggered unsteadily to Nighthawk.

"Let's go," he said, throwing his right thumb over his shoulder. "Out!"

Nighthawk raised his face slowly, cast a dark shining eye on Carl, and smiled, chilling the red-faced man. *Voodoo.* Nothing scared Carl like a crazy man, and this crazy man was five crazy men.

"Woo-woo-woo!" Harvey called. "Hey, Mr. Mason, woo-woo." He danced around Nighthawk, holding a centerfold for Carl to see. It was from *Garden Fresh*: A large, freckled woman in pigtails displayed the bulbous end of a crookneck squash from her vagina. Her thighs were puckered with cellulite. She wore high black sneakers. Her vagina was rouged. "Woo-woo-woo!" Harvey said.

"Harvey! Get up there and throw 'em off, a bunch at a time, for crissakes. You can read 'em later." Then to Nighthawk: "All right, Ellis. Last chance. These magazines are Camp Property. They're on my land. . . . Faster, Harvey! Use two hands!"

Pages, torn and flesh-colored, scattered across the campground now in a steady morning breeze. Some floated like loons across the surface of the pond, while others tumbled along the grass and clung to trees and bushes.

"All right, that's it !" Carl said. He snatched the blue baseball cap off his head and bunched it in his hand. He turned toward the Camp Office and feigned a step. "I'm calling the cops on you, Ellis."

Then, still gazing into the smoking sticks, the black man moved his lips. "Luthor Ellis is dead," he seemed to say, but the low breath of his voice was carried off by the wind. Carl scowled and leaned toward him, trying to eke meaning out of the message, when he suddenly raised his painted face with such drama that goosebumps skittered up Carl's sides. The black Indian breathed: "Nighthawk lives!"

The timing was God-perfect—a tiny spark jumped out of the smoke, and a deep, fiery blast blew Carl back against a blue spruce, fighting for breath against the blinding heat. The flames roared twenty feet in the air, surrounding a faint, dancing silhouette at the top of the mound. "Woo! Woo! Woo!" it called.

"Just save what you can, Harvey, then get outta there!" Carl hollered.

A flaming magazine flew off the pyre, then another, and then Harvey himself followed, falling down the flaming mountain with a stack of burning magazines in his hands. "Waa! Waa! Waa!" he cried.

"Into the pond, Harvey" Carl yelled, pointing, and Harvey ran, trailing his flaming pajama pants from one ankle. He entered the pond on his knees, sizzling, then flipped onto his back under water, still holding the smoldering magazines safely in the air.

Just then Harvey's wife, Jean, appeared at the bonfire. She was curious. She was excited. She eagerly began feeding the blaze with saved magazines.

"Don't do that," Carl said resignedly. (He had once watched Harvey and Jean Duckoff try to squeeze an eight-track tape cartridge into their car's cassette deck. By the time they had given up, they had broken not only the cartridge, but the cassette player and the car's antenna.)

"What?" she grinned, tossing on a *Beaver*.

A distant cry pierced the crackle of flames: "Ayyee! Ayyee!" It was Nighthawk, high up on the ridge above the right side of the pond, dwarfed by distance and obscured by smoke, but plainly naked, waving his longbow in the air.

Carl shot his middle finger high above his head. "You keep right on goin', you crazy bastard!" he hollered through cupped hands, crouching for volume. "And don't come back!"

"Ayyee!" Nighthawk whooped. Then he turned and disappeared into the woods.

Above Carl's head a scrawny blue spruce suddenly crackled into flame. It squealed violently and in a second was totally engulfed, throwing off heat and sparks and a strangely satisfying fragrance of campfire.

Jean giggled at the cover of *Transsexual Temptations* and tossed it on the bonfire.

Carl smiled warmly at her and cocked his head. "You know, you're a real friggin' idiot," he said sincerely, as the flaming cover of *Forbidden Sex Digest* lifted off the pyre and sailed onto the open window of a nearby cabin.

Wind In The Pines

CAMP WIND IN THE PINES
Swimming, Fishing, Boating, Hiking, Picnics
HOOKUPS
Nightly, Weekly, Seasonal, Year Round

The sign was badly weathered. Only a shadow of paint remained, though the sign couldn't be seen anyway, hidden as it was by the cover of leaves that had grown up in front of it. It hung low on a dead elm on the River Road where a rutted dirt road abruptly left the highway and cut into the woods, apparently leading nowhere. At the dirt road's entrance, beside a large gray mailbox, was another sign spiked into a utility pole. Its letters had once been red:

UNWaNTeD PeTS LaiD AWay
See EarL ROOT—DOWN THe ROaD

An arrow pointed up the pole, meaning down the Camp Road.

Still a third sign was visible, if only for a couple of hours each week. The poster, in bold black letters on white, would say:

SWIMMING PROHIBITED—WATER UNFIT
Norwood Department of Health

It was stapled onto the camp sign every Tuesday morning by Norwood's health inspector, Rutus Sny. By noon it would be gone. When questioned about it once, Carl Mason shook his head and said, "Damn kids again. Now whaddya suppose they want with a sign like that?"

The camp's reputation in town was beneath contempt, the tenants there unworthy of even the most sordid gossip. They were nameless and faceless, the social dregs, the welfare cheats, the slum rounders who were welcome nowhere. They never paid a dime in taxes, yet sent their dirty and infected children to the town schools, where they were given free lunches and milk in exchange for head lice and impetigo.

Carl Mason, however, did not fall into that category. He and his family were, and always had been, townspeople and as such, open to town scandal and derision and lots of envy for their acquisition of Wind In The Pines. Fell into a pile of shit and came out smelling like roses, people said. Indeed, the Masons had lucked into the choicest property in Norwood, a potential gold mine; and nobody, not even their friends and neighbors, was happy for them.

Still, there had been a time—before Carl had bought the campground—when they were just another Norwood family: Shirley belonged to the PTA in those days, Carl to the Lions Club. Together, they bowled for the Mill Day Shift team in the Norwood Mixed Bowling League, and were both quite good, though Carl was once suspended for fighting. He had just turned fifty and was loaded on whiskey when it happened. But his suspension was lifted after a week, due to his strong influence on the board—some called it politics—Carl Mason was also Norwood's source of football cards and numbers betting, a lucrative sideline he conducted on the job, at the Stevens' Woolen Mills loading platform.

Which was where he met Old Man Rogers, the man who sold him Camp Wind In The Pines. Rogers was a steady, compulsive gambler in those days and, following his wife's death, a heavy drinker too. The two men became fast friends. They drank shots and beer together at the Ol' Mill Cafe nearly every afternoon and most every Saturday. It wasn't long before Carl began spending occasional Sundays at Rogers' campground, fixing a water line or mending a leaking roof for his friend.

By that time, sadly, Rogers had neglected the campground for so long it had grown as wild and reckless as an ungrazed field. A hippie community slowly took root in funky waterfront shacks thrown together of tin, asphalt, and whatever scraps of wood they could forage. They raised cows and hogs and sheep. They swam naked in the pond—only in the evenings at first, but then in the sunlight, discreetly—down at the marshy end of the beach. Finally, inevitably, during the late summer weeks, they migrated to the main beach, where they dived from the dock and floated in tire tubes with their suntanned genitals and breasts exposed. Shocked day swimmers and campers would march straight to Rogers and threaten to call this or that agency. But the old man didn't care. "I say live and let live," he'd tell them. On many an afternoon, back from town with whiskey in his blood, he too would shed his clothes and join his naked tenants on the beach.

In time the pond became polluted, and the campground was posted UNFIT. Campers stopped coming, and Rogers's money ran dangerously low, while his shantytown swelled and diversified, attracting not only his many feckless grandchildren, but still more hippies and resolute, real-world misfits. One morning a motorcycle gang from Bluffton—the Mutants—evicted an extended family and took up residence in one of the shacks, and it wasn't long before the communal spirit of Wind In The Pines disintegrated to looting, bad-drug-dealing, and downright Meanness.

But Rogers didn't care anymore. His TV got good reception, and he managed to collect enough rent from his tenants for food, booze, and football cards. But not for back taxes. When the town finally placed a lien on the property, he borrowed two thousand dollars from his friend Carl Mason to take up the slack, and he lost it on the horses.

Everybody agreed it was a damn shame: Two hundred of the choicest acres in Norwood—or anywhere, for that matter . . . property worth a fortune—wasting away on a bunch of hippies, welfare cheats, and motorcycle bums. A motion was carried at town meeting to set a timetable on Rogers's tax bill: 60 days. A week later, First Selectman and Health Inspector Rutus Sny offered Rogers $90,000 for the land, but Rogers just laughed and said, "Where would I go with that kind of money?" They both knew the property was worth three times that much.

So when Rogers abruptly sold the property to Carl Mason for fifteen thousand—the amount he owed in back taxes—with the stipulation that he could remain in his little campground house *forever* (that's how the deed read)—gossip spread through the town like the plague. Mafia muscle was cited, gambling debts, even blackmail. At least, thought the townspeople, the trash element would finally be evicted from Wind In The Pines—and from Norwood itself. Carl Mason was not a man who'd put up with the sort of riffraff that lived on the pond.

But it was not to be. Sure, there were people at Wind In The Pines that Carl disliked—mostly everybody. But he needed their rent. And as long as they paid it (he evicted those who didn't) he could overlook their transgressions.

Carl Mason had a unique method of collecting rent: food stamps. At the end of every month, everybody—even the Mutants and their women—turned over half of their allotment of food stamps to Carl Mason. Then he and Harvey Duckoff would take the Camp Truck to Atlas Grocers in Bluffton and trade the food stamps to Dixie Clark—third shift foreman and Carl's successor in the football cards racket—for generic groceries—wholesale. By dawn, they'd return to Wind In The Pines and unload the goods at the Camp Store, and Carl would mark up prices 25 percent and insist that *All tenants buy all groceries at the Camp Store*. This they would do with their remaining food stamps—until those ran out—and then with welfare, unemployment, disability, energy assistance, or pension money. It was a rental system that satisfied all, especially Carl Mason. It earned him a little over twenty thousand dollars his first year in business, money which he added to the profits from the sale of his split-level in town to enlarge the Camp Store and add on to it a new log home/office for his family: wife Shirley and daughter Susie.

Carl earned another $250 a month wheeling and dealing, as he'd always done. He had a furniture and clothing department in the rear of the Camp Store that was stocked from dump trades, lawn sales, and visits to Goodwill on tag days. Harvey Duckoff, his only employee, was his best customer.

In March Carl traded two dozen golf balls to Clyde the dump-keeper for a ripped Naugahyde studio couch with three legs. He nailed a short two-by-four on the bottom where the missing leg had been and mended the rips with green duct tape. He told Harvey and Jean that the couch had probably sold for $600 or $700 new, being genuine imitation leather. Harvey was impressed. So was Jean. The sale was clinched when Carl flipped it open and it became a green imitation leather double bed. "Wow!" Harvey said, brushing the earwigs off. "How much?"

"Gotta get two-fifty," Carl said.

"Oh, I dunno," said Harvey, eyeing his wife craftily. "Lookit all the bugs on 'er."

"Two hundred," Carl said, kicking the bed back into a couch.

Harvey pointed a finger at Carl. "Sold," he said.

"Awright!" said Jean, clapping. They paid a hundred dollars cash, and Harvey agreed to work a week for no pay. In this way Carl managed to retrieve most of Harvey's $5000 salary.

But despite Carl and Shirley's efforts to better the place, Camp Wind In The Pines registered only thirty overnight guests during their first year—seven families (none returned)—for a total of $90. Townspeople wondered how the Masons could manage to raise the $11,000 in annual property taxes on their meager business and still flaunt their Lincoln around town. Most hoped they would fall on their faces.

One would see to it they did.

A year after they acquired Wind In The Pines, an official letter came from Rutus Sny at the Town Office. The property had been reassessed. Doubled. Suddenly they were looking at a $22,000 tax bill. And their future, once a shared vision of soft, green comfort, began dissolving like a morning dream. They now faced a future with corners, dark and uncertain; and trouble, that wouldn't go away.

4

Zippy and Ruth

Zippy considered the fire a mystical experience. His wife Ruth was at the Masons' when it started, discussing Christianity with Shirley Mason, and he was home naked, cross-legged on the bed, rewriting "Our House," the Crosby, Stills, and Nash song.

He had a knack for altering a song—whether by varying its chords, or modifying its melody by a note or two, or maybe just changing a crucial word—he'd craft small, nearly imperceptible changes—the Zippy touch—and the song would be forever enriched. This was his gift. When he'd complete a song alteration he'd mail it to the composer with a note saying: Don't Send Money. Spread Love. Zippy Jones.

He had altered most of the songs of the late sixties (all the Dead songs). He had even altered "White Christmas" after reading in *The Guinness Book of World Records* how popular the song was, but he replaced Don't Send Money with a typewritten note that read: "Song alteration by Z. Jones, *Specialist*." He hoped for a windfall, even from the sixties musicians to whom he wrote Don't Send Money, and he met the mailman on the highway every day with High Hopes.

The mystical thing about the fire was that Zippy had been in deep concentration, singing the opening line of the song over and over: "I'll light the fire . . . ," and trying out different chords on the word "fire," just as the flaming cover of *Forbidden Sex Digest* sailed through the window and lit on the bed, torching the ragged window curtain beside him.

Somehow the urgency of the fire eluded him, dwarfed by the weight of its portent. He believed he had started the fire telepathically. "Far fucking out!" he breathed.

A stack of cardboard boxes beside the bed—a bureau of sorts—caught fire about the same time the bedspread and windowshade did. The hair on his leg spun and singed, and Zippy, realizing the fire would spread, jumped off his bed and carried his guitar outside.

Upwind, Carl Mason and Jean Duckoff stood beside a roaring, blowing bonfire in the pavilion area. Jean was feeding the fire with magazines. Harvey Duckoff was walking naked out of the pond, holding a black bunch of magazines above his head, his mouth open in a wide, disbelieving grin. He was red—cooked like a lobster.

Zippy was also naked. He approached Carl and said, "Hey, man, my house is on fire."

Carl spun around, looked over Zippy's shoulder, and saw flames leaping from two windows, pushing waves of black smoke up the eaves.

"Jesus!" he cried. But he didn't move. It was obvious the cabin was finished. He just sighed deeply and shivered, letting the wave of adrenaline wash over him. He took another deep breath and blew it out forcefully, then glared into Zippy's eyes, searching deep and hard.

Zippy stared back with a twinkle. "What a trip," he said. "I was just singing this song about lighting a fire . . ." Suddenly his eyes filled with terror. "Oh, no!" he cried. "My transceiver!"

He dropped his guitar and bolted for the burning cabin. He threw the front door open and dived into the thick, brown rolls of smoke. A moment later he barged out the door again, trailing plumes of smoke from his body. In his arms was a smoking cardboard box—in the box, a dark bulky machine that fell to the ground with him—the transceiver. He leaned over and kissed the machine, then snapped back with a yelp, rubbing his lips with the back of his hand.

Sunday morning. Carl Mason strode into the low rising sun, arms grandly swinging, as if they, and not his legs, propelled his short, barrel-chested body. He was a man who walked taller than his stature, who carried his chin higher than what seemed comfortable—almost defiantly so. And as he walked, his head turned with the rhythm of his stride—left, right, left—always watching, always alert. He was a hot-blooded man with a red face that, even in winter, seemed on the verge of perspiring; he had quick green eyes that, along with an eager confederate smile, invited mischief—even in normal conversation. His brown hair, which had once been waxed in a thick flattop—and which now barely covered his pink scalp—was itself covered with a blue baseball cap adorned with a shadow of the letter B. (Carl had torn the red B from his Red Sox cap during the fourth week of the 1981 baseball strike.)

He took his place behind an old church podium in the pavilion area and surveyed his tenants. The morning sun cast soft, speckled light on their hard faces while they squirmed on ragged lawn chairs and rough wooden benches. He turned up the volume on his milk-gray megaphone and pulled the trigger, unleashing a fierce reptilian squeal.

"Okay, let's have it quiet," he said through the squeal.

The Mutants, dressed in their greasy colors—sleeveless denim jackets with MUTANTS printed in blood-red letters across their backs—grew louder. There were four Mutants and three Mutant Bitches. They lived together in a wide, low-roofed, asphalt-shingled shack nestled in the pines in the Masons' backyard. Machine parts, appliances, and rags surrounded their place.

"Hammer—now, if you don't mind," Carl said to the Mutant leader.

"Yes, sir!" Hammer shouted, standing and saluting. The other Mutants snapped to attention and raised their hands in a Nazi salute. "Heil Mason!" one shouted. Another laughed, saying, "Is he gonna evict us?" It was the tedious standard procedure at these Sunday meetings.

"At ease, men," Carl said, playing along.

"Can't evict us," one of the Bitches chimed. "He'll go broke!"

"Ladies—please."

"Bitches," corrected the Bitch, still standing.

"Bitches," Carl said. Shirley shot him a disdainful glance. "Okay, let's start the week off right, Shirl."

Shirley Mason came forward and took the megaphone from him. This, more than anything about Wind In The Pines, displeased her. A breeze came up and pressed her light flowered skirt to her thighs as she greeted her tenants with a cautious smile. As her gaze passed over the Mutants, her smile waned, and they in turn mugged and exaggerated her slightly patronizing tilt of the head. She directed the megaphone at them and pulled the trigger: "Let us pray. . . ."

She had objected at first, flat-out refused, and now she wished she had stuck to her guns: "No," she had said, shaking her head adamantly. "No way."

"Wait a minute, wait a minute," Carl had said. "What do you mean, 'no way'?"

"I mean, that's just what I mean: No! I'm not going to stand up there and make a fool of myself."

"What do you mean? Just a little prayer and the Pledge of Allegiance, that's all. Is that making a fool of yourself?"

"It would make me a hypocrite, and you know it. I haven't been to church in thirty years and neither have you. I'm not going to do it, Carl."

"Look, I'm not asking you to cut off your goddamn arm, am I? What have I ever asked you to do around here? Huh?"

"So, do it yourself, if it's that important to you."

"Daaa, they'd know I was full of crap. C'mon, Shirley, for crissakes, these people need it. Jesus, I bet most of 'em have never been near a church. They need it, honey—the self-respect, the fear of God, a little goddamned patriotism."

"Carl, no. Don't ask me."

"All right. Forget the Pledge of Allegiance. Just say the prayer. Just a couple of sentences, you know, just simple stuff like, uh, 'Dear Lord, bless us today, and forgive us our trespasses' . . . whatever comes to mind."

"No. It's a stupid idea. I—"

"Shirley, honey, please," he had said, squeezing her thigh. "It means a lot to me. What else have I asked you to do?"

She had sat silently then, watching the whirl of steam on her coffee. It *was* the only thing he had asked of her. "Goddamn you," she had said.

". . . Oh, Lord, we thank you for your blessing on us this week, and we ask that you show us, each and every one, how to become better and more productive citizens." (She said this with a glance at the Mutants, who made a point of sitting upright and patting down their hair, smirking at one another. Weasel saluted her.) "And please guide more campers to our campground as the new season opens . . . and join us in our prayers for Harvey Duckoff's speedy recovery from his burns. We ask these things in Your name. Amen."

Dolly Root farted.

"Amen," Ruth Jones sang in echo. Shirley looked at her and smiled nervously. Carl took the megaphone.

"Okay, as most of you know, we had a little fire yesterday, and Zippy and Ruth Jones lost all their possessions." A short laugh went up as Zippy Jones stood, holding a charred Holiday Inn towel around his waist. He acknowledged the laughter with a slow grin and a wave. Ruth pulled him gently down. "So if anybody has any extra clothes for them, it'd be nice.

"They'll take over the Ellis cabin now that the Ellises have vacated, which, by the way, Luthor Ellis may still be in the area, and if anyone sees him, call the funny farm. Or the cops. I don't want him around here anymore. Also, as you know, the Weymouths and that crowd in the school bus have been evicted for grocery and rent violations. And they won't be the last—

"Now listen up! It's come to my attention that there are still groceries on the premises that are not being purchased at the Camp Store." Carl held up an empty can of Progresso minestrone soup and an empty package of Pepperidge Farm Zanzibar cookies. He looked slowly from face to face. "This hurts, folks, it really does. Haven't we been decent to you, Shirl and me? Well? Haven't we?"

There was a general nodding of heads. Even the Mutants sat without comment.

"And this is how you repay our kindness? Well, I'll tell you this," he shouted suddenly, his finger in the air, the megaphone squealing. Zippy slid off his wooden bench and out of his towel, to the delight of the Mutants, who stood and cheered as he slowly, red-faced, picked his naked self up. Ruth, smiling lovingly, cupped her forehead and shook her head in embarrassment for him.

"Sit down and shut up!" Carl hollered, throwing the megaphone to the ground. His face was scarlet and his finger trembled as he pointed. He walked around to the front of the pulpit and spoke slowly: "When I find out who's responsible for these illegal groceries, they'll be out of here so fast it'll make their friggin' head spin!"

"Carl!"

"Awww," he answered in disgust, sweeping an arm across the air like a scythe. He walked away, right through the sapling hedges that bordered the pavilion, leaving his small, tattered audience absolutely transfixed. No one moved. No one dared break the silence. Finally Dolly Root farted softly.

"Is the meeting over?" Jean Duckoff asked in a loud voice, and everyone rose and left in silence.

5

Susie and the Cheat

Susie Mason became horny in the sixth grade, and her horniness swelled with age; unfortunately, so did her surliness. Now eighteen, she despised her parents, hated the campground and everyone in it, and, since having her first furtive taste of *le sport*, dwelled endlessly on sex.

She had a small, taut mouth set in an oversized jaw, and big, big breasts which, on her short body, looked massive. Mr. Rogers would shake his head and refer to her as "that poor horse-faced girl." Her hair, which she hated, was dark red and permed.

Susie worked days in the Camp Store; she read romance paperbacks while customers waited at the cash register. When Harvey Duckoff hobbled to the counter with a can of baked beans and a Popsicle pressed between his bandaged hands, a dollar bill and two quarters clenched in his teeth, she was reading a story from a charred magazine she had found in a pile marked ADULT MAGAZINES. SOME SMOKE DAMAGE—$1.99.

Harvey's face was pink, his eyes still bloodshot from the fire, and he dangled like a poorly made marionette, balancing from one leg cast to the other. Saliva collected in his throat. When he tried to swallow it, the quarters fell into his mouth, and he feared he would choke on them, so he lowered his head and tongue-flipped the quarters against his teeth—but when he tried to get another bite on them, the saliva escaped from his mouth and ran down the dollar bill onto the counter.

Susie heard the dribbling and slammed her magazine shut.

The dollar bill fell with a soft slap, and the quarters followed with a jangle.

"They let me out," Harvey said, grinning. "Bandages'll be off in a couple of days. Prublay. The doctor said I'm lucky to be alive. Damn lucky."

"Watch your mouth," Susie said, stooping for a paper bag, allowing a full view of her abundant cleavage.

"Oh, I didn't say that word. The doctor did. I was just. . . "

"Here's your change, Einstein," she said, dropping three coins onto the counter and returning to her magazine.

With his bandaged mitts, Harvey could not get a grip on the coins; he could only slide them along the counter from one paw to the other. Susie pretended not to notice. "Oh, well," he shrugged. "Better luck next time." As he hobbled out the door he heard the ring of the cash register and the clatter of coins falling into its drawer.

"Moron," Susie said, not softly.

The large hippie community that flourished in the late sixties had dwindled to only three members under Mason's management. The others, for wanderlust or career decisions, had moved on. Of the three remaining, only one resembled his former self, and that was Zippy Jones, aptly named for his lack of vitality, attention, or ambition.

Zippy was a ponderous man, slow yet seldom deliberate. He had come of age in Haight-Ashbury in 1966, in the heyday of Experience—black-lit, liquid-lit, laser-lit, hairy-naked-acid-tripping, music-lit Experience. And thus enlightened, he saw no reason to trudge on the heels of those who departed for the bourgeoisie.

He owned little. Only his guitar and transceiver survived the fire; two pairs of gloriously patched bell-bottom jeans and his humble assortment of paisley shawls and peasant shirts burned. Zippy had never been employed and meant never to be.

He might have been a casualty of nature if not for his loving wife Ruth, whose real name was Lois. (She had undergone four name changes in ten years. In 1969 she became Herring during an acid trip at Marconi Beach on Cape Cod. Then in 1971 she became Trippy because it rhymed with Zippy. In '74 she changed to

Saandra, because she liked the sound; and finally, when she found Jesus, she became Ruth.)

Ruth and Zippy were married in the pavilion area of Wind In The Pines by Rutus Sny, Health Inspector, First Selectman, and Notary Public, and her life began to change. She began wearing bras and knee-length dresses. She cut and bobbed her hair, and every morning she'd draw a fine red line of lipstick on her lips. Ruth looked a lot like June Allyson in *The Secret Heart*, a movie she had seen on television one Sunday morning. In fact, she tried to. She spent hours cultivating the look, the mannerisms—the black-and-white essence—of the 40s American starlet. She had the same boyish, diminutive stature, the same businesslike forehead and nose. And her voice, like June Allyson's, was low and raspy. Her one plaid dress which survived the fire was gray pleat with a white ruffled collar—a rip under its arm allowed a tuft of sandy underarm hair to poke through whenever she raised her arm. But for the most part her transformation was complete. Like Shirley, whom she visited every morning for Christ and Coffee, she read *Family Circle*, *Reader's Digest*, and was decent, honorable, and Moderate.

The third member left over from the hippie community was Angel, which was her real name. She had been the Earth Mother of the group, and as such had once worn heavy brass bells around her neck. It was on the basis of her decisions that the group had acted, presumably due to her wisdom and assertive nature and her sometimes devious politicking and caustic tongue. Actually, it was her promiscuity—she fucked all the guys. Then, either through blackmail or the promise of more favors, she held reign over them. The women loved and admired her and competed for her favor, while their men—though they'd not admit it—were terrified of her.

Angel lived in a camper-trailer on the left end of the pond where the cattails and lily pads grew. Maurice, her taut gray poodle, stayed outside on just enough chain to reach the front steps, or, when fully extended—as when the dog was in midair, attacking—to within an inch of a cowering visitor pressed hard against the trailer's side. Maurice was not a dog to be taken lightly, and Angel loved him dearly. She fed him steaks from town, grilled hamburg, and hot dogs.

Small animals were also a part of Maurice's diet—and his passion: mice, squirrels, frogs, June bugs, and kittens—Susie's kittens. One morning Angel found Susie's kitten's head cradled between the sleeping dog's front legs. She picked up the tiny golden head and stuffed it in an empty Kellogg's Pop-Tarts box and threw it in the trash. It was the third of Susie's cats to vanish in as many months.

Although Angel was no longer the clear voice of authority and no longer wore brass bells, she still held peculiar powers over people. For example, she was the only tenant regularly excused from Mason's weekly meetings and the only person at Wind In The Pines who wasn't taunted by the Mutants and Mutant Bitches. In fact the Bitches came to her, one at a time—secretly—for counsel.

The visits would seem innocent enough: a little drink, a little cocaine or pot. Girl talk. But Angel was like a poultice on a wound—she would draw out secrets. They would ooze out at first—just skin-deep privities—then suddenly the clot would be torn aside, loosened by narcotic and matriarchal trust, and the raving and tears would pour forth. By the end of a visit the woman, donning her filthy colors, would smile timidly and ask, "You won't say anything to anybody about. . . ," and Angel would take her in her arms and give her a strong, motherly hug. She had the Bitches but good, right down to their steel-shanked boots.

Angel's appearance belied her past—as well as her present circumstance: Her shorn hair was streaked squirrel brown on black and very cosmopolitan, her clothes très chic. She had rich brown eyes, strong cheekbones, and seductive, full lips. She wore three tiny gold rings through each earlobe and drove a late-model Volvo—very middle class, very expensive, and very curious, thought the Masons, since she paid her rent in food stamps.

One night in March, when Shirley had gone to town, Carl walked next door with an armload of seasoned firewood. He was curious. "This oughta keep you warm tonight," he said to Angel.

She measured him, then said, "And how are *you* going to keep warm?"

"Oh, you know, we've got a little woodstove in the parlor. . . ."

"You know what I mean," she said, pouring a short glass of Jack Daniel's. "Like a quickie?"

"Mmm." He took the glass, cleared his throat. "Whiskey," he said. "Nothin' like a quick shot o' the good stuff."

She drank from the bottle and wiped her mouth with the back of her hand. "Look, you wanna get laid tonight or not?"

Carl's temples throbbed. He snorted and downed the whiskey with a vague grin, and she refilled his glass.

"I'll bet you're hung like a fucking horse," she said huskily, running the back of her hand up the front of his pants.

He fell back a step. "Nope," he laughed, reaching for the door-knob. "Just ordinary." He backed out her door, grinning foolishly, and hurried back to his cabin dazed, the full glass of whiskey still in his hand. Safely inside, he locked the door. Then he unlocked it. He turned on "M*A*S*H" and paced like a caged bear in front of the TV, occasionally glancing out his window—seeing her lights on—seeing her moving past her window. She was waiting for him, he knew it. And, he supposed, she knew he knew. He gulped the whiskey absently and found himself at the door, going outside, hurrying to her elegant camper to finish what he had begun—an affair that was consummated without another word. And he was back home before "M*A*S*H" ended. Angel had Carl Mason, too.

She had Dixie Clark as well, the nightshift foreman at Atlas Grocers in Bluffton. She bought her own groceries from him— Pepperidge Farm, Progresso, Maxwell House—wholesale—and never spent a penny at the Camp Store.

"Susie," Carl said one evening at supper, "you *must* know who hasn't been buying their groceries at the Camp Store. Honey, we're going under here, and somebody's beatin' us on the rent."

"Oh, you're so paranoid," she said, wrinkling her face. Angel had Susie too, and it was a master stroke. Susie's contempt for her father reached new heights—as did her admiration for the woman who had seduced him. She would literally sit at Angel's feet for wisdom:

"See, you get 'em by the balls, and you keep 'em by the balls—so when they get out of line, you just squeeze."

Yes, Angel had Susie in a big way. Every Sunday night she would load Angel's illicit trash into the trunk of the family Lincoln and drive to the town dump, where she'd toss the bags over the locked gate.

6

The Letter

Nothing from Jerry Garcia. Nothing from Neil Young or Dylan. Zippy sifted through the thick wad of mail—mostly other people's bills—at the Camp Mailbox on the highway, when something sparked his curiosity—something in the mail he had passed. So he thumbed back slowly through the envelopes until he came to one marked: Harold Jones. Harold Jones? That was his own name, he thought—although it had been years since he'd heard it. Harold. It sounded odd. Harold . . . Harold Jones.

Turning back onto the Camp Road, pondering his name and the distant past, he didn't notice the stealthy rustling of leaves in the brush nearby. When he passed Carl Mason, who was carrying a can of red paint up to the highway, he looked at Mason and shrugged his shoulders as if the man were as perplexed by the mail as he. When he got back to the former Ellis cabin he found Ruth on her knees stripping the yellow waxy buildup from the linoleum floor.

"Hey, honey," he said, holding up the letter. "Something for Harold Jones."

"What?" She looked up.

"Harold Jones," he repeated with a crooked smile.

"That's you."

"I know."

His dark hair, thinning on top, hung like seaweed down his back; his wispy beard draped, gnarled and knotted, onto his chest. The tip of his tongue sucked against a hole where a front tooth had once been—a nervous gesture. The gestalt of this man puzzling over his own printed name made Ruth wonder for a fleeting instant how they had come so far together. It had indeed been a long, long time.

"So open it, Zip."

"Where's my transceiver?" he said, dropping the letter onto the table. "You open it."

"It's your letter." She picked it up and said, "There's no return address on it—maybe it's from Dylan." She was being cruel. She watched the slow gleam build in Zippy's eye as he took the letter from her.

He broke the seal, beaming at her. "Dylan doesn't know my real name. How could he?" He pulled the letter from its envelope and read it aloud:

Dear Harry,

How they hanging, Bro? Long time, no sea, as Lewis and Clark once said. Get it? Hey man, don't be surprised if you see me knocking at your door pretty soon. I just graduated. Mom sends her love. Pop says you still owe him four bills—ha ha ha—Don't worry, I'll take care of it one of these days, soon as I'm flush. Keep it in your pants.

Peace,

Larry

"Larry?" Zippy said angrily to the letter. "Larry?"

"That's your brother," said Ruth. "He's coming here?"

"Oh, shit," said Zippy.

"Oh, shit," said Ruth. "Praise the Lord."

7

A Worried Song

Carl walked to the highway with a can of fresh red paint. The season was a little more than two weeks away, and he wanted things to be Right. Wind In The Pines needs campers, he thought, and we're gonna get us some campers. Or else. He did not finish the thought. Anyway, it was just a matter of PR—public relations—a little fresh paint, some advertising, an Image Change.

All winter long he and Harvey had been preparing new campsites down at the pond and up behind the cabins on Lookout Hill—twenty new campsites in all, with picnic tables and fireplaces—a potential for $240 extra a night, in season. Good money.

As he opened the paint can, something caught his eye. The health department's WATER UNFIT notice was stapled again to his Camp Sign. "Hrr," he muttered. "It's Wednesday." (He had taken down this week's notice on Tuesday—just yesterday—as he always did.) But there was something else about the new notice: Someone had crossed out the $500 from the small print, which read: $500 FINE FOR TAMPERING WITH THIS NOTICE, and penned in $1000. The change was signed by Health Inspector and First Selectman Rutus Sny. "Sonsabitches," Carl said, ripping the notice down and stuffing it into his pocket.

"Ho, Mister Mason." It was Rutus Sny himself, stepping out from the brush, smiling. "Guess we finally caught those kids, eh?" Two local cops, Sgt. Pauley Johnson and a deputy, came from behind him. The deputy held a Polaroid print in his hand, and both cops watched tilt-headed as the photograph came to life. Sny said:

"How'd she come out, boys?" The deputy responded by making a smug circle with his thumb and index finger.

Carl clenched his fists and took a step toward the deputy, who put a hand on his holster. "What are you gonna do, shoot me, you puny bastard?" Carl said, looking up at the young man, who was a head taller than himself.

"Easy does it, Carl," Sgt. Johnson said, gesturing with his palms down. Pauley was an old friend and bowling partner—a good man, Carl thought, when he's on your side. "Sorry about this, Carl, but you're going to have to come down to the station. You can take your own car if you want, you know—save the embarrassment."

"Yeah, yeah," Carl said, as Sny stapled another notice to the Camp Sign.

"Let's hope the kids don't take this one down, right, Mason?" he laughed.

"A thousand dollars?" Shirley said that evening. "They can't do that, can they?" Carl sat on a low footstool by the coffee table, his head down, his arms resting on his knees. He watched blankly as his fingers made changing geometric shapes over his shoes. Susie was locked in her room, playing records at three-quarters volume, and dancing. The glassware in Shirley's oak hutch tingled, the water in the aquarium churned. A goldfish looked out at the television with wide, worried eyes. She's a heavy girl, Carl thought lamely. Too heavy.

"We'll have to sell the Lincoln," Shirley said.

Carl went to the kitchen and poured himself a tall glass of whiskey. There was comfort in its fragrance, in its warm amber hue. He gazed through the glass into the fluorescent light.

They had turned their first blind corner at Wind In The Pines, and the future suddenly loomed clear: They were going under.

8

Cocaine

Angel had Weasel too—Weasel, the Mutant drone—loyal as dogs to Hammer and the Mutants, and cruel as a chicken—even at twenty-four he still pulled the wings off dragonflies. He was small—wiry and angular, and his pale blue eyes were outlined by an almond of black lashes, making hypnotic his already menacing stare. He combed his blond, grease-dirty hair stiffly to the side with a wide-tooth comb, and he walked with a splay-legged bounce, so the hair flapped on his head like an oilcloth but never came uncombed. The one inconsistency in his otherwise desperado image was his accent: He and his widowed father, a British bone surgeon, had moved to America from Cornwall, England, when the lad was eight, and a trace of highbrow Cornish still lingered in his speech. He said things like, "You're a bit of a pigfucker, now, aren't you?" and "'old 'is bleedin' ahms so I can thrash 'im."

Weasel was uneasy around women, having spent most of his life in male-populated institutions. On the rare occasions when the urge for sex struck, he would fulfill it with the same expediency with which one fulfills hunger or thirst. One night, just after the Masons had taken over Wind In The Pines, Weasel fulfilled the urge by climbing through Susie Mason's bedroom window. For him, it was nothing more than scratching an itch. But for Susie, it was the night she had longed for—and a night she would never forget. It was the night she became a woman. And ever since that night, Susie had tried every subtle means in her female arsenal to lure Weasel back into her arms, but to no avail. Women simply held no interest for the young man.

Weasel was the only Mutant without a Bitch and so seemed an unlikely object of Angel's manipulation. But she had him good. And she had good reason: She wanted his leader. "Hey, don't tell Hammer what I said, whatever you do," Weasel would say as he left her trailer, "or I'll kill you."

He sat naked on her bed now, lines of dirt overlapping on his skin like oil on the shore. A large blue tattoo on his chest said MOM'S DEAD.

"God, you stink," Angel said, kicking him onto the floor. "You're just a worthless collection of molecules." She lit a cigarette. "Garbage wrapped in skin, right?"

"Yeah, right!" he said proudly, though he groped for a more apt tone. "Hey," he said, pulling his jeans from off the bed, "I almost forgot. Lookit." He reached into the pocket, withdrew a fold of black paper, and unfolded it on her night table. "Check this out," he said. It was just under a gram of cocaine. "Hundred twenty dollars if you want it—nearly pure." He took a scalpel from his cuff and separated four skinny lines from the pile. They snorted two lines apiece through a rolled-up hundred-dollar bill, and Angel soon felt the familiar tingle, like a fine pink laser, in her brain. It was indeed fine coke.

"This sucks," she said. "Where'd you get it?"

"None of your concern now, is it?" He made four more lines and they greedily sucked it up.

Angel felt electric and superfine. She imagined Weasel on a skewer. "Put your clothes on," she told him. "You're disgusting."

He pulled the dungarees up his legs. "Want some more?" he offered. "We got plenty."

"We got plenty," she mocked, while he set up two more lines for her.

Weasel snickered and looked sideways at her. "I shouldn't tell you this," he said, "but my friend Hammer's a big man in this part of the country."

She knew. In fact, "big" was an understatement. Hammer was

The Man, and, contrary to appearance, he was a very wealthy man—coke wealthy. For the last four years he had supplied Bluffton County dealers with cocaine he purchased off fishing boats in the dark coves along the ragged mid-Maine coast. He'd pay the Colombians $40,000 a kilogram for the coke, and the next day he'd double its weight and distribute it to local dealers at $30,000 per pound, more than tripling his investment—overnight.

Hammer's introduction into the lucrative trade forged his reputation as a sharp, ruthless businessman. Four years earlier, just before the Mutants moved into Wind In The Pines, when cocaine was just a rumor to Maine folks, a supplier from Miami came north with three pounds of the precious white powder. The man disappeared. A deep, charred crater was discovered a few days later on a woods road in Lovell. The man's license plate, still attached to the car's twisted bumper, was found in a cow pasture a quarter mile away. Then, a month later, bird hunters scouting the Lovell woods came upon half a car engine wedged in the crotch of an elm not far from where the crater had been found.

Yes, Hammer was The Man, alright. And he was the one man Angel had been unable to get purchase on.

"So Hammer's a big man, is he?" She sniffed a line and put the bill to her other nostril. "If you ask me, he's just another turd in the cesspool."

With the speed of a viper Weasel grabbed her hair and mashed her face into the table. The bill forced up her nostril until it broke skin, then it mercifully folded against the table, draining her nose blood into the cocaine. He hissed into her ear: "Maybe you'd like to retract that statement, now. Huh? Maybe you're unaware that right now, even as we speak, he's over there sittin' on more blow than you've ever seen. Five fucking pounds—pure. So now who's the turd, huh?" He ground her face into the bloody coke. "You are, now, aren't you?"

The sensation was overwhelming. Five pounds, she thought. Thousands and thousands and thousands of dollars. Hundreds of thousands. She could taste her own salty blood in the bitter coke now. He rubbed her face in it harder. "Who's the turd? Who? Answer me."

"Mmmm!" she moaned into the table, lapping the cocaine with her tongue.

Weasel jumped back. He grabbed his denim vest from the floor. "You're one fucked-up chick," he said, as she rolled onto her back, moaning, red powder matted on her nose and chin. He snatched the bill from the table, then went to the refrigerator and opened a soda, a Schweppes Ginger Ale. He returned to her blue Persian bedroom and grabbed her by the hair and said, "Don't tell Hammer what I said. Don't tell anyone, or I'll kill you."

Weasel opened the trailer door and stepped onto the porch. A sudden snapping of chain links alerted him, and he turned just in time to kick a steel-pointed boot into the airborne poodle's throat. Maurice kii-yiied, twisted violently in midair, and dropped to the ground, where he lay heaving and glassy-eyed beside the porch, sniffing the air deeply.

The night was thick. A spring heat wave had enshrouded the northeast for three days, and tonight silent bursts of lightning climbed the clouds above the pond. As he swaggered past the Mason cabin, Weasel could see Carl in the kitchen, staring through a glass of whiskey at the fluorescent light. He could hear the incessant thud of rock 'n' roll from deep within the house. He felt surly and fine. He tossed the can of ginger ale onto the roof. "Have some mixer, asshole," he sneered. The can cracked against the metalbestos chimney, then rolled down the metal roof and fell to the porch in a spray.

Carl heard the noise and put his glass down. He flicked on the porch light and went outside. Ginger ale trickled off the eaves in front of him, and the empty Schweppes can lay spilling at his feet like a smoking gun. He picked up the can. A shadowy figure turned the corner around his cabin, and Carl stepped quietly off the porch to follow. The dark figure headed, finger-snapping, along the side of the throbbing cabin and into the backyard, where it stopped in the light cast by Susie's window and looked inside. Carl recognized the face and the greasy vest: MUTANTS, it said in red letters, deep as blood.

9

Strength

Carl Mason waded back into his kitchen and drank the tumbler of whiskey. He chased it with a gulp of generic cola, then poured more whiskey and was drinking that when Shirley walked in, instinctively concerned, sensing she shouldn't interfere, but—

"Carl, don't. We'll manage—we always have. . . "

"They're outta here tonight, Shirley, the whole filthy lot of 'em."

"What? Who?" She reached for the bottle before he could pour another glassful, but he spun away and poured, his temples pulsing. Whiskey made him mean, but she'd never seen him drink like this—purposely to get mean. "Who's out of here?" she demanded.

"See that?" He pointed his nose at the empty Schweppes can on the counter. "Schweppes!"

She scowled uncertainly.

"I found out who's been beatin' us on the groceries. That bunch out back—and they're outta here tonight. Right now!"

She understood. Shirley herself had wanted the Mutants out since the day she had arrived at Wind In The Pines. "You *are* going to call the police," she said, fearing he would not, "aren't you?"

"Yeah, right! The day I need this goddamn crooked police force. . . " He stopped to drink. "I'll kill that filthy bastard. I caught him looking in Susie's window." He poured another glass and drank it. "Why can't you get her to pull her shades down?"

"Don't go over there alone, Carl," Shirley said. "I mean it." She touched his wrist, too softly, and he found himself struck by a dizzying surge of tenderness for her—his eyes burned. Then, just as suddenly, his rage returned, and he dashed his whiskey in her face. "Okay, I won't go over there alone," he sneered. "I'll get Harvey to come with me. Come on, Harve boy," he mocked, swinging his hands simianlike by his ankles. "'Okay, Mr. Mason,'" he answered in a goofy voice. "'Let's get 'em.'"

"Bastard," Shirley said, her voice muffled behind a dishtowel.

Carl turned away and refilled his glass. "Or how about ZZZippy? Oh, ZZZippy," he called softly up to the ceiling, "oh, ZZZippy, where are you? Come out and help me, you friggin' acidhead space-shot."

"Carl, listen to me!"

"Or what about Old Man Rogers? We haven't mentioned him." He drank more, then pounded on his solar plexus for relief. "Hah! Sure, I'll get help, you . . . goddamn. . . " He slapped his glass on the counter. "They," he said, poking his finger at her, "are . . . out . . . uh . . . here . . . right . . . now!"

Mr. Rogers was there already, as irony would have it, sitting between Bruiser and Crabs, who leaned in battered lawn chairs against the asphalt-shingled shack, their Bitches in a sea of empty generic beer cans at their feet. They were keeping watch while Hammer cut and packaged cocaine inside.

"Awful horse-faced girl, though, wouldn't you say?" Rogers asked seriously.

"Ugly as sin," Crabs agreed. They toasted.

"Nice tits, though," said Bruiser. Their women laughed.

Fifty feet away, bathed in yellow light, Susie danced before her bedroom window, sweat-soaked and nearly naked, bucking like a rodeo pony to the locomotive beat of Z Z Top. Her sheer baby-doll top clung to her body and flounced wildly on her with a life of its own, and when she gathered her red hair in her arms and turned away from the window, teasing, her buttocks bulged and her thighs puckered with each fall.

Inside the Mutant shack, Hammer sat quietly at his kitchen table. A five-pound block of cocaine lay like a huge, raw gem before him on the Formica table between a stainless-steel scale and a bag of manitol (which he added in equal portions to each plastic bag of coke he made up). A sawed-off shotgun lay, cocked, across his lap. Only loyal Weasel and Hammer's Bitch, Kitten, were allowed inside, and they were closed in the darkened front bedroom—Kitten on the bed humming, and Weasel with his ear pressed to the window screen, listening to Bruiser and Crabs for whispers of treason. Weasel knew what kind of trouble easy money could bring. It drew out the worst in a man.

Carl Mason didn't see his daughter dancing. He lumbered past her window with drunken purpose, falling into each heavy step. The music was his battle hymn, and the light from her window cast his squat shadow twenty feet long before him. He strode fearlessly, brandishing the empty Schweppes can like a saber.

"Ah well, good Mr. Mason," Rogers proposed, raising his beer. "Here for the show, are you?"

Carl peered squarely through the darkness at the two Mutants. He held up the Schweppes can and threw his thumb up. "Out!" he commanded, the motion jerking him backward. But he reeled ahead again, floundering past them to the door. He smacked the doorlatch with his empty can, and the door swung open, creaking.

Bruiser and Crabs jumped. "Hey! Stay outta there!"

But Carl was already in the doorway, now just slowly perceiving the raised shotgun as he tripped over the doorsill. "Freeze!" he called, falling forward, displaying the can like a badge.

By the time Hammer recognized him, he had already pulled the trigger. The shot blew past Carl's right shoulder and tore the upper doorjamb off the house, driving the door out on its twisted lower hinge, so that it settled crookedly in the threshold like a funhouse ramp.

Crabs and Bruiser charged up the ramp. "Don't shoot!" Crabs yelled, covering his eyes with his forearm, and Carl lunged, hurling a mighty roundhouse punch at the doorway. It caught Crabs on the nose and snapped his head back into Bruiser's face, pitching both men onto their backs on the ramp. Carl reeled again and socked Hammer's ear with his fist, just as the Mutant leader was dropping another shell into the shotgun chamber. The chair kicked out from under him and Hammer went down hard against the wall, spilling both shell and shotgun.

Then Weasel ran in from the bedroom, stretching a short chain between his hands. He climbed Carl's back, snapped the chain against his throat, and rode his landlord around the kitchen like a cowboy breaking a bull. In the meantime Hammer reloaded his shotgun and rose to his feet. When Weasel saw the weapon aimed he dropped off Carl's back and rolled across the floor.

Carl spun and faced Hammer. He saw the feral eyes, the black, oily shotgun maw pointing at his chest, and he raised the empty soda can to protect himself.

"You're dead, pigfucker," Hammer snarled. And in the next helpless instant Carl Mason watched curiously as Hammer lowered his shotgun and blew apart his own foot. His mouth opened, his eyes bulged, his face reddened. He leaned back against the wall and roared, uncomprehending, pinned there by a red-blue-yellow hunting arrow through his shoulder.

Weasel moved to help him when a second arrow whizzed past his ear and tore into the wall clock, stopping it forever.

"Hey," Carl objected, sinking to his knees. He knew that arrow—he recognized its gaily colored feathers. They shimmered, they spun, they caused him to lie down in dizziness and close his eyes.

From the bedroom Kitten cried frantically, "What? What? What?" while Weasel, unable to yank the arrow out of Hammer's shoulder, snapped off its end and pulled his leader off the dripping arrow stub, screaming. "What? What? What?" Kitten cried.

Outside two Harleys kicked into a double roar and tore through the campground onto the River Road—Bruiser and Crabs and their Bitches escaped Wind In The Pines. They left Norwood, drove all night, and slept in a Pennsylvania Rest Area. When the sun came up they abandoned their Mutant colors without ceremony in a state rubbish barrel and headed west.

Weasel switched off the light.

"Quiet," he whispered. Carl snored softly in the dark. Another arrow came in from the night, passed silently through the kitchen, and smashed through a bathroom window.

"What?" Kitten shrieked from the bedroom. "Somebody tell

me!" And getting no answer—believing the cabin under siege and her man dead—she wrapped herself in a blanket and dived through the window. She found Hammer's chopper, wrestled it off its kickstand, and gunned it through the darkness out of the campground.

"Ohh," Hammer groaned.

"Shhh," Weasel whispered. "Can you walk?"

"Ohh, man."

"Can you crawl?"

"I'm sleepin'," Carl mumbled. "Le' me 'lone."

"I don't know," Hammer said. "I'm stove up good."

Weasel bellied over to him, lugged him to his knees, and led him down the door-ramp, crawling—staying low. An arrow whistled above them and pierced the refrigerator. Weasel heard the muffled breaking of glass behind him. "Bitch," he muttered. "I'm gonna kill her." Under the cover of darkness Weasel found his chopper. He quietly lifted his leader onto its seat. Then he climbed on and turned the key.

Hammer put his mouth to his ear. "The coke," he breathed. "On the table."

Weasel squeezed his arm in understanding. He dismounted and ran low for the doorway, but as he stepped onto the ramp, it shifted and snapped, and he got hit from behind. The arrow shot through the bend of his leg and came out his knee, crumbling him in fiery red pain. He howled and rolled off the ramp, yanking the arrow from his leg in the same motion, then scurried three-legged to the chopper.

"They got me too," he whispered with a muted, brutal laugh. He kicked thunder into the machine, and they escaped the campground in a spray of gravel, without headlight, storming for St. Vincent's Hospital in Bluffton.

Weasel's leg hung from the bike, burning, filling his boot with his hot blood. He held Hammer's feeble arms around his waist with his own arm, feeling proud, ecstatic—the wounded warriors returning from the fray. He had risked his life for his leader, and he had saved him. "It was Angel," he yelled back to Hammer. "I'll take care of her." He opened the throttle and the bike surged ahead.

They rode east on Turner's Ridge, overlooking the scattered farmhouse lights of Norwood, the warm spring air blossoming at intervals with the fragrance of pine, then lilac, then water. The night throbbed—Weasel's pain was exquisite. He opened the throttle wider and the big machine soared. "Hold on," he yelled. "Just another ten miles." He drew a sharp breath and took the chopper hard and low into a curve. Too low. Hammer's mangled foot dragged between the footrest and the flying asphalt. His ankle snapped, and as the bike jolted upright, he was torn from Weasel's grasp and sucked down to the racing pavement, where he catapulted at once into the guardrail and died with his blind face against the railpost.

The uprighted motorcycle could not negotiate the curve. It slammed straight into the low guardrail and went somersaulting over the top, Weasel still clutching the throttle with his right hand. He hit ground thirty feet down the steep embankment, then bounced and tumbled over stumps and rocks and sapling trees until he finally came to rest in a moist pine grove, faceup, his glassy smile embedded in his lip, his right hand squeezing screams of agony from his broken chopper into the wild, peeper-filled night.

10

·

Timing

The River Road was dark and strange to Larry Jones. He had asked directions to Camp Wind In The Pines at a small store in town, but the man had only laughed and told him to use his nose. So Larry drove slowly, peering above the steering wheel for any sign or turn-off, confident that his luck would steer him right.

He trusted his luck—it had gotten him this far in life: thirty-five, no debts, no wife or kids to care for, slick car, college degree. He had earned his Bachelor of Arts Degree from Kubinack Community College in Massachusetts after seventeen years and six different colleges, and after this summer vacation he would decide whether to go for his Master's degree or look for a job. He'd probably go for the degree, he thought, since his work experience was so limited. And unfulfilling.

Larry had been an Electrolux salesman—at the insistence of his second wife's father, an Electrolux branch manager. He had lasted six weeks and cost the company $1500—never sold a vacuum cleaner; not even a vacuum cleaner bag. He just wasn't a salesman, he had told his wife, who waitressed in two restaurants to support their children. He was an entrepreneur, lack of funds or direction notwithstanding.

He and his buddy Jack would spend entire days planning their fortunes over beers and joints and loud, loud music in his Camaro. They'd cruise the city streets in winter, the beaches in summer, saying, "Wouldn't it be great to have a car wash with all naked women," or, "How about we open a restaurant where you weigh the people coming in and weigh them going out, then just charge them by the pound!" Or Larry's favorite: "We'll open a park up in Maine, right on the ocean. We'll get big-name rock bands to play every Saturday night." "Outtasight!" "And every Wednesday, like at Hampton Beach, fireworks! But really huge, like, atomic fireworks . . . and rides—for the little kids, you know—roller coasters, Ferris wheels, ponies and things." "How about an animal park?" "Oh, yeah! An animal park, yeah, and a movie theater, with a huge Cinerama drive-in screen . . . and skin flicks on Friday nights." "Yeah, but late, when the kids are asleep." "Right, that shit's no good for kids." "Hey, *Deep Throat*, right?" "Oh, yeah." "On a Cinerama screen." "Here, gimme that."

Suddenly a motorcycle shot out of the woods into his high beams. It was a wide-eyed girl, riding without lights. Larry stomped on the brakes and watched her fly darkly out of sight. Then he backed up and turned the car to the left to see where she had come from. WATER UNFIT, the sign read, in bold black letters.

Larry turned down the dirt road. Tire tracks had worn deep ruts in the gravel, while a tall ragged hump rose between and scraped at the Camaro's underbelly.

As the road turned left through the woods, the landscape opened up. He could make out a pond to the right and trailers and cabins all around, amidst a scattering of pines. The night seemed full of sounds: strange, incessant, high-pitched peeping sounds and the deep, rhythmic thud of nearby rock 'n' roll. Then suddenly another motorcycle roared and went weaving without lights past him—this one with two riders—the one on the rear was slumped against the driver. In the glare of his headlights he could see blood on the driver's leg.

Larry aimed his headlights across the grass to where the chopper had come and saw an old man bent over a body, struggling. He got out of his car and trotted across the tire-worn grass for them.

"Is he hurt?" Larry asked.

The body itself answered with a drunken slur. "Hell, no. Wanna campsite?" He raised a crumpled Schweppes soda can in his hand.

"It's time to bring good Mr. Mason home," the older man said. "Will you assist, sir?"

"No sweat. Where does he live?"

"Hawaii," Carl said, gazing up at the swirling stars.

"Right there," Mr. Rogers answered, waving a finger across the horizon. Larry turned and immediately spotted the girl in the yellow-lit window. He squinted. She was dancing. She was doing the monkey. She looked naked. He looked quizzically at the old man, who put his face to Larry's ear.

"Awful horse-faced, though," he wheezed, coughing deep and hard. He grabbed Larry's arm for support but slowly sank to one knee, retching. "Too much beer," he said between coughs.

"Too much whee," Mason said, his eyes closed. "Whis-key," he enunciated.

"C'mon, let's take you home," Larry said, hoisting Carl upright.

"Take me home, country roads," Carl sang. Then he suddenly pulled away from Larry and punched wildly at him. "I'm awright," he snarled, spreading his legs. "I'm allll . . . right." He fell backwards. Larry pulled him up again to his knees, then to his feet, and this time Carl accepted his arm.

"Got shot at t'night," he said. "Sombitch try kill me."

"Oh, yeah?" Larry watched Susie in the window.

Carl spun around, wheeling Larry with him. He pointed at the Mutant shack. "See that? S'all yours. Take anything you want— they won't be back. I 'victed 'em."

Larry spun him back around.

"I mean it. S'all yours," Carl said.

Beautiful tits, Larry thought, watching the man's daughter.

When they stumbled onto Carl's porch, Shirley was waiting at the door. Carl saw her and made a triumphant "out" sign with his thumb, nodding smugly, a nod that remained on his chest, forming three chins. She saw a trace of blood in the folds and looked, suddenly distraught, at Larry.

"What. . ."

"L.A. Jones," he said to the attractive blond woman. He let go of Carl, who nestled heavily into a pile on the floor.

"L.A.?" she said.

"Like the city—L.A.," he said. "L.A. Jones. Well, Larry, actually. I'm on vacation for the summer. Just graduated. College."

"Oh, I'm Shirley Mason, and this . . . is my husband Carl. Whom you've already met. He's had some trouble tonight evicting some . . . unpleasant tenants."

Suddenly the pounding electric bass and drums ceased—and Larry remembered the naked girl in the window. He heard a door slam somewhere in the house, and all at once she was there in the kitchen doorway, a sheer pink baby-doll nightie not quite concealing her full, moist figure.

"Mother!" Susie snapped. "You could've at least told me we had company!"

"I'm sorry, dear," Shirley said. She looked at Larry with an embarrassed, apologetic smile. "My daughter Susie."

Larry looked at Susie's breasts and nodded. "L.A. Jones. Just graduated."

She noticed his dark styled hair, his strong jaw and black mustache; his snug designer jeans. She wanted him. She ran her hands down the front of her nightie, pulling the silky fabric tight against her breasts. Her nipples pointed. "Well, I hope you're satisfied, Mother," she spat. "You've embarrassed me again!" She wheeled on one heel, stormed into her bedroom, and slammed the door. Carl covered his head.

Larry abruptly bade Shirley goodnight. He hurried off the porch and turned the corner just in time to see the light in Susie's room go out. He could hear her voice through the window: "All right, you don't have to yell. I'm not deaf, you know. Jesus H. Christ."

"You watch your tongue, young lady," yelled Shirley, her voice muffled from within.

"Drop dead," Susie muttered, but only Larry heard. He walked to his car, shivering, started the engine, and turned on the headlights. They shone through the open doorway of the Mutant shack, illuminating a toppled kitchen chair and a box of cereal on the floor. He remembered Carl's offer—"Take anything you want." So, not wanting to arrive at his brother's house empty-handed, he got out of the car and wandered in.

The first thing he saw when he switched on the light was the white powder on the table. Flour? he wondered. Sugar? Laundry detergent? *Cocaine?* He saw the blood then, a dark, gummy pool of it in front of the refrigerator; and the shotgun, and the arrows, and the black ragged hole in the floor (a musty breeze blew up).

Cocaine!

His mouth dropped. His life changed. Larry knew very little about coke, but once when he had half a gram he got laid three times in one night—by three different chicks. His heart pounded. He looked around the kitchen for something, and he found a grocery bag, to put it all in. He threw the half-full plastic bags in first, then the block, and then he bulldozed the loose powder into the bag with the sides of his hands, and followed it all with the stainless-steel scales. He thought of the dancing girl as he left, and of her attractive mother, and of his sister-in-law. Born lucky, he chuckled. Just born lucky.

11

The Warrior Returns

Shirley Mason sat down. She had gotten Carl into bed, she had put the cat out, she had taken the dishes out of the dishwasher, and, finally, she sat down to watch the "Tonight Show."

Then came a knock at the door.

"Good God," she moaned, hammering the chair arm with her fist. "Now what?" She combed her fingers through her hair and tied her housecoat around her waist and walked through the kitchen to open the door. But what she saw there made her gasp and back away.

It was Luthor Ellis—Nighthawk—tall and dark and swollen in the doorway—and naked, except for a rabbit skin tied around his genitals (its ears hung down between his legs). A leather quiver of arrows was strapped to his back (the arrows were fledged blue, yellow, and red) and rolls of birch bark were wrapped around his feet (moccasins). His brown skin was peppered with welts and specks of blood, and his face was so puffy that his eyes were little more than sparkling slits—the delicate and continuous work of blackflies. He held a longbow in his right hand.

"Nighthawk hungry," he said, thrusting four fingers toward his mouth.

Sensing his earnestness, Shirley repressed a laugh. She cleared her throat, smiling. "Carl," she called hoarsely. "Carl . . . Mr. Ellis is here."

"Nighthawk need food," he said in a deep voice. It occurred to her that he spoke with the same inflection as Tonto, and in truth, he did. Tonto's was the only real Indian voice he had ever heard, and he had mastered the TV Indian's timbre. She went to the refrigerator and began filling a plate with leftovers.

"To go," Nighthawk said, sweeping his hand across the room.

"To go," she repeated, setting the plate on the counter. "To go. Okay, I'll get a bag. Just . . . wait there." She hurried into the bedroom and closed the door. "Carl," she whispered, "Luthor Ellis is here." She shook him and spoke slowly, emphasizing each word. "Luthor Ellis. He's dressed like an Indian."

Carl's eye twitched.

"Carl." She shook him again. "He wants food."

Carl fidgeted and wiped the drool from his lip. "Crazy bas'd," he slurred. "Lock'm up."

"Shhh!" she hissed. "He's right out there."

But Carl just rolled over and snored, and Shirley returned to the pantry, smiling at the patient black man as she passed through the kitchen. "Praise the Lord," she said. In the pantry she found cans of generic peas and corn, spaghetti, ravioli, tuna fish, and condensed tomato soup. She put them in a bag and folded down the top. "Well, the Lord's work is never done, is it, Mr. Ellis?" she said sprightfully, upholding an image that was becoming, distractedly, second-nature. She handed him the bag and folded her hands prayerlike as she waited for him to leave. But he balked at the door.

"What is it, Mr. Ellis?" she asked, her smile sinking like a full canoe.

"Nighthawk want off," he answered, curiously waving at her with his index finger.

"I don't understand, Mr. Ellis."

"Nighthawk want off," he repeated, now waving at himself with his index finger.

"Mr. Ellis—"

"Deep Woods Off," he said in a low, hollow voice, still working his index finger around the room.

"Oh," she said, mimicking his finger motion, "I should have known. Stupid me." But her sarcasm was lost on the large man.

She took a can of insect repellent off the refrigerator and dropped it into the bag. "Well," she said, swinging the door open for him, "okay then. Good night now."

But Nighthawk lingered in the doorway again, searching the floor for the right words.

"Mr. Ellis, there's really no need—"

"Gracias," he mumbled, scowling to himself as he left.

Shirley locked the door behind him. "Good God," she said. She cocked her head and stared for a moment at the knotty-pine pattern ingrained on the door, then shook her head as if to shake off the incident. "Crazy bastard," she said.

Carl Mason never really slept. Rather, he passed from stupor to frenzied nightmare to stupor—all under the power-driven pull of deeply implanted rock 'n' roll—to starts of jolting awakeness, which would be triggered by his glancing into the barrel of a shotgun or by seeing a man foolishly blow apart his own foot. At these moments he'd break free of his moist, twisted blankets and lurch upright, barking, "Gahk!" or "Ahhooo!"

Shirley finally left the bedroom and opened the living room couch. There, she fidgeted under a charcoal woolen blanket, unable to sleep, passing through columns of numbers—the Camp budget—with near delirious repetition, running the same figures through endless operations, and coming always to the same dismal conclusion: They wouldn't last the summer.

Every so often she'd be startled by Carl's muffled cry from the bedroom, and she'd imagine it was the call of an owl or a far-off train, and she'd slip into its tranquility. But then she would recognize his tone, and she'd be yanked back into Camp-consciousness.

She wondered how Carl had evicted the Mutants so effortlessly (she hadn't heard the gunshots earlier, or the screams; only the roar of escaping motorcycles). She didn't know what had happened, and she never would—she would never ask. They were gone and that was enough—finally and blessedly gone—and when sleep at last rolled like a slow fog over her concerns, she eased gratefully under its shroud and drifted off.

.   .   .

Across the pavilion, in a cabin that smelled of disinfectant, Ruth Jones also lay troubled, her husband fast asleep beside her. Something was nagging her, but she couldn't remember what. The smell of old beer and burnt pot on Zippy's breath suddenly disgusted her and she turned away from him.

Our Father, she prayed . . . *No—Dear Lord. Dear Lord . . . It doesn't really matter, does it? I could say Dear Bob, and You'd know I was addressing You, wouldn't You? Dear Bob: This is Ruth Jones . . . as if you didn't know. Ruth, Lois, Heron—that doesn't matter either . . . This is June Allyson.* She smiled. She chuckled.

On the kitchen floor, Zippy's twin brother Larry ground his teeth in his sleep, and Ruth shut her eyes and scowled. She didn't like Larry, didn't trust him. Identical twins, she thought with a smirk— these two were as alike as wholewheat bread and white—Zippy, of course, being wholewheat. Zippy was real, reflective, creative. She likened him to the great inventors—and likened his irony to theirs—here on earth to help society, yet too brilliant to live alongside it. Zippy was the nonconformist, the Thomas Edison just waiting to fulfill his destiny. And one day his genius would bear fruit— maybe not as a songwriter, maybe not as a space pioneer or an inventor (he had sent plans of his transceiver to Carl Sagan)—but one day the world would be a better place because of him.

Dear Lord, I mean, Dear Bob: Now as I was saying, something's wrong. . . .

And then there was Larry—white-bread twin Larry. Larry, who had stayed in high school in '66 while Zippy had quit for San Francisco. Larry, the favored son, who'd gone on to college, flunked out, gotten married, gone back to college, had two children, flunked out, gotten divorced, returned to college, gotten remarried, dropped out, had another child, returned to college, gotten divorced, and finally graduated—Larry's life was a road map of superficiality. He was insincere, self-centered, hung up on the material world, and he thought himself sexy (he had come on to her years ago, when her name was Heron, and would probably do the same thing this visit; when he kissed her hello, he had mouthwash on his breath). And he was so perfect: perfectly styled hair, perfect straight nose, new designer jeans, leather sneakers—he looked like a young TV detective.

Dear LordGodBob: This is LoisRuthJune. Thank You again for everything You've provided, especially this new cabin, which we both love. But something's bothering me, and I can't seem to put my finger on it . . . like when you can't sneeze—you know it's there, but it just won't come? I think it's Zippy, Lord. Don't You think if he was a little straighter, You know, and didn't smoke dope all the time, or if he'd just cut his hair a little, or . . .

She had suggested once that he get his hair cut and shave his face; or even find some clothes that fit. But of course he'd just teased and called her Mrs. Middle-class.

Was she tiring of him?

Is that what's bothering me? Am I tiring of him? No, I don't think so, that's not it. I know I still love him, Lord.

Yeah, but are you tiring of him?

Maybe it's just that I keep changing, while he keeps staying the same. Maybe if he could change too, You know, his hair or his beard—or his clothes. I think he'd look a lot better. You probably do, too.

So you're sick of him.

Well, he can't stay the same forever, can he?

She had been imagining for weeks how he would look changed— clean-shaven, hair cut—how nice they would look together. And now she pictured him again in her mind, the new Zippy, and she gasped.

No!

That was it—the new Zippy . . .

would look like Larry.

She tried to rearrange his face, to make it back the way it was, but found she was unable. He just stood there in her imagination, looking like his superficial, handsome brother.

God, I don't really want him like that. Do I? I mean, do You?

She heard the call of a lonely train—or maybe an owl—in the distance. She opened her eyes again and gazed out the window. The moon had risen above the trees and hung crazy and oblong behind the racing, piling clouds. A silent flare of heat lightning fluttered up the sky, and a soft breath of wind whistled through the screen. And peepers chirped desperately in the night. While far away, high on the ridge, she heard a soft, steady metallic rapping, like someone beating a tin can with a rock.

Part Two

12
·
Sny

Carl awoke too early. His right hand ached, his dry tongue stuck to the roof of his mouth, and his head throbbed with every step he took to the bathroom. As he ran icy water over his knuckles, dreamlike fragments of the night before raced through his mind, and he wondered what really had happened. Were the Mutants gone? Had he evicted them singlehandedly? His unmarked face and swollen fist told him he had. He rinsed his face and shivered.

He walked outdoors, shutting his eyes against the brightness. The air was dry—clear and crisp—the way it should be in early May. Puddles dotted the Camp Road—it had been a hell of a rainstorm. He remembered darting naked through the hallway in the middle of the night with a baseball bat, hollering that someone was throwing slush at the house. You're only dreaming, Susie had shouted, it's just rain on the roof. Shut the light off and get back to bed, he had yelled back at her, I know when I'm dreaming!

Goddamned tin roof.

He climbed Lookout Hill behind the cabins and found Harvey building a picnic table in the thick of the blackflies. The boy was ambitious and hardworking, but he had to be supervised.

"Nice day," Carl croaked.

"Hey! I didn't see you coming."

"Should have built my house up here, Harve. I coulda set right here all day and looked down on the whole campground—seen who's beatin' me, know what I mean?"

"Yup, 'cept for these old blackflies bein' so bad."

Carl tipped his cap back on his head and put his hands in his pockets. "Harve, wouldn't you say that table's a bit on the high side?"

"Huh?"

"The picnic table—it's a little high. It's about five feet off the ground, isn't it?"

"Yeah. I made 'er high so you could see over them pinetops." The seats reached Carl's waist.

"Too high, Harve. Christ, you'd need a ladder just to sit down."

"No, I'm gonna build a step. Already figured that one out."

"I don't think so, Harve. Too high."

"But. . ."

"No, Harvey."

The boy tugged at the top of his ear, swollen and bright with welts. He stepped back, contemplating both the table and the rolled blackfly corpse in his fingertips. "Okay, if you say so," he sighed, stalking the table with the claw end of his hammer. "Guess I oughta take 'er apart then, huh? Start over?"

"No, no. Just say a couple of feet off the legs. No problem. Then we'll pull the table over near the edge there, cut down that brush, and you'll be able to see *around* the pinetops." He tapped his own head. "Gotta think, boy. Think."

"A couple of feet off?" Harvey said, scratching his leg.

"Yup."

Carl stepped to the edge of the hill, parted some branches, and looked down upon the vista that was his campground. He swept from left to right, trying to be objective.

"What a mess," he muttered, thumbing a blackfly behind his ear.

Over on the left, at the edge of the marsh, where cattails made indistinct the line between water and land, Angel's trailer perched on cinderblocks, patiently rusting at the seams, and sagging so severely that a fold of rust ran straight across its roof. In the short bog between trailer and pond a circle of mud was inscribed—mud and dogshit—by Maurice, her poodle, who nervously paced the outer limits of his chain. Behind the trailer, at the end of the gravel Camp Road, stood a rusted industrial loom, sunken inches into the quagmire like some beached iron maiden—massive evidence of the homesteading era when there were sheep at Wind In The Pines and plans for a communal mill on the pond. In the thorny brush beside the loom was Angel's outhouse, surrounded by scattered mounds of spent toilet paper. Two Valiants—one turquoise—and a wringer washing machine sat under a tall pine tree nearby. A clothesline was strung from the tree to a car handle.

To the right of Angel's trailer was Carl's own house, reflecting the sun off its metal roof. It was a comfortable log house, cozy and warm, and, attached to the original Camp Store, it was a large and impressive structure—out of place amidst the squalor there.

Behind his house was the dilapidated shack the Mutants had occupied. Their eviction would cost him a big chunk of his annual income. (Flash of memory: a glimpse of a grisly blown-off foot.) In fact, he thought, it might spell doom for Wind In The Pines. But they had been cheating on their rent, and an example had to be made for the rest of the tenants. Besides, as Shirley had always said, their presence at the campground discouraged the weekend camper, whose business was crucial to the Camp's survival. A coat of paint and a little soap and water, and the place would be good as new.

To the right of the Mutant shack, at the bend in the Camp Road, was Harvey and Jean Duckoff's trailershack—half camper-trailer and half pressboard shack—Harvey's attempt at expansion. The pressboard addition was layered with scraps of asphalt siding—patterns of octangular gray slate or granular brick. The roof was a patchwork of asphalt shingles and scraps of metal (a stop sign and a flattened stovepipe were nailed down to stop leaks), and the entire trailershack slanted enough so when Jean or Harvey spilled milk in the kitchen it would run into the trailer for the cats to drink.

Farther along the Camp Road lay the charred cinder chimney that had once been Zippy and Ruth Jones's cabin: a rectangle of rubble surrounded on three sides by an outhouse, two greasy washing machines, and two vans, all in various stages of dismemberment.

Across the road from the rubble was Mr. Rogers's place, a small, pale house in need of painting. A peeling picket fence lay on its face in an overgrowth of weeds, and the ruins of a delicate arbor stood collapsing upon itself, entwined in bleached dry vines—all traces of a once pastoral home.

To the left of that stood Zippy and Ruth's new cabin, the former

Luthor Ellis house, its lawn green and trim. Ruth was outside now, circling the house with a lawnmower. Since moving in, she had gone on a cleaning binge that approached the obsessive. She had dug up Luthor's buried relics from the yard and taken them to the dump (although Zippy had salvaged many of the things and returned them to a small shed out back). She had reseeded the lawn and even planted a small vegetable garden behind the house, a perfect brown square marked off with string. But hers was the only sign of humanity in the campground, an ominous sign two weeks from opening day. Carl hawked and spat a blackfly down the hill.

Central to Wind In The Pines—across the Camp Road from his own house, and to the right—was the pavilion area, site of all official meetings. Formerly a pen for the commune's hogs, Carl had gravelled the rutted mud rectangle when he first took over. The pavilion area was a thing of beauty now—neat rows of chairs and benches faced a pulpit—a row of sapling hedges lined its borders.

Beyond the pavilion area, lining the shore, barely visible through the scattered pines, were the dozen campsites he and Harvey had built. There was a stone fireplace and a wooden picnic table at each one. He made a circle with his index finger and thumb and nodded approvingly at the sight.

Then he scowled. Interrupting the tidy line of campsites was Earl and Dolly Root's trailer—a sixty-footer—stretching along the shore almost to the ridge. The pale red, white, and blue beast took up the choicest shore frontage on the property, and despite Carl's pleas and his offer of a septic tank and indoor plumbing if they would move it back behind the Camp Road, the Roots stubbornly refused. Dolly Root was Mr. Rogers's daughter, and as kin to the original owner, she claimed protection by the same clause which enabled Rogers to remain forever in his own house.

The Roots stayed inside most of the time. They were fat people— 700 pounds of fat between them. And they farted freely—probably farting right this very instant, Carl thought. And eating pastry, and watching game shows on TV. If God had made people out of rubber, Carl had told Shirley when he had first seen the couple, they'd be just like the Roots.

The Root children, seven in all, had gone to school at their own discretion until they were sixteen, when they quit and moved to a different part of their grandfather's campground. Jean Duckoff was a Root offspring, the only girl and the only one Carl hadn't thrown out of Wind In The Pines. (He had ejected Chickie and Tiny when he caught them breaking into the Camp Store; Squeaky and Peanut after police had found half a dozen stolen cars hidden in the woods behind their shack. The two oldest boys, Junior and Slug, the first to make their way in the world, were now serving time in the state prison for a three-state Root family fencing operation—too many reported items—TVs, cameras, stereos—had shown up at Root flea markets to be written off as coincidence.)

The Roots were a large source of Carl's income. Their monthly store account often came close to a thousand dollars: six hundred in generic pasta and pastry, another hundred in cola. The Roots were a pockmarked, bilious gold mine. So for the time being he was stuck with them—and their trailer.

As his eyes swept up to the ridge he noticed something unusual. Right at the top of the ridge, forty feet up on the rocky ledge that overlooked the right side of the pond, there was something growing—something man-made—low and rust-colored. And there was someone moving just beyond the structure. It was Luthor Ellis. Crazy Luthor Ellis. Nighthawk.

The arrow!

Carl suddenly remembered the arrow that had pinned Hammer to the wall—the blue, yellow, and red arrow—Nighthawk's arrow. And now he recalled the shotgun again—the shotgun that Hammer had blown apart his own foot with.

It had been aimed at him!

"Uhhh," he grunted, clutching at a branch. The crazy bastard Indian had saved his life. Yes, it was Ellis—Nighthawk—there on the ridge. And he was building.

A long, silver El Dorado interrupted his thoughts. It came gliding into sight below him. Carl knew the car—it belonged to Rutus Sny, First Selectman and Health Inspector of Norwood. Sny had been after Wind In The Pines for years, and Carl had been expecting his visit—but not this soon. "You prick," he said, hurrying down the path.

"Huh?" said Harvey.

Carl found Sny at the pond, cupping a handful of water to his nose.

"Ah, Mr. Mason. Can't say I enjoy your blackflies much, but it's a lovely morning just the same."

Carl stood back and folded his arms. "What do you want?"

"Water has a smell to it, wouldn't you say? Shame, it's a damn shame the old man let it go so far."

"I haven't got time to—"

"I'm here to make you an offer for this," he said, motioning distastefully at the campground. "As you know, your tax bill is long overdue, and Norwood simply can't wait any longer for remittance. It just wouldn't be fair to the other taxpayers." He shrugged. "Frankly, I don't see how you could expect to make ends meet with the, let's say, quality of the tenants here."

Carl turned to leave.

"I've done a little investigating, Mr. Mason—I hope you don't mind. I spoke with my brother-in-law Ed Stevens at the bank, and he told me that he refused your request for a second mortgage. He also told me you threatened him. If you ask me, Mr. Mason, you're between the proverbial rock and hard place, so I suggest you listen to what I have to say."

Carl folded his arms and squinted across the pond. "Your brother-in-law Ed Stevens is a goddamn crook," he said.

"Well, be that as it may, Mr. Mason, I have the capital to turn Wind In The Pines into a veritable paradise. And, as you must know, I could pay you quite handsomely for the property as well. What do you say, Mr. Mason? Let's talk turkey, shall we?"

Carl resisted an urge to swing at the man. He adjusted his base-ball cap on his head and rubbed the back of his neck.

Then Sny handed him a small notepad and a ball-point pen and said: "What figure do you think would reflect a fair profit for you?" He withdrew a checkbook from his pocket, a slow smile growing like a rash on his face. "I'm prepared to make the transaction imme-diately."

Carl scratched his chin, walked a few paces back toward the office, and then returned to the shore. Water lapped gently at the sand and he balanced the sole of his shoe on its surface. Finally he let out a long, tortured sigh and scribbled something in the notepad. "You got me," he said sadly, handing the notepad back to Sny. He clipped Sny's pen in his own shirt pocket.

"Oh come, now, Mr. Mason. This is business, nothing personal. Please." He unfolded his glasses, adjusted them on his nose, and peered arm's length at the notebook. On it was written: TEN MILLION. Sny looked up without humor.

"Ninety thousand, Mr. Mason, the same figure I offered your predecessor. Pity for him he didn't take it, too, I'd say."

"Get outta here," Carl said with a jerk of his thumb. He started walking away but then stopped, saying, "No. Wait." He turned slowly, contemplating his swollen fist for a moment, fighting the growing urge to punch his adversary. He looked at his feet and drew an uneven breath. "Lemme tell you something," he began. "You know why Rogers didn't sell to you?"

"I couldn't—"

"'Cause he hates you, same as I do. And you know something else? I'm not going to sell the place to you either. I might donate it to the Y, maybe the Girl Scouts. I might even burn it to the ground. But you'll never get your hands on it."

Sny laughed. "Of course I will. Of course I will. It's inevitable. It's a fact of life. And you know as well as I do that you can't afford not to sell it to me." He pointed at Carl. "But even if you don't, the next sucker down the line will—or the one after him. It's a fact of life, Mr. Mason. Face it. And profit from it."

"No, sir. And the reason you won't get it, Sny—I wanna tell you this—is because it's people like me and Rogers that's gonna keep it—workin' people." Carl turned and faced his property. "Everything—everything you see, from that car to that house to those new campsites—everything—I had to work for. I didn't marry money, Sny, like you did. My old lady isn't a Stevens. Hey, lemme tell you something about the Stevenses. You know, I busted ass all my life for that family, and I'd still be bustin' ass for them today—except for I got my chance, Sny. I got my chance. One chance, that's all I got. One chance. And this is it. But that's something you wouldn't understand."

"Carl, I do understand, and I sympathize with you wholeheartedly. And that's why I want to help—"

"Help? Listen, I know your wife, Sny. Her name's Tiffany. She used to come down to the mill with her father. She got my buddy Tommy Stone canned one day—claimed he whistled at her—Tommy Stone, with five kids at home. She had me drive her to the airport one afternoon, and you know she sat in the back seat the whole way, like I was her chauffeur. Never said a word to me, never even said thank you. And now she wants Wind In The Pines for a country club. And you're telling me you want to help me. The only help I need from you, Sny, is a couple of months to raise the tax money. Other than that we'll do just fine here—"

A soft cry interrupted them, and they turned just in time to see the small, flailing figure of Harvey Duckoff riding a picnic table out of the trees on Lookout Hill. The table rolled down the steep embankment, pitching Harvey out of sight into a thick growth of brush, and finally slammed with a sharp crack against the side of an old spruce, sending a broken seat flip-flopping in the air to the bottom of the hill. Harvey appeared from the brush, waving.

"You've got five days, Mr. Mason, and not a minute longer. I hope for your sake you make the right decision."

"Get the hell out of here."

13

Bugs

"Isn't she a cocker, lad?"

Warren G. Rathbone III sat up in his hospital bed and peered through slits in the bandages that covered his face.

"Four-wheel drive, as well. Climb the walls of this hospital, I'll bet."

It was a picture of a new Chevy pickup, ultra-sleek and ultra-black—blacker than possible—it glowed black. And its cab was encircled by an array of lights—green, red, yellow, and blue—with a warlike chrome searchlight on top. It was a fine black carnival on oversized wheels.

"And it's all yours," Dr. Rathbone said, dropping keys onto the night table. With the chrome searchlight on top, it wasn't difficult to persuade the boy to forget his crushed motorcycle.

"Nnng," Weasel said, closing his eyes, lying back down.

His father looked sadly upon him. What could he possibly have done differently, he thought? Had the boy been destined for such a life of pain?

The trouble had started when the boy was eight, when Mrs. Rathbone died. The lad was crushed. For weeks he stayed in his room, secluded and depressed. Dr. Rathbone called in psychiatrists, psychologists, even checked the boy into the hospital for lithium tests—but the depression only deepened. Finally, when the youngster strangled the family cat, his father decided to put distance between them and their misery. They came to America, to Hartford, Connecticut, to begin a new life. There Dr. Rathbone placed young Warren in a private school, hired a nanny, and even found a private psychologist to resume the lad's treatment. But Warren's attitude only declined.

A year after the move, little Weasel was institutionalized for the first time, after brain-damaging his psychologist. The psychologist's young receptionist testified that she had found the youngster sitting cross-legged on the floor with her boss's bloody head in his lap, crying bitter tears at his inability to pull the halves of the man's skull apart along the fissure he had so carefully made with an egg-shaped glass paperweight.

Ironically, Warren and his psychologist were admitted to the same Massachusetts institution, and Dr. Rathbone relocated there to be near his son. Three years later, due to the doctor's influence on the review board and several generous contributions to the home's library fund, Weasel was released.

But he couldn't adjust to public life. A week after his release he set a neighbor boy on fire and was sent to a boys' reformatory in southern Maine. Once again Dr. Rathbone relocated, this time accepting a position in a Portland hospital. But it was three years before Warren would come home. And by then he had grown into a sullen, brooding teenager, with a decided penchant for spear-hunting turtles and other small, moving things.

Still, the doctor and his son managed to live together peaceably for almost two years in their large seaside house in Falmouth. Weasel attended a nearby alternative high school and visited a counselor twice a week—improving by leaps and bounds, his father told everyone. And the boy might have stayed the course too, had Dr. Rathbone not gotten him a job at the power company. How the doctor rued that terrible day.

For it was on the ground crew that carved ten-foot-deep utility pole holes in ledge and swamps and the sides of mountains that Warren G. Rathbone III first discovered dynamite. And the discovery changed him forever.

One day at the end of summer, when Weasel was feeling anxious about the onset of another school year, he stole a softball-sized chunk of the mysterious claylike substance. That night, with a detonator fashioned out of a twelve-volt battery, and a hundred feet of electric wire, he blew up a Jersey cow on a nearby farm. Of

course, a marble-sized piece of dynamite would have been suffi-
cient, but, as it happened, the exploding cow blew apart the barn,
which in turn collapsed the attached shed on the farmer's wife,
breaking her back. On the day after Labor Day, Warren Rathbone
III was formally enrolled in a four-year program at Thomaston U.,
the Maine state prison.

The doctor gently laid a hand on the boy's shoulder and Weasel
bolted up, wild-eyed. Dr. Rathbone eased his son back down. "Let's
get you back to sleep now, skipper," he said. He took a syringe from
a silvery tray and eased the needle into Weasel's thigh. "You'll want
to conserve your strength, won't you?"

"Nnng."

Dr. Rathbone pulled the cord on the blinds and they skittered
down, cutting off the outside light. Weasel closed his eyes, felt the
drug pull him like grease down a kitchen sink, spiraling down to
another world, deeper and deeper and deeper.

He saw her kneecap first—a teardrop of blood spattered on it—
then he panned up along the pale moors of her naked body—her
dark, fetching pubic mound, her flexed, sunken belly, her soft white
breasts, up along the strained muscles of her arms to her wrists
shackled high above her head to the wall. Her brown eyes were
glazed with fear—exquisite animal fear. He pried open her jaws and
rammed in another fistful of dynamite, then laughed in his sleep as
he watched her try to spit it out—she could only swallow it. She
writhed, and he massaged her throat so she'd swallow more. And
more. And more—until finally the dark gray putty slithered out her
vagina in a long, slender, glistening line—like it was being squeezed
out of a frosting tube. He pulled on it and spelled her name in a
delicate script on the floor:

ANGEL.

He knelt before her and struck a match. Her eyes widened. He
touched the flame to the fuse and it flared along the loops of her
name, then climbed to her pitching, grinding vagina. "Payday!" he
screamed, and the room exploded in pure white ecstasy.

"Bugs."

"Yeah, they're stuck on, Mr. Mason. I couldn't get 'em off."

"Well, Harvey, they gotta come off. The guy's coming tonight to look at the car."

"I dunno. I tried as hard as I could."

"Look. Just get down and scrape 'em like this."

"But the wings. They get up under your fingernails. And there's millions of 'em."

"So what am I paying you for? I don't care if you get wings under your fingernails. I don't care if you get wings under your fingernails and your toenails. I don't care if you got wings comin' out your ass—I just care that I sell this car. Do you hear what I'm sayin'?"

"Uh-huh."

"Oh, and Harvey, I think you oughta take a look at that color TV I told you about. It's a beaut, really; big, too. And clean? You could eat off that set, Harvey. To tell you the truth, I don't think it's hardly been used. I know Jean'd love it. You gotta keep the little woman happy, Harve—happy and well-fed—know what I mean?"

"Yup, 'cept she don't hafta be no more well-fed. She's turnin' fat on me. Tubby, that's what I been callin' her lately."

"Yeah, well, anyway, come over to the store when you're done and I'll give you one heck of a deal on the television. Now do a good job on the car, Harvey. I'm gonna go inside and have some lunch."

Zippy was on his way to the Camp Store for cigarette papers when he saw Harvey on his knees scratching at the long white Lincoln.

"Hey, man, what are you doing?"

"Tryin' to get the bugs off'n 'er."

"So why don't you wash 'em off? You like gettin' the wings up under your fingernails? Gaah, it's turning my stomach."

"Mine too. But Mr. Mason wants 'em all off so's he can sell the car. And they don't wash off. I already tried."

Zippy stroked his beard. "Hmmm." He formed a picture in his mind, a magnified picture of the car's surface, so that it looked like an endless sheet of curved ice—and the insects, spindly and frozen into the ice, were the size of dogs. He imagined a giant thumbnail, like a great curved scythe, trying to scrape them up.

"Won't work," he said. "You need a flatter blade—one that'll adhere to the surface—and some device where they won't jam when you scrape them up."

"Huh?"

"Wait there, Harvey—and take it easy. I've got just the thing for you."

Zippy hurried home and found the box in the shed—the cardboard box of Luthor Ellis relics Ruth had dug out of the ground. He had known there would be a use for them one day—it was all such perfect junk. It was the Auto Sucker he was after—a small, battery-operated vacuum cleaner—and he found it, still in its box. He flicked it on and it buzzed in his hand like a honeybee.

Next he needed a blade—something sharp yet pliable enough to conform to the curves on a car's body without marring its finish. He visualized the magnified sheet of ice again—and the frozen dogs. A monstrous vacuum was riding toward him from the horizon, sucking a clear, shining swath as it came, cleaning the flat areas as well as the rises. As it came closer Zippy tried to make out its blade. Was it metal? It came closer. Rubber? Bearing down on him now—his sneaker laces began fluttering toward its vacuum. Was it a card of some sort—a playing card? The machine's roar was deafening now, and he fought against the gale that threatened to suck him in. Plastic? Yes, yes—plastic! He dived out of the monster's path just as it passed, and looking back over his shoulder he saw the blade clearly: It was a giant, single-edged credit card.

"What are you doing?" Ruth asked.

"Making something for Harvey," said Zippy. "The Bug Shaver."

Larry looked up. "Is that why you've been filing down that credit card? I was afraid to ask. What's the clamp for?"

"You'll see. Hey, don't bogart that joint, brother."

"Good stuff," Larry said, handing the joint to Zippy. "What's the vintage?"

"Homegrown Afghani—last year."

"Tastes Colombian," Larry said, absently thumbing a black ant on the table. Another ant, close behind, latched onto the dead one and began pulling it along. Larry reached out to squash it.

"Wait! Don't kill it," Zippy said. "Did you ever think—listen— you know, that might be the best ant we've got here. I mean, that little guy might be the greatest ant around. Think about it—the cleverest, the wisest, the most holy, the strongest, the most compassionate, the greatest warrior—the greatest ant in Wind In The Pines. Ever. The greatest little ant—a giant among ants—the greatest ant in the town of Norwood. The greatest ant ever in the whole state, the whole country—the greatest fucking ant in the entire history of the world! Have you ever thought about that? And here he is, right here on our table. We've got him."

"That's deep," Larry said.

"Yeah. Hey, guess who I am." Zippy flicked on the Bug Shaver and sucked up the ant.

"Zippy!" Ruth said. "That's cruel."

"No, really. Guess."

"You're not funny," Ruth said.

"Barnum and Bailey," Larry guessed. "No, Ed Sullivan—the way you said, 'right here on our table.'"

"He wants you to say 'God,'" Ruth said, leaving the house.

"Ah, that's sick," Larry agreed, and he followed her out the door.

14

Love and the Barter System

Earl Root turned the corner and wheeled his shopping cart down
the bakery aisle—the "Root Aisle." His cart was overfull, mounded
at the top with a stevedore's precision even before he began ravaging
the pastry shelves; and after, when he pulled the cart to the cash
register, it was heaped up like a Macy's float. "Gettin' some awful
hot again today, ain't it?" he wheezed.

Susie slapped her magazine on the counter and sighed.

"Yessuh, gonna be another muggy one, I guess. Leastwise that's
what they're sayin'."

She didn't reply but started sliding the food past, item by item,
punching the register keys, watching neither the price-markings nor
the keys, though sometimes she'd shake her head in disgust as when
she counted out thirty boxes of cookies, or twelve gallons of ice
cream, or six twelve-packs of generic cupcakes.

"What was you readin' there, anyway?" the fat man asked. He
wore a white satiny short-sleeved shirt adorned with tiny pink bub-
bles and an ancient breast-stain that looked like a jellyfish had once
slept there; and despite his honeysuckle cologne, the stench of his
sweat surrounded him like a yellow-brown aura.

"Nothing," Susie said, turning to switch on the fan.

"*Mountain Girls?*" he said with a big red smile, reading the
magazine's title. "Some cover." A large blond girl was photo-
graphed naked from the back. She appeared to be dancing—or
wrestling—with a llama. She looked back over her shoulder and

smiled for the camera. Earl guessed the llama was trying to get away from her. "That for sale?" he asked.

"Nope. I'm reading it."

"Mind if I look?" Without waiting for an answer, he grabbed the magazine and began thumbing through it. By the time she rang up his groceries, he was red-faced and wheezing like a leaking bellows.

"Five bucks," he said, pressing the magazine to his chest.

"What?"

"I'll give you five bucks for it."

"Look," she sighed, snatching it from him, "there's a whole pile of 'em right there. I told you I'm reading this one."

He spotted the magazines behind the counter and pushed past her, panting, to get at them. Susie imagined his fetid exhalations displacing all the air in the store. She went to the door and propped it open with a chair, taking a deep breath of fresh air before returning.

"Two hundred thirty-seven dollars and thirty-eight cents for the groceries," she exhaled, holding her hand out on the counter.

"Two bucks apiece for the magazines, huh? How much for all of 'em? I counted about fifty in all."

"You counted wrong. There's seventy."

"Whoops. So how much?"

"Two times seventy—a hundred forty dollars. Plus tax."

"Aw, gee. No break for buyin' the lot, huh?"

"Nope."

"I'll give you seventy bucks, cash money."

"That and your good looks'll get you thirty-five dirty magazines."

"All right, all right, you got me. You're quite a young businesswoman," he laughed, straining under the whole stack. "Guess we'll have to put some of this food back, though."

"What?" she said, slapping the counter.

"I said—"

"I heard you."

"Hi," said Larry. He was leaning in the doorway, propping his shades on the top of his head.

"What do you want?" Susie answered, attending to her register tape, wondering how long he had been standing there.

"L.A. Jones," he said. "We met last night."

A drop of sweat formed on her chest and began rolling down her cleavage. She caught it with her fingertip and rubbed it into the counter. He came closer.

"Work here every day?" he said.

"What do you think I do here? Play?"

"I don't know," he teased. "Do you?" He liked the way that line came out, easy and cool as chrome. He folded his arms and posed to the right.

"That's for me to know," she teased back, fanning herself with the front of her haltertop, "and you to find out."

"Miss—" said Earl Root.

"I'm sorry," said Larry, "I forgot your name."

"Susie," she said, suddenly more friendly. "What's yours again?"

"L.A. Jones."

"I mean your real name."

"Well, Larry, actually. But nobody ever calls me that. You probably know my brother Zippy."

"Zippy?" she exclaimed like she'd just chewed a rotten peanut. "God, he's so weird."

"So this is your campground, right?"

"Well, really my father's. He put it half in my name—to try to keep me here, you know—the only daughter, and all that. But I hate it here. I'm going to Fort Lauderdale as soon as we lose the place. I've got a cousin down there—"

"What do you mean, as soon as you lose it?"

"Oh, they raised the taxes on us and closed the beach—they say the pond's polluted—probably is, too. So no campers, no money. They're gonna take the place for back taxes. Either that or the first selectman is gonna buy it from us."

"Sorry to hear it."

"I'm not. If you ask me, I can't wait to get rid of the place. It's so gross. And the people you have to deal with—no offense to you— they're such pigs, you just wouldn't believe it. Can you imagine me dealing with this trash every day? Don't make me puke."

Earl Root: "So what about my groceries?"

"Wait a minute. I'm busy."

"And what do you do when you're not working?" Larry asked.

"Oh, this and that." She smiled coyly. "Mostly that."

"Oh, yeah? Tell me what 'that' is." He was closing in. Already he was tracing a line with his finger up her forearm, making the fine hairs on her arm rise like smoke.

She answered him in a low voice: "Maybe if you're lucky you'll find out some night."

"Maybe, huh?"

"Maybe."

Harvey was scraping bugs from the same car door when Zippy returned with his invention, saying, "Okay, man, stand back—here goes." Harvey stood, furiously wiping his fingertips on his pants, and Zippy began mowing rows of insects from the car.

Harvey's mouth sprang open. "Wow!" he said. "What is it?"

"It's called the Bug Shaver, son, and it's all yours."

Carl Mason ran onto his porch. "Hey!" he yelled. "What are you doing there? Get away from that car."

"No, no," said Harvey, "it's a Bug Shaver, Mr. Mason. Zippy made it for me. Lookit what a job it's doin'."

"It's gonna scratch the paint."

"Wrong," pointed Larry, just emerging from the store. "It's only plastic, Carl—a simple credit card."

"Who the hell are you?"

"You don't remember? Last night—I helped you home."

"So what?"

Larry walked around the car. "Not bad," he said. "Not bad."

"Lincoln," said Harvey.

"Yours, Carl?"

"I'm sellin' it. What's it to you?"

"How come?"

"None of your goddamn business."

Harvey said, "He's gonna put the ol' Buick back on the road. Right, Mr. Mason? Ain't much—seventy-three Apollo, three-fifty—but she always was a good ol' beater."

"You know, Carl, that's a good idea when you come right down to it," Larry explained. "Better to have a good old car than a bad new one." He looked at Carl and nodded. "Think about it."

Carl turned to Harvey and said, "Who is this?"

"It's my brother," Zippy said. "Larry."

"You can call me L.A., Carl."

"You can give me some money, Larry," Carl said. "You slept here last night, right?"

"Well, I stayed with Zippy and Ruth."

"Do me a favor then, would you? Go inside there and give my wife some money."

"No sweat, man. But, you know, I like it here, Carl, and if the price is right, I might just decide to stay for a few weeks. Maybe we can work out a little deal on the rent, huh?"

Carl folded his arms. "So you're a wheeler-dealer, are you?"

Larry folded his own arms and held Carl's gaze.

"Carl," he said, "Wheelin' and Dealin' is my middle name."

15

Cash Money

Larry scrubbed the wooden floor of the old Mutant shack, washed the blood and the years of dirt and machine oil out of its pores. The agreement was two days' work for one week's stay at Wind In The Pines. On the surface it was a deal that favored Carl, but Larry had another motive: He believed that by ingratiating himself with Mason he would be allowed more latitude with the man's daughter.

He was carrying out a boxload of trash when a pink Trans-Am came slowly down the Camp Road and stopped. A man in a pink Stetson rolled down his car window and called to him: "You a friend of Hammer's?"

Larry shielded his eyes from the sunlight. "Might be," he answered.

The man laughed nervously and stepped out of his car. "I take it nobody else has been out to see you—I know it's against policy, but under the circumstances—you know how sorry I am, by the way—" He touched his brim. "Anyway, as soon as I heard the bad news I thought I'd take a chance and drive out here to see if any of Hammer's partners took over the business, if you get my drift."

Larry did, suddenly. He knew exactly what the man wanted. His heart pounded, but he kept cool. "Me," he said, extending his hand. "L.A. Jones. I mean I think it's safe to say that I've taken over the business."

"Excellent." He shook Larry's hand. "Name's Pinky," he said. "Gosh, I've been waiting—we all have—for weeks. People are dying for the stuff."

"I'll bet they are. Well, you came to the right place."

"Great. So if you've got a pound for me, man, I've got the bread. Same price?"

"Same price," Larry agreed. "Wait here." He trotted across the campground to his Camaro. He took a plump plastic freezer bag from the trunk and ran back again, clutching it at his side like a football.

"I think you'll enjoy this," he said when he returned.

"Yeah, great," the man said, shoving the white bag under his pink jacket. "But shouldn't we be a little more discreet? What say we duck into your house, if you don't mind?"

Inside, the man produced a tiny silver spoon from his jacket pocket, dipped it into the cocaine, and sniffed it into a nostril. He repeated the ritual for his other nostril, then beamed.

"Very nice," he said. "Very, very nice." He walked out to his car and came back with a bulky manila envelope. From the envelope he pulled a thick stack of hundred-dollar bills wrapped in an elastic band. "I think it's all there," he said, handing the stack to Larry.

Larry remained nonchalant. He tried to nonchalantly stuff the bills in his pocket.

"You really should count it, man, just to make sure."

"Yeah, right." Larry dropped cross-legged to the floor and dealt the bills like playing cards into a scattered pile. "Thirty thousand dollars," he said finally to himself. His hands trembled. His mouth was dry. "Thirty grand," he yawned. "Looks right to me."

"A little high," Pinky said, "but this is some high-grade blow. I'll be able to get rid of it in an hour."

"Damn straight," Larry chuckled, gathering his money, walking with him into the sunlight.

"Listen," Pinky said as he climbed into his car, "you wouldn't have any more of this stuff, would you? I mean, if it's not promised out—"

Larry folded his arms. "I've got another eight pounds for sale," he said.

"Same price?"

Larry nodded. "And I'll throw in half a pound to boot."

Pinky drummed on the side of his car. "Gimme a few hours to come up with the bread," he said, "and I'll be back for it all. Is that cool with you, man?"

"Yeah, it's cool. But not tonight, man—I've got plans."

16

·

The Offering

The evening descended with promise. Its clear peach horizon graced a wide slate sky, still but for the rich and varied creature calls of spring. Conrad Rogers stopped by the shore, unscrewed the cap from a bottle of brandy, and let the nectar splash off his tongue and run down his throat, thinking to himself: This is the most wonderful evening I have ever seen—a thought he had on many such evenings.

"Any luck, sir?" he said when he saw Zippy—as he did on many such evenings.

"Not yet," Zippy answered, drawing on a joint. "Not tonight anyway."

The old man sat down next to him at the picnic table and studied the silently blinking red lights on the black box. "Good night for it, though, I should imagine." He passed the brandy bottle to Zippy, and Zippy handed him his joint.

Zippy took a long swallow, wiped his mouth, and said, "I haven't tried her since the fire."

"Oh? You don't say."

"Yeah, man. Lots of delicate parts in here." He patted the heavy metal box. "I had to replace a few resistors, a few diodes, a couple of chips, too. But I think she's okay now."

"Couple of chips, you say."

"Yeah," Zippy said. "Computer chips, man. They operate the spectrum analyzer."

"Spectrum analyzer. I'll be darned."

"Yeah, man. The spectrum analyzer monitors two hundred and fifty-six channels at the same time." He took the joint from Mr. Rogers, handed him the bottle. "It scans space for any unusual signals."

"Is that so?"

"Yup. And there's a digital decoder in here, too—it'll decode anything, man—Morse, ASCII, EBCDIC, whatever—and then convert it to written English on the readout screen."

"I'll be darned."

"And I've got a speech analyzer in here, too, so I can speak into her, and she'll translate whatever I say into digital code. And then, with a push of this magic button, she'll transmit the coded message into space at fourteen hundred and twenty gigahertz—that's the radio-wavelength of atomic hydrogen."

"You don't say."

"Oh, man, I'm telling you, this little baby's a marvel. It's got a two-stage gallium arsenide amplifier with an overall noise temperature of sixty-five degrees Kelvin."

"Yessuh."

"And the entire box is lined with zinc."

"Zinc, you say."

"Yeah, man. Wilhelm Reich found zinc to have unusually strong receptor properties. You know Reich—he invented the cloud buster and the orgone box."

"Well, by the Christ, Zippy. And this box is your invention, is it?"

Zippy drew smoke from his joint and puffed it out in slow, concentric circles. "Not entirely, man. It's a pretty conventional homemade radio telescope I built with a couple of Berkeley freaks about ten years ago. The zinc was my idea, though. And the antenna."

They turned to gaze at Zippy's antenna. It was a wooden frame, eight feet square, made of rough-cut two-by-fours, lying flat on four cinderblocks. Chicken wire was stretched across the frame. A black antenna wire soldered to the chicken wire ran back to the transceiver.

"It ain't exactly a satellite dish, but it does the trick. With this baby, I can receive and transmit up to ten light-years away."

"Ten light-years, you say." Mr. Rogers took a long gulp of brandy.

Zippy pushed a softly glowing button on the transceiver and said, "Hello." He turned to Mr. Rogers and explained, "Now that hello is traveling through space at the speed of light—it's already way past the moon—and it'll keep travelin' that fast for the next ten years. Can you imagine how far it'll go—one little hello in space?"

"And you're hoping somebody out there'll answer you."

"Yup."

"And it'll be twenty years for their answer to get back?"

"Yup."

Mr. Rogers reflected. He took another gulp of brandy—Zippy took another hit of pot, and they exchanged again. "You going to be here in twenty years, Zip?"

"Who knows?" He pushed the button again. "Knock, knock," he said into the transceiver, grinning at the old man.

"There it goes," said Mr. Rogers, looking up.

"Wanna try it?" offered Zippy. "Wanna send a message to somebody?"

Mr. Rogers took a hit of pot. He scratched his chin. "I might just do that," he said, sliding closer to the machine.

"Just speak slow and clear," Zippy instructed, "like I did."

Mr. Rogers cleared his throat. He leaned over the machine as Zippy pushed the button. "Hello, Millie," the old man said. "It's Connie." He waved Zippy's finger off the button, then sat back to watch the sky. He took the brandy bottle from Zippy and emptied it into his mouth. "Well, sir," he said, "I think I'll park right here for a spell, if you don't mind."

"Not at all, man. But we'll need more of that stuff. Looks like you're dry."

Rogers patted his pocket and his ring hit glass. "I think we're all set, boy. For a while anyway."

"Far out," Zippy said, looking out at the North Star, just rising.

Susie found the black silk panties underneath her mattress and slid them on, adjusting them so the open slit in the crotch allowed just a wisp of red pubic hair to poke through. She stood before her mirror and turned around, craning to examine her buttocks in the glass. Then she pulled on her tightest white jeans—so tight that she fell down and rolled on her back like a roped calf getting into them. She felt sexy and hot. She slid into a vibrant pink haltertop, then sat at her vanity and worked on her face: a little cherry blush for her cheeks, black mascara for her lashes, pale lip gloss, violet eye shadow, soft brown eyebrow pencil, and finally, a dab of Animal Passion perfume under her chin, behind her ears, deep into her cleavage, on her inner thighs, and down her ankles. She thought as she passed the mirror that she might have overdone it.

So did Shirley who, seeing Susie at the door, said too innocently, "Going out, dear?"

"Drop dead," Susie answered.

It was just growing dark as she stepped off the porch and sauntered toward the Jones cabin. The night swelled with the musky fragrance of the pond and the passionate warbling of young, hot frogs. As she drew near the cabin she saw Zippy and Old Man Rogers sitting at the picnic table, looking up at the sky—the hippie and the wino, she thought—a likely pair. She walked by, ignoring them, then circled the cabin close enough to listen for Larry's voice through the screened windows. She cleared her throat, hoping he'd hear.

"Hi," he said from behind his Camaro.

She jumped. "Jeezum!"

"Sorry. I had some work to do in the trunk."

"Always work in the dark?"

"I've got a flashlight," he said. He was wearing a light V-neck sweater—the dark hairs of his chest filled the V—and a warm glow rose in the pit of Susie's stomach. He closed the trunk and leaned back on the car. "I thought maybe you could show me around sometime."

"Maybe I could," she said, starting slowly, not speaking, toward the shore. He followed.

"He shouldn't have let them put that trailer so close to the pond," Larry said, catching up to her. "The sewage. Doesn't he know?"

"Yeah, he knows. But they won't move it, and he can't afford to evict them."

"And that outhouse over there—is that what it is? Too close."

"So what are you, the health inspector or something?"

"Where's the playground?"

"What playground?"

"Come on. No playground? Nothing for the kids? No wonder the place is going under, if you don't mind me saying."

"Don't mind a bit. Like I told you, I got a cousin in Fort Lauderdale. She owns a bunch of hot dog stands, and she's just waiting for me to move down there. She's gonna set me up with my own stand—right on the beach. No snow, no blackflies, no morons to deal with. I'll tell you, the minute this place goes, so do I."

"Hey," Larry said, drawing closer, "ever do coke?"

"Whaddya mean, cocaine?"

"Yeah."

"No."

"Want to?" He took a bag from his pocket and shook it.

"I dunno, I guess. What'll it do?"

"It'll make you feel great. Really. Give you lots of energy. It's real nice."

She took his arm. "There are other things that make you feel great, you know."

"Watch," he said. He dipped the tip of a small screwdriver into the bag, then lifted it out again, a pinch of powder on its tip. He put it to one nostril, closed the other with his finger, and sniffed. "Here, you try it."

"I don't know," she said squeezing his arm, pressing her body against him.

"Come on, you sound like a virgin—'I don't know,'" he mocked.

She grew rigid and turned away from him. "So what if I am?" she sulked.

"What?"

"A virgin."

"Are you?"

Her eyes searched the moss at her feet. "I'm afraid it'll make me sneeze."

"You won't sneeze." He put a pinch of coke on the screwdriver and held it up for her. "Sniff," he said, and she did.

"So, big thrill," she said. "I don't feel a thing." She filled her nostrils three more times before they moved on, and then she said suddenly, "When the North Star is there—right where it is now— and the sky looks all flat like that, and sort of tinny . . . that's what I like best." She inhaled through her teeth with a hiss, hugging herself. "I love it, don't you?"

"Fort Lauderdale, huh? When do you think he's going to sell the place?"

"Oh, I don't know. Soon, I hope."

"Hey!" he said, snapping his fingers.

"What?"

Larry bowed his head for a second, deep in thought, then turned and looked at Wind In The Pines in one sweeping gaze.

"Larry—"

"Oh. Nothing. Just had an idea—one of my brainstorms. I have them all the time. So, tell me," he said, continuing a past thought, "are you?"

"What?"

"You know—a virgin."

"I dunno."

They stopped walking. "What do you mean you don't know? Either you are or you aren't, right?"

"So, what's the big deal if I am?"

"No big deal. Just asking, that's all."

They continued along the shore in silence, each absorbed privately, until Larry spoke in midthought: ". . . a drive-in screen, with X-rated movies, way up there on the ridge."

"What?"

"Adult movies—for the guests."

"You mean like *Deep Throat*?"

"Yeah, on a huge, monstrous, Cinerama screen." They looked up at the ridge, a piney silhouette now against the starry sky, and imagined it.

"Tsk," Susie said.

"And a water slide off the ridge. For the kids. Is the water deep there?"

"It's polluted. Have you ever seen *Deep Throat*?"

"Hey, let's go up there," he said, leading her toward the ridge. "This place could really be something, you know. I'm serious."

"Let's sniff some more," Susie said. They stopped and looked up at the ridge—a steep, forty-foot-high path had been worn in the hill so that the exposed tree roots made a natural stairway. They sat on a gnarled root at the bottom and snorted cocaine until Susie felt goose bumps dancing inside her skull.

Larry took her face gently in his hands. The moon had risen over the pond, a fine orange crescent, and it reflected in her eyes like an inner flame. "You're beautiful," he said.

"You are too," she said, kissing his wrist. She wet her lips and paused, inches from his face. "I am, you know," she lied in a low voice.

"Huh?"

"A virgin." She kissed him lightly on the lips. "But we could change that tonight." In that instant they plunged into a full-tongued kiss, and his right hand shot awkwardly down the front of her haltertop, seizing her right breast. As the kiss continued they jostled for position—he tore his hand out of her top while she tried to get hold of his buttocks, then he slid both hands up underneath her haltertop, finding both breasts—all the while driving his right thigh into her crotch.

Suddenly an acorn bounced off his head ("Unp," he said), followed by a skittering of pebbles, which struck them both repeatedly.

"What the—"

"Shh!"

They stopped and listened and, in the stillness, heard the sounds of a struggle above them—a dragging, scuffing sound and soft, labored grunting. They looked up and saw, high above them on the crest of the hill, the silhouette of a man dragging something—something heavy—on a rope.

"Who's that?" Larry whispered.

"Shh—"

The figure then came erect—whatever he was hauling was snagged—and Larry could plainly see a feather reaching from the top of his head. Indian? They heard him grunt louder now, straining against the taut rope. Then, finally, with a snap, he came trotting straight down the path toward them, pursued by the sliding dark form on the rope. Before they could move, his trotting escalated to a full, desperate gallop, and the thing rolled up his heels and overtook him. The Indian tumbled into a wild somersault, careening down the hill enmeshed with the dark mass, and slammed to the ground beside the lovers. "Wowwff!" he said.

"What is it?" Larry asked.

"How should I know?" said Susie.

"Buck," Nighthawk answered, struggling to separate himself from the animal. "For Mason." He tugged at the rope, trying in vain to untangle it.

Larry whispered, "That guy's no Indian."

"Don't ask," Susie said.

"Nighthawk need help," the black man said.

Larry got up and stood behind the man, took hold of the rope, and pulled with him. He was hammered by the stench of sweat and insect repellent on the Indian.

"It's snagged," he told Susie. "Go get help."

She hurried off and the two men were left in a long silence. Larry spoke first.

"So, what's this, now? Deer, isn't it?"

"Buck."

"Buck? Looks like a deer to me. Must be what kids call a reindeer, right?"

Silence.

"So, you a basketball player? I mean, judging by your size . . . Were you? In school or something?"

More silence.

"By the way, I'm L.A. Jones. I'm here for a couple of weeks or so, visiting—"

Mercifully, Susie returned with Zippy and Mr. Rogers. "Oh, wow!" Zippy said, shining a flashlight on the buck.

"A fine animal," Rogers said, running his palm along an antler. "Gonna mount it, boys?"

"He caught it," Larry said.

"Gift for Mason," the Indian said, "from Nighthawk."

The four men took hold of the rope and proceeded slowly toward the Camp Road, dragging the quarry behind. Susie followed dourly.

Harvey and Jean Duckoff were outside in lounge chairs, eating generic cookies and milk and watching color TV when the procession drew by.

"Whaddya got?" Harvey called.

"Reindeer," Larry answered.

They ran over to examine the animal. "Awww," Jean whined, wringing her hands, "don't kill it."

"Jeez, it looks dead already," Harvey said, getting a hand on the rope. "Right?"

"Yeah, the Injun killed it," Larry said.

"Nighthawk's arrow flew true," Nighthawk said, perturbed at his unintentional rhyme.

"Awww," Jean said. She ran ahead and rapped on the door marked OFFICE.

Carl turned on the porch light and opened the door. He saw Jean standing there, a wide milk mustache gracing her smile.

"What?" he said.

"We got a surprise for you," she teased.

He waved her away with the back of his hand and closed the door.

"A big, big surprise," she called.

He opened the door again. "Just tell me, okay? Don't screw around."

"Something big," she sang. "And dead."

Then he noticed the crowd moving into the light, with Nighthawk at its center. He stepped out cautiously.

Nighthawk offered him the rope. "For Mason," he said.

"What the hell is it?"

"Buck," Nighthawk said. "For Mason."

Carl rubbed the back of his neck and cleared his throat. He looked around suspiciously. "What's goin' on?" he asked.

"Take the rope, man," Zippy said. "The buck's yours. It's a gift."

"What do I want with it?"

"I am your brother," Nighthawk said.

"No, you're not," Carl said, waving away the ludicrous idea. But then he remembered how the Indian had saved his life the night before. "Okay, okay," he said, taking the rope. "I suppose it is on Camp Property."

"I am your brother," Nighthawk said again, holding up a flattened palm.

"Yeah, yeah. Look, ah—about last night—I guess I owe you. So let's put it this way: You can stay at Wind In The Pines. Okay? Just don't go lightin' any more bonfires." He turned to Mr. Rogers with a grin. "Besides," he said, "I'm still cashing his disability checks.

"Okay, folks, party's over. Let's not stand around attracting bugs. Harvey, you stick around. We'll have to butcher this thing right away. Go in through the house and unlock the store, and I'll meet you at the door with this thing."

As the people walked away, Carl examined the dead animal— lifted its head to gauge its weight. He stooped and hauled the buck's head over one shoulder, then tried to stand, but the dead weight was too much for him. He dropped it, cursing. Then he grabbed the antlers with both hands and tried dragging the animal to the store.

"Your speech broke me up," a soft voice said, startling him. It was Angel, stepping out from behind a stand of poplars. "You blew it, you know. You had a chance and you blew it, Stoneface."

"Go home, would you?"

"Mason, these people love you, don't you know that?"

"Is that what it is?" he grunted, inching the carcass along.

She folded her arms and smiled. "Portrait of The Yankee—rugged individual to the end. Shows no heart, no kindness. Accepts none. He stands—and he falls—alone. Right?"

Carl ignored her. All his concentration was focused on his straining back muscles and his trembling legs.

"Need a hand, Yankee? You're not going to make it alone, you know."

"Watch me," he said.

"Mother, Larry has some great ideas for this place," Susie said.

Shirley looked up curiously from the television to see Susie and Larry holding hands in the doorway. It was the first time in weeks her daughter had begun a conversation that wasn't baited or acid-tongued.

"Oh, I didn't even hear you come in."

"Larry says the pond can be cleaned up."

"That's right, Shirley. You know the way people purify swimming pools with chlorine? Well, you could do the same thing with this pond. Just use more of it, that's all."

Shirley looked at him—then at her daughter—and asked: "Why are your noses white?"

"Oh, Mother," Susie sighed.

"Jelly doughnuts," Larry explained.

Just then Carl came in through the door that led from the store. He saw Larry and scowled. "What does he want?" he asked Shirley.

Susie said, "Larry knows how we can clean up the pond."

"Oh, before I forget," Shirley told Carl. "The man called about the car. He'll be here on Sunday morning to pick it up." She saw fresh bloodstains on Carl's tee-shirt and a bandage on his arm. "Harvey said you were butchering a deer. Did the whole thing fit in the freezer?"

"Nah. I put some of it in the cooler. We can sell it to the Roots as hamburger. So he's gonna pick up the car Sunday, huh?"

She nodded her head, exchanging a look with him that eluded the young couple—a grave look of camaraderie and doom. Carl rubbed the back of his neck. He pulled a handkerchief from his back pocket and blew his nose. Then, without a word, he went to his bedroom.

"Well," Shirley said, "early to bed, early to rise." It was a hint for Larry to leave, but he didn't respond—he still had the impression of Susie's breasts on his palms. "Don't be up too late," she said to Susie with a smile, leaving the room.

"Tsk!" said Susie, turning her head violently away from her mother. "C'mon," she said to Larry. "Let's sit down." She flicked off the lamp and removed the cushions from the back of the couch. And then they leaned back against the wall, listening to the muffled mutterings in the next bedroom, waiting for the silence that would tell them her parents were asleep. And when that silence finally came they lay down, kissing, in the dappled, pulsating light of the color TV.

In the next room, Carl rolled onto his side, then onto his back. He rubbed his eyes and breathed irregularly, considering his alternatives. Rutus Sny had made him a decent offer for Wind In The Pines, and he knew the man would pay even more. But if he held out or refused to sell, the town would simply claim the land for his unpaid taxes—and Sny would grab it before it ever reached public auction. Either way, the bastard would get Wind In The Pines, just as he had said.

Carl heard a knock on the wall behind him. He ignored it.

And what would Sny do with the place? First of all, he'd evict everybody. Then he'd declare the water safe and start building his country club. (Another sharp rap on the wall.) And where would the Masons be? Back in town, in some chintzy split-level house. And Carl would be right back on the loading dock at Stevens' Woolen Mills. (Another knock at the wall, harder. Carl flinched and rolled onto his side.) And what about Mr. Rogers? The old man had virtually given the campground to Carl, trusting that he'd have a place to live out his life. Where would Mr. Rogers go? Probably to Bluffton, to the projects. (Three more knocks, heavier, and in rapid succession.) Carl rolled to his side and laid his arm across his ear.

While in the next room Susie and Larry lay on their sides, locked in an endless French kiss—Larry's hands kneading, massaging, rolling, pinching, fondling, and generally misusing the girl's mammaries—Susie struggling to remove her jeans, occasionally knocking the back of her head against the wall in her furious struggle. Until finally, with a mighty thrust, her pants ripped apart at the seams and her elbow slammed into the wall, dislodging the family portrait from over Carl and Shirley's bed. The picture came down flat on Shirley's forehead, spraying broken glass all around.

"Gahrrl!" she yelled with a waking slur.

Larry was just struggling out of his own pants when the light came on, followed by a shrill whistle. He looked up and saw Carl's plug-frame in the doorway.

Up went the thumb. "Out!" he cried, stalking the couch with the driving compulsion to punch the kid's lights out. But this was no kid, Carl told himself. This guy was fifteen or twenty years older than Susie. He clenched his fists.

Larry stood. He stretched and yawned. "Hey, oh boy, what time is it? Guess I dozed off there." He buckled his belt and turned away from Carl to zip his fly.

Carl targeted the tip of his nose. "C'mere," he said, beckoning with his index finger.

"Daddy!" Susie snapped indignantly. But her protestations carried little weight as she squirmed on the couch, pulling her ripped jeans over her hips. "Larry," she warned, but the handsome young man was already following Carl out of the room, tucking in his shirttails as he walked.

When they reached the kitchen, Carl kicked a chair along the floor to him. Larry sat down. "All right, mister," he said, arms tightly folded, still resisting the compulsion to punch, "what's goin' on here?"

"Excuse me?" Larry said, dusting off his jeans.

"College boy, huh?" Carl said. "You been to college?"

A strange question, thought Larry. "Yeah, I just graduated."

"How old are you?"

"Thirty-five."

Carl nodded, measuring him. "Thirty-five, huh?" He came closer—within inches—to Larry and looked him in the eye. His voice was low, steady, and in tight control. "Do you know how old my daughter is?" he said.

Larry shrugged.

"Eighteen," Carl said. "She's eighteen years old—half your age, for chrissake!"

Larry reflected for a moment. "No," he said, "not really. Think about it, Carl. Two times eighteen is thirt—"

Carl's fist shot out—Larry flinched—but the fist turned into one stubby, pointing finger, which poked repeatedly into Larry's chest. "You think about this, mister," he growled. "That's my daughter in there. You got that, hotshot? My little girl." He rubbed the back of his neck. "She's just a kid—a teenager. She still lets me take the barrettes out of her hair at night, goddammit!"

Larry cleared his throat and took a breath to speak, but Carl continued.

"All right, no bs," he said quietly. "I was your age once—not too awful long ago, either—and I know what it's all about. Young girl;

good lookin'; innocent; single; good build—you're not bullshittin' anybody." Larry looked at his watch. "But I'm gonna tell you this, mister. And you best remember it good: If you do anything to hurt that girl—if you so much as put one teardrop in her eye—so help me God you'll live to regret the day you were born. That's a promise."

Larry remembered the puddle of blood in the Mutant shack and nodded meekly.

He said, "I know we just met, Carl—I mean Susie and me—but there's a kind of magic between us. Really. Call it chemistry, call it fate, call it love if you want. All I know is the way we feel about each other. And believe me, I'd never hurt that girl."

Carl nodded. "Lovely," he said. "Just remember what I told you. Now get out."

17

Cowboys on the Moon

How often at night, when the heavens are bright,
With the light of the twinkling stars,
Have I stood here amazed and asked as I gazed,
If their glory exceeds that of ours.

Home, home on the range!
Where the deer and the antelope play,
Where seldom is heard a discouraging word,
And the skies are not cloudy all day.

"The big bang—know what that is?" asked Zippy.

"Oh, I guess. S'what makes the world go round, wouldn't you say?" Rogers chuckled, breaking the seal on another bottle of brandy.

"No, man. The big bang is how the universe was formed."

"Just a theory, that's all," Ruth called out the screen window.

"That's what she thinks. The big bang happened about fifteen billion years ago. There was this particle, see, tinier than an atom, but superhot and superdense, and dig this—it weighed as much as an entire universe. 'Cause it *was* the entire universe, man—just supercompressed. And then, bang—it exploded, and the universe was formed. And it all happened in a tenth of a thousandth of a millionth of a billionth of a trillionth of a trillionth of a second— the big bang, man."

"You don't say."

"Yeah, no kidding. It's all about density, man. Everything's just a matter of density."

"Hey, boys, how they hangin'?" It was Larry, coming to join them on the picnic table.

"Well, if it isn't my old friend Country Roads," said Mr. Rogers. "Zippy, have I ever introduced you to my old friend Country Roads?" He pulled Larry by the arm and laughed as he had the night before.

"Yeah, we've met, man. He's my twin brother, Larry."

"Call me L.A."

"No," Rogers said with an air of disbelief. "Brothers, you say? I'll be darned." He put a hand on each of them. "Good boys. Good boys."

"Where you been, Lar?"

Larry sat up on the table. "Oh, I've been making the rounds with Susie."

"Susie," Rogers reflected. "Carl Mason's girl. Big knockers, that one."

"Big—and soft," Larry bragged.

"Awfully horse-faced though, wouldn't you say?"

"Oh, I don't know," offered Larry, taking a hit of the old man's brandy. "You oughta try her in the sack."

"Woe-woe," Zippy said. "Listen to Mr. Cool; Mr. Fast Mover here."

Ruth called out the window again, "Would you mind changing the subject?"

"Good girl, though," Rogers said, turning solemn.

"Yeah," Larry said. "We're thinking about getting married."

Zippy looked across the darkness at him. "Bullshit."

"Hey, no lie. Don't say anything to anyone, though. We don't want it to get around." He took a hit of a joint and then said casually, "I'm also thinking about buying into this place."

"Gimme a break," Zippy said.

"Used to belong to me, you know," Rogers began. "Belonged to my wife's family before that, back when it was a farm. Big farm it was, too. Had some trouble with black bears one year, I remember—bears everywhere that year."

"You know you could compress a black bear to the size of an atom?" Zippy said.

"Trash compacter?" Larry asked.

"Density, man. You could compress all the molecules of, say, the White House into the size of a grain of sand and it would still weigh as much as the White House."

"What?"

"Yeah, that's a fact, man. You know how dense that would be—a grain of sand as heavy as the White House?"

"Hey, that must be good weed, brother."

"Pretty fucking dense, man, denser than anything imaginable. And it would sink—it would fucking plunge—right to the center of the earth. Nothing could stop it—not granite or steel or diamonds—nothing. It'd just plunge!"

"Gimme another hit, would you?"

"That's how black holes are made, you know. Black holes in space. Ever hear of a black hole, Mr. Rogers?"

"I don't recollect—"

"Yeah, when some stars die, what happens is, the whole thing, in the tiniest fraction of a second, plunges to its own center—it becomes dense—super, super dense—and the entire star collapses, man, with such incredible force that it disappears from the universe and goes into the anti-universe. The anti-universe, man. It becomes a black hole. It becomes anti-matter. It even sucks time out of existence. Anti-time, man. Anti-everything."

"Hey, that's real awesome, brother. You know the first thing I'd do if I owned this place? I'd get that trailer back away from the water—"

"So if I wandered into the black hole, you know what'd happen?"

"What?"

"Boop—the universe would have a negative Zippy on its hands—"

". . .and I'd build a playground for the kids—"

". . .a negative Zippy and a positive Larry. Matter and anti-matter, just like in the beginning. Matter and anti-matter." Zippy took a long draw on the brandy bottle. "And you know what happens if matter and anti-matter meet?"

"Ah, gee, no, brother. What?"

"They annihilate one another. Poof! Matter, anti-matter, density, that's what it's all about. So, brother, if I ever get sucked into a black hole, stay the fuck away."

"By the Christ, I remember the year when this black bear come down with a case of rabies. Went wild, it did. Got into the hen house, ate up the hens and chickens, and then—as if they weren't enough for it—it went into the barn and got after the milk cow. Tore the bejesus outta that poor old cow—"

"Wait!" Zippy said. "Shhh!" A tiny green light glowed on the transceiver and two yellow lights began blinking in a pattern synchronous with its high-pitched beeping.

"What's that thing?" Larry asked.

"Shhh!" Zippy hissed, waving him quiet. "Holy shit, man!" he whispered. "I'm getting something!" He looked down at the readout screen and dusted it off with his finger. "'Cow, cow, cow, cow'— that's all it says." He pushed a softly glowing button. "Okay, be real quiet now, boys," he said, and then he spoke into the transceiver, slow and robotlike:

"I . . . am . . . Zippy."

There was a long pause, followed by a flash of yellow lights: "Cowboys," came the reply on the readout, and the machine fell quiet again.

"Cowboys?"

Then the machine erupted, blinking and beeping and conveying the same message over and over: "cowboys, cowboys, cowboys, cowboys, cowboys, cowboys, cowboys, cowboys, cowboys, cowboys, cowboys . . ."

"C'mon, what's happening here?" asked Larry.

"I . . . am . . . on . . . the . . . third . . . planet . . . from . . . the . . . sun," Zippy said, pushing the button again.

"This is pretty weird if you ask me."

"I . . . desire . . . a . . . meeting. I . . . desire . . . space . . . travel. . . . Will . . . you . . . come . . . for . . . me?" He released the button and waited for a response. "Oh, man," he said, "please say yes."

The reply came immediately. "Yes."

"Awright!" he shouted. "They're coming for me! They're com-

ing, they're coming!" His finger on the button was trembling.
"Where . . . are . . . you . . . coming . . . from?" he asked.
"*Third planet from the sun,*" came the cryptic reply.
Zippy lowered his head in confusion. "How could they be? We're
on the third planet from the sun!"
"Maybe you're picking up ham radio," Larry offered.
"No, it's coming from up there somewhere. . . ." Zippy looked
up at the sky, contemplating. And then it hit him. "That's it, man!
They are here—right up there. They're on the moon!"
"Come off it."
"I know it, I know it! Watch this," he whispered. "I know they're
on the moon."
"What . . . is . . . your . . . location?" he said.
"*Moon.*"
"They are! They're on the moon!" He could hardly believe it
himself. He gulped Mr. Rogers's brandy, and the three of them
raised their heads together and gazed at the thin, silvery crescent.
"Cowboys? On the moon?" Larry asked.
"Hey, man. They're coming down to get me. I gotta get some
things together."
"Wait a minute, brother. You're not serious." He looked at Mr.
Rogers. "He's not serious, is he?"
"When are they coming, Zip?" Rogers asked. "Maybe you
should ask?"
Zippy pushed the button: "When . . . will . . . you . . . come
. . . for . . . me?"
"*Moon.*"
"Huh?"
"*Moon.*"
"I don't understand. I ask them when they're coming and they
keep saying 'moon.'" He tried again, this time rephrasing the question: "Come . . . for . . . me . . . when?"
No reply. The machine fell silent and dark. They huddled
around it waiting for another message—listening, watching, waiting, as a cool breeze picked up and shooshed through the pinetops.
After a while Larry's eyes got heavy, and he began to drift. He stood

and stretched and started for the cabin. "I'd love to stay, boys, but I've got a busy day planned for tomorrow." He went inside.

Soon afterward Mr. Rogers began to snore. Zippy lit a joint and drew deeply, considering the cowboys on the moon, wondering if perhaps they had once somehow been sucked into a black hole for a microsecond—a century in earth time—then redeposited on the moon. He wondered what they ate, how they breathed, how high they could jump.

"I'm awake," blurted Mr. Rogers.

"I guess that's all for tonight," Zippy said.

"Yup. Time to hit the hay." The old man stood and dragged himself home, while Zippy laid his head sideways on his arms and looked across the water to the darkness beyond. The moon was new and not yet bright enough to cast its own reflection on the pond. New moon, he thought as he dozed. Then his eyes opened wide.

"Yeah," he breathed, looking up at the moon. He smacked the table with his hand. He turned once again to his machine, pushed the button, and said: "Will . . . you . . . come . . . for . . . me . . . on . . . the . . . next . . . full . . . moon?"

The reply came in a single yellow burst:

"*Yeah.*"

18

Love, Supply, and Demand

Saturday morning dawned crisp and bright. A cool gust of wind and the revving of a car's engine jolted Zippy awake on the picnic table.

"Excuse me, my man. Sorry to wake you," said the man from his slick pink car. I'm looking for Larry Jones. Know where I can find him?"

Zippy rubbed his eyes.

"That's me," said Larry, emerging from the cabin and buckling his belt. Then, recognizing Pinky, he nodded and pointed at him.

"L.A.," Pinky said. "Can we talk?"

Larry pointed again, and nodded, and winked.

"Was that a yes or a no?" Pinky asked.

"Right on," Larry said, stepping into the car.

Zippy rose stiffly and stumbled off behind the cabin to urinate. He walked into his house just as Ruth was getting out of bed.

"You didn't come to bed again last night, Zip," she said to him.

"Yeah, I know. Sorry. When's the next full moon?"

"I don't know. Why?"

"Well, where's the calendar?"

"What calendar?"

"The calendar we've had for the last three years," Zippy said with an uncommon edge.

"It burned in the fire with everything else."

"Oh, no."

"There's a calendar in the store, I think. What do you need it for?"

"That's right, the store," he said, hurrying out. "I'll check that one."

Ruth followed him outside and watched him break into a stiff-armed gazelle trot across the pavilion area, heading for the store. She turned to go back inside when something drew her attention to the picnic table: tiny blinking red lights—Zippy had left the transceiver on. "Oh," she sighed, "that machine again." Then, almost in answer to her, almost mocking, the transceiver began beeping. A green light glowed in its center, and two yellow lights blinked rapidly in time to the beeping. The readout screen repeated one word over and over: "*Again, again, again . . .*"

"Zippy, Zippy, Zippy," she said, shaking her head, flicking the transceiver off. "Boys and their toys."

When Zippy reached the store, Dolly Root was just going in, laden with a heavy stack of magazines. She squeezed through the door and slammed the magazines on the counter.

"I want my money back for this filth," she demanded, upturning a palm on the counter.

Susie looked up, uninterested. She said, "No refunds," pointing with her thumb to a sign on the wall which said NO CHECKS.

"What?" the fat woman demanded. "That don't say 'no refunds.' I want my money back, now." Again she slapped the back of her hand onto the counter.

Zippy picked a magazine off the stack and began thumbing through it: *Naughty Nurses.*

"Sorry," Susie said. "Store policy."

"Oh, no you don't, girl. You don't pull that policy horseturds with me. We gotta eat over there, and we can't eat no policy horseturds."

"Sorry," Susie said, humming to herself, examining her breasts. She noticed Zippy then.

"What do you want?" she barked.

"One hundred and forty dollars!" the woman yelled. "Plus tax!"

"Don't you yell at me!" Susie shouted back at her. "Go yell at your husband—he bought 'em."

Just then Carl appeared. He had heard the exchange from the back room. "Give Mrs. Root half her money back," he said to his daughter.

Dolly Root wheeled around. "Seventy bucks? No way! We'll run out of food by Monday. A hundred twenty-five."

"A hundred, and that's the best I can do. Take it or leave it."

"Well, that's better," Dolly snapped with grim satisfaction. She snatched *Naughty Nurses* away from Zippy and returned it to the pile. "I'll just get a hundred dollars' worth of food then—if you don't mind," she said to Susie, smiling pointedly.

Susie shrugged. "Knock yourself out." Then she turned to Zippy. "Are you still here?"

"I guess so," Zippy said, examining himself comically. But his humor was lost on Susie.

"Well?"

"Have you got a calendar?"

"Maybe."

"On the wall," Carl said. "By the door."

Zippy studied the calendar and found a small circle—FULL MOON—on May 25th. Someone had circled the date with a thick black marker. "Hey," Zippy said, thinking someone else had been contacted. Then he saw the scribbled note next to the circle: *Opening Day!!*

"Far out," he exclaimed. "Two weeks."

"Far out," Susie mocked as he left. "That's where I'd like to be. Far outta this dump."

Outside, Zippy noticed Larry and the man in pink standing in the overgrowth of weeds beside the Mutant shack. They were shaking hands and laughing. Get a load of Mr. Popularity, Zippy thought to himself as he plodded across the pavilion area, upsetting one of the chairs Shirley Mason had set up there. "Mr. Popularity," he said to her, indicating Larry, but Shirley turned away from him as he passed.

"Get a job," she muttered.

Carl turned up the megaphone. "Attention! Attention! Everybody to the pavilion area. Special meeting. Nobody excused. Everybody to the pavilion area. On the double."

In minutes, the area was filled—even Angel came, although she stood off to the side, looking mightily annoyed. Earl Root sat alone on a wooden bench. His wife Dolly sat opposite him, munching on generic cupcakes and candy, glaring at her husband as she chewed. Nighthawk trotted down from the ridge and settled cross-legged on the ground in front of the podium. Susie came last, searched the gathering for Larry, and, not seeing him, stood with Angel apart from the rest. Carl took the podium solemnly. "Shirl," he said, "start 'er off, honey."

Shirley Mason rose and took the megaphone. Her voice echoed back from across the pond as she spoke. "Lord," she prayed, "bless us all, your servants, as we gather today. We thank you for your many blessings and ask vengeance on our enemies. In Your name we pray, Amen."

She returned the megaphone to Carl and sat down. He sighed loudly, then began: "I've got something to tell you that I wish to Christ I didn't have to say, folks." He spoke softly, almost inaudibly, surveying each captive face. For the first time he felt almost responsible for his tenants. "Now I won't mix words. I know some of you have heard rumors, but I want you to hear it straight from the horse's mouth."

"The horse's ass," Angel whispered, and Susie guffawed. Shirley shot her a vicious glance.

Carl continued: "We're losing Camp Wind In the Pines, folks. We're selling out. The town doubled my tax bill on the place, and I just can't raise the money. So we're selling."

Mr. Rogers stood and jabbed a finger into the air. "Rutus Sny," he said. "Am I right?"

Carl avoided his face. "I probably shouldn't say."

"He never could be trusted, that Sny," Rogers said. "No sir, he's a bad one. Tried to steal the place right out from under me, he did—but I wouldn't have it. No sir."

"I talked to Mr. Sny earlier this morning," Carl said dryly, "and he made me an offer. We haven't got any choice in the matter, folks. We're going to meet with his lawyers on Monday morning. I just wanted to let you know so you could start making plans. I also want you to know that we've been—both Shirley and Susan and me—real, uh, proud to have you all as tenants, and especially Harvey there, with all his help, and, well . . . all I can say is, we gave it our best shot. . . ." He lost his voice for a moment, lowered his head, and cleared his throat.

"Yea!" Jean Duckoff cheered, clapping her hands. Harvey joined her, standing. Carl waved them quiet.

"If there's anything I can do—for anybody—don't hesitate, okay?"

"Ask him," Jean whispered, prodding Harvey with her elbow. "Ask him."

Harvey shook his head, tried to wave her quiet.

"C'mon, ask."

"What is it, Harve?" Carl said.

"Well," he said, "when do you think we'll be gettin' cable TV down here?"

Meanwhile, in Bluffton—

"Wow, you look like The Mummy. What did you do, break out of the hospital and steal them wheels? Man, that's one mean black mother of a truck."

"Nnng," Weasel chuckled, holding the steering wheel with bandaged hands.

"Oh, you're bad, man," he laughed. "The baddest."

"Nnng nd mng nn ngnng—"

"Uh, it's a little hard to understand you with your jaw wired up, man. Save your voice. I got your note, anyway, and the stuff's right here." He loaded a wooden box wrapped with black wire into the back of Weasel's truck. "This box is your detonator," he said, "and there's a hundred feet of wire all connected for you." He gingerly laid a small cardboard box beside it. "There's enough stuff here to blow the side off Mount Washington, so watch your ass, bad boy. Just mold the stuff to whatever size or shape you need—make sure you wear gloves—then put the wire leads into it and get behind something heavy—far, far away—and push the plunger down. Ka-boom—mountain's gone."

"Nnng," Weasel said, starting the truck. He tossed his last gram of cocaine out the window for the man.

"Thanks. Remember this, though. That's Highway Department

stuff. If anything goes wrong—if you get caught—you found it, right?"

Weasel floored the accelerator, laid thirty feet of rubber on the road, and was gone.

The afternoon sun shone full on Larry's legs. He sat on his rear bumper, partially shaded by the hood of his opened trunk, surrounded by money. He lay back into the cash and closed his eyes— he was swimming in money, basking in the glow of wealth: nearly three hundred thousand dollars! And he still had half a pound of blow left over for himself. That's what Pinky had called it—blow. You the cat with the blow? That's right, man—L. A. Jones—the cat with the blow. He grabbed a fistful of bills and sprinkled them on his face. L. A. Jones, man. The cat with the blow—cat with the dough.

The first thing Larry bought was a camera—a ten-second instant camera at K-Mart in Bluffton. Susie asked him why—why had he insisted she leave the store and come with him—just to buy a camera? But he wouldn't say. Then he drove to Big Al's New and Used Cars. He pulled in and asked for Al.

"He's busy now. Can I help you?" the salesman said, a big, dark-haired, middle-aged man in a blue plaid suit and white shoes.

"Yeah, I'd like to try out that convertible there, the silver one."

The salesman hesitated. He bobbed a bit, feinting left and right with his head. His ears were gnarled, his nose crooked as a root— evidence of younger days spent in the ring. "Can't," he said, with a slight duck. "Nobody takes that one out of the lot. That's a Porsche 944—twenty-two grand."

"No problem," Larry said. "Got it covered. I'd like to sit in the driver's seat just to see how it feels, if you don't mind." He handed Susie the camera. "Can we put the top down?" he asked the salesman.

The salesman weaved and snorted. "I'll get Big Al," he said.

"Just push that red button when I tell you to," Larry told Susie, "and make sure you hold the camera still."

Just then Big Al appeared in a puff of cigar smoke. "Beauty, isn't she? Best car made, this one." He held out his hand, palm down, and pumped Larry's. "Big Al, everybody's pal," he smiled. He wore a cream three-piece suit and a cream fedora hat with a turquoise feather tucked in the band. "Now what can I do for you kids?"

"L.A. Jones," Larry said with a confident nod. "Would you put the top down for me?"

"Know what that is, kid?"

"Yeah, it's a Porsche. Big deal."

"All twenty-two thousand bucks of her," Big Al laughed.

"Is that all?" Larry said, putting on his shades, examining himself in the window of the car.

Big Al raised an eyebrow and opened the car door for Larry. "Sit right in there, son, and I'll have Carmine bring the keys."

"What do you think?" Larry asked Susie.

"I think my old man's gonna be some ugly that I left the store. Tell me what you're doing, Larry. You're not really gonna buy a car."

Big Al handed him the keys. "Start her up, Larry, if you wanna hear a real kitten."

"No, just put the top down."

Big Al obliged. Larry reclined in the bucket seat, laid his left elbow out the window, and held the top of the steering wheel with his right hand.

"Take the picture," he said to Susie, raising his chin.

They examined the photo together on the car's hood. "Not bad," Larry mused. "I should get one of those racing gloves, though."

"Can we go now?" Susie said.

Big Al folded his arms. "Look, folks, it's about closing time—"

Larry dipped into his pocket and withdrew a hundred-dollar bill. He offered it to Big Al without looking at him, and the big man snatched it.

"Larry—" Susie protested.

"Would you put the top down on that green one? What is it, a Jag?"

"That dark green convertible? That, my boy, is a Mercedes 380-SL. Best car made. I'm afraid that's probably out of your league, though."

Larry turned slowly and looked straight at Big Al, without expression. It was a long, hard squint, the kind of look that made Clint Eastwood wealthy. "I doubt it," he said.

Big Al snapped his fingers. "Keys," he snapped, and Carmine hustled to the office. "You look like the adventurous type to me," he said to Larry. "Are you?"

"I've been told," Larry said, sliding into the car.

"Well, then, this is the baby for you." Big Al unlatched the canvas top and lowered it.

"Watch the glare on my shades," Larry told Susie, as she snapped his picture.

"You a movie star or something?" Big Al asked. "Television?"

Larry smiled and turned to Susie. "What do you think, baby?" he said to Susie as they watched the photo materialize. "I think this is the one." He compared photos, then pondered for a second. "Definitely the Mercedes."

He turned to Big Al and said, "I'll take it. Just make sure it's got gas in it."

Big Al squeezed his salesman's arm. "Put gas in it," he laughed. "Did you hear that, Carmine? 'Put gas in it,' the man says."

Then to Larry: "Now how do you want to handle financing, Mister Jones?" But Larry had gone to the Camaro and was sifting through its trunk. Susie looked at Big Al and shrugged her shoulders. He returned the shrug.

"How much?" Larry called.

"How much what?" Susie asked.

"No, Big Al—how much for the wheels?"

"That's forty-four, eight-sixty-seven, plus tax. Call it forty-seven and change."

"Thousand?"

"Yeah. Forty-seven thousand."

Larry walked toward him with a grocery bag in his hand. "Take cash?" he asked.

Big Al reached for his heart. "Kid, you're killin' me."

Fifteen minutes later, when the paperwork was done, Larry pulled the forest-green Mercedes out of the lot and headed downtown.

"Where did you get all that money?" Susie asked, nearly shrieking.

"I'm a counterfeiter, didn't I tell you?"

She wasn't sure if he was joking. "Did you see the look on his face when you dropped the bag of money on his desk? He almost croaked!"

Larry smiled and said, "Some people just don't know how to handle money."

They pulled up to Tubmann's Jewelry Shoppe on Main Street just as the small, bald owner was sliding a steel bar into place on the front door. Larry hopped out of the car, raised his shades, and said: "One minute there, pops. How about staying open another fifteen minutes?" There was a fifty-dollar bill between his thumb and forefinger.

They drove back to Norwood against the setting sun, the cool evening air whipping around the low green car and caressing the backs of their necks. Deep in their leather seats, drenched in the punch of rock 'n' roll from the car's radio, drenched in luxury, Susie held Larry's arm and pulled herself close to him, kissing his ear as he drove. She eyed her new ring at different angles, tilting the back of her hand toward the sun, then away from it, letting its fading brilliance dance off the diamond in glorious pinpricks of color.

"It's like a star," she said. "It burns and burns—it just doesn't stop. Like making love." A wave of ecstasy overwhelmed her. "I'm so happy," she said, "I could shit."

Larry put his arm around her and buried his hand in her blouse. "Tonight," he said, "I'll show you what real happiness is."

She squeezed her thighs together and leaned forward, gasping. Her face flushed.

"Hurry," she whispered.

19
Intrusion

The peeping of frogs cascaded like raindrops over the poodle Maurice, and like a robin in a spring shower he waded into the thick of it, nose twitching along the damp ground—stalking—until his chain suddenly snapped tight.

The peeping ceased.

He hunkered down in the reeds and waited, perfectly still, barely breathing—*Patience is the hunter.*

A flute trilled. A trumpet squawked. A bass viol plucked, and suddenly the air rained again with the thrilling cacophony of beckoning frogs. Maurice licked his lips.

Then he spotted her—climbing over a sprig of pale, dead grass, eyes dark and dumb, moving closer, blindly closer to ecstasy—her egg sacs were full and she could do nothing but heed the beck of her mate. Maurice waited, nearly whined with eagerness as the inches between them diminished, and when he could wait no longer he lashed out against the tug of his chain. But he caught only her rear quarter, severing her leg from her body in his growling fervor, and so he watched helplessly as the plump, wide-eyed morsel tumbled just beyond his reach.

He gulped the leg whole, tasting nothing but a trace of bloodsalt on his muzzle. Nevertheless, it was exquisite, and he craved more—straining against his chain for her. But she was gone, kicking and turning foolishly on one leg, with one purpose, kicking for the bog.

Then suddenly a brown leather boot dug its side under the frog and nudged it back, and Maurice, with a lunge and two gulps, devoured her.

"That's my good dog," Angel said, scratching behind his ear. "Maurice likes his froggies, doesn't he?" She dropped a small piece of steak on the ground in front of him. "Mama's got some business in town, baby, but I can't take you with me. So be a good boy and I'll be back in an hour or two, okay?"

Maurice's ears perked and he attacked the steak, first throwing it in the air and then diving after it. For Maurice, the hunt was everything. Even after Angel's Volvo had crept along the worn Camp Road and disappeared, he still cradled the meat in his paws and teased it, gauging with an inner sense its pain.

All at once Maurice dropped the steak and raised his nose into the air, sniffing deeply. A low growl rose in his chest, a mean scent on the wind.

It was he—the adversary.

Maurice slunk toward the trailer, listening with ears grown perfect to the distant snap of a twig, the steady hush of decayed leaves under foot. Here he would lay for his enemy, unseen behind the porch step—just a twitching nose poking the air. His heart raced. He salivated freely.

And then he saw him, the adversary, at the edge of the woods— shadowless, the color of snow—walking stiffly, like a stick-man, three-legged man. It was a disguise. But Maurice was not fooled. The scent was true.

The day was quickly losing its color, giving way to the slate and shadow of evening. Weasel leaned against a fir tree to catch his breath. He surveyed the area: The trailer was dark, the Volvo gone— just as well she's not home, he thought, I'll take her by surprise. He adjusted the wooden crutch under his arm and hobbled to the huge industrial loom behind the trailer. Then, kneeling, he took the detonator box from his pack and tucked it on its side under the overhanging hulk. The bitch would pay tonight, he promised himself. Angel would pay. "Nnng," he said aloud, backing slowly toward the trailer, unraveling the electric wire behind him as he went.

Closer and closer the stick-man came. Maurice rolled his lips over his teeth, gnawed on his own leg, and whimpered.

Patience. Patience.

He lay like a rock, listening for the first footfall on the step. And when it finally came, he sprang up and seized the leg, biting down till his jaw ached. But something was wrong. There was no warmth, no salt in the bite. No pain. He looked up. The adversary was grinning, raising his other leg—no—it was a stick, and something gleamed at its end. Maurice tried to release his bite, but his teeth stuck. Then the stick came down onto his neck, and he screeched, twisting and falling from the man, rolling in the dirt, mindlessly trying to bury the terrible pain. And the shame.

Weasel gloated. "Nnng," he laughed, wiping the dog's blood from the spike he had driven into the bottom of his crutch. He made another threatening move at the poodle, who whimpered and slunk away. Then he slipped on a pair of thin white gloves and went inside.

He searched the bedroom first—Angel's blue bedroom—emptied her bureau and jewelry drawers onto her Persian rug and rolled the rug against the wall; stripped the bed of its teal silk sheets, then overturned the mattress and box spring. He went into the bathroom next, tore through the medicine cabinet and opened every bottle, spilling the contents onto the floor. Still he found no cocaine, no money.

Dizzy and winded, he hobbled back to the kitchen and sat down, feeling an overwhelming need to sleep. He rested his head on the table and shut his eyes. Must get ready, he thought—must be ready. Must stay awake. He took his pistol—a .22 snub-nose—from his pack and laid it on the kitchen table; she'd tell where she had hid the stuff. He took a coiled rope (she would have to be tied in the chair) and spread it on the table.

A car's lights swept across the window curtain. Weasel's heart fluttered. He drew the curtain aside and peeked out. The car came slowly down the Camp Road and stopped in the light of Mason's porch—a forest-green Mercedes. "Nnng," he exclaimed. Nice wheels. But it wasn't Angel.

Must get ready.

He took the dynamite from the pack and gently rolled the heavy gray ball onto the table. Enough to blow the side of a mountain apart, he mused—ought to take care of a lying bitch.

. . .

Rutus and Tiffany Sny were entertaining—a spontaneous celebration—the Ridgewoods were there; so were the Moweys and the
Van Nostrands. The men drank Chivas and played eight ball in the
billiard room, talking local politics and investment credits, while
the women basked in the downstairs Jacuzzi, sipping brandy and
listening to Tiffany hold forth about the impending Norwood
Country Club. This was the day, she gloated, that she'd positively
ached for. Worrying over that vagrant camp had given her two
lifetimes of migraines.

Then Henry appeared by the pool table—Henry, from Northern
Domestic Services in Bluffton—butler for the evening. He called
Sny aside and said, "There's a young lady to see you. She wouldn't
tell me her name, but she seems quite perturbed about something."

"Perturbed, is she?"

"She said to 'get his shiny butt inside pronto' or she'd put me in a
boys' choir."

"We'll see about this, then," Sny said. He marched through the
house, threw open the inner doors of his vestibule, then, seeing his
guest, closed them quickly behind him.

"Are you crazy? Don't come here, don't ever come here!"

"Now, Rutie," Angel said, wagging her finger. "Watch that blood
pressure."

"Shhh! For God's sake, my wife'll hear you!"

"Good. And that's not all she's going to hear, poopsie." Angel
crossed the room and stood face to face with Sny. "I hear you doubled
the taxes on Mason's campground. You're forcing him out so your
old lady can turn the place into a country club. Is that right, Rutie?"

"I don't see why that's any concern of yours. It's just business,
that's all. Just business."

Angel reached down and grabbed Sny's genitals. His knees went limp.
He swallowed hard and grabbed at her wrist with both hands. "Ahh," he
croaked. She squeezed harder and he went down to his knees.

"Oh, but I *am* concerned," she said, kneeling with him. "The
man's a friend of mine, and he's worked his tail off for that place.
Now you either lower those taxes or I'm going to have a little talk
with Mrs. Sny. Understand?" She squeezed in earnest. "Wouldn't
we have some stories to tell her?"

"Mmm," he moaned, nodding his red, contorted face. "Blackmail," he gasped. "But even if I do lower the taxes, he'll still sell. He has to. He's broke!" Perspiration streamed down his face.

Angel paused, relaxed her visegrip on him. "What?"

"Truth," he groaned, rolling his head dizzily. "The banks won't touch him. My brother-in-law Ed Stevens, the bank president, told me himself. The man's finished."

Suddenly the doors opened and Tiffany Sny entered, standing imperiously in the doorway, wrapped in a lavender bath towel. Rutus looked up, unfocused—his eyes were crossed.

"Oh, sweetheart," he said, "there you are. This young lady just stopped by—let me introduce my wife Tiffany. Tiffany, this is— now what did you say your name was?"

"Shirley Temple," said Angel, standing.

"Right. Shirley . . . er . . . Miss Temple."

"And?" Tiffany scowled, folding her arms.

"Just a little question about her taxes, sweetheart. I'll only be a second."

Tiffany shook her head. "Let me tell you something, dears, and I suggest you both listen very, very carefully. Town business—and any other sordid business you two might have—is conducted at the Town Office—or anyplace else that might suit you. But never, never in my home. Is that crystal clear, Rutus?"

Rutus nodded vacantly.

"Hmmm?" the blue-haired woman pressed.

"Yes, of course, dear. Town Office."

"And you, Angel—I believe that's your name—I trust you understand."

Rutus glanced from one woman to the other, his expression crossed with concern and surprise. How did she know about Angel? He started to speak, but Tiffany cut him off.

"I couldn't help noticing you kneeling on the floor, dear. Let me guess. This is the new you I keep hearing about, right?" She laughed haughtily at her own joke, then wheeled and left.

Rutus slowly picked himself up, though he remained bent at the waist, trying to catch his breath. He said to Angel, "I assume that was your trump card."

Angel heard apprehension in his voice. Even though he was

making it clear he could no longer be threatened with his wife's jealous wrath, there was something else—something he was hiding. But she hadn't a clue to what it was. "Please don't let her do it," Angel appealed in a pleading voice that surprised even herself.

And then she saw the gleam return to his eye, that tiny beam of stealth and greed that distinguished the man. He straightened, put a paternal arm around her shoulder, and said, "You know, this is most unusual, but I'm going to do exactly as you requested with Mason's taxes. That's right—the other selectmen are here with me tonight and, well, the very minute you arrived we were talking about the reevaluation of Camp Wind In The Pines. And the general consensus was that we had made a mistake there. Yes, I think we will be cutting those taxes by more than half. Funny how things work out sometimes."

"Real funny." Angel honored him with a momentary expression, new to her, a look of confusion and defeat: the hunter trapped by the game. Rutus Sny shut the door on that expression and returned to his guests with a new cause to celebrate: He'd just lowered his own taxes.

Carl threw a shovel onto the porch and came into the kitchen. "Whose Mercedes—" he began, but then he saw Larry and stopped. He took a beer out of the refrigerator and started to leave the room.

"Carl," Shirley said in a queer voice, full of delight.

Carl stopped and turned curiously.

"Well?" She prodded her daughter. "Show him!"

Susie held her hand up to the light. Her diamond ring sparkled.

Carl turned to Larry. "What's that?" he asked, jerking his thumb at his daughter.

"Five carats."

"Ten thousand dollars," Susie added.

Carl took his daughter's hand in his, brought the ring close to his eye. "You're kidding."

"Have you set a date?" Shirley asked abruptly, and by the silence that followed it was clear they had not. Carl turned again to Larry for an explanation.

"Two weeks," Larry said. "Saturday after next—Opening Day at Wind In The Pines, right?"

Carl snorted and looked at the floor. "You'll never get married then."

"What do you mean?" Larry asked, feigning ignorance.

"We're selling out—losing the place."

"Oh, no," Larry said, shaking his head forlornly, showing too much concern. Then he snapped his fingers. "Hey, I just had an idea. Since I'm going to be family now, what if I were to buy into the business, you know, become a partner—pay you, say, half of what it's worth—"

Carl snickered.

"No, really."

Carl shook his head. "Then you'd lose a quick hundred grand. The place is a dump—a losing proposition. The water stinks, the air stinks, the whole stinkin' place stinks. Besides, you don't have that kind of dough."

It was a peach of an opening. L.A. Jones—the cat with the dough. He looked at Carl with a confident nod and said, "I've got it."

Carl studied Larry suspiciously. "You were flat broke a couple of days ago—you couldn't afford to pay me rent."

Larry chuckled. He shot a glance at Susie, as if she shared his humor—but she, like her parents, stood waiting for an explanation. "No, Carl, I was only pretending to be broke," he said. "I couldn't let on who I really was until I was sure everything here was on the up and up—you know, with Susie and the campground. A single man with bucks is an easy mark, you know." The Masons stared breathlessly. "You see, I'm not exactly new to this business. I was involved with Disneyworld down in Miami."

"Orlando," Carl said.

Larry shrugged. "Same difference."

"So how'd you make your money?" Carl asked.

"Daddy—" Susie said.

Shirley interrupted. "Maybe he'd rather not say."

Larry silenced her with a gesture. "No, no. I don't mind. I had some real estate—a little property in Orlando. Let's just say I made what we in the business like to call a killing."

"Tell me about it," Carl said.

Larry folded his arms and sat on the kitchen table. "To tell you the truth, I had an uncle—one of the founders of Disneyworld—he owned quite a bit of the Orlando coastline—property worth millions. When he died I inherited a share."

Susie's eyes opened wide. Shirley's heart fluttered. Carl said, "Orlando is thirty miles from the ocean."

Larry laughed. "You think I mean Orlando, Florida, right? No, no. Orlando, California. Uncle Walt owned half the town."

"Uncle Walt?" Susie cried. "Walt Disney?"

Larry glanced at Carl, saw his sullen, skeptical stare. "No, no. Uncle Walt Jones—Walter Jones, the famous campground architect."

"So your brother Zippy must have inherited a fortune, too," Carl said.

Larry cleared his throat. He slid off the table and walked across the kitchen, shaking his head. "Nope. Uncle Walt wrote my brother out of his will after Zippy's business with the Russian government—" He stopped abruptly and grimaced. "I'm sorry," he said, "I've said too much already."

Carl shook his head. Susie and Shirley scowled at each other in deep confusion.

"Anyway, Carl, did you say a hundred grand?" Larry asked, suddenly dealing hundred-dollar bills into Carl's hand.

It took Carl a moment to fathom the depths of what was happening. He looked at Larry with a suspicious scowl. Then a wide, conspiratorial grin crossed his face. "You son-of-a-pup," he said, holding his hand out under the steady slap-slap-slap of hundred-dollar bills. His eyes took on the sparkle of his daughter's ring. He beamed. Then his thoughts turned to Rutus Sny, and his face turned crimson. "Oh, that bastard," he laughed, flashing a savage smile at Shirley. "Ohh, that bastard."

Soon the money spilled out of Carl's hand, and Larry began dealing banded stacks of bills onto the kitchen table. Carl could no longer stand, his knees trembled so. He flopped into a chair.

Then suddenly his smile disappeared. "Wait. Wait, wait," he said, shaking his head. "I can't take this from you. Stop."

"Why not?"

"'Cause you're not married yet. You're not family."

"Oh, Daddy," Susie said, "we'll be married in two weeks. What's the difference if you take it then or now?"

He folded his hands on the table. It was her he was worried about—his little girl—he didn't want any fortune hunter deceiving her, breaking her heart. He pushed his chair away from the table and turned his back on the money. "Just—just to keep things copesetic, here, you take your money back. Pay me when you're married."

Shirley intervened. "What about the taxes, Carl? They've got to be paid."

"Hmmph," he grunted. "The taxes."

Larry held up his hands. "No problem, no problem. Look, I'm loaded—keep the money just so you know my intentions are sincere. Call it rent, call it a deposit, call it whatever. In two weeks we'll all be legal. Deal?"

Carl looked at his daughter, studied her eyes, and when he was satisfied that she was happy, he scooped the money off the table, turned a circle on the kitchen floor, and then sat back down. Tears welled in his eyes. "I'm overwhelmed," he said to Shirley, shaking her head. He had never used that word before, she thought, but it was apt. He began talking in fragments: "Hey . . . I'll tell you what, you kids . . . I'm gonna buy . . . wait, that's your car out there, isn't it? I'll be damned . . . Shirl, get some beers—no, no, no—get the good stuff, hon' . . . I'm going to build you kids . . . ohh, that bastard."

Larry, despite his nonchalance, was ecstatic himself—one of his own fantasies was materializing. He had the amusement park he had dreamed of, and the nearly inexhaustible funds to transform it into a playground that would rival even Old Orchard Beach. He held out his hand to Susie, and she took it in her own.

"We're going out," she said to her parents, and they headed out the door with but one goal. Turning left off the porch—away from the Duckoffs and the Joneses and the Roots, away from Nighthawk and her parents and anyone else who might interrupt their lovemaking—they walked straight for the deep shadows of the forgotten industrial loom behind Angel's trailer. And there, without ceremony, they undressed each other and made a soft nest of their clothes on the ground. Susie lay in it first and opened her arms and legs, writhing in ecstasy even before Larry touched her—and his first touch was entering her, hardened and with immediate jackhammer thrusts.

Inside the darkened trailer Weasel rested his head on his hand, peering out the window with eyes nearly closed—occasionally dozing—watching the Camp Road for Angel's car. He had prepared everything for her entrance. The dynamite was molded and placed out of sight in the shadowed gap between the top of the refrigerator and the cupboards above it, the rope was tied loosely around a chair so he would have only to sit her down and tie the knot; his pistol was in his hand, loaded and cocked. He saw Carl Mason now, and Shirley. They came onto their porch an sat down in its soft yellow glow. They were drinking. Carl stepped off the porch and circled the Mercedes. He was smiling. He cupped his hands around his mouth, threw his head back, and whooped.

"Hey, hey," Shirley said. "Take it easy. People will think you've lost your marbles."

"Good. Hey, look at the stars, Shirl! Have you ever seen so many stars?"

"I know."

"And smell. Can you smell the pines?"

"Shh," Shirley said. "Listen—what's that?"

"What?"

"Shush! It sounds like somebody's hurt."

The animal fire grew in Susie's loins. Spasms racked her spine. Larry bit softly on one of her nipples and pulled. "Ohhh," she moaned.

"There it is again," Shirley said. "Didn't you hear it?"

"Naw, it's just the wind in the pines." Carl smirked. "Get it?"

A car wound slowly through the woods from the River Road, sweeping its white beams across the greenery that bordered the campground. Then suddenly it emerged fully on the Camp Road, coming in a blaze of headlights straight down the drive: Angel's Volvo.

Inside her trailer Weasel came alive. "Nnng!" he said. He pushed to his feet and hobbled into the darkness of the bedroom to wait. His heart raced. "Nnng!"

"Now," Larry gasped. "Now."

"No, wait," Susie whispered. Her belly trembled.

"I'll tell you something about that kid," Carl said, shielding his eyes against the Volvo's headlights. "I didn't think much of him at first, you know? Figured he was just some idiot college kid who didn't know his ass from a hole in the ground. But I'll tell you something—I was wrong. That kid's a go-getter—a real ball of fire—"

"Wait," Shirley said. "Listen."

"Now!" Larry growled. He snorted. His body stiffened and he grabbed Susie's ears.

"Oh, God yes!" Susie cried, quaking, throwing her arms over her head, reaching, desperately grasping for something—anything—to hold, and finding a smooth, cool handle, she clenched at it and squeezed, still rising, rising in blind passion to meet her lover. "Arrggg," she snarled.

"Hey!" snapped Carl, turning toward the loom.

Susie's eyes opened wide, her body jerked convulsively: "Uh! Uh! Uh! Uh! . . ."

"Hey!" Carl hollered, breaking into a run.

And then, with a deep primal roar, Susie Mason pushed off into ecstasy.

The force of the blast lifted the industrial loom almost an inch off the ground. It threw Carl back-somersaulting onto his face and broke windows all over the campground and in houses a mile away. It drove Angel's refrigerator through the trailer floor and launched the kitchen cupboards through the exploded trailer roof. It blew Weasel out the bedroom window into the backyard, where Maurice raced wide-eyed and hang-tongued in an ever-tightening circle around his tether-stake. It caused a shower of canned goods to rain down on Mason's roof and yard, so that a can of V-8 Juice snapped their antenna mast in half; Carl himself was struck on the back by a can of Hunt's Tomato Paste.

"God," Susie breathed. "That was my first true orgasm. Can you believe it?"

20

Sent From Heaven

Carl refused to call an ambulance for Weasel. This place got a bad enough name already, he said, so he and Larry heaped the broken, bleeding body onto a pile of newspapers in the back of Larry's Mercedes (Shirley insisted they not carry him in the trunk), and they drove him to the hospital themselves.

On the way, they stopped at the Norwood Superette for beer. They polished off a six-pack in the half-hour drive to Bluffton, then stopped at a convenience store for more. When they reached St. Vincent's Hospital, they pulled into the visitors' lot and parked, suddenly wondering what to do with Weasel—whether to take him into the emergency room or to the front desk—or whether to take him in at all. There were bound to be questions. Carl suggested they take him to the dump, where he belonged. Larry thought they should drop him beside the highway, then call the cops anonymously. Carl thought he'd look good wedged in the claws of the bronze lobster statue at City Hall. They turned the radio to a country and western station, opened another beer, and debated the question.

Outside Carl's house, Maurice lay chained to Angel's Volvo, dazed and panting; while inside the house, Angel lay, dazed and lamenting, on Susie's bed. She had lost everything, everything except her car, her dog, and the clothes on her back. Yet her lamentations were not for her possessions. You just wouldn't understand, she told Susie.

"Probably not. But maybe just talking would help." Susie ached

to tell of her own blossoming romance, her engagement, but she
sensed the timing was wrong; she would wait for the proper opening. "You know, maybe hearing about somebody else's happiness
might make you feel better."

Angel laughed sardonically. "Feel better, huh?" She fell back and
closed her eyes. "I don't feel a thing. In fact, I don't remember
when I've ever . . ." Her voice dropped and she swallowed.
". . . when I've ever felt anything." A tear rolled into her ear. "No,
I take that back. I have actually felt, you know. I've felt greed. And
envy. Hatred. Lust. And revenge—yeah, revenge, that's a good
one—"

Susie refrained from touching her. "Did you have insurance?"

Angel snorted. "Insurance? Insurance on love? Sorry, ma'am, we
don't cover that."

"No, really, on your things—your clothes and everything. God,
if I lost some of the clothes you did, I'd puke for a week I'd be so
sick. Oh, I almost forgot to tell you, you know that guy Larry that's
been around?" She twisted her ring up to the light.

Angel rolled onto her stomach and mused, "'Insurance on love.'
Sounds like an old Supremes song, doesn't it? Oh, God, listen to
me! Some wacko tried to kill me—God only knows why—and now
I've got the hots for him."

"Weasel? You and Weasel?"

"Messed up, huh?" A point of light from Susie's diamond pierced
Angel's eye. "I don't know. I don't know why I'm attracted to him. I
think maybe—"

"I love his accent," Susie blurted. Angel looked up at her.

"Yeah, there's that," she said. "But he's like a little boy, you
know? Scrappy and cruel. And so bad. Fucking him is more like
breaking windows than making love."

"Fucking?" Susie sat up—too fast. She felt momentarily dizzy,
like she'd been shaken. Her heart jumped. She stared numbly at the
herringbone pattern on Angel's back, imagined they were sharks'
teeth. Wished they were sharks' teeth. She said, "You and Weasel,
huh? So when did all this—"

"He's so rough . . . I mean, he actually hurts. He's bony, and
small, but—"

"Yeah. I know."

"But—you know, this might sound schizoid, but when I came down the drive tonight and saw my trailer blow up in my face, I knew it was him—and you know what else? I sat in that car and I came, and I came, and I came—all the while my pots and pans and pieces of my home are falling all around me, and I could see my bed wrapped around this pine tree, and all my clothes fluttering down—and I just came and came and came."

"Look," Susie said, thrusting her ring close to Angel's face.

Angel scowled and pushed it back into focus.

Susie said lightly, "I'm engaged."

"What?"

Susie rolled onto her side close to Angel, propped her head on her hand, and twisted the ring up to the light. "To a guy named Larry. Maybe you've seen him around. Larry Jones? We're getting married in two weeks."

Angel shook her head. "Whoa," she said. "Slow down, girl. You're not pregnant?"

Susie shook her head.

"So how long have you known this guy?"

"He's been around for a couple of days. But he's so incredible, I can't believe it. We're really in love."

Angel eyed the diamond. "One would have to admit he's got good taste in jewelry."

"He's a sharp dresser, too. Real cute. And wicked smart."

"Money?"

Susie grinned. "He's rich. He owns real estate. Maybe you saw his—our—new car on your way in."

"I didn't see too much."

"Oh, and this—" Susie knelt on the bed and dug into her back pocket. "Have you ever tried this?" she whispered, unfolding a small wad of paper. "Cocaine."

Angel sat upright. She ran her fingers through her hair. "I need some air," she said, and she left the house.

The Mercedes slowed to a stop on the River Road, shining its bright lights at the weatherbeaten Camp Sign. Carl drained a bottle of Bud, threw it into the woods, then opened another. "Well, that's my good deed for the day," he said, opening another bottle for

Larry. "But I'm not sayin' any prayers for the kid. Know what I mean?"

Larry took a long drink from the bottle and smacked his lips. He said, "Look—you can't even see that sign there. And that's what I've been trying to tell you. I know about these things, Carl. Advertising and all that. Now I'm talking billboard, partner. Billboard. Lights, pictures, the whole nine yards. Like they say, don't throw good money after bad." He took another gulp of beer. "Think about it." He waited for a response, but none came. He could hear Carl nose-breathing, could feel him staring through the darkness. "All right, to show you how sure I am about this, I'll tell you what. I'll spring for a new sign out of my own personal funds. No sweat." He turned onto the Camp Road. "And you really ought to consider what I said about raising the rent around here, Carl. It's not going to kill anybody here to pay a little more, you know. I'm thinking profits. And, hey—if they can't afford it, well, that's life. Let 'em go somewhere else. Love it or leave it, right? Just between you and me, I think it'd do the place some good to get some classier people in, you know, some good-looking chicks—I mean just to attract more . . . I'm thinking profit, partner, all the way."

"All the way, pal." Even as drunk and unusually cordial as he was, Carl refrained from calling Larry "partner."

"And, Carl, the next time you need somebody evicted, why don't you let me handle it. I'm pretty good with people, you know. I've read just about all the psychology books. A little psychology, Carl, and then they don't come back and dynamite your property, you know what I'm saying? Just let me handle it."

"Yeah, I guess I pissed 'em off, didn't I? Well, one thing—if that poor bastard lives, you can be sure we'll never see his face around here again. Besides, he couldn't have picked a better place to blow up. Not that I want anybody hurt, but she was cheatin' on her rent and, well, these things happen when you get that sort—"

"You reap what you sow."

"That's right. Besides, that's the perfect spot to build your new house. Right next to the office and store."

"And right beside you."

"Damn right. So you're going to call the builders tomorrow?"

"The Diablo Brothers? Yeah, I'll call 'em."

Carl stepped out of the car and talked through the window. "These guys are friends of mine, Larry, like I told you. They're good, and they owe me a favor. The old man himself built my house—preassembled log cabin—ten days from start to finish. And they'll do the same for you. Course, the way Shirley is, religious and all, it's probably not a good idea for you two to move in until you're married, you know?"

"No sweat, partner." Larry gave Carl the thumbs-up sign. "Think profit," he called, backing the Mercedes toward Zippy and Ruth's.

When he got out of the car, he poured his beer on the ground. He noticed Zippy, wearing a mosquito net on his head, slumped on the picnic table. In the darkness, beside the blinking transceiver, he looked alien. Larry slapped a mosquito on the back of his hand and was starting for the cabin door when he heard a soft hiss behind him. He stopped.

Psst.

He turned toward the pond.

Psst.

He noticed an alarming silence—the crickets had stopped chirping. Then a dark shadow came from behind a tree. It beckoned him with a wave of its hand. "Hello?" he called softly. The figure didn't answer, but began moving toward him. He strained to see, to hear, but the night had grown black, cloudy, and blowing. He began backing toward the house.

"Don't go," the figure said in a low and breathy female voice, dark as the very night. It stopped Larry cold. She came closer. "So you're Larry," she said softly. "I've been dying to meet you." She extended her hand toward him, and he reached out to shake it—but he found it wasn't his hand she was after.

"Call me L.A.," he said, putting his arms around her.

"Call me Angel," she said into his ear, and in that one moment, a personal record for the woman, she had her man.

Part
Three

21

The Haunting

High on a rocky ledge,
I'll build a wigwam,
Close by the water's edge,
Silent and still.

Blue lake and rocky shore,
I will return once more,
Bum-didda, bum-didda, bum-didda, bum-didda,
Bum-didda, bum-didda, bum-didda, bum-didda.

The sky is liquid green—greener than possible, separated from earth by a low, long line of clouds, puffed up white along the horizon as if exploded; while rice paddies, lying lush and flat on both sides of the dirt road, stretch unbroken as far as the eye can see. *Green*. And now there is a truck bisecting this moist emerald world, a drowsy lumbering American truck, freshly painted red over accumulations of older paint. Farm red. Yet its grillwork is turquoise and its headlights, half painted—winking—are lemon yellow. The truck is overburdened with . . . pumpkins. The pumpkins are over-ripe: hot, shimmering orange pumpkins mounded up over the side-rails. The truck growls and brushes this landscape with a slow, thick line of color and a wake of dust and smoke.

But there are soldiers in the pumpkins and soldiers in the truck: Americans. They are puffing on Thailand ganja from cigar-sized joints so that their faces are shrouded in smoke. And they are singing an American song: "Sittin' in the morning sun (the pumpkins throb: *orange, orange, orange*), I'll be sittin' when the evenin' come . . ."

They approach a village. Small black-haired girls in creamy, gossamer gowns are playing near the road. ". . . Watchin' the ships roll in . . ." Smoke fills the cab. ". . . Then I watch 'em roll away again . . ." The truck is not responding. The soldiers are laughing in the cab. The driver cannot see. The girls are in the road. The driver brakes the truck, but the truck does not respond. He pulls the truck hard into a thicket. Pumpkins fill the air, drumming onto the cab like hoofbeats, *bum-didda, bum-didda, bum-didda, bum-didda*. Laughter fills the smoke.

". . . Sittin' on the dock of the Bay, watchin' the tide roll away . . ."

The girls are shrieking outside the truck. The soldiers are shrieking inside the truck. Smoke fills the shrieking. The truck cannot respond. The driver leaps from the truck. A small, black-haired girl is caught beneath a wheel. Gold pours from her mouth. Her mother is kneeling in the pumpkins, pulling on the girl's legs. The truck is overburdened with pumpkins. It does not respond. The mother is staring at the driver. Smoke fills her eyes. Her eyes are shrieking. The driver is raising his weapon. The truck does not respond.

Crackkkk!

Nighthawk sprang to his knees in the darkness, spinning, groping for his weapon, while lightning crackled steadily outside and rain drummed like hoofbeats onto the roof. His heart raced. Red clay slurry ran bloody past the flashing, open windows. Another crack of thunder shook the ridge, and he heard in it the tearing of a great elm by the Mighty Spirit; while silent, white lightning shot his shadow onto every wall—like a trembling cave drawing—crouching, bow in hand, listening for the telltale rustle of cloth, or a careless breath—but hearing only the lowing of thunder from faraway hills. This is not my dream, he said to himself. No longer my dream. And he escaped his shelter for the storm.

22

The Push

The megaphone squealed: "ATTENTION!" and startled trees, with a sudden thrashing of leaves, shed their songbirds into a shattered pink morning sky. Carl turned to the cabins and sprayed them, as if with machine-gun fire: "On the double. Let's move! Yadda-yadda-yadda!" The pavilion was puddled from the pre-dawn thunderstorm—trees still rained cold, crystalline drops with each pale breath of wind. He waited at the podium, sipping coffee and scanning the *Bluffton Sunday Telegram*, barely noticing the staggering arrival of his first puff-eyed tenants. He studied instead a "late" story on page 1:

Man Hurt in Mysterious Hospital Fall

BLUFFTON—A patient believed missing from St. Vincent's Hospital yesterday was found by sanitation workers shortly after midnight this morning on the ground beside the hospital's dumpster. Although Warren G. Rathbone, 24, of Norwood, is believed to have fallen from his third-floor private room sometime yesterday afternoon, some facts in the case don't quite add up, a hospital spokesperson said. Cited as examples were canine teeth marks on the man's leg cast and burns on his back. Further evidence of possible foul play was the fresh blood samples taken from the side of the dumpster itself.

"It's as if somebody tried to lift him up into the dumpster," the spokesperson said. "We're waiting until he regains consciousness so we can learn the true story." Rathbone is listed

in serious condition this morning with a concussion, three frac-
tured ribs, and lacerations of the face and hands. Investigation
into the mishap is pending.

Carl snickered and looked up. A sparrow soared. The pavilion
was full. He looked at his watch, squeezed the megaphone trigger,
and began: "Okay, everybody. Thank you. I know that it's early
Sunday morning, but I've got some important news, so let's look
alive. First of all I want to congratulate you, each and every one, for
setting a new Camp assembly record: four minutes and twenty seconds, by my watch." The tenants stared blankly. "And as usual,
Harvey Duckoff was the first one here. Harvey, take a bow." Harvey
stood and bowed; he wore only Jockey shorts, grayed and sagging,
rippled at the waist. His face was rubbery and matted with pillow
lines. Carl stepped out from behind the podium and casually
handed him a new twenty-dollar bill, which Harvey brandished
over his head like a trophy.   .

"Outtasight, Harve," Zippy called, applauding soundly. The
Roots exchanged expressionless looks from opposite sides of the
pavilion. Then Earl Root leaned in his chair and administered a
full-volumed fart, his first of the day—generally his loudest. It
echoed back at the congregation from a cove across the pond, where
a pair of nesting ducks scattered.

"Okay," Carl said, motioning Larry to his side. "I've got some
good news and some bad news. Which do you want first?"

"Good," said Earl Root.

"Bad," said Dolly, looking away. Dolly was dressed, as always, in
her green pants-suit—a plain, ribbed suit in a shade of green one
might see on a beach umbrella or picnic tablecloth—gay yet not
overly clownish, a vibrant green that occurs more on five-and-dime
waitresses than it does in nature. The suit was old and well-worn.
The elbows and knees had faded noticeably, and her generous pos-
terior was three feet square worn nearly transparent.

The megaphone squealed. Carl rapped its rim against the
podium. "Okay, bad news first. As you all know, we had a little
accident last night (thumb-pointing to Angel's blossomed trailer).
The perpetrator—the guy that did it—an old friend of ours—one of

our motorcycle buddies—is in the hospital, pretty broken up over what he did. And I hate to say it, but I don't think we'll be seeing any more of him." Despite his sarcasm, Carl was not smiling.

"Aww," Jean said.

"So, as of now—today—Angel here will be occupying the vacant cabin—"

"Pigsty," Angel interjected sourly.

"—the vacant cabin vacated by our old biker friends. And seeing's how she doesn't care for the groceries we provide in the Camp Store—and hasn't for some time—her rent will be strictly cash basis"—he looked at his watch—"as of now."

Angel sat forward on her chair, resting her chin in her hands, showing no signs of emotion.

"And now for the good news. I'd like you all to say hello to my future partner, and your new . . . I guess you'd say future co-landlord—Mr. Larry Jones."

"Hello," Jean Duckoff said.

"Larry," Earl nodded.

"Because of Mr. Jones here, we are staying put. Camp Wind In The Pines will not be sold. No one has to leave. I'll be seeing Mr. Sny tomorrow to give him the good news." The group applauded politely. "Now . . . now, wait. Not only is Mr. Jones—"

"Call me L.A.," he smiled. Larry had prepared for the meeting—he wore a white linen shirt (opened to his solar plexus), a tan leather vest, snug designer jeans, and shades.

"Not only is he my future partner. Not only that, he's also . . . my future son-in-law." There was a confused turning of heads. Most people looked at Shirley. "That's right, Susie and Larry are tying the knot Saturday after next—Opening Day here—so there'll be lots to celebrate. I might even take a drink or two myself. And you're all invited to the festivities, too." More polite applause. "Of course, after they're married, Susie won't be working in the Camp Store, so—" A spontaneous burst of cheering interrupted him. Dolly stood and whistled through her teeth.

"Stuff it!" Susie snarled. "You can all go straight to hell for all I care, you filthy pigs!"

Shirley leveled a punitive glance at her daughter.

"Okay, okay, folks—all in good fun, honey. So anyway, we'll be taking applications at the office for a replacement."

"What's the pay?" Dolly asked loudly.

"Mrs. Root," Carl said with a smile, "something tells me that you guarding my store would be like an elephant guarding the peanuts."

"What the hell's that s'posed to mean?" she spat through a mouthful of doughnut.

"He means you'd eat the place dry!" Susie called, and more laughter erupted in the pavilion. Even Earl pointed at his wife and said, "Gotcha."

Dolly Root was indignant. She lumbered around and addressed the crowd: "I s'pose you think it's funny bein' overweight!" But she was quickly drowned out by Susie's loud staccato guffaw. Carl held up a hand.

"All in good fun, all in good fun," he said. "Now I've been talking quite a bit to Larry here about ways we can improve the place, and he's got some terrific ideas, so with your help, understanding, and cooperation, I think we're gonna straighten out ol' Wind In The Pines. I think it can—and will—become the kind of campground it was meant to be. The kind of place we can all be proud to call Home. Now the first change we're going to make, later on today, is the relocation of the Roots' trailer to a more suitable part of the campgrounds."

"Oh, no you don't!" Dolly shouted, struggling again to her feet.

"I'll second that one!" Earl said, thumping his fist on the bench.

"Now wait a minute, folks. Hear us out—"

"No way, Jose. We're not budging," Dolly said, pointing at Carl.

"You tell him!" Earl said.

"Oh, shut up, you!" Dolly barked.

"Shut up, yourself, y'ol' cow!" Earl snapped, clawing the air at her.

Larry took the megaphone from Carl and smiled benevolently at the fat couple. He turned halfway around, studying the pinetops, contemplating. And then, as if in prayer, the young handsome man extemporized, "Now what was it someone once said?" By the silence that followed it was apparent that nobody, not even Larry himself, could remember what it was that someone had once said, but neither his smile nor his confidence waned. "Think of it," he

said, "as an investment in your future." The Roots scowled suspiciously at him. Larry nodded assuredly to Earl Root, then handed
the megaphone back to Carl.

"Think of it this way," Carl said, venom creeping into his voice.
"If you don't move it back away from the water, we'll move it for
you—back and out!" The thumb went up. "All the way out!"

Dolly leveled her finger at him. "You touch one hair on that
trailer," she hollered, "and you might as well say, 'Kill me!'"

Carl dropped the megaphone and came toward her, a grin forming slowly, like a thundercloud, on his scarlet face. His fists were
reflexively clenched. "'Zat right?"

"Carl—" Shirley called softly.

"Yer goddamn right that's right!"

"You know, I oughta—"

"You oughta what, pudface?" Dolly sneered, pushing his shoulder. He sprang back and faced her nose-to-nose.

"Our father," interrupted Shirley, standing beside the podium,
hands folded, head bowed, eyes shut tight, "we are gathered this
morning in celebration of joy at the engagement of our daughter
Susan to Mister Larry Jones, and at the saving of Camp Wind In
The Pines. We ask that You help our Camp prosper by letting
certain people understand that some things they are asked to do for
the good of the Camp are for their own good, too. In Your name,
we pray. Amen."

Dolly spun around, raised her face to the heavens, and clasped her
hands high in the air: "Our Father, Who art in heaven, Please help
those of us who got nothin' but a tiny, worthless piece of land and the
love of our families . . . keep what we worked so hard to get!"

"Dear Lord," Shirley countered, "please bless today those people
who have never worked a day in their lives, but instead, live off our
government and never gave two hoots about their own children—"

"Oh, God, hear me now!" Dolly sang, beseeching the very
clouds—"Wait a minute, that's a goddamn lie!" And then, as if
erasing her comment, she wiped furiously at the air, saying, "I pray
now! I pray now!" while Shirley continued her own prayer:
". . . And please forgive those who take Thy name in vain . . ."
Dolly: "I pray now! Just where the hell do some people get off

judging others? I say let 'em cast the first stone, let 'em mind their own goddamn business! That's what the Bible says, am I right? Amen!"

"Amen!" Shirley shot back.

"Amen!" Dolly snapped, glaring.

"Amen!"

"Ah-men!" hollered Dolly, punctuating each syllable with a jab of her finger. "Ah-men! Ah-men! Ahhh-men!"

Then something caught Harvey's wandering attention. He slowly rose to his feet, as if witnessing a supremely splendid vision. "Hey," he breathed. "Hey! Hey!" he yelled, jumping, pointing up at the office porch. "Customers!"

At once the entire gathering stood, silenced. "Go get 'em, Shirl," Carl said with caution, as if he were helping her land her first rainbow trout. Shirley turned abruptly from Dolly Root, hiked her shoulders, straightened her back, and began a spritely, smiling walk up the short grassy rise to the office.

"Ahhh-men!" Dolly called after her.

"Go shit in your hat," Shirley said through her smiling teeth, not turning, never breaking stride. The elderly couple on the porch returned her smile weakly, as those do who miss a joke. Dressed in matching L.L. Bean khaki safari suits, they fidgeted and lowered their heads so Shirley couldn't see their faces under their white beach hats. She bit her lower lip. "Baby kittens," she said warmly. "They just love to go sit in your hat—not *your* hat, I mean, but just anybody's hat . . . they're so tiny. And cute. But then they get old and cranky . . . and fat!" she called over her shoulder. "Oh, those cats." The elderly couple was still peering down at the gathering in the pavilion area. Shirley explained, "We like to get together with the guests every so often and shoot the breeze. It gives Wind In The Pines a sort of family atmosphere, which . . . oh, well, I'll stop blabbing now . . . are you interested in a campsite?"

The man looked curiously from his wristwatch to the gathering. "Seven-thirty," he said. "Is that right? We've been driving most of the night."

"I think so," Shirley said. "Near enough." The couple looked again at the crowd, now edging closer, then glanced at one another.

The woman said: "We stayed here about twenty-five years ago, and we were just curious to see if it still existed."

"Still here," Shirley smiled.

"But I remember it as being a very *nice* campground."

"Well, it still looks very nice," the man said. "We'd like a trailer hookup, if you have any available—"

"Preferably on the water," said the woman.

"Yes, we do. And how long would you like to stay?"

"Might stay the whole summer," said the man, "if we like it."

Shirley motioned them in the office door. "Please excuse the mess," she said. "We're right in the middle of spring cleaning. . . ."

"I noticed the sign at the entrance saying something about water pollution," the woman said.

"Oh, that," Shirley laughed, waving it off. "Don't be concerned." She leaned close to the man, as if sharing a secret. "The water's the same as it's always been; it's the tests that change."

"Well, we're both too old for swimming anyway," the woman said. "We just enjoy the tranquility. Of course he likes to torment the fish every morning—"

"Probably just bacteria," said her husband. Shirley smiled.

While she was registering her new guests in the office, Harvey was up by the store, eyeing a heaped army blanket on the ground. He was intrigued by the growing swarm of flies that buzzed around the mound. He wondered if it was perhaps a manure pile or somebody's garbage under there. He kicked at it, and the flies scattered. Probably somebody's garbage, he figured—but then why cover it with a blanket? Jeez, he thought, it's gonna pick up some awful smell. When his curiosity finally peaked, just as Shirley was ushering the elderly couple off the porch, he threw off the blanket.

"Aw, jeezum!" he cried. "Dead cow!" It was a small, fawn-colored Jersey heifer, with two arrows deep into its side. Its long pink tongue draped out of its open mouth, buzzing and crawling with flies. A small brass cowbell hung silently from its neck.

The guests were transfixed. The woman absently pinched the skin on the back of her husband's hand.

"Oh, lovely," Shirley said, glaring at Harvey. Then, noticing her startled campers, she added with folded hands: "The Lord certainly does provide in mysterious ways, doesn't He?"

23

Wheelin' and Dealin'

Ed Stevens made his confession Monday over smoked pheasant and fifty-dollar-a-bottle Bordeaux. Even for a bank president it was an expensive luncheon. He reached across the table and dipped his fingers into her palm.

"I'm telling you this only because I know I can confide in you." Angel squeezed his hand. He lowered his voice. "I just need to get it off my chest."

Angel lit a cigarette. She poured more wine for him. He slid to the chair beside her.

"I broke the law," he said, surprising even himself with the statement. He looked at her and shrugged, then took another drink of his wine. "I'm not proud of what I did, Angel—I'm a church deacon, for heaven's sake. But it was a family thing—this damn Wind In The Pines business."

Angel dragged on her cigarette and blew the smoke over his head. "Sny?" she said. "I might have guessed."

"I didn't know what to say to him," he said. "My sister's got him so fired up about that property—last week he begged me not to write Mason a second mortgage on the place. He offered me a thousand dollars. I mean, the man is desperate."

Angel nodded. "So that's what he was hiding," she said, crushing her cigarette in the ashtray. "And I never even saw it."

"I didn't take his money," Stevens said. "I told you, that's not my style. I refused Mason's mortgage as a family favor to Tiffany." He leaned closer to Angel. "But then Rutus came into the bank Friday and said he needed to withdraw . . . well, a good deal of money—"

Angel's leg rubbed against his. "How much?" she asked.

He shook his head. "I can't," he said. He finished his wine, and Angel poured him another glass. The waiter started for the table, but Stevens waved him away. "He said he needed cash—right away—said he had Mason backed into a corner, and he wanted to flash a wad under his nose. Wanted him to smell the money."

"So you gave him the money. What's the problem? The Snys must have a fortune in your bank."

"Of course they do. But that's not the point. You see, you just can't withdraw that much cash whenever you want—even from your own account. We have to file what's called a currency transaction report on any cash withdrawal of ten thousand dollars or more. It goes to the Internal Revenue." He picked up his wineglass with a shaking hand. But it, and the bottle, were empty. "This is federal," he said.

"So why didn't you just file the report?" she said, motioning for the waiter to bring another bottle.

"It takes ten days. And like I said, he wanted the money right away. Besides, he didn't want Tiffany to know about the withdrawal—he wanted to surprise her."

"So you gave him the cash."

"No, I refused. My God, I told him, I had already turned down Carl Mason on a second mortgage—and was feeling damn uneasy about that. See, Angel, this stuff just doesn't agree with me. I've always considered myself an honest man. I really do. I mean, sure, this thing between you and me is . . . well, look, it's a vacation of sorts, with the wife down in Connecticut for the week—"

"So you didn't give him the cash."

"Not at first. But then he offered me twenty-four thousand dol—"

The waiter suddenly appeared at their table, uncorking a new bottle of wine. Ed Stevens covered his mouth, coughing. The waiter handed him the cork to sniff, but Stevens waved him away. "Twenty-four thousand dollars," he whispered when the waiter had left. "For an unreported weekend loan. He guaranteed to have the money back to me before the banks closed today."

"Twenty-four thousand?" she said, squeezing his leg. His knee jerked and hit the table, bouncing silverware and china.

"Shh," he said, sitting up in his chair, red-faced and smiling.

"Do you mean to tell me that you charged your own brother-in-law fifty percent interest for a three-day loan?"

"Ten," he said, and immediately wished he hadn't. His eyes darted.

Angel whistled softly. "That's some bank loan," she said.

Stevens shot her a stern look. "This is strictly confidential," he said.

"Of course," she answered, running her fingers up his thigh under the table. "So you just gave him the money on the spot?"

"No. We don't have that kind of cash in our vault. Especially on a Friday. When the banks closed, I went to each of the branches—there are six of them, you know. I took—borrowed—forty thousand from each one. And it'll be back—every penny—tonight."

Angel sighed. "All that for Wind In The Pines?"

"I'm telling you, Tiffany's driving him crazy—threatening divorce. But it looks like she finally got her way." He looked at his watch. "They were supposed to meet this morning. I imagine Rutus and Tiffany are celebrating right now."

Angel dragged on her cigarette. "Mason won't sell," she said.

"My dear," he said, "Carl Mason won't be able to refuse." He looked her in the eye, took her hand, and said, "One should never underestimate the power of legal tender."

Under the circumstances, it was needless advice. When they had finished their wine and Stevens had paid the check, they left and spent the rest of the afternoon shopping. Angel's new appliances arrived at Wind In The Pines before she did, courtesy of Mr. Edward Stevens.

The meeting was not going well for the Snys, however. Their attorneys had left the town office after several unanswered phone calls were placed to the Masons' residence, and now only Rutus and Tiffany remained. When Carl barged in, he was over two hours late for the closing.

"Well, Mr. Mason," Sny said, rising from his black leather and chrome office chair. "Better late than never." He wore a tan smoking jacket with brown leather elbow pads over a pale blue shirt and striped tie: maroon on navy blue. He extended his hand, palm down, for Carl to shake, but Carl pretended not to notice. He turned instead to Tiffany, who sat in a soft orange office chair against the wall, as far away from Carl—and Rutus—as she could. She wore a bright, color-spattered summer dress that looked to Carl as if it had been peppered with fresh fruit.

"Good morning, Mrs. Sny," he grinned at her. "And don't you look charming today? Tough food fight, was it?" Delighted with his own humor, Carl turned again to Rutus. He held out his hand— palm down—and Rutus shook it. "Good to see you, Rutie. Big day for the Snys, huh?" He pulled up his dungarees and sat in the wooden chair beside Sny's desk.

Sny at first was taken aback. He tried to read Carl's flushed grin but was unable to. He assumed the man was drunk. "Well, Mr. Mason, I must say you're taking this better than I thought you would. After the way you treated Ed Stevens at the bank, I thought I might need bodyguards." He laughed haughtily, then pushed a red button on his desk and spoke into the intercom: "Yes, get Mr. Marks and Mr. Roberts back here right away." He turned again to Carl and offered him a cigar from a wooden humidor on his desk. Carl took three and put them in his tee-shirt pocket. He winked at Mrs. Sny.

"I certainly am glad to see you're feeling better about our transaction, Mr. Mason," Sny said, standing and crossing to the window, "because, frankly, I'm—we—are having second thoughts about buying that overpriced unsanitary landfill." He chuckled softly, still gazing out the window. "Yessir, you almost took me—almost took me but good. Imagine my offering you ninety grand!" Sny looked at Mason and beat on his own head: "I must've had a screw loose."

"Yeah," Carl said. "More than one, if you ask me."

"Nevertheless, as I was saying, the quality and condition of that land being what it is, I'm afraid we really can't meet the purchase price we had originally discussed. Do you hear me, Carl?"

"Loud and clear, Rute."

Sny came back to his desk and sat down, worked a gold ball-point pen between his fingers as he spoke: "To tell you the honest truth, the board of selectmen recently reexamined its reevaluation of your property and unanimously came to the conclusion that it's worth considerably less than we had originally thought."

Carl smiled. "I'll be darned," he said, rubbing his neck. "I guess those taxes'll have to come right down then, won't they?"

Sny studied him. Why is he smiling? he wondered. He chose his words carefully. "One would assume so, wouldn't one, in a case such as this?"

Carl's smile broadened. He stood slowly and leaned on Sny's desk, looked directly into his eyes, and said, "You know, you're really something, Sny." Rutus leaned back in his chair. Carl's face glowed like a rib roast—the veins in his temples throbbed. "I mean, you're a goddamn peach! Sorry, ma'am—you're a goddamn peach, too. I mean, with all you've done for me and my family, and now you're giving me a break on my taxes—you will reimburse me for the difference in last year's taxes, won't you?"

"I have the check right here," Sny said, holding it up. Carl snatched it and stuck it in his tee-shirt pocket with the cigars.

"What I mean to say," Carl continued, "is that you've been so generous—both of you—well, I just don't know what to say. What do you think a fair price would be for Wind In The Pines? Eighty thousand?"

Sny sighed. He glanced slyly at his wife, then drew a long, critical breath through his teeth. "Eighty thousand, you say." His heart surged, he drummed his pen against the desk. "God only knows how much it's going to cost to clean the place up," he mused. "Frankly, I was thinking of a lower figure."

"Okay," Carl said. "You're a tough cookie, Sny. Let's say an even seventy grand."

"Mr. Mason," Sny said, opening his desk drawer, "I want to show you something." He reached into the drawer and pulled out a handful of hundred-dollar bills. "I've got fifty thousand here in this drawer—cash money. Looks pretty good, doesn't it?" He waved it back and forth. "Quite a windfall for a guy like you."

Carl folded his arms and lowered his head in thought. He drew a deep breath, then looked up at Sny. "Make it sixty," he said.

Rutus Sny rose to his feet. He walked around the desk, offering his hand. "Say no more, Mr. Mason. You've got a deal."

Carl looked directly at Tiffany. "I'm not selling." He smiled and turned for the door.

"What? Wait, wait, Mr. Mason! Is there some problem? Negotiations aren't complete here . . ." He reached over his desk and pulled stacks of bills from his opened drawer. "Look," he cried, beseeching with hands full of fan-shaped hundreds, "I mean, we're still prepared to go the higher figure—if we have to—"

Carl turned slowly, his grave expression silencing Sny. He looked at Tiffany sitting on the edge of her chair, her lips dumbly slack. He pulled a cigar from his tee-shirt pocket, unwrapped it, and stuck it between his teeth. "Let me just savor this moment," he said, unsmiling. "I want to remember you two assholes—just like this."

Earl Root sat low in a worn, cushy recliner. He was dressed in polka-dot boxer shorts and was eating baked beans, ham, and fried doughnuts from a wide platter on his lap. With a tablespoon in his right hand and a fork in his left, his feeding was a continuous, greedy dirge of left, right, left, with only an occasional break to suck in oxygen or swill milk from a red plastic cup. A small black and white television—one of seven Root TVs—sat on the kitchen table tuned to "The Price Is Right," not Earl's favorite show, but a show nonetheless. On the other side of the table Dolly sat, eating in a manner identical to her husband—left, right, left—but watching her soap, "Mothers' Lonely Days," on a separate television backed against Earl's. The volumes of the sets competed not only with each other, but with the sounds of the Roots' feeding. From the outside, the trailer fairly resounded with a weird cacophony of panting, grunting, organ music, gnashing, prize giveaways, confessions, burping, weeping, farting, wild applause, canned laughter, floor wax commercials, and throat clearing.

The tide of anger had shifted with the Roots. No longer was Earl pandering to Dolly with groveling, transparent comments such as, "Any more rats in the trap this morning?" or "Still got the runs, honey?" to which she would only reply "Mmmp" or "Mmmp-mmp." No sir, no more of that. A man got to keep his pride, can't be led around by no nose ring. Now it was her turn to grovel. "More," he said, holding out his platter, and Dolly silently shoveled on another half-dozen fried doughnuts. "More," he said after eating them, knowing there were no more.

"No more," Dolly said. Earl rapped the platter twice on the table, still not looking at her—a clear signal to go out and get more. She balked at first but he rapped the platter again, so she rose, snatched her handbag from off the refrigerator, and walked out the door.

She wasn't gone but a minute when Earl heard the approach of a tuneless whistle and a knock at the door. He grunted, lifted himself out of the chair, and went to the door, where he found himself face to face with a magazine cover: *Tender TuBBies*: two spherical, naked young ladies frolicking in a child's blue plastic swimming pool filled with turkey legs, cream pies, cupcakes, strawberries, peaches, cheesecakes, blintzes, bananas, eclairs, and half a roasted pig. The tubbies were coated with oil. One poured cream from a pink porcelain pitcher into the other's mouth, so that the cream overflowed and ran down her massive belly into the dark, hidden abyss of her crotch. Earl Root looked from the flesh to the food to the flesh and began wheezing.

"Good morning, Earl," Larry smiled, extending his hand.

"Whadda you want?" Root asked, making a slow grab for the magazine. Larry pulled it away.

"So how's business, Earl? How's life been treatin' ya?"

"'S' been better—"

"Yeah? You figure people are killing their own pets nowadays, or what?"

Earl looked down at the steps beside Larry and saw a stack of magazines over two feet high—the whole lot! A thin, sandy curl of hair fell onto his forehead and became ensnared in sweat. "All right," he said, squinting, "what's goin' on here?"

"Oh, I thought maybe we could help each other out—you know, you wash my back, I'll wash yours? That kind of thing. So how do you kill 'em, Earl? Lethal injection? Electrocution? Hanging?"

Earl leveled a mean, pig-eyed stare at Larry, then held his breath and farted. "Gas," he said, without humor. "And that's why I been losin' business, too."

"Why?"

"Cause-uh the gas. It used to be better." In truth, UNWaNTed PeTS LaiD AWay had never been better. It had never even been good—fifteen customers a year at best. But the Roots' home business did help to keep the nagging welfare people at bay.

"Used to be better, huh? How did you used to do it?"

The fat man put two fingers to his head and pulled an imaginary trigger. "That's how I used to gas 'em," he said, curling his lip. "Bang."

But Carl Mason had put an end to that practice one summer day after a frenetic, head-wounded German shepherd staggered head-shaking, bloody, and snarling through the day-swimmers on the beach, hotly pursued by Root in his blue boxer shorts, ordering the swimmers to stay back, stay back, stay back, and pumping four rounds into the animal from a police-show crouch.

Later, under Carl's orders, Earl built a large plywood doghouse and attached two propane gas tanks to it, while Dolly spray-painted the entire structure enamel sky-blue. A valve protruded through the doghouse roof, on which were painted three words in blue-streaked enamel red: OFF, SlEEp, and KiLL. A saucer of milk placed in the doorway and a fresh piece of gristle tossed in the back ensured that the unfortunate animal's final journey would be, if not peaceable, at least a palatable one.

"Yep," Larry said, shaking his head glumly, "those musta been good ol' days, all right."

"So, uh, what's with the books? You still ain't told me what you're up to."

"Six campsites and a clean pond, Earl."

Earl looked cockeyed at him. "You don't make sense, boy."

"Think about it. Six campsites and a clean pond. That's what we'll have here if you let us move your trailer—and that blue doghouse out there."

"Killhouse," Earl corrected him. "We call that the killhouse. No way. We ain't budgin'. So, these your magazines, or what?"

"Well, Earl, I'll tell you, I was going to burn 'em, but then I thought, 'Wait—I bet Earl Root, being a regular kind of a guy, might like to have 'em.'"

"Christ a'mighty," Root laughed softly, opening the torn screen door, peering over Larry's shoulder for signs of Dolly, "don't burn 'em, boy. Bring 'em right in here."

"Not so fast, Earl. Let's talk turkey, if you get my drift."

Earl nodded his head knowingly. "Sure, I get it. You give me the books if I move the trailer, right?"

Larry allowed a slow, crafty grin. "You guessed it, my friend. You know, I think we're on the same wavelength here, even though your wife said—oh, never mind, I probably shouldn't say—"

"What? What'd that ol' cow say now?"

"Nothing important, Earl, really. I wouldn't want to start trouble between you and the missus. That's not how I operate. In fact, I hope you don't mind my coming over while she's not around. It's just that I've got a little wager—a little side bet—with Carl. He told me, 'Don't waste your time dealing with Earl, 'cause Dolly's the person to see in the Root family if you need a decision.' He told me she calls all the shots. 'Hey,' I said, 'I don't believe that for a minute!' I think I know you better than that, Earl. Am I right?"

"She calls the shots, huh?" Earl's head was bobbing like a boxer on the skids.

"That's what she told him, anyway," Larry said.

"Gmph." he said, still bobbing in the doorway. "Gmph." He opened the door again. "You bring them friggin' magazines right in here, boy. Slide 'em under my recliner there. Way back so she don't see 'em. And I'll tell you what. I'll get her outta here tomorrow night. It's our anniversary, see? I'll take her to Bonanza or someplace for supper, and you can move the trailer then. But not too far back, all right?"

"Nah," Larry said, "just twenty feet or so." Larry pointed at the fat man. "You're my kind of man, Earl Root. I knew I wasn't wrong about you."

Mosquitoes whined in the darkness at Ruth's window, futilely poking their stingers through the screenholes. If I run my hand along the screen, she wondered, would their stingers all bend so they'd get stuck there, like in the cartoons? Probably not. Instead, she popped the screen with her finger. But the whining only intensified. She laid her hand on her forehead, hearing, yet trying not to hear, the mosquitoes, or the rhythmic knocking of Susie's head on the linoleum kitchen floor, or Zippy's blustery snore beside her.

As usual, Zippy slept back-to. It had become a relentless pattern of nights without love, days without conversation: Tolerance— that's all their love had become—tolerance and occasional contentment. And though she always believed tolerance and contentment would carry her through, now—just now, for this moment—she longed for something more.

She closed her eyes and remembered her passionate years with Zippy—the underblanket fucking on a crowded Chicago Trailways bench; their sixteen-hour lovemaking on psilocybin at Marconi Beach; she remembered acid tripping with him on a muddy, rain-drenched hill at Woodstock, openly fornicating in plain view of a half million pilgrims, when suddenly he had risen and walked off naked to find "the bus." She had closed her eyes then and fallen into a hallucinogenic sleep only to awaken hours later at the bottom of the muddy hill, her peasant dress bunched up under her shoulders, being mounted by a crazed Canadian who called himself The Archer—Ah, yes, those sweet, sweet days—her salad days—her days of passion. And now she wished for that passion in her life again.

Lying there, listening to Larry's frenzied lovemaking, she suddenly wished she had never consented to his moving in with them; yet in the same thought, she whimsically imagined herself in Susie's place, making love to him. Yes, it was romance she longed for. She allowed herself more images of Larry: the square of his chin (it occurred to her that she had never seen her husband's chin); the stubble on the back of his neck. She imagined a life with him: window shutters and shrubbery on a quiet, maple-lined avenue, children, neighbors, him coming home from work in the cool of the evening, her meeting him at the door with a gentle kiss on the mouth; him, with manicured hands, lifting her by the bottom, pressing her soft, yearning vulva against his hard flannel thigh, his sweet, warm tongue snaking into her mouth . . .

Enough! she scolded herself. Larry was her husband's brother. And besides, he was engaged to another woman.

Still, she had glimpsed something new in Larry today, something that brought him spiritually closer to her. He too, she had discovered, had been Born Again. She never would have known if she hadn't stumbled upon him kneeling by the trunk of his old Camaro. Are you okay? she had asked; oh sure, he had answered, I'm just praying.

He had asked her to go into town with him tomorrow so that he might buy her some "decent" clothes; Zippy had become sanctimonious—possibly a bit threatened—and accused her of having middle-class values. He had gone on about Ethiopia. He had gone on about Babylon.

She sighed and thought to herself, I will go into town tomorrow with Larry.

24

Tex's Wild Animal Kingdom

Early Tuesday morning workers arrived. Some bulldozed the remains of Angel's trailer into a pile while others hauled it—and the
industrial loom—away in a dump truck; meanwhile, a backhoe
began digging a septic hole and leachfield for the Roots' new site;
and another crew laid forms for a slab foundation onto which the
newlyweds' prefabricated log home would be assembled; still others
began construction of a thirty-foot dock and diving board, while a
siding company took measurements of all the cabins for false-faced
plasti-log siding. Then the bulldozer crew scraped up the burnt
remains of Zippy and Ruth's former cabin and loaded that into the
dump truck. During all this activity Carl walked from one project to
the next, swinging his arms proudly and whistling "Love Letters in
the Sand." Inside Angel's new house—the former Mutant shack—
Harvey whitewashed the ceilings and walls, while Angel shopped in
town for furniture, clothes, and drapes (Ed Stevens and Larry and
several other members of the community had donated generously to
her cause). High atop the ridge Nighthawk packed fresh clay and
straw on his roof. It was hardly noticed when, about eight-thirty, the
season's first customers drove quietly out of Wind In The Pines,
never to return.

"I'm thinking of changing my name," Ruth said to Larry as they
drove into Bluffton.

"Oh, yeah? To what?"

"June."

"That's a nice name. You look like a June." Larry didn't know how to take Ruth. He never had. She was a quiet woman, serious and reflective, always seeming to be sizing things up—people, situations, relationships—as if her world were bunches of categories that always needed sizing up; yet on the other hand, she was so simple and forthright. Still, he wanted to get into her pants. "But Ruth is, well, a real nice name, and it's from the Bible. Why change it?"

"I don't know, I guess I just feel like a June lately. Do you know what I mean?"

"Sure, I know what you mean," he said. "But what about the old man, what does he think?"

"I haven't told him yet." She laid her head back against the headrest. "Maybe I won't."

"Won't what?"

"Won't tell him." Her eyes darted then and she laughed at herself. "No, I guess I'd have to tell him, wouldn't I?" She laughed some more, then stopped abruptly. "I'd actually like him to change his name. I'd like for him to be Harold, I think—his real name. Maybe if I start calling him Harold, he'd start acting like a Harold." She chuckled softly to herself, and then they drove a mile in silence. "Haar-old," she called suddenly, as if calling a dog. "Oh, Haaa-rold." She laughed again, and he laughed with her this time, although he didn't know why.

They drove on until they came to a shopping plaza. "There"— Ruth pointed—"Sears." And they spent two hours in the store building her a wardrobe—a very conservative wardrobe, at that, for the girl whose name had once been Seagull. She left Sears wearing a chocolate tweed skirt and matching jacket over a light blue ruffled blouse. "That was very generous of you, Larry," she said when they were on the road again.

"Don't mention it," he said, looking at her nyloned calf. Great legs, he thought to himself. "How about dinner tonight?"

"No, I really can't. I've got to get back and make dinner for Zip . . . Harold . . . Harry . . . Oh, I don't know—what's-his-name." She laughed.

They stopped briefly at The Sign Shop so Larry could check the progress of the new Camp Sign; he wanted a change, if it wasn't too

late. In amongst the words SWIMMING, FISHING, BOATING, HIK-
ING, PLAYGROUND, PICNICS, Larry wanted the word SOUVENIRS.
He emerged from the shop with a confident wink and a thumbs-up
sign. Ruth thought to herself, I am enjoying him; I am enjoying
myself today.

Then Larry sought out Atlas Grocers on a long, seldom-used
country road, the slow, winding, seventeen-mile back road to Norwood. In Bluffton it was called the Norwood Road; in Norwood, the
Bluffton Road. There was a time, before the Bluffton Mall was built
in the center of the city, even before the seven shopping plazas
sprang up on the outskirts, before the barrel mill and the button
factory had gone under, when the road was a busy one. Its small
businesses thrived then. But now only their relics remained: empty,
ivy-covered shops with dark, smashed-out windows; boarded-up gas
stations whose asphalt and concrete grounds had long since split
under the relentless upward siege of weeds and frost heaves, whose
cracked and peeling walls were spray-painted with phrases like "68"
IS GREAT!!, BEATLES FOREVER, and SUCK.

It was along this stretch of modern wasteland that they saw the
tall, free-standing green and white sign:

TEX'S WILD ANIMAL KINGDOM

On both sides of the weed-covered parking lot, almost completely
hidden from view by alders, were the tall, weathered remains of
once magnificent totem poles.

Larry saw the totem poles, pumped his brakes, and swung into
the lot. There were only three other vehicles there: an old Cadillac
up on blocks, another Cadillac with TEX written on its license
plates, and a beefy, steel-bedded International truck with circus art
on its sides and weeds growing into its doors. On the boarded-up
ticket booth behind the sign was a faded poster:

Selling Out—Everything Goes

A black, wrought-iron fence which enclosed the kingdom was
opened beside the ticket booth. Larry and Ruth walked through.

They followed a shattered sidewalk through tall quack grass straight into the empty, overgrown heart of Tex's Wild Animal Kingdom, where cage after opened cage stood vacant, on whose floors still lay remnants of grit and sawdust, and whose worn signs— MOUNTAIN LION, OSTRICH, BENGAL TIGER, AMERICAN BUFFALO —still hung neatly on the bars. The sidewalk led to a small, tattered mockup of a western ghost town: a jail, a saloon, a bank, and a general store. Through the dark, cobwebbed windows papier-mâché dummies could be seen, frozen in time. An Indian Chief stood in the jail cell, adorned in full battle dress, clutching at the bars, a ferocious sneer on his painted, corroded face. A sheriff sat smugly with his gun drawn and his feet up on his desk (one boot fallen sideways revealed a two-by-four leg); his nose fell askew and an ear hung down. The sweet-acrid stench of urine hung heavily in the doorway.

"Welcome to Tex's Wild Animal Kingdom," a voice said. They turned and a stranger in a ten-gallon hat seized Larry's hand, pumping it. He tipped the hat to Ruth. "Ma'am," he said. He was a short, bespectacled man, dressed in full cowboy regalia right down to his chaps and rhinestones, though his advanced age and overall paunchiness detracted from the image. He had a pink, baby-fair face and a small, baby-fair grin, which further detracted. To Ruth, he looked more like a inflatable beach toy than a man. "Guess who I am?" he said.

"Tex," Larry guessed, pointing.

"Got me," Tex laughed, raising his arms in surrender. "You know, a young man tall and handsome like yourself'd look downright proud in some western duds—an outfit like the one that sheriff's got on, for instance."

Larry said, "Tex, I'm mighty obligin' for the compliment, but the plain and simple truth is, all I want—and I'll pay ya handsomely— are them two totem poles you got out front o' yer spread."

Tex looked at him with a mixture of admiration and distrust. "Well, I'll be. You know, you talk like you was from Cheyenne."

"I got cowboy in my blood, Tex," Larry said with a nod.

"Five hun'rd for them totem poles, son," said Tex.

"I'll give you a hun'rd apiece," Larry said.

"Two-fifty," Tex said.
"Two hun'rd," Larry said.
"Apiece," Tex said.
"You got it," Larry said.
"Sold," Tex said.
"Delivered?" asked Larry.
"Extra hun'rd," said Tex.
"Gotcha self a deal, pard'nr," Larry said, shaking his hand.

Carl climbed the ridge-path, no longer whistling. Shirley had told him at lunch that under no condition did she ever want another dead cow or deer left at her doorstep. She told him he would have to tell Nighthawk—in a tactful way, of course—before the situation got out of hand. So he climbed. He would simply tell the Indian that he had no facilities to deal with large, dead animals.

But of course it wasn't that simple. He crested the ridge and spied Nighthawk kneeling beside a smoldering campfire, bent over a fallen squirrel.

Holding in his hand a gleaming, leather-handled hunting knife, Nighthawk rolled the limp rodent onto its back and sank the blade into its belly, ripping upward to the throat, so that a puff of steam escaped the parting flesh. Carl's throat contracted at the sight, but he kept silent. Then Nighthawk went inside the animal's tiny ribs with the blade, sawing. After a soft snap he lay the wet knife on his thigh, pinched out a small iridescent organ, and popped it into his mouth. Chewing, he said to Mason (though still not looking at him), "We join spirits."

Carl stepped onto the ridgetop. "What the hell was that?"

"Heart," Nighthawk murmured through bloody lips.

Carl's stomach clenched. He grimaced. "Mmm, lovely," he said.

Nighthawk stood, went to the edge of the ridge, and began hauling a long rope, hand over hand, up from the pond forty feet below. At the end of the rope was a shortening can, half full of pond water. He set the can down, then squatted beside the fire to rustle its embers with a stick. "Stew," he explained with pride.

Carl peered at the murky water in the can. An ivory foam blinked on its surface. "You're not going to drink that shit, are you?"

Nighthawk smiled patiently, still tending the fire. "My land is my woman," he said. "She is as I take her, and I take her as she is. She is my food, my drink—"

"*My* land," Carl corrected. "Just for the record, okay? This is *my* land. I'm the guy with the deed, the guy that bought it." He rubbed his thumb against his forefinger. "Money," he said, raising his eyebrows, as if to coax understanding from the Indian.

Nighthawk, still not looking at Carl, rose to his feet. "Yes," he said with a sigh, "money. You know money. It is your food, your drink, your woman." He bent for the shortening can. "But you do not know the land. You do not speak to it, as I do. It is not of your spirit." He turned to Carl. "No, Mason, the property is yours—but the land—it is mine." He put the can to his lips and, staring hard into Carl's eyes, drank deeply.

Carl's stomach rolled—he swallowed to repress a gag. Then, shaking his head, he turned and started down the ridge-path muttering as he walked, "Mmmm. I'll bet that's real tasty!"

It was late in the afternoon when Larry and Ruth reached Atlas Grocers. Larry went in alone and spoke to the office receptionist. Yeah, he said, I need about eighty thousand gallons of chlorine. Got a big load of laundry? she asked. Nope, big swimming pool, he answered. Anyway, can I get a break in price if I order eighty thousand gallons? Are you serious? she asked. Very serious, he replied in a low, oily voice. She pressed a button on her intercom. An hour later, after a five-hundred-dollar deposit had changed hands, Larry emerged triumphant. Atlas had arranged, as brokers, for a chemical company to ship one hundred twenty fifty-five-gallon drums of industrial sodium hypochlorite to Wind In The Pines, and yes, they would deliver day after tomorrow—for an extra fifty dollars. No sweat, Larry had said.

It was well after six o'clock when they got back into Norwood, and Larry still had one more stop. I'll just be a minute, he promised.

"That's okay," Ruth said. "If Zippy—I mean, Harry—gets hungry, he can make himself a peanut butter sandwich. I think I like Harry better than Harold, don't you?"

Larry parked under a full maple tree in the peaceful upper-class neighborhood and strolled up the flower-lined walk to the front door. He rang the chimes and waited, studying his reflection in the glass. In a moment the door parted and Rutus Sny poked his head out. "Yes?" he snapped.

"L.A. Jones," Larry said, offering his hand. "I'm a new businessman in town, and I just wanted to introduce myself around, you know, rub elbows and that sort of thing?"

Sny was unimpressed until Larry stood aside, allowing the health inspector a view of the forest-green Mercedes and the smart-looking woman in the passenger seat. During this brief period of silence they could hear the smart-looking woman saying to herself: "Harry; Harold; June and Harold; Harold and Ruth; June and Harry; Harry and June; Ruth and Harry . . ." Sny raised an eyebrow and opened the door wider. "Is that your car?" he asked.

"Oh, that? Yeah. Picked it up the other day. Sporty little thing, you know? Good for breezing around."

"Yes, yes, I see," Sny said, smiling. "Now what may I do for you, Mr. Jones? Sorry for the brusqueness just then. It's just that, well, nowadays you never know who's going to be knocking at your door, and I had just sat down to dinner—not that I mind the interruption . . . er, visit, I should say." Sny laughed. "So, won't you come in, Mr. Jones? And your lady friend, as well?"

"Well, we're a little pressed for time, Mr. Sny, so I'll lay it right on the line. I need a water test done at my new campground."

"New campground? What campground?" Sny knew of only one in town.

"Wind In The Pines," Larry said with pride. "I just bought into the business."

Sny furrowed his brow. "Can't help you," he said, closing the door.

"Wait," Larry called after him. "We need a test done. I'm cleaning the water day after tomorrow. I'm purifying it so we can get the swimmers in."

"Can't do it," Sny repeated from behind the door. "My time is too valuable to be chasing around that swamp. Besides, I just did a test there a few months ago, and I can assure you that that water will never be anything but a malaria breeding ground. If I had my way, I'd donate the whole goddamn campground to the government to bury their nuclear waste in."

"How valuable?"

"What?" Sny cracked the door and peeked out.

"How valuable is your time?" Larry said, digging into his pocket. Sny reached out and pulled him into the foyer. Three minutes later, when Larry emerged, he was unburdened of another four hundred dollars, but Rutus Sny had consented to test the pond water.

Driving back to Wind In The Pines, Larry turned suddenly to Ruth and said, "You know, June, you should have been a model. Or an actress."

She tilted the rearview mirror to study her face. "Really?" she asked, a little embarrassed. She tried to picture herself in the Sears catalogue, then shook her head. "No, I don't think."

Larry looked at her with a dark smile. "I mean it," he said, throwing a casual hand on her knee.

As soon as they drove into the campground, Harvey ran to the car. "Hey," he said, peering from behind a pair of new sunglasses, "we got these things here some guy bring for ya, toadin' poles, and Mr. Mason wun't around, 'cause him and Mrs. Mason went to town. Nobody knows nothin' about 'em, so I figgered you did. So whaddya want me to do with 'em, anyways? Can't carry 'em by myself, they're wicked heavy. Jeezum, y'd need four, five guys to lift 'em."

"We're going to bring 'em up to Indian Village, Harvey."

"Huh? Where?"

Larry stepped out of the car. He raised his sunglasses onto his forehead, put an arm around Harvey's shoulders, and pointed with his entire hand toward the ridge. "Look up there, Harvey." Harvey raised his own sunglasses as Larry had. "Now tell me what you see."

"House made of mud," Harvey said.

Larry chuckled. "You know what I see, Harvey?" Harvey stiffened. He wasn't sure he liked Larry's arm around him; didn't like any guy's arm around him. Made him feel funny. "Indian Village,

Harvey, that's what I see. Indian Village—wild animals, teepees, gift shops, a giant water slide coming off into the pond. And kids, Harvey—thousands of kids. And you know what else?"

"What?"

"I see a real live Indian up there running a gift shop—selling souvenirs. Training wild animals. That's what I see up there, Harvey."

Harvey looked at him. "Wow," he said. "I don't see none o' that."

"Yeah, pretty good, huh?" asked Larry. The question was rhetorical and actually meant for Ruth. Just the same, Nighthawk answered.

"Me no like," he said in a gruff voice.

Larry jumped. "Oh, Cochise," he smiled. "Didn't hear you sneakin' up on me there. Must be the moccasins. Oh, no moccasins. Must be those bare feet of yours." He studied the Indian for a moment, the first time he had seen him in the daylight. Were it not for the raccoon cradled in his arms, the big man would have been a fearsome spectacle.

"Where them go?" Nighthawk snapped.

"Where them go?" Larry asked.

"The toadin' poles," Harvey explained. "Where them things go?"

"Oh. Them go up there"—Larry pointed—"for an entranceway to Indian Village. And you, Cochise, are going to be the main attraction."

Nighthawk scowled. He worked his face into a fearsome frown. "White man loco," he said.

Larry moved to put an arm around his shoulder, but Nighthawk jumped back and went for his knife. Larry jumped back in the same instant, holding up his hands. "Whoa, whoa, hey! C'mon, Chief. Kimosabe, remember? Kimosabe. Listen, we only want to make you famous. Hey, we'll pay you, too. C'mon. It's for the kids, for the kids . . ." Then suddenly he snapped his fingers. "Hey!" he exclaimed, "have you ever done any high diving?"

Nighthawk looked up to the ridge, high above the pond, and his frown deepened. There stood his wigwam, of which he was proud, with its new thatched roof and polyethylene windows; and the animal skins—rabbit, woodchuck, squirrel, and buck—that hung from the sides drying in the low evening sun. He was becoming a noble brave, and when he turned his head to speak, he looked almost reverent. "White man," he said, shaking his head sadly, "bring trouble."

"Trouble?" Larry exclaimed, incredulous at the suggestion. "Trouble?" Then he wheeled to look at the Roots' trailer. "Oh, no!" he said. "Have they gone yet?"

"Yup," Harvey answered, nodding his head. "They went out to eat—"

"How long ago?"

"Um . . ."

"Never mind!" He grabbed Harvey by the arm. "Quick!" he said. "We haven't got much time. Get the Big Truck and back it up to that trailer."

"You mean—"

"Quick, Harvey!" Larry shouted. "Run!"

25

The Move

Larry and Harvey handled the move alone, and though their work
wasn't particularly good, it was so fast that by the time Carl and
Shirley returned from town the trailer—and Earl's killhouse—were
already in their new location—not twenty feet back, as Larry had
promised, but clear on the other side of the Camp Road, backed
into the brush.

First Harvey backed the Big Camp Truck to the trailer and
clamped the hitch onto the truck's towbar. Then Larry gave a signal
to go—knifing his hand down like a guillotine. "But she's up on
blocks," Harvey protested. "And you gotta take them propane tanks
off the front of 'er."

"Go! Go! Go!" Larry called. "The gas tanks are attached right to
the trailer. They'll be all right. Now go!"

Harvey shrugged. He dropped the truck into four-wheel-drive
and raced the engine, slowly easing up on the clutch until the truck
shuddered . . . and stalled. He tried again. He raced the engine
faster this time so that the trailer at least became aware of the truck's
intentions. It groaned and sagged—a window popped—and ul-
timately resisted. The truck stalled again, blue smoke rising from
under its hood. "Wait," Larry called. "She's hung up on this cinderblock." He ran to the store and returned with a sledgehammer. "Try
again!" he called, holding the twelve-pound hammer like a golfer's
driving iron.

Now Harvey floored the accelerator till the engine screamed. The truck dug in. All four wheels began spinning slowly, independently. The trailer appeared to stretch.

"Fore!" Larry cried, swinging the sledgehammer against a cinderblock. Then, with a deafening crunch of metal and jangle of breaking glass, the trailer lurched forward, immediately overrunning its severed, hissing propane gas tanks, rising up with a *creeaaak*, then falling again onto its rotted, flattened wheels with a muffled yet lingering *bang* and *craash* from inside, pitching like a barge across an angry, hardened sea. "Keep going! Keep going!" Larry cried, waving both hands wildly, as Harvey drew the trailer in a grand arc away from the pond and across the Camp Road, leaving behind a trail of tumbled, half-buried cinderblocks, a live power line swinging from a pond-front birch, two rolling, sputtering propane gas tanks (one hissing fire), a broken waterpipe spraying water out of the ground like a fountain, and one thin trail of white liquid—probably milk from the kitchen, Larry thought. Oh, well, some breakage was bound to occur in an operation like this.

Larry slept late Wednesday morning. He had spent Tuesday evening dividing his time between his women—talking religion with Ruth, screwing Susie in the Mercedes, and then, after walking her home, sneaking to Angel's where he spent the night sniffing cocaine and having sex.

With Angel, cocaine tended to make Larry confessional: "Don't say anything to Susie about what I've been telling you. I want to break it to her gently, you know, for the good of the Camp." With Susie, the drug made him philosophize, made him marvel at his own mind. He told her that sometimes he believed he knew everything. What do you mean? she wanted to know, snorting cocaine through a hundred-dollar bill. "I don't know, I just think my brain is, well, advanced. Like, I think about things that nobody ever thought of before. For instance, have you ever wondered why there are big holes in the earth where the oceans are?" No. "Or how about UFOs—did you ever wonder if we're really alone? I mean the things I think about are really incredible. And how about reincarnation? That's pretty heavy, I don't want to scare you; or ghosts?" With Ruth, on the other hand, the coke—which he hid from her—made him cool and modern, except when they were in Zippy's presence, when he became cold and competing—disrespectful of their brotherhood: "If you need financial help, just come to my private office and I'll see what I can do," he gloated after presenting his brother with a letter, typed by himself but signed by "The Camp Committee," which raised the couple's rent.

He woke up on Angel's bedroom rug with the high morning sun in his eyes, even as his fiancée Susie was into her third miserable day of training her replacement, Jean Duckoff, in the Camp Store; as Ruth, in a modest new peach sundress, was having coffee and making wedding arrangements with Shirley in the Masons' kitchen; and as Carl and Harvey were preparing to pour cement at the six new shorefront sites. They had been up since dawn with the Diablo Brothers, bulldozing the Roots' former site and outhouse and hauling away the debris, and then building wooden rectangular forms on each of the sites.

The operation in the past three days had already cost "The Camp Committee" many thousands of dollars, but it was the face-lifting Wind In The Pines had needed for years. Why, the place even smelled better—the satisfying fragrance of new lumber filled the air: cedar from Larry and Susie's new log home; pine from a load of new picnic table lumber which had been dumped by the shore—enough for eight new picnic tables; and oak from the new wooden dock—painted flat gray—set firmly in place thirty feet straight out from the shore, with eight brand new rowboats tied to its side and a sparkling diving board at its end. (Carl and Shirley had walked out on the dock late the previous evening. Carl had playfully gone onto the diving board, like Tom Sawyer fence walking, and bounced up and down.)

Yes, things were looking up. As Carl saw it, there were only two complications in his life: (1) The pond water was still polluted, and (2) Dolly Root was inside one of the campsite forms, reclining in a red flowery upholstered chair and watching a small black and white TV on a rusted TV stand. A hundred-foot orange extension cord led like an umbilical cord back across the Camp Road into the ravaged trailer she had abandoned. She wouldn't be budged, she declared, until her home was repaired and returned to its rightful place, the same home that was now being connected by plumbers to a great dark underground hole—the septic system Carl had promised. She was adamant: "You can cement me right here where I sit, and I hope you do, because this is my land, and I'm never leavin'. I want everybody, including God Himself, to see what bums you really are."

The cement truck churned noisily, and when the mix was ready the men poured the first four forms without a glance at the fat woman, nor she at them. She simply folded her arms in grim defiance and watched her game shows at full volume, occasionally muttering (so they could hear) various invectives concerning the Mason family and members of the animal kingdom. But when they poured the fifth form right beside her, she was no longer able to concentrate on TV. "Oh, big, big men!" she snapped at them, her jaw protruding. "Turn a poor woman out of her home. Kill me, why dontchas, take a gun and shoot me in the head, bang!"

Finally Carl went to the Root trailer to reason with Earl. "Call her off, Root, or I swear to God I'll pour the cement right where she's sitting, and she'll never get out."

But Earl was just as cantankerous. "Well, you go right ahead, mister, 'cause I feel the same way she do," he complained. "We was tricked into this! That ol' Larry promised he was just gonna move the trailer twenty feet back, and lookit where he put us. And lookit the mess! Everything's stove up, all the windows too. And by the Christ, every step I take now in this God-forsaken trailer I feel like I'm goin' right on through the floor. Listen to 'er crackin' under me. And right over by that chair, can you see how she sags? And look up here—that's sky showin' through my ceilin', mister. Sky! You could throw a cat through that crack! I'm tellin' you, Mason, somebody's gotta put this right." He was making his point by hammering his chubby fist on a tabletop magazine: *Grade School Groupies.*

Carl threw up his hands. "I don't have time for this, Root," he said, leaving. "Talk to Larry about it. But I'm warning you, we're pouring that concrete right now."

Earl caught the screen door and followed Carl to the shore where his wife sat, merrily scolding them both like a jaybird. Earl said:

"Stick to your guns, Dolly. Don't move a muscle." (He secretly wanted some time alone with his trove of pornography.)

"Out of my life, you lily-livered milksop," she commanded, pointing majestically. "If you was a man, you'd stand up and protect my"—she shook her jowls, searching for the right word—"rep-u-tation!"

Carl motioned to Harvey. "Get Shirley," he said. Then to Mrs. Root: "In one minute we're pouring, Mrs. Root. I don't want to do it, but you're not leaving me much choice. So if you want your favorite chair ruined, and those shoes and socks—nice socks, by the way—and that gorgeous TV stand you got there, well, you just sit right there. Be my guest."

Just then Shirley came out her door, hurrying across the pavilion area with Ruth. Jean Duckoff ran from behind the ladies, overtaking them with great, long-legged strides. Susie followed glumly, uninterested, angrily scanning the area for Larry. (She had stolen from her house after midnight the night before and gone looking for him but found he was not at home.) When she saw her mother take a stand beside Carl in the face-off, she stood beside Dolly Root.

"Mrs. Root," Shirley said firmly, "just what are you doing?"

"I'll tell you what I'm doin', Miss Prissy, and that's not movin'! Nobody's movin' this woman off'n her land."

Shirley smiled condescendingly. "Now, Mrs. Root—"

"That's right," announced Susie to her mother, patting the large, defiant woman's shoulder. "She doesn't have to move. She's got her rights."

"I'm on your side too, babes," said Earl.

"Jesus Christ," said Carl. He turned away from the pond and rubbed the back of his neck, seeing, but not comprehending, Larry running from tree to tree down to the gathering from Angel's new house—Angel herself followed slowly. Finally he let out a long sigh and gestured to the man in the cement truck. "Okay, junior"—he shrugged—"let's pour."

The man looked down from the truck at Dolly Root, her hands folded prayerlike on her lap. "I can't do that," he said to Carl.

"All right, never mind," Carl said, "I'll do it myself." The driver climbed down, Carl climbed up, and Harvey held the chute near Dolly's left shoe.

"Sorry, Ma," he said.

"Don't you Ma me, you ungrateful pup!" she snapped. Then suddenly her eyes widened. Cement poured down the chute like a thick gray lava flow and covered her feet, rising to its level height just below the tops of her sweatsocks. "You'll be sorry!" she bellowed. "You'll regret this, all-uh-yuhs. Lookit my chair! Lookit this chair!"

Larry couldn't figure out what was going on. He sidled up to Susie to ask her, but she ignored him. By the looks of the situation—a woman voluntarily sitting in cement—he had the feeling that it was probably his doing, and therefore, he reasoned, it was up to him to undo it—or, better still, to make the most of it. Yes, that was his thing—snatching victory from the bowels of defeat. And just like that, it came to him: *Brainstorm!* He pointed to his head so Susie could see. But she looked away. And then he was gone, running up to the office, pulling Harvey along behind him.

They came back minutes later wearing the new official Wind In The Pines uniforms—red V-neck tee-shirts and matching shorts. Green letters on their backs said in a semicircle, WIND IN THE PINES. On Larry's breast was also written MANAGER; on Harvey's, HARVEY. "Woo-woo," Harvey said, showing off his new uniform to Jean. "L.A. got one for you, too. Says 'Jean' right here." He then added, without malice, "I hope it'll fit. Jeez, you get fatter every day." Jean lowered her head in unarticulated embarrassment.

Larry said to Carl, "Yours is in the office, partner. Go put it on. I had 'em write 'Manager' on it." Carl raised a skeptical eyebrow. "I got one for you, too," Larry told Susie, putting an arm around her waist.

"Big thrill," she said, pulling away from him. "Is that what your big idea was?"

"Nope. You'll see. All I can tell you is, you've only got about three minutes to get into your uniforms. This is a major brainstorm." He turned again to Carl. "Go on, change into the Camp Uniform. Really. You girls, too. Come on, trust me on this."

They were distracted then by the arrival of a long blue station wagon. The words BLUFFTON DAILY JOURNAL were written across the car's side. Carl scowled suspiciously at Larry, and Larry nodded confidently in return. "Trust me on this, partner," he said. "Just trust me."

In seconds a staff photographer was out of the car, framing Dolly Root against the pond, while a reporter held a cassette recorder up to her fuming mouth. Carl pulled Larry aside.

"What's goin' on?" he demanded.

Larry tapped on his own head. "Always thinking," he said.

Carl's eyes darted. "You? You did this?"

"You know what they say, Carl: 'All publicity is good publicity.' Think about it."

"Jesus Christ," Carl spat softly. He bent from the waist, fists clenched, looking like a man about to vomit. "Je-sus Christ!"

The reporter, a young, tanned woman with frosted hair, spotted Carl and approached him. "You don't seem too happy about all this," she said.

"No comment," he said, waving her away, still bent at the waist.

"Mr. Mason," she said politely, "how long will you make Mrs. Root sit here before one of you gives in?"

Carl turned to leave. "No comment," he muttered.

"Opening day," answered Larry Jones. "May twenty-fifth."

"That's more than a week away," the reporter said. "Will you really make her sit in cement that long?"

Larry smiled for the camera. "She's a good sport. Besides, where else could she sit and watch swimming, boating, fishing, and, if she looks up there on the ridge, Indian Village? For the kids."

The reporter motioned to her photographer. "Very interesting," she said to Larry. "Can we get a picture of you beside Mrs. Root?"

"Right," Larry said. "And let's get Harvey in the picture too. He's got the uniform on."

So Larry stood behind Dolly's left shoulder, Harvey by her right, and their picture was taken. When it appeared in Thursday's Journal, Harvey's eyes were closed and his face grimaced in the throes of a violent sneeze which also dislodged his sunglasses from one ear and caused his knee to jerk up to his chest, so that his image was blurred like a ghost's. Larry, in his Camp Uniform, had turned slightly inward to show his best profile despite a request by the photographer to face the camera. Between them Dolly Root sat stiffly, gazing heavenward with exaggerated reverence, like the religious record-album covers she'd seen advertised on TV. The caption below the photo read: "*Cementing Relations*—Mrs. Root 'stuck' on campsite." The article read:

NORWOOD—Here at Camp Wind In The Pines, workers are feverishly preparing for opening day. And no one hopes more for that day to come than Mrs. Dolly Root. Mrs. Root, in a unique protest at having her mobile home moved away from its beachfront site, has had her feet and favorite chair embedded in cement on her former home site, and she vows to "stay put" until the campground officially opens for the season.

Camp co-owner L.A. Jones commented about the incident, "She's a good sport."

The camp, which officially opens on May 25th, will offer swimming, boating, fishing, and something special for children.

Carl laid the newspaper down beside his coffee cup. "That son-of-a-pup," he said with a grin.

"Hmm?" Shirley asked.

"He was right, this is great publicity."

"Carl," Shirley scolded, "that poor woman didn't sleep a wink last night, and I didn't either, what with hearing her crying all night. I must have gone out to check her a dozen times. The poor thing was nearly eaten alive by mosquitoes."

"Mosquitoes won't hurt her," he said bitterly. "She'd choke a bear."

"Tsk. That's not funny. Carl, why can't you compromise? At least go down and talk to her. Show her that you care, maybe she'll give in."

"I don't care," he replied lightly. "Not a bit."

She pulled up the blinds and looked curiously out toward the pond. "What are the boys doing with all those barrels?" Lately she had begun to refer to Larry and Harvey as "the boys."

Carl leaned across the table and looked out. Down by the dock Larry and Harvey, both dressed in their bright red uniforms, were huddled in a squat forest of fifty-five-gallon drums. They appeared to be counting them. Dolly Root appeared to be heckling them. "Oh, I dunno," Carl said. "Larry must've gotten a deal on trash barrels, I guess. Looks like he got more than he bargained for."

"Shouldn't you go down and check on them, Carl?"

"Nah, he knows what he's doin'. The kid's got good business sense. Besides," he said, getting up from the table, "I've got to take the Big Truck into town and pick up a few things—lumber and pipes and things. The new sign's going to be ready today, too. Wait'll you see it, Shirl. Larry designed it. It's a billboard, for cryin' out loud—it's even got lights. And the best part is, he paid for it. Small fortune, I'll bet, but a sign like that'll make a big difference." Shirley thought to herself that she had never seen her husband so happy, even despite his problem with Dolly Root—or possibly because of it. He got up, checked his pockets for keys, and opened the door. "Whoops," he said to someone outside, "don't do that, sonny." (A small, blond-haired boy was throwing rocks at the Duck-offs' trailershack.) He closed the door again and said to Shirley with quiet excitement, "Psst, hey—customers! A lady and a kid in a van."

26

The Cleanup

Harvey felt for his mustache. It had been a week since he'd shaved, and now the sparse, golden-red stubble was beginning to show. He wondered how long it would take till it was as thick and dark as Larry's. He adjusted his sunglasses and tucked his red Camp Tee-Shirt into his Camp Shorts. He slapped the top of a drum and said, "What're we gonna do with all of 'em, L.A.?"

"Gonna clean up this pond, once and for all, Harvey."

"So what's in the barrels, clean water?"

Larry chuckled. He pried the cover off a fifty-five-gallon drum and pushed the barrel over, spilling the chlorine into the water at their feet. "Whoa!" said Harvey, shaking like a wet dog. "Smells like a dang washin' machine."

"Or a swimming pool," Larry said pointedly.

Until now Dolly had sat, only mildly interested in the proceedings, but now, with Larry's intentions clear, she cackled loudly. Larry ignored her. "Okay, Harve," he said, rubbing his palms, "where's that raft I told you to build yesterday?"

Harvey took a deep breath. "Sorry, L.A., but I didn't have time. I spent all day puttin' together these picnic tables—eight of 'em."

Larry took off his sunglasses. "Didn't have time? Didn't have . . . Harvey, Harvey, c'mon, man. How are we supposed to get these barrels out to the middle of the pond without that raft? Huh?"

Harvey looked sheepishly at him and shrugged. "But Mr. Mason told me—"

"Harvey." Larry sighed as if with great patience, moving closer to the fan-eared boy. "Let me tell you something about Carl Mason. And me." Larry turned him in an awkward circle. "Look around you. See that new dock, those new rowboats, these new barrels, these new campsites? That new log cabin going up? Even your new picnic tables there—do you see all that? Well, that's *me*, Harve— that's the kind of stuff I'm into—new stuff, the kind of stuff that'll put this place on the map. But Mason's not like me, you know what I mean? We're on different levels, him and me. Nothing against the man, but, how can I put it, he just doesn't have what it takes to run a campground like this. Now, just between you and me, Harvey, when I bought into this place, I kind of took over, you know? Took control. Carl—Mr. Mason, that is—still likes to putter around and all, but you're gonna have to realize who's running the show here. Me. Right?"

"Yup."

"Okay." As he talked, Larry continued dumping drums of chlorine into the pond. "So now you're telling me we've got no raft, and so I've got to come up with an idea to haul these barrels out to the middle of the pond. Right?"

"Right."

"But that's okay, Harvey. It's a mental challenge, and I love a mental challenge." He furrowed his brow and turned slowly, stroking his chin. "I'm thinking," he told Harvey.

"Pump the stuff out with a long hose," Harvey suggested.

"Shh."

"Row 'em out," offered Harvey.

Larry raised a finger to silence him. Then he raised his head. "That's it!" he exclaimed, snapping his fingers. "I've got it."

"What?"

"You'll see. Quick, go get Carl's outboard motor, and bring some rope, too."

While Harvey was gone, Larry dumped more barrels along the shore until sixteen were emptied, and then he sealed them up again, watertight. Slowly his brainstorm took shape. The eight new picnic tables were pressed into service as rafts: two empty barrels— floats—were jammed lengthwise under each table between the benchseats, and then the tables were tied together in a convoy.

Harvey mounted Carl's fifteen-horsepower outboard motor onto the lead picnic table—the tug table, Larry called it—and then they pulled the convoy up alongside the dock where they loaded on full, opened drums, two to a table. They found after losing eight barrels that loading them one at a time would not work, as their weight forced the picnic table to slant, kicking the float drums out from under the table and pitching the full drum into the water. So they learned to wrestle two drums onto each table simultaneously. They lost another twelve drums doing that, but by early afternoon the convoy was loaded and ready for its maiden voyage.

All during the operation Dolly Root shouted discouraging words at the industrious pair from her cemented upholstered chair, most often making fun of their red uniforms, but also cajoling them when they'd lose a barrel, or just needling her son-in-law for the sport of it. "You'll never make it!" she shouted uproariously as they took their positions on the barge.

Harvey pulled the starter cord and the motor began to purr, gurgling gaily in the shallow water. "It's a heavy load," he called back to Larry, opening the throttle. "I hope she'll pull it."

"Bon voyage, imbeciles!" Dolly shouted through cupped hands. Coming from a woman with her feet cemented to the ground, the remark drew an audible snort from Larry.

Harvey scowled back. "What'd she say?"

Larry felt the tug at his table. "She's just mad 'cause I outfoxed her," he said, watching the dock back away. "But she'll be the first to thank me when this pond is cleaned up." Standing on the rear table between two black drums of chlorine, legs spread for balance, Larry cast an heroic figure—he thought of Humphrey Bogart, John Wayne, Harrison Ford. He checked the shore for his women— Angel, Ruth, Susie—he hoped they could see him. He loosened his hair with his fingers and let it blow back in the wind. He looked back to the shore again. Mrs. Root gave him the finger.

When they reached the middle of the pond Larry hollered, "Cut the engines, matey!"

Harvey jerked his head around with a confused, open-mouthed expression. His table rocked beneath him. He shut off the motor and said, "What? I couldn't hear you with the motor goin'."

"Just say 'aye-aye,'" Larry called.

"Huh?"

"Say 'aye-aye.'"

Harvey only smiled.

"Say it," Larry yelled.

Harvey shrugged his shoulders.

"Never mind, matey," said Larry. "Let's dump 'em!"

The chain reaction that followed was so predictable, like a domino line, that Mrs. Root gleefully began applauding on the shore before it began. Unfortunately, once it started there was nothing Larry or Harvey could do to prevent its outcome. In the same instant—on Larry's command—they both dumped their end drums overboard, creating a sudden weight shift that pitched their picnic tables forty-five degrees out of the water, simultaneously ejecting the float drums and spilling both man and drum onto the tug rope, severing it, and then into the drink—but only after jarring that next table enough to cause its end drum to jump into the water after them, which of course threw that table up out of the water, freeing its float barrels and forcing the remaining full barrel down onto the tug rope of the next table—the fateful pattern continuing until finally the last two tables, bound together in a V-shape by the rope and weighted by the last two converging drums of chlorine, plunged straight to the bottom of Norwood pond.

Larry and Harvey, weak swimmers both, surfaced amidst the wreckage, sputtering and choking, eyes burning with chlorine. Larry found the corner of a picnic table above water and held on, while Harvey struggled to board one of the many float drums that bobbed in the water about them.

"Over here!" Larry shouted, and Harvey began paddling to him in a blind panic, splashing stiff-armed the foaming, bubbling water. "Open your eyes!" Larry yelled. When Harvey reached the table he grabbed its corner next to Larry and hung there panting. Then he opened his eyes and stared at Larry, horrified. "You're bleeding," he gasped.

"So are you!" Larry said, but upon closer scrutiny they discovered that neither was bleeding, despite the bloody appearance. Their bodies had simply absorbed the bright red dye their clothes had lost—only their Camp Uniforms were bleeding.

It was Mr. Rogers who rowed the pair into shore a short time later, amidst the catcalls of Mrs. Root, the quieter buzzing of others assembled along the shore, and the splash of small, flat, skimming rocks hurled by a blond-haired boy hidden in the brush. "Gunnar!" a woman's voice hollered.

Larry climbed out of the boat with a merry skip, fixed his hair, and said casually, "Okay, folks, excitement's over." He turned to the pond, folded his arms, and struck a troubled pose, looking toward the high, piney horizon. Shaking his head solemnly, he mistakenly thought his good looks and *angst* transcended his pink face.

"What are you gonna do now, you goddamn fool?" Dolly Root chortled.

Larry turned slowly to the woman and said, "Madam, I have just begun to fight." It was a rich statement, obviously made for the others, but they were already walking away, afraid perhaps of being pressed into service. Only Susie and Jean remained by their men, Susie looking at Larry with more than an inkling of doubt.

"Do you know what you're doing?" she said.

"Do I know what I'm doing?" he replied indignantly. "No, I don't know what I'm doing. What do you think?"

"I dunno," she said lightly, walking away. His red legs hadn't helped.

"Harvey," he said with bravado, "if at first you don't succeed . . ." He left the end of the proverb for Harvey to fill in. Mrs. Root guffawed. Harvey looked at him blankly—his ears looked like tomato slices. "C'mon, Harvey, finish the sentence. If at first you don't succeed . . ."

Harvey looked at his wife Jean for assistance. She said, "E-I-E-I-O?"

"Try, try again," Larry said.

"Hi-oh, the dairy-o?" Harvey guessed.

"No," Larry said. "*Try, try again.*"

"Jeez, I dunno," said Harvey. "We been tryin'. We give up."

It took the rest of the day to finish dumping the drums of chlorine, but, as Larry explained, what's a day's work compared to a clean pond? He dumped at various points along the shore, while Harvey went under water—wearing a face mask—to pry the lids off the drums lost earlier beside the dock. Later, in a rowboat, they managed to rescue six of the capsized picnic tables. One of them, the table which held the outboard motor, was spotted suspended a foot below the surface, but in maneuvering it they accidentally sent the motor plummeting to the murk and chill of the bottom, to rust its silent life away in the company of sixteen opened fifty-five-gallon drums and four drums wedged in a V-shaped configuration of picnic tables.

By the time Carl returned with the new billboard tied to the inside of the Big Camp Truck, he noticed nothing amiss other than the almighty stench of chlorine in the air—and Larry's pink face. "What the hell is that smell?" he asked. "Did you open up a Laundromat while I was gone?"

"That 'smell,'" Larry boasted, "is our new pond, partner."

"What?"

"Yeah. Don't you remember? I told you I was going to clean up the pond."

Carl scowled. He climbed down from the truck and gazed through the trees at his pond. He sniffed the air deeply.

"Chlorine," Larry said. "It'll do the trick, guaran-goddamnteed."

"I don't know," said Carl, shaking his head. "You really think you shoulda dumped that stuff in the pond?"

Larry pointed at him. "Hey," he said.

"Hey what?"

"Hey, let's get that sign up, partner."

A smiling, bikinied woman leaped high in the air, gracefully poised in the apex of a swan dive. Below her, beneath the words FAMILY CAMPING, a fat rainbow trout gleefully broke water. Carl thought for an instant the woman was going to dive into the fish's mouth, but then his attention was drawn to the four sailboats and water-skier beside the trout, and the Indian chief in the clouds, and the mountain climbers scaling a snowy cliff on the right. Along the top of the billboard, just below a bank of six spotlights, were tall green letters in a semicircle:

WIND IN THE PINES

Down below the trout, in red letters:

SWIMMING, FISHING, BOATING, HIKING, PLAYGROUND, SOUVENIRS
Year round, Seasonal, Weekly, Nightly
JONES AND MASON, PROPRIETORS

Larry and Harvey dug the postholes while Carl clamped the tall cedar posts to the billboard's back. They worked in silence on the side of the River Road under a darkening evening sky. A chill had fallen in the air, and Carl found goosebumps raising the hairs on his arms as he worked. But the evening chill was a sign of a clear day ahead, so he didn't mind. Perhaps, he thought, the chlorine *will* clean the pond. After all, Larry was pretty bright—college educated and all. And the water couldn't get much worse.

When everything was prepared, they carefully raised the billboard with ropes and wrestled it over to the holes, then dropped it in. Surprisingly it went up without a hitch. It even looked straight and level. They had backed into the road and were admiring their handiwork when a rock whizzed over their heads and struck the bikinied diver. Carl wheeled around and spotted a slender, light-haired youth set to throw another. "Hey, you little weasel," he snapped, "screw!" The boy let the rock fly, then spun on his heels and bolted into the woods.

"Let's plug it in," Carl said, barely disguising his pride, "and see what the lights do for it." He gave the end of a two-hundred-foot power cord to Harvey and sent him running down the Camp Road to plug it in at the Roots' trailer, the closest source of power, while he and Larry stood silently watching the ring of power cord uncoil at their feet and go snaking after Harvey. Then suddenly it stopped. Carl and Larry stepped back into the road to witness the billboard lighting. They watched and waited, but it didn't light up.

Instead, Harvey returned, saying, "He says, 'Plug it up your ass.'" The boy pondered for a moment, then added, "He meant yours, not mine."

"Okay," Carl nodded with a smile, "we'll see how he likes his new rent. Well, where's the next nearest place?" He paused in thought. "I guess it'd have to be your place, Harve. Plug it in at your place."

"No," Larry said, "I think Zippy and Ruth's is closer. Go plug it in at Zippy and Ruth's.

Carl looked sideways at Larry. He spat on the ground and said, "Your place, Harvey. Plug it in at your place."

Harvey looked to Larry for a final decision, but Larry didn't press the point. Instead he added, "And hurry up, Harvey—run, run, run!" He folded his arms and kicked at the bed of pine needles at his feet, whistling, feeling the burn of Carl's glare. Then, finally, he broke their silence. "Look, I know you're a little worried about the pond, Carl, but believe me, the chlorine'll do the trick, just like it was a giant swimming pool. Hey, a promise, from me to you—I'll have you drinking that pond water one of these days. Guaran-goddamn-teed."

Suddenly the power cord at Carl's feet snapped taut, and in the helpless instant that followed, he watched it stretch, then heard a pitiful groan from the top of the billboard, and finally ducked as the bank of floodlights flew off the billboard and crashed in an unholy shattering of glass and metal at his feet. Of the six lights on the circuit, only one remained intact, and it suddenly lit up, casting its severe white light on Larry's glowing face.

The pink-faced young entrepreneur shrugged, straightened his hair (a gesture that was becoming increasingly annoying to Carl), and then, as if obligated to say something, he shrugged and said, "Zippy and Ruth's, partner, like I told you."

27

A Vigil

Zippy gave up early. He had been trying again to confirm his flight with the mysterious moon cowboys, but Mrs. Root's television and Mr. Rogers's relentless conversation had been too much distraction. He shut off the transceiver. "Oh well," he said.

Mr. Rogers took a deep slug of brandy. "Yep," he replied. They sat quietly then, eventually turning their attention to the TV show that Dolly was watching down by the shore. There, the soothing banter of melodramatic dialogue, the crescendi of incidental music, and the cold blue light of the television all made Mrs. Root herself seem like a television character, motionless except for the mechanical hand to mouth, hand to mouth feeding of chocolate. "That's my daughter, you know," Rogers said. "Always was a stubborn one, that Dolly."

They went down and sat at the picnic table beside her. "So," said Mr. Rogers to the sizable woman, "how's my little one tonight?"

Dolly pointed the remote control switch at her TV and shut it off, darkening everything around them so that the moon, in its first quarter, threw dark, distinct shadows onto the ground. "Terrible," she said. "Seems this TV's the only friend I got."

"So why not let us dig you out of there?" her father said.

"Nosuh. This is my fight and I'll see it through to the end. If I don't stand up to that guy, then no one else will either."

"Stubborn, same as always," Mr. Rogers said with a father's tenderness. "But Carl Mason's a good man, Dolly. He's a man of his word. Didn't he put the flush toilet in your trailer just like he promised?"

"I know, I been listenin' to it flush all day," she said with thinly disguised envy. She reached under the skirt of her chair and brought out a generic coffee can covered with a plastic lid. "Daddy, empty my can for me? Earl ain't been down in a while." After Mr. Rogers had walked a few paces and spilled the can's contents on the ground, she continued: "Anyway, it's not Mason I'm fightin'. It's that new one, that pretty boy."

"Oh," Zippy said, "that's my brother Larry."

"That's your brother?" she exclaimed. Dolly was never fond of Zippy—in fact, on better days she taunted him. "Well, thank God he don't look like you."

"Ah, but he does," Zippy announced. "We're twins."

Rogers said, "Zippy here's going on a space ride next week."

Dolly didn't respond. The three of them just sat for a spell listening to the water lap the shore. Then Mr. Rogers spoke again: "Dolly here's seen a UFO or two in her time, haven't you now?"

"Well, I have, if you want to know the truth, but I don't make it a point to go around tellin' everybody and their cousin."

"Yep," Rogers said. They sat a while longer. "To the moon, isn't it, Zip?"

Zippy lit a joint. "Uh-huh."

"Oh, God," said Dolly, "that's all I need. Blow that stuff the other way, will you? I don't want to get sick smellin' it. This friggin' bleach smell is bad enough."

Mr. Rogers persisted: "Seems there might be some cowboys up there . . ."

"Up where?" said Dolly.

"Moon," Zippy coughed.

Dolly fanned her face with her hand. "Oh, did you read that too?"

"Read what?"

"About them cowboys," she said. "I read it a while back in one of them supermarket papers, where some scientist proved that this famous gang of outlaws that disappeared a hundred years ago was actually picked up by a UFO. And that's why they was never heard from again."

"Outlaws?" Zippy said. "Which gang?"

"I don't remember. Some gang."

Mr. Rogers slapped his knee. "There you go," he said.

Dolly asked Zippy suspiciously, "So how do you know about 'em?"

Her father answered. "He contacted them the other night on his machine—the transceiver. What'd they say, Zip, tell her."

"They said they were coming to pick me up next Saturday—on the full of the moon."

Dolly had heard enough. She flicked on the TV again and reclined. "I think you been smokin' too much of that stuff, that wacky tobacky," she said. Her voice was not unfriendly, though.

The old man drank from his bottle and looked out over the pond. It glistened strangely—silvery. "Prettiest night I've ever seen," he said nearly in a whisper. "Look at how that pond sparkles." After another while he said, "So tell me, Zip, just what are you planning to bring with you?"

"Oh, I don't know. Deck of cards, guitar, toothbrush. Couple pairs of jeans, ounce or two of weed, sweatshirt, winter jacket, some fresh fruit."

Rogers leaned over. "Don't forget rubbers," he said softly, nudging Zippy with his elbow.

"I heard that," Dolly said. "Dirty old man."

28

The Harvest

In his waking dream Larry stood waist-deep in the pond and drank from a silver cup. "Crystal clean, Mason, just like I promised." Rutus Sny verified the analysis with a thumbs-up sign, which caused the crowded campground to erupt in wild applause.

"Right again, L.A. Jones!" Carl Mason called, wading into the water to take a drink.

Angel cried out, "Let's hear it for L.A. Jones! Hip, hip—" and everyone rammed their fists into the air, shouting, "Hooray!"

"Hip, hip—"

"Hooray!"

"Hip, hip—"

"Hooray!"

"Hip, hip—"

"FISH!"

It was a woman's voice, somewhere outside Larry's dream-world—a real-life, frantic woman's voice. "FISH! FISH!" it screamed. Larry shook his head to wake up. "FISH!" He pulled on his dungarees and ran outside, only half awake. Down by the water Dolly Root had risen to her feet and was somehow bouncing hysterically. "FISH!" she screamed.

Larry looked down at the pond. A soft chlorine mist hung like gauze above the water, and beneath that gauze, across the entire pond, the morning sun gleamed in sick, silvery flashes. He looked closer, and his knees buckled. The entire surface of the pond was covered with dead fish.

"FISH!" Dolly wailed.

"Harvey!" Larry called.

"FISH!"

"Harvey!"

Suddenly the entire campground had awakened with people creeping out their doors and migrating to the shore, as if to behold a miracle. Larry looked warily toward Mason's house and saw Shirley standing in the window, covering her mouth with her hands. Then Carl banged out the front door, a single-minded look of destruction on his face. He came straight for Larry, who in turn backed to an overturned rowboat and picked up an oar. He leaned on it nonchalantly, as if on a cane, but it was strategically placed between Mason and himself.

Harvey raced down in his bleached uniform to see what was the matter. Like Larry, his face was watermelon pink. "Harvey," Larry scolded, raising his hands, "I told you that was too much chlorine."

"You fuckin' idiot," Carl said to Larry. His fists were doubled.

"Yeah," Larry said, looking at Harvey.

"I'm talking to *you*, asshole!" Mason snapped, yanking the oar from Larry's hands and heaving it away, into the fish-covered pond. Larry noticed Angel watching and gave her a quick, casual smile. He hoped Carl didn't see. "What's so funny?" Carl growled.

Suddenly Larry grew alert. "Hey!" He pointed over Carl's shoulder to the Camp Road. "Isn't that Rutus Sny?"

"Where?" Carl said, turning to look.

Larry sidestepped him. "All right!" he announced to the gathered crowd, "we're going to have a little contest this morning. I've got a hundred dollars in my pocket for the person who can collect the most fish and load them into these empty drums along the shore. A hundred dollars, ladies and gentlemen, and, of course, our guest campers are welcome to join in the contest as well. There are enough boats for everyone. So, without further ado, ready . . . on your mark . . . get set . . ."

"Are you serious?" Susie called.

"All right, big deal. I'll make it two hundred."

"Five hundred," Dolly Root hollered.

"Yeah, five hundred!" the woman camper yelled.

"No sweat," Larry said, shrugging. "Five hundred it is. Now we've only got until ten o'clock—that's three hours—so let's get started. Everybody choose your boats . . . and . . . GO!"

By the end of the first hour hundreds of fish had been collected and dumped into the numbered barrels, yet the pond was still thoroughly littered. Larry called the Diablo Brothers to come dig a pit to dump the fish in.

In the second hour the race turned nasty. There were complaints of pilfering, and Earl Root officially protested that his daughter Jean Duckoff had tried to capsize his boat; Dolly Root, the self-proclaimed contest judge, awarded one of Jean's barrels to Earl. Zippy, who had foregone a boat and was waist-deep in the cattails with a barbecue fork, spearing the fish that drifted across the pond, was leading the pack with six full barrels, while his nearest rival, Earl Root, had only five—counting the one awarded to him by his wife. Carl Mason was working on his fourth, having wasted the first half hour searching for his outboard motor. He had finally given up and begun scooping up fish in a wire trash basket stolen from the highway department. There had been cries of foul at first, which Dolly quickly sustained, but Carl himself had overruled her.

As Dolly sat in her upholstered flowery chair alternately cheering her husband, watching "Mother's Lonely Days" on TV, and passing judgment on the contest, she was mildly startled to see a small boy standing nearby, quietly watching her. As she eyed him he moved closer to her, slowly, cautiously, as if he were timid. But the look on his face spelled something else—an odd look for a little boy, one of pluck and purpose, a slight, deft smile on his thin lips.

Dolly didn't like small boys. When he took another step closer she flung a scowl his way. But he was not deterred. His smile seemed only to brighten, and he came nearer. "Go on," she spat, shooing him away with the back of her hand, "beat it!"

Then, very slowly, very deliberately indeed, the fair-haired youngster raised a long, green plastic squirtgun, brought it to arm's length, and squirted her. The first blast hit her chest, but the second found a better mark on her chin. Dolly tried foolishly to stand. "You stinkin' little . . ." she began, but his third shot filled her mouth— vinegar! "Plahh!" she spat. He hit her eyes next—one! two!—and she fell back in her chair, fiercely rubbing at them, crying out for help. But no one heard, and the little boy began peppering her unmercifully, wetting each of her breasts in turn, then refilling his weapon with chlorinated pond water and emptying the gun against the back of her thrashing head. His final assault was on the helpless woman's television. As Dolly flailed in her chair, bellowing for assistance, he opened up on it, back and front, until it began emitting a high-pitched squeal. Then with a loud POP! the picture sucked itself into a tiny white dot, and a deathly blue smoke rose from the back.

"You die," she threatened in a voice so level, so sincere, that he turned and ran off. Dolly cried to her husband, who was feverishly scooping fish not far from shore, "Earl, get me outta here! Hey, I'm callin' you! Come set me free!"

"Can't now," he yelled back, thinking to himself: Ain't that just like her, when I'm about to make five hundred bucks! Ain't that just like that woman, keepin' me down!

During the final half hour of the contest all the fish, and so all the contestants, were at the end of the pond where the cattails and lily pads grew, everybody by this time drenched with the chlorinated pond water. Ruth Jones's neck and face were blotched indigo from a new summer dress, although her arms and legs were a lighter blue from the constant rinsing in the pond. The green from Shirley Mason's blouse had run onto her chin and arms, while her red shorts had painted gruesome pink streaks down her thighs. Carl's brown shirt had made his face look Jamaican, while Earl Root in his flowered shirt was multicolored.

When the last fish was snared and the barrels tallied, Carl Mason, with nine barrels, was declared the come-from-behind winner. Amidst discontented mutterings from the others he explained that the five hundred dollars would be used to stock the pond with trout—should they ever again be able to survive, he added, glaring at Larry.

The fish were hauled in a bucket loader and dumped unceremoniously into the huge pit behind the nearly completed newlywed home. Then dirt was mounded up into a small hill over the unhallowed ground, so that when Rutus Sny arrived an hour later the campground looked as it always had. He did not waste time nor words. He simply walked out onto the dock and dipped a stainless steel bucket into the water, filled a sample bottle with it, then repeated the process in two more locations and drove off.

The next day at noon he telephoned Larry at the office. "You can drink the water, Mr. Jones," he gloated, "if you want to contract hepatitis—or how about diphtheria—or leprosy?" He laughed. "That water is so filthy it probably won't boil."

"What's wrong with it?" Larry asked.

"You mean, aside from the human excrement, animal excrement, decayed animal matter, decayed vegetable matter, detergents, chemical residue, and chlorine? Nothing." He laughed again.

"Well, I thought the chlorine was supposed to purify it," Larry said.

"All that'll do, my friend, is turn the shit white. Sorry."

Larry hung up the phone and tried to avert Carl's brown-faced stare, the nodding I-told-you-so look. "Good move, college boy," he said. "How much did this one cost you?" Larry was afraid to add it up. He waved off the comment and walked out the door.

"Good move, college boy." It was Susie, lightly turquoise, sitting on the porch drinking her morning coffee. She had wanted to see him crawl, but now, seeing the look of defeat in her man, she softened. She stood and put her arms around him. "Wanna help me check the stockroom?" She nuzzled against him.

"I don't know," he said, slipping her hold and turning away.

"Now, now, baby. Do I have to bribe you?" She furtively placed his hand on her breast. He tried to smile.

Then suddenly Larry's eyes lit up. He backed down the porch, pointing to his head. "Later," he said, running off. "Brainstorm!"

29
·
Grease

Rutus Sny lived on a quiet, maple-lined avenue where, in spring-
time, songbirds by the thousands migrated to perch in the pale
green canopy that came together over the road—where days, even
weeks, went by without sight or sound of a child—where houses
were opulent and generously spaced apart, their grounds vast,
weedless, and toyless—miniature kingdoms unto themselves, of
hedgerows, landscaped gardens, and underground sprinkling sys-
tems. These were the elite of Norwood, the old-monied, who for
generations had built their wealth in cities like Portland, Lewiston,
Portsmouth, Kittery, and Oxford, then retreated to the quiet of their
country-suburban Norwood homes.

Saturday afternoons Sny routinely played golf at the Bluffton
Country Club, but today he had decided to stay home and follow a
golf ball around his own trim backyard, first putting it here, then
there, always looking up toward the road when a car passed, waiting
for that forest-green Mercedes. His sixth sense, the sense of Easy
Money, honed so fine by years of experience, told him to expect a
visit from Larry Jones. The young man had so easily parted with
hundreds for a routine water examination, Sny was certain that his
wallet would pour liquid gold for a falsified permit. He had baited
the hook over the telephone an hour ago by so dramatically overstat-
ing the facts concerning the water test. The truth was, that while the
pond at Wind In The Pines did indeed fail the test, it did so only
marginally. In fact, under other circumstances Sny might have
issued the permit. But not in this case. That sixth sense of his told

him there was a windfall coming. So now where the hell was Jones, he wondered—could he have misjudged this ambitious young man?

No. The Mercedes came. Very slowly, very quietly—but it came. Sny pretended not to notice. He bent over a golf ball with his putter and feigned concentration even as he heard the car door open and close, heard Larry's footsteps tread up the walk. He visually measured the shot—mentally measured Larry's distance, and gauged by his footfalls whether he carried the money on his person or in the car. He drew back the putter, poised to shoot . . . and then stopped, pretending sudden awareness—and annoyance—at Larry's presence. He dropped his head with a terrible sigh and then slowly raised it again, eyeing Larry with a scowl. "I'm busy," he said. "See me in my office on Monday."

Larry pointed at Sny's feet. "Try putting off your front foot more," he said. "Really—try it."

Sny folded his arms and stared at Larry.

"Nice backyard," Larry said, admiring the greenery. "Oh, yeah—there's something I wanted to show you," he added, backing down the walk, beckoning Sny with his finger, "down in my car."

Surely, Sny thought, I have baited this hook most sweetly. He dropped his putter, hiked up his shorts, and followed Larry down the sidewalk to the forest-green Mercedes. He saw the same girl sitting in the passenger seat—the one he had seen talking to herself the first time Larry had come. The lower half of her face was blue; her lips, as before, were deep lipstick-red. The fool shouldn't have brought her this time, he said to himself.

Larry went to the trunk of the car and fidgeted with the lock. He was a little nervous. Sure, he had paid off Sny the other day, but that was merely payment for services rendered. But this—this thing that he was about to do was heavier stuff: Bribery. Larry knew he had to choose his every word and action with hairtrigger precision. The trunk flipped open and he said: "Hey, look at all this money, will you?"

"Shhh!" Sny said, smiling, revealing no obvious body language to the neighbors. He leaned over the rear quarter of the car and peered into the trunk. And there, on a Hawaiian shirt in Larry's open suitcase, like some rich tropical fruit dessert, lay a fan-shaped wad of twenties.

"A hundred of them," Larry said softly, hoping he'd need say no more.

Sny looked impassively up and down the street. "Two thousand bucks," he croaked quietly, sounding to Larry like an unoiled door-hinge. Ruth, hearing his voice, checked under her seat for frogs.

"It's worth a lot to me," Larry said. "I've got my honor at stake, if you know what I mean."

"You'd *think* it'd be worth a lot to you then," Sny agreed. "So what's this?" He indicated the trunk's contents with two hands. Insulted, he folded his arms and turned away.

"Three then," Larry pleaded, touching Sny's shoulder cautiously, as one tests a hot iron. But Sny was firm. He turned to Larry, spread his fingers into a fan, held them against his heart, and mouthed the word: "FIVE."

Larry took a deep breath, let out a long sigh, then dug under his clothes in the suitcase and found a pack of hundred-dollar bills. He counted out thirty hundreds—three thousand to add to the two thousand—staying low in the trunk to hide his actions from the neighborhood, and clumsily stuffed both wads of money into an empty Junior Pie box. He handed the box to Sny. "Five," he said. A drop of perspiration rolled down his forehead and he brushed it aside.

"You okay?" Sny asked. "Your face is flushed."

"Yeah, I just hate to part with money, that's all."

Sny grinned, suddenly amicable. "So you like money, do you? Well, so do I, so do I. But one thing confuses me, Mr. Jones. If you hate parting with money as much as you say, why on earth did you ever get mixed up with a place like Mason's?" Larry shrugged. He thought for an instant of Susie's breasts and shrugged again. "A little free advice, Mr. Jones: The longer you hold on to that place, the more of your considerable money will find its way out of your pocket and into somebody else's. Believe me." Larry raised a finger to protest, but Sny turned away saying, "Wait here." He walked effortlessly, nearly danced, up the walk to his house, and when he returned he handed Larry a document, signed and stamped with the official Norwood seal: TOWN OF NORWOOD, DEPARTMENT OF HEALTH.

Larry took the document and felt a sudden sense of initiation into the rites of covert politics. His coy smile caused the first selectman a pang of fear.

He looked hard at Larry and drew closer to him, whispering, "Does the little lady know?"—meaning Ruth. Larry shook his head, lying. "Good," Sny said. "And don't ever tell anybody—not your mother, not your best friend, not your partner—especially not your partner—not anyone. Don't trust a soul. Capisce?"

"Capisce," Larry answered.

Sny followed him to the driver's door. He put a hand on Larry's shoulder and said, "You've got good business sense, Mr. Jones. Like me. And you know, it's people like us that get to the top in this man's world." His free hand rose in front of them like it was helium-filled. "So, my friend, when you decide you've lost enough of your money on that dump, why not give me a call. Maybe we could work something out." Sny turned and walked away, straight up his flower-lined walk. "Enjoy," he said, waving casually over his shoulder, looking at no one.

When Larry got back to Wind In The Pines he noticed a large, mustard colored tent pitched on the shore beside an old dark blue station wagon with Virginia plates. On the other side of the tent was a spectacle that had not been explained to the campers: a flowery upholstered chair and a rusted TV table facing each other, both embedded in a cement slab.

Larry pulled up to the office, then sat in his car with the ignition off and the radio on, drumming on his leather steering wheel to an old Beatles song. He watched Carl hurry out of the office with a pair of oars and two life jackets in his arms, his face still a rich chocolate brown. Larry blew the horn as Carl passed, causing him to spill the oars and life jackets, then wheel and face the Mercedes in a vicious simian crouch.

"Hey," Larry said nonchalantly, holding the document out his window.

Carl ignored him. He spat on the ground and bent to pick up his gear. But Larry persisted. "Hey," he called louder, rattling the paper, looking casually away from Carl to the horizon. Finally Carl took a deep breath, threw the oars and life jackets back on the ground, and snatched the paper. He read it with a frown, then reread it with a deeper frown. Then he looked slowly up at Larry. "What did you do?" he scolded.

Larry, still not looking at him, raised his left hand and made the universal money sign: thumb rubbing the index finger.

Carl shook his head. "You're really something else," he said, showing more disgust than humor. "How much did this cost?"

"Hey, no sweat, partner, I took care of it." He nodded to the orange tent by the shore. "More customers?"

"Yeah. A couple of fishermen from Virginia," Carl said. He started down toward them again, then turned and came back to the Mercedes. He put his face in the window, near Larry's, and said, "I didn't have the heart to tell them there were no fish in the pond." Larry shrugged. Carl shrugged. And then the short, wide-shouldered, brown-faced man began to laugh. And he laughed until his brown face grew purple and his eyes teared. His whole body shook. He looked at Larry, shaking his head. "What a fucked-up place," he said.

When Larry walked into the store, Susie regarded him coldly, not even looking up from her romance paperback. "Hey, I fixed the water test," he said, laying the document on her open book.

"How?"

"Let's just say I've got good business sense. So, you wanna check out the stockroom now?" Susie shrugged her shoulders and, still not looking at him, came around the counter and took his hand. They walked together down the paper goods aisle to the stockroom door.

"Watch the register," she called to Jean, who was bent over in the next aisle straightening boxes of generic corn flakes with a yardstick, "and don't let anybody in the back room."

The stockroom was concrete, dank and musty, where a thoughtless maze of precariously stacked, half-filled cardboard boxes gathered dust under a single web-enshrouded light bulb. A pile of oars lay on the floor below four orange life preservers that hung from nails stuck in the concrete wall. An oil furnace, water pump, and water heater stood together in a dark, cobwebbed corner, and a workbench littered with tools and small machine parts stretched along the opposite wall. A disassembled outboard motor lay on the floor behind some boxes, its grease-covered parts strewn on brown, slick pages of newspaper.

Susie flattened a cardboard box and laid it beside the motor, then flattened a second box to overlap the first. She peeled off her clothes, exposing her lush, turquoise breasts and her dark gray bottom and thighs, and lay seductively on her back. Her pink man climbed quickly on top of her and immediately tried to enter her— persistently poking and poking at her dryness like a June bug bouncing again and again off a window screen.

"Jeezum, just a second," she hissed. "Not so fast!" It was always the same with him: no tenderness, no lovemaking to their sex, just a quick, hard fuck and then he was gone, escaping sometimes even as he ejaculated. Sighing, she twisted her upper body and reached above her head to a plastic tub of brown wheel-bearing grease. She filled her fingers with the thick, cool stuff and brought it down between their bodies, where she smeared it on his dry shaft. Immediately, and with a warm groan, he plunged deeply home, and her legs, with sudden lives of their own, splayed and kicked furiously in the air above him. She loved the feeling. She squealed and arched her back, locking her ankles around him, squeezing. "Kiss me," she breathed, "kiss me hard."

He kissed her on the mouth and her face began rotating against his in small, grinding circles. Then he kissed her on the neck, his hot breath electrifying her. He kissed her again on the shoulder and a steady tingle shot down her sides. And then he kissed her again and again and again until she threw back her head in ecstasy, basking in his attention, becoming so hot she thought her body must have lost its feeling. She could hear him kissing, but she could no longer feel his kisses. She opened her eyes and raised her head and saw him, eyes shut tight, in the throes of animal passion, kissing his own shoulder.

"Kiss *me!*" she snapped.

He stopped and looked up with distant, pondering eyes.

"What's the matter?" she said.

Without answering, he pulled out of her, wiped the brown grease off his penis, and smeared it on a box of generic macaroni. He pulled his pants up as he hobbled to the door.

"Come back here," she threatened.

"Can't now," he said. "Brainstorm!"

When Sunday's *Journal* came out, Larry's brainstorm was spread across a full page in the sports section. Decorated with a woman diving from a diving board and a huge, wide-mouthed striped bass breaking water for her, the ad read in thick headline type:

FISHING CONTEST! FISHING CONTEST!
$5000 FIRST PRIZE!!!

Camp Wind In The Pines
off the River Road in Norwood

BRING THE WHOLE FAMILY!!
(Look for our new sign—You can't miss it!!!)
Saturday, May 25—8 A.M. to 5 P.M.
All entries must be registered campers for the weekend.

MOMS!! AND DADS!! SWIM IN OUR **CLEAN** NEW POND!

HEY KIDS!! VISIT OUR ALL-NEW "INDIAN VILLAGE"
Totem Poles, Petting Zoo, Real Live Indian

$5000 FIRST PRIZE FOR THE BIGGEST FISH CAUGHT

WIND IN THE PINES

Swimming, Diving, Boating, Indian Village, Souvenirs,
Playground, Hiking, Convenience Store, Tent and Trailer Sites

L.A. Jones and Carl Mason, Proprietors

Carl read the ad while he ate his Sunday breakfast. "Get him," he said to Susie without emotion.

"Get him yourself," she said, but there was no need. He opened the screen door and swaggered into the kitchen, holding a copy of the ad in his hands.

"What do you think?" he said with a cocky grin, seeing the paper laid out on the kitchen table. Recalling his abrupt departure from Susie the day before, he added, "Now you know why I left in such a hurry yesterday. Quite a brainstorm though, wasn't it?" Susie and Carl both looked at him with the same furrowed eyebrows. It was easy to see they were father and daughter. "Hey," he said, holding up his hands in surrender, "no sweat, partner—we're not going to lose a penny." He looked at Carl slyly. "Think about it—all the fish are dead. We're gonna clean up this weekend! Customers, customers, customers!" He held up a hand for Carl to slap.

"Real live Indian?" Carl asked, ignoring the hand. "Petting zoo?"

"Yeah, Nighthawk and his raccoon—don't worry, he'll do it, I'm gonna work on him—and I'll go out and buy a sheep or a goat or something. Hey, the kids'll love it."

"Playground?" Susie sneered.

"So I'll have Harvey build a sandbox. I'll run into town and pick up a swing set. No sweat. Hey, come on, lighten up, you two."

"Yeah?" said Susie. "Well, you forgot something else."

"I did?"

"Yeah, pinhead—our wedding! You gonna squeeze the wedding in there sometime between the fishing contest and the Indian show?"

He cuffed his forehead with perhaps more drama than he needed. "Darn," he said, "I almost forgot."

Susie pitched an English muffin over the table and it glanced off his shoulder. "Bastard," she said, going outdoors.

"But, Susie—" he implored, following her, thumbing the margarine off his Camp Tee-shirt. He caught Carl watching him with amusement, and he raised his eyes in a gesture of helplessness.

"Hey," Carl said, stopping him. "Saturday, right?"

"What?" Larry said.

"The wedding. It's at three on Saturday, right?"

"Sure thing, partner," Larry said, his thumb up.

Carl said measuredly, "I'd suggest you don't call me 'partner' anymore—until it's official. Know what I'm sayin'?"

Larry glared. "Sure thing, Dad," he said, with the tone of someone held to a hastily made bargain. Carl stared long and hard after him as he slammed the screen door and headed down the steps.

30

The Fishing Lesson

"Mornin', boys," Larry said to the two fishermen eating ham and eggs at their picnic table. "How's the fishing been?"

"Stinks," the younger man said.

"Fished eight, nine hours yesterday," said the elder, "me and my boy here, but we never even got a nibble." Larry thought of the upcoming fishing contest and chuckled unintentionally, a gesture which, under the circumstances, puzzled the men.

"Something funny about that?" the "boy" said, a tough-looking man in his forties.

Larry choked. "No, no," he garbled, "just some toast in the throat."

The older man took a sip of coffee and asked, "So what do they generally catch here?"

"Oh, we've got just about everything in here," Larry said. "Trout, perch, bass, catfish—you name it, we've got it."

"How about chlorine?" the younger man said bitterly. The bottoms of his trousers, and his father's, were bleached pale.

"Yeah," Larry chuckled nervously, "that too." He folded his arms and gazed across the pond, sucking the cool morning air through his teeth. "Not even a nibble," he said, shaking his head in mock sympathy.

"So how do you catch 'em?" the older man asked. He was cordial, not unfriendly like his son, and his question was sincere. "What sort of bait do you use?"

"Oh, you know, nothing fancy. Worms and things."

"Worms?" the younger man said with volume. Larry didn't know how to read him.

"Yeah, worms, bobbers—" Larry's sneakers began to dig at the sand. "Night crawlers really, if you want to get technical."

The son started to play him. "Use a fly rod, do you?"

"Oh yeah, sure." Larry searched the horizon for a way out. "Well, busy day ahead," he said, turning to leave.

"So what kind of bait do you use on your fly rod?" the young man persisted, with a playful glance at his father.

"Oh, a little bit of everything, when you come right down to it."

"Then why don't you come right down to it and tell me what kind of bait you use?" he said with a sneer.

"Worms," Larry said, "and night crawlers, like I said. Rubber worms, flies, bees, marshmallows. My fishing motto is, 'You never know what works unless you try it.'" He turned again to leave, saying, "Think about it."

"Wait a minute, wait," the young man said. "Do us a favor, would you?" He stood and picked up his fly rod, a long, flexible graphite rod. He walked out onto the dock, unhooked the fly from the reel handle and let the line swing free. Then he yanked some slack out of the reel and began whipping the line back and forth over his head. "Look, just watch me for a minute and tell me what I'm doing wrong." With every flex of his rod he pulled more line from the reel, until soon there was twenty feet of fine brown fly line whipping in a gracefully suspended S-shape over his head. Finally the fly at the end of the long, transparent leader touched down like a mosquito on the surface of the water, sending out delicate, concentric rings in the still water. In an instant it picked up, flew twenty feet behind the man, only to return to the same exact point in the water.

Larry nodded approvingly. "Good form," he said. Then, shaking his head, he said, "They're just not into flies today. If I were you I'd go with the worms—like I said."

"Hey, Pop," the young man called to his father, "bring us a worm, would you." He looked at Larry and said earnestly, "We don't have any marshmallows." The older man came onto the dock and handed his son a fat, slippery night crawler, and the son in turn handed both the worm and the rod to Larry. "Now let's see how you do it," he said.

Larry glanced at his watch. "Tsk," he said, "I don't know if I've got the time right now."

"You've got the time," said the younger man, smiling but blocking his exit from the dock.

By now Carl and Harvey had come to the shore to watch, having seen the activity from the pavilion area where they had been building the new lavatory. "Watch closely, Harve," Carl said, loud enough for Larry to hear. "Mr. Jones is going to give us a fishing lesson."

Larry looked at Carl with a mixture of humiliation and threat. He took the fly in one hand, the night crawler in the other, and sank the fly's hook easily through the middle of the fat, writhing worm— it left a slimy film on his fingers which he wiped on his designer jeans. Then he held the line up and examined the bait: the night crawler hanging heavily by its middle, bowing its body in pain, a yellow and gray fly rudely protruding from its middle. His stomach churned, but he nodded approvingly, gaining confidence by his own cockiness. The fishermen agreed they had never seen such a lure. "It's my own thing," Larry assured them.

"Very unusual," said the older man. To the delight of his son, he was playing along. "I can see now how a trout couldn't resist."

"Bobber," Larry said, holding out his hand.

It was an order, and the younger man eagerly danced off the dock to find him one. His father told him, "There might be one in the bottom of my tackle box, way down there somewhere." Then he looked at Carl and winked. Carl nodded back.

Larry put the red and white plastic bobber on the line with ease, about a foot up from his fly/worm concoction. In his mind he was already casting: drawing the line from the reel with his left hand as he had watched the man do, swinging the rod back and forth over his head, and finally, with a deft whip, launching the bait gracefully out to the depths.

The actual demonstration, however, was less impressive. "Back up, boys," Larry warned, planting his feet like a wrestler on the dock. Then, with an agile backflip of the wrist, the bobber and bait lifted off the dock and sailed back over his head. When he saw it had gone far enough, he swung the rod forward while pulling on the line with his left hand—but he wrongly pulled the slack rather than the reel line, so the line abruptly whipped in the air behind him, snapping the night crawler into two spinning pieces. When the bobber and fly made their speedy forward return he was still drawing slack, and now bending at the waist, holding the rod high to avoid being struck by the hurling plastic missile. The bobber, racing to the end of its flight just above his head, swung hard over the tip of the rod and smacked the side of the dock with a spray of plastic. When he straightened, all that was left of the bobber was its red plastic core pinned to the line. The rest of it, shards of white and red, sank lazily through the chlorinated water and disappeared from sight.

Larry examined the rod. "Is this new?" he questioned. Nobody answered. "That's your problem right there—too much whip."

31

Betrayal

"I'm going to miss you."

Ruth looked up from her needlepoint. A soft yet ironic smile crossed her lips. She had just been wondering if she would miss Zippy when they parted. "I'm going to miss you, too," she said, although she wasn't altogether sure it was true. Not after last night.

Zippy laid his guitar on the floor and sat Indian style at her feet, leaning back against her legs. "I don't know," he said, thinking about the moon. He ran his fingers through his hair till they got snagged in the knots. "Maybe I shouldn't go." He was looking for direction, but Ruth could offer him none. Instead, she tried to untangle his hair from his fingers.

She was wearing a new dress, a pleated dress of soft green and yellow plaid which she had let down to an inch below her knees. She shaved her legs irregularly, not for a week now, and the stubble on her shins scratched his back. He rubbed back and forth, contemplating.

"Maybe I'll just tell them I've got work to do here—"

"What will you do if you don't go?" she asked. The notion that perhaps there really were no cowboys on the moon, or that the transceiver—or even Zippy himself—had made a mistake, had not occurred to her. Such was her faith in him. "Have you ever thought about raising a family, you know, having kids of our own?"

"I don't know," Zippy reflected. "I don't know anything about cowboys, you know? What they're really like."

"We could buy a house of our own . . . if we had some money."

"Yeah, what if they expect me to, you know, ride the range and all that?" He cried softly, "Hi-o-Silver." Dwelling on the thought, he jumped, as if out of a dream. "Bummer," he whispered.

". . . We'd have a paved driveway, a little ivy-covered garage, a maple dining room with dark oak furniture, a nice big kitchen. You'd come home from work and I'd say, 'Hi, dear, how was your day?' And you'd say, 'Oh, fine, what are the boys up to?' Could you see us like that?" She laughed a little.

"I'll just tell 'em, 'I kin ride, I kin punch cattle, I kin play guitar—but Ah ain't no gunfighter.' What do you think?"

"I'm thinking about changing my name," she said, staring at the bald spot on top of his head. Just a wispy whirlpool of hair covered it.

"Hmm?"

"Do you like June?" she asked.

"Eh. I don't like the mosquitoes much, as you know—"

"No, the name June, as in June and Harold? June and Harry?"

"June on the moon?" he asked. "Come with me, babe."

"What, to the moon?"

"Yeah, they won't mind."

"Oh, I don't know," she said, lowering her face to kiss the top of his head, suddenly wrestling with a new problem: whether to raise a family or go to the moon.

Or marry Larry.

Yes, Larry had popped the question last night—of course, only after she had spurned his sexual advances. But he had seemed sincere. His marriage to Susie was bound to fail, he had told her. They were never really serious about it anyway—it had just been part of his bargain with Carl, that along with a share of the campground he take the man's daughter. The wedding would have to occur—it was the only honorable thing to do. But then he'd be free.

"Zip—Harold?"

"Mmm?"

"Oh, nothing, I guess." She thought of Larry again, and those few close moments they had shared last night. How was it they had come to be together in her bedroom? Was it, as they say, fate? Had he really come in to borrow her Bible? It had been just a matter of moments—and inches—the inches that slowly diminished, as in the movies, when their lips met, drawn together with the inevitability of colliding planets. She licked her lips, still feeling the tingle there. But she had pulled away last night—and pushed him away—and her heart had thumped in her breast all night long.

"I think I'll stay behind," she told Zippy. "I've got some thinking to do."

Angel sat alone in the almost darkness. She poured herself a snifter of cognac and took a quick, hard belt.

She was losing her touch. In the past she never would have pleaded with the likes of a Rutus Sny—for the likes of a Carl Mason—only to be shot down in the end. In the past, she would have seen through Sny's deceit—and she would have had him, but good. Instead, she had let him ridicule her. And no one had ever done that before. And certainly no one had ever tried to kill her before. Until Weasel.

But why? Because the Mutants had been evicted? Because Hammer had been killed? Because Weasel had dumped his bike and landed in the hospital? Certainly those things weren't her fault. So why then? Had the Mutants really been ambushed, as she'd heard, and their cocaine stolen? And was he blaming her for the setup?

She took another drink. What was happening to her? In the past she would have known the answers.

And then there was Larry Jones. In the past she never, never would have allowed someone like Larry Jones to come to her house whenever he damn well pleased. But that was the crux of it all, wasn't it? Larry Jones was an anomaly—a mystery. Here was a man with a seemingly limitless supply of money—who acted like a lottery winner. Could he have somehow stolen the Mutants' cocaine? Impossible. The Mutants had been too cunning, too ruthless for the likes of a Larry Jones.

But . . . but if he had . . . if by some miracle he had, then he was in the clear! Because Hammer was dead, and Hammer alone had done business with his customers—the county dealers. The other Mutants had merely been pawns in his operation—never privy to those transactions. Besides, they were long gone. And

Weasel, if he lived to find whoever was peddling the cocaine, was unlikely to ever find out who had supplied it. Dealers just didn't reveal their sources—to anybody. And Pinky was no different. Angel had worked on him all night long—for nothing. All he would tell her was that a silent partner had fronted him the cash. She gulped her cognac. In the past, he would have told her everything. In a minute. Yes, she was losing her touch.

She looked out her window now and saw Larry hiding behind the Duckoffs' trailershack. Was he hiding on her? No, he was coming to her, fast, like the sheep-hunting wolf in a Bugs Bunny cartoon, darting from tree to tree. No, she thought, Larry could never have stolen that coke.

Still, she would test him.

Later, when they were in bed, she lied in a casual voice, "I visited an old friend in the hospital today—that guy Weasel that tried to kill me. He used to live here, you know. He said as soon as he gets out he's got a score to settle with somebody over some stolen cocaine." She watched Larry closely, but he didn't flinch.

"Oh, yeah?" he said, just as casually. "That's nice."

Ten minutes later, however, he was sitting on the edge of her bed, humiliated, pulling his pants on. "It must've been something I ate," he said, avoiding her eyes. "Honest, that's never happened to me before. Never."

"Maybe the muscle's just dead," she teased, "from overuse."

Larry made a noise with his nose.

Learning his secrets, Angel thought, is like gleaning gold from river sand. One needed only the patience to sift through the surface grit, the layer of falseness that he wore like a sleek designer shroud, and then he'd be laid bare.

He stretched. "So this guy Weasel—when's he getting out?"

She bent for a line of cocaine on her night table, filled both nostrils, and closed her eyes. "Mmm," she moaned. "I'm sorry, what did you say?"

"When's he getting out?"

"The doctors say he should be out in a couple of days." The truth was, Weasel was still unconscious. Angel had sat at his bedside that

day, waiting for his pale eyes to open, waiting to tell him that it was
not she who had double-crossed him. But he hadn't stirred.

"Has he found out anything about his coke?"

"Well," she lied, "he said he's going to call this local dealer
named Pinky to find out who he bought from." She studied Larry.
His lungs sucked air. "But Pinky won't tell him," she continued.
"Dealers never reveal their sources."

Larry turned the gasp into a yawn, even as perspiration seeped
onto his forehead. He stretched again.

Angel nodded, thinking, Aha! I've got him. But her face registered no such thoughts. *Patience is the hunter.* "Pinky'll tell me,
though," she lied again with a smile. "He's a special friend of
mine."

Larry cleared his throat. "Listen," he said, "I've been seriously
considering hiring somebody as a personal secretary—somebody
with a lot of your qualifications. There wouldn't be a heck of a lot of
work—actually, no work, but the pay would be pretty good—"

"Pretty good?"

"Well, by that I mean, really good—say, two thousand dollars."

"For doing nothing?"

"Well, it would mean just being confidential about certain
things, if you get my drift, you know, keeping certain secrets?"

"What secrets? You mean like where Weasel's coke went to?"

"Yeah, things like that. And also keeping me informed about
other things—like, for example, if Weasel finds out anything."

"Wouldn't that make me sort of a spy? I thought spies were in a
higher income bracket."

"Okay, look. Five thousand bucks. And you don't know anything. Deal?"

"My lips are sealed," she said, smiling broadly. Perhaps the old
magic wasn't dead after all. "Gee whiz, I didn't know secretary work
was so hard."

Susie lay on her bed, staring at the swirls in her ceiling, feeling a
dull, persistent ache inside—like an old wound flaring. But she
couldn't pinpoint it, tangled as it was in the larger confusion she

faced. She had somehow fallen into a mire from which she couldn't escape: She had fallen in love. And she had been loved in turn—or so she had imagined.

But, no. Now the truth glared: Larry had never loved her. He had simply used her to buy into the campground. And suddenly she felt just as certain that she had never really loved him. Or anyone, for that matter. That her life was, and always had been, loveless. She was incapable of loving. And incapable of being loved.

But she would go through with the marriage. She had to. Because if she didn't, her father would lose Wind In The Pines. And she would not see that happen to him.

She turned off her room light and took off her clothes, standing at her window, watching the Mutant shack—Angel's house. And the ache grew—the hollow, shadowy ache that one feels after the betrayal of a friend. As she watched, a dark, familiar figure crept from tree to tree into the light of Angel's door, and the ache suddenly broke over her like an ocean wave, knocking her backward onto her bed. It was Larry out there walking into Angel's arms.

Yet in her pain her imagination revealed something different. It was someone else out there, someone cruel and savage and beautiful—the man who had first made her a woman, who had crawled drunkenly through her bedroom window and taken her in hot, brutal silence—who had taken her completely. It was Weasel out there walking into Angel's arms again, and Susie's tears boiled down her cheeks as if they would never stop.

32
·
Thursday

The newlywed log cabin was finished on Wednesday evening, ten days after it was begun. To celebrate, Susie went shopping for furniture on Thursday. Larry had declined to go with her, but had given her the Mercedes and four thousand dollars to spend. She thought of the things her mother had always wanted—the early American brass and maple hutch at Bourassa's Trading Post, the pastel colonial living room set at Standard Furniture, the crystal chandelier at Bob's House of Lights—Susie would buy them for her own house. She felt better today about marrying Larry—if she couldn't have his love, his wealth would compensate nicely. Yes, by Thursday she felt fine indeed.

And so did Carl. For by Thursday morning every tent and trailer site had been reserved for the weekend (many for the entire week), and people were calling every few minutes, pleading to sleep in their cars and vans for the weekend just to be able to enter the fishing contest. Carl and Harvey were hastily constructing camping sites to accommodate them, hustling pre-built picnic tables and cinderblock fire pits onto every spare plot of land they could find. Yes, once again Larry's brainstorm had paid off. Between camping fees, store profits, boat rentals, firewood and ice sales, and the newly instituted guest fee of two dollars per day, they were looking at a possible three-thousand-dollar weekend.

Already two families from Worcester had arrived for the long Memorial Day weekend and parked their campers on the Root site along the shore. The men, both vacationing mail carriers, were anchored in a motorboat beneath the ridge. One mailman was shirtless, casting flies beside a large, pyramid-shaped boulder that rose out of the pond, while the other fished with a fat, "wounded minnow" plug. They had come early to study the feeding habits of the trout and bass—having agreed to split the $5000 prize money. But despite trying every lure in their tackle boxes—and fishing up and down the entire pond—they hadn't got a nibble.

Their wives and children lazed on the narrow sandy beach under an unseasonably hot sun, the ladies in lawn chairs, smeared with coconut tanning oil, alternately reading and chatting. Their children built mud castles in the colorful foam at the shore, while another skinny, yellow-haired boy was off by himself defacing the sparkling new diving board with a red crayon. The boy's mother sat on the beach away from the other two women, sipping screwdriver mix from a quart bottle and occasionally screaming, "Gunnar, you know you can't swim! Come down from there right this minute! Gunnar! Did you hear me? I hope you fall in and drown, you goddamned little brat!" Carl had warned her twice already about profanity in the campground, and she had apologized, but she seemed unable to stop, so he ignored it. Besides, no one else seemed to mind.

After roughing out six new tent sites behind his own house—in Angel's front yard—out of Maurice's reach—he and Harvey put the finishing touches on the new Camp Lavatory down beside the pavilion area. It was a proud, sturdy pine building with two doors—MEN and WOMEN—complete with two toilets and three pay shower heads in each side. And a urinal in the men's side. Carl whistled "Love Letters in the Sand" while he hammered, a tune he hadn't been able to get out of his head for days. Harvey enjoyed it, especially the way Carl ornamented the end of each phrase with a trill. He said it made the song sound like "that violin and bugle music."

But Harvey was troubled about something, and for four days he had planned and unplanned and replanned the best way to approach Carl about it: It was his salary. On Sunday Harvey's friend Orrin had humiliated him about his salary in front of Jean. He had asked Harvey how much he made. And when Harvey told him, he had said, "What?" and smacked his head. Three times. Right in front of Jean. And then he told Harvey (as if he were an older brother) that he had to ask for more money. "That guy's robbin' you, Einstein. Tell him you want a raise in pay or he kin take that job and shove it," he said. "That's what I'd do."

So now Harvey was ready. He had put in sixty hours of work in four days, and now he was ready to ask. And so he did, as they were finishing up the new lavatory. "Hey," he said.

"What?"

"Nothin'."

"Okay, Harve."

"Well, umm, I don't know how to say this, but . . . sometimes when my friends ask me how much money I make, you know? Well, it sorta embarrasses me to tell 'em."

There followed an agonizing moment of silence before Carl responded. And then he said, "So don't tell 'em. That's nobody's business but your own, Harve. Right?"

"Um, yeah, I guess. But—"

"There's no 'I guess' about it, Harve. It's none of their business."

The Roots, meanwhile, were spending the day by the kitchen table, their marital troubles resolved. Dolly relaxed in her orange loveseat—a wide, S-shaped piece of furniture that Carl had sold to Earl as an antique (he had told Shirley when he brought it home from the dump that it looked like an animal slide from the circus). She was contentedly munching on generic pies and telling Earl about the lad who had squirted her with vinegar and ruined their TV. "That little boy is possessed by Satan himself, Earl, I know it. I seen pictures in the newspaper where other kids was possessed the same way, and they had that same evil stare in their eyes. Just like that little girl in that movie there, The Exorcist. I just pray to God I never have to look in them eyes again." Earl, in his cushy recliner, slowly devoured a ham and cleaned his pistol.

They had had a busy morning. Since Carl had stopped by to say that Larry was coming over in the afternoon to assess the damages to their trailer, they had proceeded to attack their home with pinch bars and hammers, widening cracks in the ceiling and floor and poking holes in furniture and walls. They were hoping for a new trailer—or at least a bigger used one—maybe a seventy-footer—maybe a Detroiter! So in their fervor they inadvertently destroyed more things than they had intended—everything that had survived the move, actually—with the exception of two televisions and the chairs they sat in: Dolly's because of its sentimental value, and Earl's because of the treasure of pornography still concealed beneath its skirts.

Inside the store Jean Duckoff was alone—soloing—and it wasn't a good day. Already she had needed customers' help making change. And when she was making hamburg patties she knocked the fan into the vat of hamburger. Then, when she was picking the dead bugs out of the hamburg, a little blond-haired boy ran from the store with a fistful of candy, and before she could chase him down she had thrown up into a grocery bag. And then the store toilet got stopped up when she tried to flush the bag. By the time Angel came in for the newspaper, Jean was sobbing.

Angel smiled at her. "Got the blues?" she said. It was the first time she'd ever spoken to Jean.

"Naw, just sad. Nothin's goin' right, and I got the grippe, too."

"You've got the grippe? You mean morning sickness, don't you?"

"I threw up, that's all I know."

Angel smiled again.

"You think that's funny?" Jean blubbered.

"No, I'm just happy for you, that's all." Angel shook her head plaintively. "God, you don't know how lucky you are. I'd give anything to have a baby of my own." It was another of her recent statements that surprised herself—why, she thought, would she want a baby?

"So what's that got to do with the price of worms?" Jean snapped, shaking her head disdainfully. She'd always mistrusted Angel, always gone out of her way to avoid her, thought her witchy and strange, and now the citified woman had just proved her suspicions. "How come I'm lucky? 'Cause I got the grippe and you want to have a baby?"

Angel studied the pale-faced girl. Was it possible she didn't realize? "No, because you're going to have a baby."

"Gaaa. Get outta here," Jean said, lifting some hamburg as if to throw it. "You better watch it! That ain't nice teasin'." But then she stopped, and suddenly her dark eyes shone with the clear light of understanding. She threw down the hamburg and dropped her hands onto her belly, feeling its hard roundness. Her mouth opened in a disbelieving oval and tears welled in her eyes. She flashed a look at Angel that changed from accusatory to a plea for guidance.

And Angel surprised herself once again. She said, "You know, I've done some midwifery in the past—that is, I've helped deliver babies. I'll do yours if you'd like."

Now Jean was sure the woman was a witch. She scowled at Angel and pursed her lips angrily, bravely biting back her tears. She backed cautiously toward the door. Then she turned and ran.

When Harvey saw her coming, he called, "Hey, tubby, what's the hurry? Hey, watch this." He turned the outside shower on and a fine, comical spray fell over him. It was meant to make her laugh, but she ran right past him, sobbing.

Carl nodded in her direction. "Go ahead, Harve," he said. "I'll let you know if I need you."

"Okay, let me know if you need me."

"Yeah, okay, Harve, I'll let you know if I need you."

"Okay," Harvey said, half smiling at his own foolishness. Then quickly frowning as if to say to Carl, "Rob me, will you?", he marched suddenly away.

Just then Mr. Rogers appeared with two bottles of beer in his hands. "You, Mr. Mason," he said, admiring the new lavatory, "are a class act." He handed one of the bottles to Carl.

"Why, thank you, sir," Carl answered with mock gentility. "And you, too, if I might say so, are a class act yourself." They unscrewed the tops, toasted and drank. The beer was ice cold and flowed like a northern stream down Carl's dry throat. They touched bottles and were drinking again when Carl saw the old man's ears perk, saw him take the bottle from his lips and cup a hand to his ear, intently studying the ridge. "What is it?" Carl said.

Mr. Rogers didn't answer. Rather, he set his bottle down, threw back his head, and ululated into the air, loud and shrill, making a sound like the wild turkeys that sometimes flew overhead. And then

Carl heard a similar call returned from the ridge. The kids on the shore stood and laughed, pointing at the old man. The ladies in their beach chairs turned to look. The men in the motorboat pointed up to the ridgetop. The little lemon-haired boy bounced up and down on the diving board, mocking the old man's call.

Mr. Rogers said to Carl, "That's Nighthawk's signal for help."

"Lovely," Carl said.

33

The Moosicorn

The moose lay on the ridgetop, in a clearing fifty feet into the woods, one sunny yellow arrow pointing straight off the top of its head between the antlers. A rotted fallen birch had split like a cornstalk under its weight. Carl, Zippy, and Mr. Rogers stared awestruck at the enormous animal, while nearby, Nighthawk stood tall and proud, his raccoon cradled in the crook of his arm.

"Moose," he said. "For Mason."

Carl climbed on a stump to gauge the animal's mass. He shook his head and said delicately, "Jeez, I don't think there's room in the freezer for it."

"Well, we can't leave it here to rot," Zippy said.

"So how're we gonna get it down?" Carl said.

"Maybe we could winch it down," said Mr. Rogers.

Carl rubbed the back of his neck. "We could, but I wouldn't want any of the campers to see it, you know?"

"I've got an old canvas tarp," Mr. Rogers said. "We'll wrap the tarp around it and winch it down."

Larry appeared then, parting the brush with his shoulder. As he came into the clearing he took a long swallow from a can of generic beer and then wiped his mouth with the back of his hand. "Whoa," he said. "*That*, my friends, is a moose."

"Ain't it a beauty?" Rogers said. "First one I've ever seen here, too. I've seen bear, and, course, plenty of deer, fishers, weasels, and the like, but never a moose. Now, wait—perhaps I have seen a moose before. Yes, now that I think about it—"

Larry shrugged his shoulders. "So what are we waiting for? Let's get it down there and start selling some hamburgers."

Mr. Rogers said, "We're just now trying to devise the best way to transport the animal."

Larry nodded, then folded his arms in a confident display of thought. He walked around the animal, abstractly measuring it by waving his opened hands in the air, as if casting a spell.

"I'll get Harvey to bring the winch," Carl said. He looked up through the trees, put two fingers to his mouth, and whistled three times into the air. But there was no response. He whistled again, and again there was no response. "I'll go down and get it myself," he said.

"Wait!" said Larry, "I've got an idea."

Carl ignored him. He continued walking away.

"No, really, we can do it without the winch."

As if in answer to Larry, Carl bellowed, "Harvey!" and whistled again.

"Hold it! Hold it! Come on back," Larry said.

Mr. Rogers said, "Ho, Carl, let's hear what Larry's got to say."

Out of respect for his old friend, Carl stopped. "Awright, what?" he said to Larry.

"Now this might sound crazy, but it'll work. Guaran-goddamn-teed. We'll just drag the moose to the cliff, drop it down into the pond, and then tow it to shore with the motorboat."

Carl didn't respond. He simply turned toward the ridge and whistled again, loud and shrill. "Harvey!"

Mr. Rogers shook his head at Larry's suggestion. "Afraid it'd sink, wouldn't you think?" Nighthawk scowled at the old man's rhyme.

"No, no," Larry explained. "It'll float, really. When things die they float." He saw Carl shake his head scornfully. "Hey, I know of whence I speak, man. These things swim all the time when they're alive. Besides, it's common knowledge that the moose is a vegetarian."

Zippy wrinkled his face at his brother. "So what?"

Larry's expression turned hard. He would not allow his brother— who, after all, was his tenant—to make him look foolish. "So it's lighter than it looks," he sneered.

Zippy was incredulous. "Did you learn that in college?" The

word "college" came out of his mouth like gas. "That's dumb, brother."

Larry looked at Zippy and smirked. "Dumb, huh? *You're* calling *me* dumb?" He smirked again.

Carl said, "I'm goin' down after the winch."

"C'mon, you guys," Larry said. He squatted beside the moose's head and grabbed hold of the antlers. "Let's go. Let's drag it to the cliff." He grunted and tried to lift, but only his legs straightened. "C'mon."

Carl spun around. "Drop it!" he said, coming close enough to Larry so only the moose's head separated them. His fist was doubled into a tight, knuckled ball at his side.

But Larry didn't relent. Red-faced and bent at the waist, he held fast to the antlers, defiantly trying to lift the animal higher, but managing only to raise his own head into the air. "C'mon, brother," he grunted to Zippy. "Are you with me or not?"

"No, man, not this time."

Larry glared at his brother.

"Drop it," Carl warned, "or I'm going to punch you in the nose." He glared at Larry.

Larry glared back at Carl.

The moose opened one dark eye and glared at Larry, then with a mighty twist and a beastly scream, it scrambled to its feet, throwing Larry into the thicket, and attacked a large blue spruce. The impact snapped the arrow in two and drove the beast, rubbery legged, down to his knees. But then it rose again, snorting, spinning in circles— an adrenaline-socked, brain-damaged monster with half an arrow in his skull—and it slammed straight into the same blue spruce. Again the moose went down, this time rolling onto his side, and with a great rattling sigh, it laid its head in the dust and went still.

Larry approached the beast cautiously, on tiptoes. Mr. Rogers and Carl leaned forward to check for breathing. Suddenly its legs started pumping, its head snapped up, and it scrambled upright; reeling, scattering the men behind trees. The huge animal lowered its rack and overran a stand of sapling alders, heading for the ridge. And then, despite Carl's cries to stop, it spotted the ridge-path and galloped down into the campground with a fearsome, guttural wail.

Targets were everywhere: tents, trailers, outhouses, the new lavatory, trees, cars, a van, scattering humans. As if to decide which to attack, the moose ran to the pavilion area and began bucking in furious circles, kicking up gravel and shaking its great velvet antlers. Then suddenly it stopped and faced the pond. Its target was in sight. It snorted, it whistled through its nose. It pawed thoughtfully at the gravel. Then, with a howl straight from hell, it charged—straight for the little golden-haired youngster who watched in horror from the end of the diving board. The monster galloped headlong for the dock and leaped onto it, stumbling and sliding a few feet on his unsteady knees, and then without losing a beat, scrambled up again: *bum-didda, bum-didda, bum-didda, bum-didda.*

"Jump, Gunnar, jump!" his mother screamed, but the boy froze instead and held up his hands as if to stop the roaring beast, which, with one last aboriginal bellow, stupidly mounted the diving board and lost its legs on either side. It came down hard on its underside, and with one deathly slow bounce, the sparkling new diving board snapped, and the moose and boy plunged together to the pea-green bottom of Norwood Pond.

Gunnar's mother ran to the end of the dock. "Help! Help!" she cried, "Oh, goddammit, somebody help me!"

From inside their trailer, the Roots heard the commotion. Go see what that is, Earl told Dolly. She put her last blueberry pie down on the table—out of her husband's greedy reach—and struggled out the door into the brightness. Shielding her eyes, she looked toward the pond, where the excitement seemed to be. The loudmouthed camper lady was down there, kneeling on the dock, peering into the bubbling water. What was she looking for? Dolly stepped closer to see, when suddenly, like a rising demon, the moose's great rack surfaced—with a small white pair of hands hanging desperately on. And then its huge dark head broke water, shaking wildly to loose the wide-eyed, choking boy.

"Hold on! Hold on!" his mother cried as the moose paddled for shore, thrusting its head back and forth like a great locomotive. Dolly thought the child was riding on an inflatable beach toy—she couldn't understand why everyone appeared so concerned. Then the moose rose to his feet in the shallow water, shooting spray from its nostrils and shaking silvery, sun-reflected drops from its antlers.

"Jump off, Gunnar! Jump off!" the boy's mother cried. But he held fast.

Gunnar! Dolly heard the name. The evil boy. The boy possessed by Satan himself! She stepped back. Oh, God help me, she thought. What is he doing to that beast? She became excited and let out a shriek.

So did the moose, who immediately charged her, *bum-didda, bum-didda, bum-didda, bum-didda.*

"Let go, Gunnar!" his mother cried. "Drop off!" But the boy was frozen, saucer-eyed, flying like a torpedo toward Dolly. And she, afraid more of the evil-eyed boy than the moose—thinking that he controlled the monster—grimly made a cross with her index fingers and held it high. She was not the target, however. As if by radar, the moose angled off (Dolly crossed herself), catching sight of a new target: Santa Claus—the red and white plastic Santa Claus attached to the side of the Root trailer.

"No!" Dolly screamed at the boy, but of course the moose didn't stop. It struck the trailer a perfect smashing blow, launching the daisy-haired boy end-over-end over the top, and buckling the trailer itself, so it jumped off its moorings, shattering the two windows that Larry—and the Roots—had earlier spared. The moose, after the impact, reeled dizzily backward, opened its mouth in a yawn, then slumped to the ground, unconscious.

"Is he dead?" Dolly breathed. She meant, of course, the boy, whose ranting mother carried him, pie-eyed and pale as a morning cloud, back to her van. "You little brat," she told him. "It serves you right!"

"Stay back, everybody," Carl shouted. "Stay back." He tiptoed over to the moose, watching its twitching eyelids. He bent cautiously. Its lip fluttered. Carl jumped back. Then he gingerly touched its shoulder with his foot. When it didn't respond, he kicked at it harder. But the beast only snored, the broken yellow arrow still rudely embedded in the top of its skull.

Just then they heard a muffled, angry cry from inside the trailer. It was Earl Root's voice, cursing and shouting unintelligibly. Dolly opened the door to see what was wrong and then jumped back, horrified.

"Now what?" said Carl. He went to the door and looked inside, and there was Earl—actually, there was Earl's head—on the floor.

"Mason!" the fat, blustery head cried, glaring up through a pair of cardboard 3-D glasses—one cellophane lens red, the other blue. At first Carl thought the man had somehow decapitated himself. But then he understood. Earl Root had fallen through the floor—sitting in his recliner—its top was just visible above the hole. And he had apparently been eating Dolly's blueberry pie, because the pie was smashed in the folds of his neck. But he was helpless—his arms were pinned below the floor, in his lap. There was also a maga-zine—3-D Buns—opened on the floor in front of his face. It was a double spread: On one page was a life-sized close-up of an irides-cent, pimpled buttock; on the other page, naturally, was the other. The object of Earl's delight had been the dark area in the seam, between the staples.

"I'll see you in court, Mason!" Earl snarled. "You blue-headed jeezer, I'll sue you for every penny you got! Don't stand there gawkin', get me out!"

Again Carl whistled for Harvey, but as before, the boy didn't respond. Where was he? Carl marched over to the trailershack and pounded on the door. "Harvey!" he called, "I need you out here!"

Then Harvey did something very, very unHarveylike. He put his mouth to his open window and said, "I'm busy!" And he slammed the window.

It took a group effort to free the piano-weight man. Even Night-hawk helped. When it was agreed he couldn't possibly be lifted out, the group tore off one of the sheets of plywood that ran along the bottom of the trailer. Then Carl crawled underneath and chain-sawed three of the recliner's legs—the fourth snapped—and Earl was able, with a group tug, to crawl out. "Shut up!" were the first words he uttered when rescued. They were for his wife, who had just opened her mouth to harangue him. "Somebody's gonna pay!" he swore, kicking at the unconscious moose. Then a sudden calm befell him. He looked down at the animal and said roughly, "Guess I better lay him away, huh?"

Before Carl could answer, Larry backed around the corner, di-recting a large International truck with circus art on its cab—Carl recognized the truck—it was from Tex's Wild Animal Kingdom. On the back of the truck was a steel cage hooked to the truck's hydraulic cable winch—an arm which made the truck look like a crane.

"Right over here, Tex," Larry said, directing the truck to the animal.

"No. Screw," said Carl. "We're going to put it out of its misery."

"No way, partner. This animal goes up to Indian Village," Larry said. "You're looking at a gold mine here, Carl. Do you know what we'd have to pay for an ordinary moose?"

"Ordinary moose? You mean one without an arrow stuck in its head? One that doesn't attack trees and trailers and children?"

Larry turned to the others and said in the hollow, oratorical voice of a circus ringmaster: "This is no ordinary moose, ladies and gentlemen. This, my friends, is the one, the only . . . Moosicorn!"

It was Zippy who reacted the loudest. "Moosicorn?" he cried.

Larry squinted at him. "Yeah," he said. "You heard me. Moosicorn."

"You're out of your mind, brother."

Larry glared at his twin. "Out of my mind, huh? You're calling me out of my mind? Listen, pal, I can buy and sell you, and anybody else in this campground."

"Good," Dolly said, "'cause you owe me and Earl a new trailer!"

"Yeah, that's right," Earl said, standing by with his loaded .22, "and make it a Detroiter, a seventy-footer—furnished."

"You got it," Larry said, pointing to the Roots, but still looking at his brother.

"Well, you can't even rent me, brother," Zippy said, "'cause your money's nothing to me. And there's nobody else in this campground that's impressed with you either."

Larry nodded slowly. "Oh, is that right?" He turned to Harvey's trailershack and softly called the boy's name. Immediately the door banged open and Harvey barged out. He, like Larry, wore a new red Camp Uniform, and he, like Larry, wore sunglasses, and he, almost like Larry, had a fine dark mustache. In truth, he looked more like Larry than Larry's actual twin.

"Here I am, L.A.," he said. "What do you need?"

Zippy saw Carl quiver, saw a brief but poignant look of astonishment and dismay.

"Go ahead, Earl," Carl said, nodding to the moose, "blow it away."

"Carl, no," Shirley said. "Larry's right. Don't kill the poor thing. The children would really enjoy it."

Tex spoke up. He said to Larry, "We can put the animal inside the cage right here, boss. Then we'll tie the cable around that elm up there and winch the whole shootin' match right on up the hill."

Carl walked away.

The Lincoln was a smooth ride. Carl had always felt lucky to own it. He pressed on the accelerator, felt the long, sleek car surge ahead, felt the long, stiff shadows of trees on the River Road beat like a flickering silent movie across his face. He didn't feel lucky about too much else, though. Luck, he said to himself. Hah. Luck was of no earthly use to anybody. Here a man can plan and scheme so he's covered all the bases, and he can be the hardest-working son-of-a-bitch in the jungle, and he can treat people right so that when he needs help, there'll be someone to lend it; and he can be a skilled trader so he never gets beaten on a deal, but rather, is able to beat everyone, just a little. Yes, a man can do all these things—and then luck comes around and throws a wrench into the works.

What kind of luck, he wondered, was it that dropped Larry Jones at his doorstep with all that money to save the Camp? Was that good luck? And what kind of luck was it that brought the kid together with his daughter? Wasn't that good luck? He had thought so at the time. Well, at least Susie loves him—and that's what counts. That's not luck, that's love—that's real stuff. At least she loves the kid. Because if it wasn't for that, he'd be gone today. No, yesterday. And Carl himself would be forced to go, too, right back to the loading dock at Stevens' Woolen Mills—if they'd take him. But he wouldn't care. No sir. He'd hold his goddamn head high, because he'd given it a shot—his best shot.

He tossed his empty beer can into the woods and opened another. Fucking bottle bill.

But now he was stuck with his rich partner. Because deep inside he knew something that he'd never told himself aloud. He knew the kid was just a fortune hunter who had agreed to marry Susie to get a piece of the campground. And he realized that he had known that all along—not consciously—but he had known it in his heart, even when he took the kid's money—that he was buying his daughter a husband.

But she loved the kid. And she wanted to marry him. And there was nothing in the world Carl would do to hurt her. He hammered the steering wheel. Somehow the kid had beaten him. He was stuck with Larry Jones.

"Fuckin' luck," he said, shooting his beer can at a passing stop sign.

The bedspring dug through the kitchen sponge into Jean Duck-off's back. She considered rolling over and adjusting it, but she didn't want to disturb Harvey by untucking the sheets from under their shoulders. She wanted him to fall asleep. Because whenever he couldn't sleep he made a noise with his mouth, a whispered, unconscious breathing noise that went "Ahh-wow-wow-wow-wow-wow-wow-wow." She usually enjoyed the sound. It was soothing to her, like ocean waves, and would eventually put them both to sleep.

But tonight was different. Tonight it kept going and going. She felt around on the floor for the flashlight that never worked. She flicked its switch again and again, then banged it on the side of the bed until it flickered on.

She sat up and shined the light on his face and saw him just staring up into the darkness like a dead boy, thinking. She leaned over his face and said, "Whutcha doin'?"

"Oh, nothin'," he said, "just thinkin' some things over."

"Well, if you'd write 'em down, you'd remember 'em. Then you wouldn't have to think 'em over all the time," she said. "So whutcha thinkin' over now?"

"Havin' a baby."

"You bin thinkin' 'bout that all night."

"Well, somethin' just ain't settin' right with me."

"Huh? Whaddya mean?"

"Well, I'm thinkin', here I am. And here you are."

"Yup."

"Now what kinda baby do you s'pose the likes of us're gonna have?"

"Whaddya mean?"

"I mean supposin' it turns out like us?"

"Whaddya mean?"

"Well . . . you're pretty dumb. And me . . . well I ain't no Eye-sty myself."

"Huh? 'Eye-sty?' What the heck's that?"

Harvey thought a second . . . "Jeez, I dunno. Somethin' you get in your eye, I s'pose. I dunno. People say to me sometimes, 'Good goin', Eye-sty,' or 'How'd you figure that one out, Eye-sty?' It means stupid, I guess, but I don't know for sure. I never did know how to figure this 'Eye-sty' business. See? That's what I mean. Both of us is number than a pounded thumb. And I'm scared the baby's gonna turn out like us."

"Oh."

"Ahh-wow-wow-wow-wow-wow-wow-wow, Ahh-wow-wow-wow-wow-wow-wow-wow, Ahh-wow-wow-wow-wow-wow-wow-wow, Ahh-wow-wow-wow-wow-wow-wow-wow, Ahh-wow-wow-wow-wow-wow-wow-wow, Ahh-wow-wow-wow-wow-wow—"

"Hey."

"Wha'?"

"I just thoughta sump'n."

"Wha'?"

"You know what I hope?"

"Wha'?"

Jean said softly, "I hope the baby turns out just like you."

Harvey made a noise with his nose. Then he lay for a long spell in silence. "I just thoughta somethin' myself."

"Wha'?"

"I hope it turns out just like you." He rolled over and pulled her close to him so their naked bodies were together. Then he gently parted her legs with his knee and made a warm spot to lie in.

"Uh-uh," she said. "We can't do nunna that now."

"Why not?"

She was flabbergasted at his thoughtlessness. She sighed deeply and said, "You think I want twins?"

"Daooww," he said, sounding like a punctured tire. She heard him strike his forehead. "That ain't how you get twins. That's only if you do it with somebody else after you do it with your husband. Then you get twins. It's God's way of gettin' you back."

"Who says?"

"Everybody knows that. Jeez, you're stupider than I thought." Then he teased, "You been doin' it with somebody else and not tellin' me? Like maybe L.A. Jones? I seen you lookin' at him. Sometimes."

"Oh, gross," she said. "He's even dumber than you."

Zippy stared at the blinking transceiver lights until his eyes burned. Then he shut them and rested his head on his arms, listening to the sounds of the evening—the Earth sounds he would hear no more. Must guard against sentimentality, he thought; must concentrate on the job at hand. But he was having trouble concentrating. Something had been bothering him all evening—an offhand remark that just wouldn't settle into the day's passing. He realized that he'd have to dredge up that remark and deal with it or he would have no peace, no concentration.

Then suddenly it came into focus. It was a remark that Tex had made, the short cowboy character who had brought the Moosicorn cage. When Zippy had first seen his truck—what with a cage on the back and a cowboy backing it into the campground—he had shuddered and said to Mr. Rogers, "That's for me." But Mr. Rogers had assured him it was not. Still Zippy watched Tex carefully, listening for any cryptic messages he might have been delivering. Finally, after the moose and cage had been dragged up to the ridge and Larry was paying the man, Zippy overheard Tex trying to sell cowboy clothes to Larry, who declined. And that's when Zippy stepped forward, saying, "I'm your man, Tex," to which the cowboy replied, "You don't look like no man to me, hippie," and Larry said, "You got that right, Tex."

Now Larry's comment didn't bother him—that was just public retaliation for calling his Moosicorn idea dumb. That's all that was, just Larry wanting to outshine him. No, it was Tex's remark that had been nagging at him. Because it echoed what Ruth had been telling him all along, about people mistrusting those who looked different—about conforming on the outside so as to move easier among the people. "If you start by having their respect for your outer self—never mind how ill-gotten—then you can go about earning their respect for your inner self. But if you don't start off with their respect, they'll never give you a chance." That's what she'd been telling him for months now. Maybe she wasn't entirely wrong.

His thoughts turned to Ruth now, and he allowed himself some melancholy. He had an urge to be with her. He got up and went into the house. But their bed was empty. That's odd, he thought, it's way past her bedtime. He looked across the campground to the Masons' house. Their lights were off. She wouldn't be there. And the lights were off at Larry's new house, too. Then he saw, on Lookout Hill, way up behind Larry's house, a small, dying campfire. And he knew it was she. It was her secret place, the place she used to go for metamorphosis and relief from the others in the communal days at Wind In The Pines. He had followed her there once, vaguely mistrusting her, and found her sitting amongst the columbine and lilacs in a hollowed-out spot, and he had slipped away unnoticed. When she had returned to him after three days, she had changed her name to Ruth and begun wearing lipstick and shin-length dresses. And she had accepted Christ as her personal savior: her metamorphosis.

And now she was changing again. A butterfly changing into a butterfly changing into a butterfly.

Nighthawk saw the fire, too, high above the sleeping campground, and he felt a kinship with the tender of that fire. He sat cross-legged on the ground before his blaze, his raccoon curled in sleep beside him, its long leather leash coiled near its head. His arms had grown weary from the working of a crude flint arrowhead, and he rested them on his lap. His new arrows were fine and strong and true, not bright yellow and foolish like the K-Mart arrow in the skull of that terrible, hell-risen moose. He looked across the fire to the cage where it slept, and he thought long about the depths of the forest and the meaning of the great beast.

Then slowly, strangely, he felt himself rising. He allowed his eyes to close, and found he could somehow see right through his eyelids. He rose higher and higher, leaving the ridge, leaving his campfire, leaving his own body behind. So deep was his trance that he didn't see the shark-gray poodle silently cresting the ridge, sniffing the fragrant air, eyeing his plump, sleeping raccoon.

Maurice froze—he spotted the Indian and the caged monster across from the fire, and he shrank back into the shadows. But the monster spotted him just the same, and it glared at him, registering alarm, registering menace, yet also registering a bewildering sense of fear. It moved sideways in its cage.

Maurice slunk around the fire, heeding the sleeping man, heeding the monster, poised for flight. He pranced once across the monster's line of vision and then back again, wagging his head, watching the bewildered moose with shining, lunatic eyes. But the monster—and the sleeping man—remained motionless.

Maurice turned to his prey. He could almost taste its flesh. His belly fluttered. But he resisted the urge to attack. *Patience.* He intended skirting the fire to get a clear attack line on the raccoon. But with his first step, a shudder crossed the raccoon, and Maurice charged.

The animals tumbled together, entwined in the raccoon's leash, and then fell apart. The raccoon recovered first. It sprang and swiped blood from Maurice's nose with its pinlike claws, then scampered up a multilimbed poplar where it settled high in the tree, grinning down at its assailant. It made a triumphant, squeaking sound.

Maurice looked up. His nose burned. He rubbed it in the sand, then looked up again, seething, unwary of the Indian, unwary of the caged monster behind him. His focus was entirely on the raccoon in the tree, and he became consumed with the need to separate one from the other. Thus seized, he charged the tree with such searing, blind ferocity that in the next instant he found himself scrambling onto the lowest limb, five feet off the ground.

Inside its cage, the monster gasped—it shrank back, wide-eyed and trembling. And high in the poplar, the raccoon clutched at a branch fearfully. Both animals believed they had seen the poodle fly.

Nighthawk soared through the night, lucidly watching each tiny movement below with perfect eyes: the sleeping breath of an exposed, motherless fawn, the streamside foraging of a raccoon, the twitching ears of a small white hare. Suddenly the hare came alive, sensing this perfect hawk in the sky above. It leaped joyously and scurried a dazzling serpentine trail through the cool, shadowless field, knowing, as Nighthawk knew, the exultation that lay beyond: *the moment of purity.* Nighthawk dived. There was a spot in the clearing, a silvery, moonlit mound where they were fated to be joined, and he swooped down upon the hare just as it arrived. He pulled away from earth with the white hare shining like Venus in his talons. It was indeed a perfect world.

Maurice bristled. He inched diagonally up the limb, then twisted and leaped in one motion, catching a higher limb under his front legs. He pumped his back legs, hauling himself up, and when he had risen unsteadily to this higher limb, he stopped, panting, to catch his breath.

The raccoon, seeing Maurice's struggle from its superior height, realized that the dog could not actually fly; that indeed he was a poor climber. So it resumed its confident posture, even came down a branch to taunt the poodle.

This was exactly what Maurice had hoped for. He looked down at the hard ground below. He looked out into the night. And with a low growl, he leaped out of the tree into the air, catching the raccoon's hanging leather leash in his teeth, so that the coon was yanked off its high perch and dropped like a fatted apple from branch to branch, easing Maurice's own descent and bruising the raccoon sufficiently so that when it finally slammed to the ground it was stunned for the instant it took Maurice to rise and sink his teeth into its throat and shake the life from it.

Seeing this, the moose was besieged by terror and confusion. He attacked the poodle: slammed into the cage door and fell back again. Maurice lifted his quarry, turned, kicked two tufts of sod at the dazed monster, then trotted casually down the ridge-path, feeling magnificent.

Nighthawk climbed again and soared over a lake so vast and still it seemed the wind had sucked the very life from the earth below. A hill rose off the far side of the lake, a velvety, sheep-grazed hill. A great black moose drank at the shore. And he realized that he had a certain knowledge of the moose, a knowledge that somehow disgraced the animal. Instinctively understanding what it must do, the beast began galloping to the top of the hill on legs faster than possible, *bum-didda, bum-didda, bum-didda, bum-didda*, and Nighthawk, having no choice but to follow, drew down in pursuit, knowing: *There will be a moment in time, beyond the hill, where we are fated to meet—our moment of purity.* The moose crested the hill and disappeared beyond, leaving only its hoofbeats resounding in the air, *bum-didda, bum-didda, bum-didda, bum-didda*, and Nighthawk crested the hill in joyous and willing pursuit.

But it was all wrong. Because he suddenly found himself flying over a jungle, black and foreboding, but he was no longer on wing, but in the open door of a helicopter, *bum-didda, bum-didda, bum-didda, bum-didda*, his imperfect hands on the triggers of an M-60, searching the blackness below. The chopper jolted. It began turning, turning, turning. Smoke filled the cockpit. The chopper wouldn't respond. "There!" someone shouted. Nighthawk turned to fire, but he was too slow. Two glowing eyes rose from the impossible blackness, and, with a long and hideous wail, the moose pulled him out of the sky.

Nighthawk lurched. His breath trembled, his heart thumped, bum-didda, bum-didda, bum-didda, bum-didda. This is not my dream, he thought, feeling for his raccoon (it was gone). He gazed across the fire to the cage and saw the beast staring back at him with dull, dark eyes. You have given me this dream, he said silently to the moose. He stood and approached the cage. He saw the foolish horn on the animal's skull (Larry had fashioned a papier-mâché horn around the broken arrow when the animal was unconscious), the horn that disgraced the animal, that gave Nighthawk knowledge over it. He put his new arrow on his bow and drew it back, aiming for the animal's chest.

But the moose stared at him with its own knowledge.

And suddenly Nighthawk shared that knowledge: This was not their moment of purity. He lowered his bow and returned to his fire, unwary of the blood there.

34

Brothers

Larry awoke to find his brother bent over him. Reflexively, he covered his face.

"Hey, man," Zippy said, "I got a favor to ask."

"Ask, then."

"I need to borrow a little bread, man."

Larry sat up cockily. He raised his eyebrows in a show of rumination, showing no sense of brotherhood. "I don't know, man, I'm not the First National Bank. What do you need it for?"

"I want to buy some cowboy clothes from your friend Tex."

Larry rolled out of bed and walked to the stove, still deliberating. "Want some coffee?" he asked.

"No, man, I just want the bread."

Larry, of course, intended to give him the money, but the play was necessary to prove his ascendancy over his brother. "To tell you the truth, I don't think it's healthy to lend money. Or to borrow it. Maybe if there was some little job we could find for you to do around here—"

"I'm not going to work for you, man," Zippy said. "C'mon, Larry."

Larry sighed. "Well, I suppose somebody's gotta look out for you." He tossed a hundred-dollar bill onto the bed. "Consider it a gift," he said, which they both realized was the coup de grace, the final stroke that solidified Zippy's servility to him.

Zippy picked up the money and said, "I need a ride, too, man."

Larry chuckled. "Yeah, no sweat. I'm going into Bluffton myself to pick up a sign."

. . .

The sign was fifteen feet across, fashioned after the rustic wooden BONANZA sign from the old TV western, but with the words INDIAN VILLAGE burned into the grain. It would hang between the totem poles at the top of the ridge-path. Larry picked up four smaller signs as well: MOOSICORN, PLEASE FEED THE ANIMALS, RACCOON, and ADMISSION—$1.00. He tied the long wooden sign to the roof of the Mercedes and headed for Tex's Wild Animal Kingdom, with a nifty new brainstorm suddenly parading inside his head: He would buy the Indian outfit off the papier-mâché Indian in Tex's make-believe jail. Nighthawk would be proud to wear it. In fact, he might be proud enough to wear it *inside* the Moosicorn cage.

"Stop!" Zippy said, hanging his head out the window.

Larry pulled quickly to the curb, saying "Get out, get out," thinking his brother was going to vomit.

"I don't want to get out," Zippy said. "I want you to back up a couple of blocks."

"Why?"

"I saw a barbershop. I want to get my hair cut."

"No." It was a statement of disbelief, not a refusal.

"Just do it," Zippy said, "before I change my mind."

Larry swung the car around in a Cumberland Farms parking lot and headed back, but by then Zippy had changed his mind. So Larry turned the car around again, but as they passed the barbershop a second time Zippy decided he would get his hair cut after all. They turned around again; and again Zippy changed his mind. After three more trips past the shop Larry stopped the car and said, "Last chance, brother. I'm not turning around." Zippy got out of the car and went in. And he came right out again.

"Let's get a couple of drinks first," he said.

They walked to a small, dark tavern on the corner and ordered a bottle of mescal, which they resolutely consumed in a booth shot by shot—the traditional way—by licking a dash of salt off the hand, downing the mescal, and chasing it with a bite of lime. Soon they began toasting each other: Zippy toasted Larry for his last day as a bachelor; and Larry toasted Zippy for his last day as an Earthling. After an hour Larry paid the bartender, and the brothers slid out onto the sidewalk into a high blast of sunlight.

Bill the Barber ran an old-fashioned, one-seater barbershop in a dingy part of Bluffton. Two barber poles—revolving red, white, and blue—stood on either side of the door, an unspoken but clear invitation to the older, wiser generation who didn't go in for styling and perming and blow-drying. When Zippy and Larry walked in, Bill considered sending Zippy out onto the sidewalk—he had never seen such an abomination of hair on anyone. But he turned his wrath to sarcasm. "Sure I can't do the job on you?" he said. "I'd do you free."

"Far out," Zippy told the barber. "Make me look like him."

Bill sucked his dentures back into place. "You think I'm God? You wanna look like him, you need a minister, not a barber."

Nevertheless, he started with two pairs of shears, snipping Zippy's dark, waist-long, seaweed hair with both hands. At one point the shears closed on something hard. The barber picked it out and shook his head in wonder. It was a small, green plastic house from a Monopoly game. "Been missing this, have you?"

Zippy looked at it, but had a hard time focusing. "Sort of," he said.

When Bill the Barber had sheared Zippy's hair to a uniform length, he scissored his beard down to a stubble. Then he led the drunken young man over to a sink, where he shampooed his hair. "Whatever made you decide to join the human race, son?"

Zippy just chuckled. It was obvious the barber didn't know the importance of his expedition. "Let's just say that I'm going somewhere where I want to fit in." He glanced in the mirror with a secret twinkle in his eye for Larry, who looked over his magazine and shook his head. It was a doubly-cryptic comment, of which Zippy was proud. Not only was it his secret way of saying he was going to the moon, it was also a covert insult to Earthlings, that he never cared to fit in with them in the first place. But Bill didn't get the meaning on either count. He led Zippy back to the chair and shaved his beard off (running once into a green wad of chewing gum and having to change razors), then trimmed and combed his mustache, and finally barbered his hair. Then he splashed some Troll grooming oil onto his hands and massaged Zippy's scalp. ("Stop that moanin'.") Finally he blazed a part down the top of Zippy's head, where a comb hadn't been in two decades, and combed his hair neatly to the side.

"Well, son," Bill said with pride, spinning the chair so it faced the wall mirror, "what do you think?" Larry looked up from his magazine, and Bill the Barber, seeing the twins' reflection in the mirror, wheeled around and stared at Larry. "I'll be damned," he said. "I'm better than I thought."

Zippy opened his eyes and looked at his reflection beside Larry's. "Oh, God," he said, "I look like an asshole."

When Tex saw them he covered his heart with his cowboy hat and said, "Thunderation! One wants Cowboy duds, the other wants Injun duds. And that's the only earthly way anybody's ever gonna tell you two varmints apart."

The Jones boys rode back to Norwood in reckless, drunken joy. "Yah-hoo!" Zippy whooped.

Larry erected the INDIAN VILLAGE sign alone. He carried the sign and a stepladder up to the ridge and nailed shelf brackets near the tops of the totem poles. All the while Nighthawk watched with folded arms. "Gimme a hand, would you?" Larry said when it came time to lift the sign. But the Indian wouldn't budge. So Larry placed the stepladder between the totem poles, balanced the sign on his shoulder, and carried it up himself. When the sign was in place, he drove a spike through both sides into the totem poles, then stepped down to admire it.

"This'll make you a celebrity, Cochise. Look down there. See all those people driving in? This place'll be packed before you know it. The chicks'll be knockin' down your teepee door to get at you." But Nighthawk was not amused. Next Larry nailed the admission sign to a tree and fixed the other three signs to the cage with wire. When he was done he folded the stepladder and shoved it under his arm. "I'll be back in a while, chief, with something that's guaran-goddamn-teed to put a smile on your face." As he descended the ridge-path, Nighthawk followed him with his eyes, thinking, Is our moment of purity not close at hand?

．　．　．

There was a tidy clearing of lilac and columbine and wild mint on Lookout Hill, far away from the main campground, far behind Susie and Larry's new house where the long hill pulled away from the bog. Ruth leaned against a dark boulder there, peeling a piece of wide grass into ribbons. Her stomach gnawed and groaned inside her, demanding sustenance, and she found the hunger increasingly difficult to ignore. Even the odor of her own stale breath made her crave food. She took a half-gallon jar out of a cool hole in the ground, unscrewed the cap, and took a short drink of water.

Confusion still played in her head, despite two days of fasting. She was angry with herself, as if she were somehow holding back secrets from herself—there was not a shadow of direction in her life. What she had been searching for were reasons to stay with Zippy. But she had found none. And to complicate things, those same thoughts of Larry kept surfacing: his stability, his worldliness, his musky-sweet fragrance, the touch of his lips, the feel of his body against hers. She closed her eyes, and in her imagination, he slowly materialized. She saw him vividly, beckoning to her. "Yes," she said aloud.

A sudden rustling nearby. She opened her eyes and gasped at what she saw, thinking she must be hallucinating. But no. It was he. It was Larry. He had come to her, as if by magic, as if she had summoned him with her very whisper—"Yes"—and now he stood at the edge of the clearing, strong and dark and handsome, dazzling in the low afternoon sun. Red rhinestones climbed up one leg and down the other. He wore a cream-colored ten-gallon hat, a blue plaid double-stitched shirt and brown leather vest, a gray lizard belt, long starchy blue jeans, and rhinestone chaps. On his feet were blue-gray sharkskin cowboy boots. He walked bowlegged.

Larry.

She rose and went to him, her breaths coming shallow and quick. A moan escaped from her throat.

He pulled the suede hat off his head and pitched it onto a bush. Quaking with passion, she ran her hands through his hair. She kissed him on the mouth. And then they sank to their knees, enraptured, undressing one another as they kissed, with no awareness of intent.

When they were naked he laid her on her back and ran his hot mouth down her breast. He took a nipple into his lips. "No," she said, pushing his head away. Then, pulling him back, she whispered, "Don't stop." His lips traced a fine light line down the wispy hairs from her navel to her abdomen, to the wonderfully aching, weeping center of her passion. She gasped. He pressed his mouth against her vagina lips, opening them with his tongue, and she writhed in the sensation of his smooth chin, raising her legs to rub his bristly head on her inner thighs. "Oh," she cried, and he slid himself along her body until their mouths met again. She opened her legs and in the same instant opened her whole being to him, slowly taking him all the way in, like the sea consuming the sun. She thought, I have found my new direction, I have found my new love. And all at once she herself was consumed: Her beautifully engorged lips and her wild, tearing eyes opened together. As if in protest, she tore bunches of wild grass from the ground beside her.

Seeing this, he held her head still and covered her protesting mouth with his own. Then he took her shoulders and rolled onto his back, pulling her on top of him. He closed his eyes, dropped his arms by his side, and moaned softly, still moving his pelvis against hers in small, slow thrusts.

Ruth looked down at him, distracted. The moaning, the closed eyes, the limp body: This was Zippy's favorite lovemaking position. She was seized by a sudden grip of guilt—and by a grip of longing for her husband. She rolled off her lover. He reached to pull her back, but she stopped him. "No," she whispered, kissing his shoulder. "Let me think."

They lay side by side for minutes then, perfectly still, a steady, dusky breeze brushing their naked bodies like a gentle hand, while busy squirrels jabbered and scattered from tree to tree above them. Ruth absently stroked his forearm with her thumbnail, and as she watched a sailing cloud slowly change shape above her, tears welled in her eyes. "I've never done this before," she said.

He opened his mouth to respond, but she stopped him. "Shh!" she whispered.

Footsteps were approaching. And voices. It was Carl Mason and Harvey Duckoff. They were arguing. "Just set it down, for crissake," Carl snapped.

"Why here? There's already one here."

"Just set it down!"

"Jeezum, can't you see that table there? Seems kinda dumb to have two picnic tables in one campsite, if you ask me."

"That's not a table, Harve. A table has legs. You cut the legs off that one, remember? That's a door now."

"It still got legs. Just 'cause they're kinda small, that's all. It's still good for kids."

"Yeah, right, Harve. And you didn't cut down these saplings like I told you, either. How's anybody supposed to pitch a tent with these trees here? Huh? Now go on back down there and get the chain saw."

"Oh, sure. I suppose it's my fault."

"No, Harvey, it's my fault for hiring you. Now hurry up."

"I'm goin', I'm goin'." Harvey's voice trailed off, muttering; his footsteps thudded into the distance.

But Carl's footsteps came closer, just beyond the lovers' cover of lilac. Fearing they'd be discovered, they sat up and quietly began getting into their clothes. Ruth slid her underpants on and clasped her bra, while her naked cowboy rolled on his back, trying to free the skin of his scrotum from the hungry zipper of his new dungarees. Suddenly a legless picnic table sailed into the air and landed atop the lilac, exposing them.

Their reactions were predictable. She became embarrassed and tried to cover her body with her dress. He said, "Whoops," more for Ruth's sake than his own, and rose, hopping, to put on his shirt and vest.

Carl's reaction was different. He strode straight through the thicket, right over the picnic table, and punched the cowboy a quick, hard right to the eye, knocking him, reeling, to his back. And then he leveled a dark, life-threatening stare and said in a measured voice, "Pack your bags, Jones, and get out—before I kill you." The thumb went up. "I swear to God I'll do it, too."

The cowboy staggered to his feet, holding his eye, looking astonished. His nose bled freely. He picked up his boots and ten-gallon hat, crammed them under one arm, and started dumbly down the hill.

"Wait," Ruth called, chasing after him. But he wouldn't stop.

So, following him, still clutching her dress to her bosom, she took a deep, shaking breath and announced: "I've made my decision. I'm going to go with you."

These were words he had craved. He stopped. His hat and boots fell to the ground. "Far out, babe," he exclaimed, turning to hug her. "Far fucking out."

Ruth's heart thumped. She heard distinctly the timbre of Zippy's—not Larry's—voice. She watched the cowboy as he turned and saw his mouth open in a slow, gap-toothed grin. She slapped his face.

Zippy fell back, covering up. He stumbled on his boots and stepped in his hat. "What?" he demanded.

Ruth recovered quickly. "Nothing," she said, turning away. "I . . . you had a mosquito." She turned back to him and gently soothed his teary, handprinted cheek with her palm. She thumbed blood from his nostril. She kissed his smooth chin.

Zippy said playfully, "You didn't tell me how you liked the new me." He turned a half circle, modeling.

She studied him curiously, the squareness of his jaw, the wrinkles of his aging skin. She smiled weakly. "You look nice, Zip," was all she could say.

He held his eye, grimacing. "Yeah, and people are treating me differently already, just like you said they would," he said, joshing her. "I just hope they treat us better on the moon."

The statement startled her. She opened her mouth to protest but didn't know what to say. Her head ached with confusion.

"Come on, let's go," Zippy said.

"No," she answered, gently pushing on his arm, "you go ahead. I'm not finished here . . . not finished thinking."

She returned to the clearing to find Carl sitting on a low rock, brooding, absently flexing his right hand. He was wondering how to tell Susie what he had seen—or whether he should tell her at all—or whether he should simply go down there and thrash Larry Jones to within an inch of his life; teach the kid a lesson about hurting his daughter that he'd never forget.

Ruth broke his concentration: "Mr. Mason," she said, still holding her dress in front of her, "I'll have a word with you."

Carl gave her the thumb. "You too. Out!" he said. "And take your hippie husband with you, too. I'm sick of looking at him."

Ruth put her hands on her hips, no longer concerned for her modesty. "That was my husband you just hit," she said.

Carl clenched his fist. He glared up at her. "You heard me. Screw!"

"That was Zippy! He got a haircut and shaved his beard."

Anger flared in his eyes. He sat up. "Out!" he said, pointing a finger at her as if it were a pistol. "Now." The pistol turned into a thumb and shot over his shoulder.

She pulled her dress on over her head. "Please, Mr. Mason, listen to me, I'm telling you the truth. That was Zippy—Larry's twin brother. He got his hair cut and his beard shaved."

Carl looked at her doubtfully, slowly shaking his head. He looked down. "Aw," he said, waving her away, "just get outta here, okay? This is my daughter we're talking about, here. My little girl."

The hollow sound of his voice, the look of sadness on the strong, scrappy man made Ruth suddenly ashamed for her intentions. Yes, she would have stolen his daughter's fiancé. She would have crushed Susie. And she would have crushed Zippy, too.

Zippy.

She thought of the new Zippy: His lovemaking had been fiery and passionate—he had taken her to a level of ecstasy she hadn't experienced in years. He had cut his hair for her, he had bought himself new clothes for her. He had made himself so . . . normal. Could a job be far behind? And a mortgage? In her mind, their future together suddenly bloomed prosperous—vital and moderate. She suddenly felt younger, like she had when she was a teenager, first finding romance. She was falling in love again—with her husband.

She knelt beside Carl and put her hand on his forearm. "There's nothing wrong," she said. "Really."

He just shook his head.

She lifted him gently. "Come on," she said. "Come down with me, and I'll prove it to you."

Angel swung her Volvo off the River Road, around the rutted, wooded corner, and then stopped in shock at the sight of the campground. There were people everywhere! Some were pitching tents, others readying campers and campsites; and children swarmed like locusts, filling the air with their thin, high-pitched laughter. Some lugged saucepans of water from the lavatory; others poked campfires with sticks; others chased inflated balls from campsite to campsite; others raced bicycles around; while still others swam at the beach, despite the anglers already crowded there, fishing.

Amidst this pandemonium, Angel's attention was seized by one tall figure hurrying across the pavilion toward the ridge. It was, or appeared to be, an American Indian in full ceremonial dress. But it was not Nighthawk. The Indian was giving a confident thumbs-up sign to all curious onlookers as he started up the steep ridge-path. Some applauded. Angel sighed. "Idiot." She pulled her Volvo onto the grass and cut straight toward the ridge. She halted the Indian near the top with a blast of her horn and a piercing yell: "Hey, Brainstorm!"

He stopped and looked down. Recognizing her car, he turned once on the path, modeling for her. With his dark mustache, he was not a convincing Indian chief.

"He's awake," she yelled up.

He shrugged, pointing to the heavy, feathered headdress. "Can't hear," he called down to her, and turned to continue up the path.

"He's awake, you idiot!" she yelled louder.

He bristled. He turned slowly to see if anyone was close enough to have heard the invective, then headed down, shaking his head impatiently. She got out of her car and climbed to meet him halfway up the path. "What is it?" Larry said. "I'm trying to do some business here."

"I said, 'He's awake.'"

"Who's awake?"

"Weasel. He's conscious. I've just been to see him."

"I know he's conscious. You told me—"

"Forget what I told you; now he really *is* conscious, and he's planning to break out. He's going to see Pinky."

"Big deal," Larry said. He studied her grim reaction to his nonchalance. "You told me yourself that dealers never tell where they buy their stuff."

"You don't know Weasel," she said direly. "He could make a dead man talk."

Larry lifted the headdress off his head and wiped his forehead with a suede sleeve. He turned in a slow circle, releasing a long, trembling sigh. "Great," he croaked, tossing the headdress over his shoulder.

"He's got to stay there for the rest of today—he's still got tubes in his arms. But they come out tomorrow morning—and so will he. And he'll be looking for you."

Larry's knees weakened. They began to shake. He backed against a tree.

"You want my advice?" Angel said. "Bring him whatever you've got left—money and coke. Every last bit of it. That's your only choice—unless you're planning a quick trip to Bolivia."

"All of it?"

"Look at it this way—it never really was yours in the first place, right?"

"Yeah, but it never really was his, either." He kicked the headdress. Two blue seagull feathers flew away from it.

"So you'll both come out on top," Angel said.

"All the coke? All the money?" He shook his head. "No way. I can't—I'll be broke!"

"He'll kill you if you don't. It's your only chance, poopsie. And even then, he still may decide to kill you."

Larry swallowed hard. He felt his bowels loosen. He tried to force a brainstorm into his racing mind, but none came. He bent for the headdress, turned, and walked down into the campground, dazed, no longer acknowledging the friendly ribbing from the campers, not even noticing the stone that stuck him low on the back. ("Gunnar!" a woman's voice hollered.) No, Larry Jones could think of nothing but his vanishing wealth—his vanishing wealth and power.

He crossed the campground to his new log house and was about to climb the stairs when he spotted Zippy staggering around the corner, holding his eye. Blood ran from his nose down his wrist, making deep scarlet lines that disappeared into the shadow of his cowboy sleeve.

"What happened to you?" Larry said.

Zippy shook his head unclearly. "I just got evicted, man. Mason just kicked me out."

"You think *you've* got troubles—" Larry began. Then suddenly his head jerked and his eyes gleamed: *Brainstorm!* "Hey," he blurted, "change clothes with me."

Zippy recognized that look. He had grown up often bearing the brunt of his brother's backfired schemes as a result of that look. (Their grandfather had sat Larry down one day and said, "Life is like a septic tank, boy. You keep puttin' the shit to her, and it gets deeper and deeper. And if you don't clean her out ever' now and again, sooner or later she's gonna back right up on you." More often than not Larry's life had backed up on Zippy.)

"No, man," he said, continuing on his way. "I'm keeping my clothes."

"C'mon, brother," Larry pleaded. "Gimme the cowboy suit. I'll have it back to you in an hour, guaran-goddamn-teed."

"No, man, I'm not wearin' that Indian stuff. Do you know how stupid you look? I'm going home and crashing, and then I'm gonna pack my bags and blow this pop-stand."

Larry stopped him. "Hey," he said, "I carry a little weight around here, you know. Did I say you had to leave? Huh? Gimme the cowboy suit and you don't have to go. I mean it. You can crash right here if you want. Nice waterbed. Put a little bag of ice on the eye, have a little snooze, and before you know it, I'll be back. One hour. Promise."

Larry stepped out onto his porch and stretched. He took a deep breath, folded his arms, and looked over his crowded campground, feeling just like Gary Cooper in *High Noon.* He put on his dark shades. He tipped his cowboy hat to a couple of campers who were pointing at him, then dismounted the steps and strode, bowlegged, around the side of the house to his Mercedes. Inside the trunk he found his last plastic bag of cocaine tucked inside his suitcase. He took the bag out and studied it. He let it sag across the palms of his hands. He squeezed it lovingly. Then he dropped it into an open grocery bag. But he reconsidered: not all the cocaine. So he split it, half for Weasel, half for himself.

He sifted through his suitcase then and gathered the last of his money into a single wad. He cradled it like one would cradle an injured robin. He gazed upon it. He flipped the bills like a deck of cards beside his ear. He sniffed the money. Larry Jones had never known such wealth, such power. And now, seeing it all come to an end, he realized that neither had he ever known such misery. He decided that he could not go through with it. Despite Angel's warning, he couldn't part with all his money. So he divided that, too—twenty thousand for Weasel and twenty thousand for L.A. He opened the grocery bag and dropped half the wad of bills inside. "Goodbye," he said softly.

Then he thought of something—it was something Rutus Sny had once said to him: "*. . . when you decide you've lost enough of your money on that dump, why not give me a call. Maybe we could work something out . . .*"

"Hey! Wow!" a voice exclaimed. It was Harvey Duckoff walking by, carrying a chain saw toward Lookout Hill. He stopped at the sight of Larry's cowboy outfit. He whistled. He came closer. "That's some wicked decent, L.A. You look just like a cowboy."

"Yep. Pretty spiffy, eh, Harve? Look, Harve, I'm in kind of a hurry here—"

"Spiffy? I'll say!" Harvey touched a rhinestone. "Where can I get an outfit like that?"

"Can't. This is the last of its kind. Roy Rogers himself gave it to me. See you later, Harve."

"Yeah, sure," Harvey said, continuing on his way. "Roy Rogers."

Larry tossed the grocery bag through the open window into the front seat and was about to open the car door when he glimpsed a flash of color ahead, at the edge of the woods. It was Ruth. She was coming down from Lookout Hill straight for him, a purposeful yet strangely intimate smile on her face. The smile was for him. He looked around furtively. Susie was in town, shopping—he was safe on that front. Shirley was busy in the office—no problem there. Zippy was inside the house—probably asleep by now.

Ruth didn't hesitate. She walked right up to him and wrapped her arms around his waist. She lifted her face to his and covered his mouth with her own. Yes, yes, Larry thought, driving his tongue into her mouth, it was just a matter of time—he had played his cards right—and now she couldn't resist him.

She pressed her mouth close to his ear. She said in a low, raspy whisper, "All I can think about is making love to you."

"Mmm," he said, kissing her again. She breathed in his ear, "Let's go to the cabin."

The timing was bad—he had so much to do—and so much at stake. Besides, Susie would be back soon—and he had promised to take her to the Yankee Fifer Inn for a wedding-eve feast. He considered asking Ruth for a rain check but decided against it—after all the time and trouble—and money—it had taken to seduce the woman, he didn't want to let her get away now. Still kissing her, he raised his wrist behind her back to check his watch. He froze. There, not fifty feet away, just at the edge of the woods, was Carl Mason—watching. He had seen the whole thing. Larry shoved her away. "No!" Larry said in a loud voice. "Are you crazy?" Then, covering his mouth with his hand, pretending to scratch his nose, he hissed, "Mason! Mason!"

Ruth took him again in her arms and looked up at him reassuringly. "Don't worry," she said. "I just had a talk with Mr. Mason. I explained everything." Larry frowned at her. He couldn't believe what she was telling him. She kissed his lips again and then said loud enough for Carl to hear: "Honey, I think Mr. Mason has something to say to you."

"That's all right, no need," Larry said. Under the circumstances, he didn't want Carl coming near him. He began to back away.

But Ruth pulled him back. "Really," she promised, "It's okay. He understands." She turned and started across the grounds toward her cabin. "I'll be waiting for you, honey. Don't be long."

Larry turned to Carl. He shrugged his shoulders and said, "Hey, what can I say?"

Carl shook his head, shrugged his own shoulders. He had made a mistake. He studied the cowboy's unmarked face curiously, tried to see his damaged eye through the sunglasses. He looked down at his own red knuckles. A short laugh escaped, but he squelched it. "Jesus, I don't know what to say," he said, trying to improvise an apology. "I thought you were . . . I mean . . ." He handed Larry a twenty-dollar bill. "Look, no hard feelings, okay?"

"No sweat," Larry mumbled, sticking the bill in his pocket. "Que sera sera, right? All is fair in love and war, and all that good stuff." He stuck out his hand and Carl shook it.

"Good," Carl said. "Look," he said, "this is a little embarrassing. What say we keep it to ourselves, huh? We won't mention it to the girls, okay?"

Larry nodded, thinking to himself, This is one outtasight father-in-law. He gave Carl the thumbs-up sign, then turned and headed straight for Ruth's cabin, Carl's uncertain gaze following him every step of the way.

Susie drove her father's Lincoln down the River Road into a bright, bright sun. This is it, she thought, shading her eyes, the beginning of the happiest twenty-four hours of my life.

She had spent the day in Bluffton—first she had gone to Flo's to get her hair set; then to Christine's to pick up her bridal gown; to Tubmann's for the wedding rings; to Mike's Costume and Uniform for the tuxedos; and finally to the Bluffton House where she had bought a summery chiffon dress to wear for the wedding-eve dinner Larry had promised her. She imagined how the low-cut dress would look on her. She tilted the rearview mirror to examine her breasts. She thought of Larry. He had given her a thousand dollars, and she had spent it. Yes, she thought, the happiest time in a girl's life.

As she pulled into Wind In The Pines and got her first glimpse of the teeming campground, an inflated rubber ball bounced in front of her car, pursued by a small red-haired girl in Dr. Denton pajamas. Susie didn't stop—she didn't even slow—she just blew the horn, issuing a majestic, brassy fanfare which drove the horror-struck little girl to her knees, then to her back, twisting away from the road. The long white Lincoln glided past, its big, whitewalled wheels flattening the green ball—POP—and the little girl staggered into the wake of dust to peel the green, metal-flecked rubber off the gravel.

There was a line of cars idling on the Camp Road, backed up six deep from the office. Susie stopped in line. She scanned the campground for Larry, but all she could see was strangers—hundreds of them. "Goddamn low-life morons," she muttered. A guy dressed like a cowboy was walking across the Pavilion Area—children were swarming to him. But no sign of Larry. She couldn't even see if his Mercedes was at their house because of the cars blocking her way. She leaned on the horn, but it did no good—the line wasn't moving. Then a car hauling a camper pulled up behind her, hemming her in. "Shit!" she spat and, still blasting her horn, pulled onto the grass, tumbling a small man in a lawn chair and mashing his gin and tonic into the ground.

From the lawn she could see Larry's car. Good, she thought, he was there. She cut back across the road past the line of cars and pulled in beside the store, almost colliding with a man carrying two bundles of firewood and a six-pack of beer. She gave him the finger, examined her face in the rearview mirror, curled her lashes with her index finger, and got out of the car.

Ruth Jones watched the cowboy through her kitchen window. He strode across the campground to her, tall and proud: the new Zippy (she thought of Dick Powell). His transformation was incredible. Even his personality had changed. In the past, he had always moved through crowds quietly, shy of stares and comments. Now he was strutting across the grass, tipping his cowboy hat, smiling and waving to the curious campers and excited children. Indeed, this was a new Zippy.

She brushed her hair behind her ears with her fingers, then rushed to the kitchen sink to brush her teeth. Her skin was oily and pungent with bug dope, and she wished she had time to bathe— but, she thought with a sense of relief, such trivialities didn't bother Zippy. She went to her bureau and found the negligee Larry had bought for her at Sears. (He had embarrassed her that day. He had picked it out and insisted on purchasing it, telling her how sexy she would look in it—and how lucky Zippy was to have her. Now she would see if he was right.) She dropped her gray plaid dress to the floor, stepped out of it, and pulled the white, lacy negligee over her head. She tied the pink satin bows in loose slipknots on her shoulders.

The door opened. She turned and saw him, tall and dark in the doorway. He threw the door shut behind him. She went to him and kissed him on the mouth. "I haven't felt like this in years," she said.

Susie found her man in bed napping, the black silk bedsheet drawn up under his chin, one arm hanging down the side of the bed, an open plastic bag of water draped carelessly over his eyes, soaking his face and hair. The pillow on both sides of his head was wet, too. They would have to leave for the Yankee Fifer soon. But she would let him sleep a little longer.

She went into the bathroom to change into her new dress. She took off her blouse and slacks. The day had been too warm, the air too still—in town it had been downright stifling. She sniffed under her arm. She found a sponge, filled it with lukewarm water, squeezed the water through her fingers, then sponged her under-arms. The water cooled her. She rubbed a bar of soap across the sponge and sponged her neck, then under her arms again. She wrung the sponge, filled it with fresh cool water and ran it down her arms. Goosebumps rose. She sponged her chest. She wrung the sponge again and filled it with colder water, and then very lightly touched a nipple, making it erect. She pressed the sponge against the breast and allowed the water to cascade freely down, falling onto her thigh, then to the floor. She drew cool air through her nose. She washed her other breast in the same way, then ran the sponge down her belly to her inner thighs. The coolness was wonderful.

She thought of Larry in the next room and felt a twinge of excitement at being alone in the house with him. She imagined his strong, hairy chest; his broad, muscular shoulders; the hard, steely lines of his biceps; she thought of his pale nether flesh, of the steamy, hairy, hard center of his manhood; his thick white thighs. She found herself breathing harder. She dropped the sponge into the sink and with both hands lifted her breasts to the mirror. Wonderful, proud breasts. They would be the centerpiece of a full and sexual marriage. She took her nipples between thumbs and fore-fingers and squeezed, raising tremors of desire deep inside her. She wanted Larry. She wanted all of him. She wanted to bask in his heat. Animal heat. She wanted to slide along the sweat of his body and cover him with her own sweat—her sweat on his. She wanted to taste him. She wanted to consume him.

She padded through the kitchen, locked the outside door, and lowered the venetian blinds. Then, quietly, she entered the bedroom and looked down upon him. A luscious wetness gathered between her legs. She leaned over him and kissed his neck, under his ear, letting her hot breath spread like oil over his skin. He moaned in his sleep. She opened her mouth and pressed her lips against his neck, letting the flat of her tongue run down his flesh until his salty taste made her heart flutter. She could think of nothing now but his loins—his hot, sinewy, sexual loins.

She lifted the sheet and crawled inside. And in the warm, musky darkness within, she lay along the length of his legs and caressed his abdomen with her cheek. He moaned again. His arms moved sleepily; he tried to roll, but she held him down. Her heart pounded. She ran her hands up his wet, slippery sides until they came into the thick, moist hair under his arms. She rounded her lips and kissed his abdomen, sucking gently and lapping him, gathering the musk and salt of his skin.

"Oh, yeah," he breathed, waking. His hands found her shoulders. His fingers came alive.

She lowered her body further down his, running her open mouth down, down, finding his penis with her hand, and holding it, squeezing it, feeling it grow thicker, hot and hard. Mine, she thought, mine alone.

He awoke. "Oh, Ruthy," he moaned. "Oh, yeah, babe."

Susie felt a rush of blood to her head. Bright, angry colors flashed behind her eyes. She closed her fist like a vise on his erection and yanked on it, so that the small of his back raised off the bed. "Easy, babe," he whispered, "slow down, Ruthy." Susie's mind raced. She dizzily desired to pull his pecker completely off. She gripped the shaft with both hands, as if it were a baseball bat, and lifted in earnest. "Ahhh!" he said. He tried to grab her hands, but found he needed them—and his legs—to push off the bed.

Ruth led her cowboy to the loft. They climbed up and knelt on the mattress facing each other. Her heart pounded. She watched her own reflection in his sunglasses, watched herself as she crossed her arms and slipped the pink bow knots from her shoulders; watched as the soft white negligee melted from her firm, youthful body. She saw his lips part, heard him gasp at the sight of her nakedness.

And all at once he was on her, parting her legs with his own leg, chafing her thighs with his new stiff denim, stinging her hot belly with his cold brass belt buckle. He was wild, grunting like a bull, unzipping his jeans even as he nuzzled her tender breasts with his rough chin. "Take me," she gasped, and his fury increased, but his jeans were tight and difficult to pull down. He humped frantically, his ten-gallon hat falling over his shades, his boots kicking repeatedly at the far wall. The new Zippy, she thought. The new Zippy. "Oh, new," she blurted, "new . . . new . . . new . . ."

"I can't get 'em down," he gasped.

"Ohhh," Ruth moaned, trying to help him. She was reborn. She was ecstatic. Tears ran down her cheeks. "I want your children!" she cried.

"Yeah," he breathed, "okay, okay."

"I want . . . I want," she panted, "a house in town—"

"Yeah. Yeah. Me too."

"A little white house . . . with a white picket fence—"

"Mmmm."

". . . morning glories, a cocker spaniel—"

"I'll tell Susie," he gasped, "tomorrow."

Ruth caught her breath. Her heart stopped. She lifted the brim of his hat and peered at him.

"I'll divorce her," Larry panted, finally pushing the jeans down past his hips, "right after the wedding . . . promise."

"Larry!" she cried out, trying to push him off. "Oh, God, get up, get up!"

"No," Larry gasped, sliding the jeans to his knees, "wait, wait—"

She pushed on his face, knocked his cowboy hat off his head, his sunglasses off one ear. She doubled up her legs and then kicked him upright with a spring of her feet. She backed to the corner of the loft and coiled. "Get out," she snapped. "Get out of here!"

But the cowboy was driven. He marched toward her on his knees, his stiff member bouncing like a springboard.

"Aaah!" she yelled, reaching out and slapping it. It bounced up again and she slapped it harder. "Get that thing away from me!"

· · ·

Susie wouldn't let go. She was crouching now, straddling Zippy under the black silk sheet and slowly rising. And he, still groggy from tequila and sleep, feared the rising sheet was some shining black nightmare demon that had crossed into his waking life to remove his penis. He tried to shout, but words wouldn't come. "Awrrrrg!" he howled. His midsection was raised a full two feet off the bed, and he couldn't lift himself any higher. "Awrrrrg!"

But Susie was slowly losing her grip on his softening muscle. Her right hand had purchase on it only by the grip of her pinky, and that was slipping. So with fierce resolve and a hearty grunt, she gave one last yank with her left, lifting Zippy's feet right off the bed. And in that same instant, while he was suspended there, she made a fist with her right and shot him a quick, hard punch to the testicles. The air forced through his vocal cords as if she had mashed bagpipes, and his body doubled and dropped off the bed like a big groaning ball of clay.

"Bastard!" she spat, stepping over him, going into the bathroom to put on her new white chiffon dress.

Larry crept closer. "C'mon, Ruth," he said, covering up to protect against further assaults. "C'mon, June. Get into it. We're safe. Get into it."

Seeing there was no reasoning with him, she leaped off the loft, grabbed her dress from the floor, and stepped into it even as she ran out her front door to the spontaneous applause from a group of beer-drinking fishermen at a nearby picnic table. Larry called out the window, "Where you going?"

She called back, "I've got to think," and headed resolutely for Lookout Hill, buttoning her dress as she walked.

Larry flew out the door after her, still zipping his jeans. "Hold it a minute!" he yelled—which only added to the loud and raucous delight of the gathering crowd.

"Go get her, Tex!" they yelled.

"Rope her!"

"Eeee-haa!"

Larry stopped. He bowed gallantly to the hecklers, and their chorus of laughter and jeering rose. He zipped his fly. He buckled his belt. He adjusted his cowboy hat and slipped his shades on, acknowledging his public with a game, cocky smile and a woeful shake of the head. "Crazy broad," he said, heading down the road with a bowlegged swagger. Then, ahead of him, Ruth suddenly stopped. And just as resolutely as she had left him, she turned and walked back again. Larry glanced over his shoulder and nodded confidently to the campers. He knew she'd come back to him. He gave them the thumbs-up behind his back and met her beside a tan Winnebago in the line of cars by the office.

"The things you told me," she said to him, "about wanting a family, and a little house in town—Larry, please, are you sincere?"

Larry folded his arms, looked across the pond to the horizon. "Am I sincere?" he said, wounded. "Am I sincere?" He shook his head sadly and sighed. He turned and looked straight into her eyes, and he put his hands on her shoulders. And then he jumped. It was Susie, coming off the porch of their new log house, walking straight toward him, walking faster than possible. Her breasts bounced inside her light summer dress like overinflated tires on a rutted dirt road. "It's Susie!" he hissed. His eyes darted. He clutched at a brainstorm. "Okay, listen, we'll tell her I'm Zippy."

Ruth scowled. "No, we won't," she said.

"It'll work, it'll work!"

"I'm sorry, Larry, but I won't lie. It's against my—"

"Whore!" Susie shouted, heading straight for Ruth. "I oughta rip your friggin' hair right outta your friggin' head!"

Ruth clutched Larry's arm. "Zippy," she said to him, "is she talking to me?"

"Far out," Larry said. "Outtasight."

Susie wheeled. "Shut your goddamn mouth, Larry, you friggin' weasel! And how'd you get out here so fast, anyway?"

"Larry?" Ruth laughed. "She thinks you're Larry. It must be the haircut."

"Oh," Larry said, pretending revelation. "Far out! The haircut! What a far-out mistake."

"What?" Susie snapped.

Ruth covered her heart with her right hand. She chose her words carefully, to avoid a lie. "Honestly," she said, "with Zippy's new haircut and shave, it's impossible to tell the boys apart."

"Yeah?" said Susie, scowling. "Well, if this is Zippy, he's gonna be some interested to know what's goin' on behind his back."

"What do you mean by that?" said Larry.

Just then Harvey's distant voice called out: "Hey, L.A.!" The boy was running down from Lookout Hill.

Susie turned a suspicious eye on Larry. "L.A.?" she said.

Larry waved it off. "Hey, man, he thinks I'm Larry. C'mon, let's blow his mind. Go along with it. It'll be a trip. Really."

Harvey stumbled to a stop beside them. He was out of breath. "I just told him, L.A."

"What's that, Harve?" Larry looked at Susie and winked.

"I told Mr. Mason that I was takin' the rest of the afternoon off. And if he don't like it, he can just take this job and shove it. 'Cause I'm takin' orders from you from now on, just like you said, right, L.A.?" He glanced behind him. "Here he comes now. You tell him."

Larry cleared his throat. He swallowed. He turned to Susie, attempting a playful, confident grin. "Your dad thinks I'm Larry, too," he said.

"Huh?" said Harvey.

"No!" Ruth blurted.

"Whaddya mean, 'no'?"

"He thinks you're Zippy. Remember?"

Larry shook his head.

"A half hour ago, by your car—the apology."

"Yeah, yeah, so?" Carl was getting nearer.

"So—he thinks you're Zippy!"

His eyes wandered. "But I thought — Oh, God! What did I do? What did I say to him?"

Harvey scowled. He looked at Larry suspiciously. "Hey," he said, "L.A.—did Roy Rogers really give you that cowboy suit?"

Larry whispered frantically: "Okay, okay, everybody, I'm Zippy. Harvey, just go along with it. I'm Zippy. I'm Zippy."

"Hey, Mr. Mason," Harvey called, pointing to Larry. "Lookit Zippy." He smiled at Larry.

But Carl was looking at something else—something very strange, inching across his campground, drawing the attention of everyone in the area. It was black and billowy and low to the ground, and it moaned with each step—like an old, hunched-over, black ghost. Except it wasn't a ghost. It was a black silk sheet. And there was something under it, though only its eyes peeked out. When the thing saw the small group by the office, it turned and came toward them.

"Jeezum," Harvey said. "What's that?"

Just then a small, dandelion-haired boy sped toward the thing on a knobby-tired bicycle—bubble gum cards sputtered like machine-gun fire in the spokes. He circled the creature three times, courageously drawing nearer with each pass. When the creature started across the Camp Road the boy jumped off his bike and crept to its rear. "Gunnar!" a woman's voice hollered. "Get your little ass the hell away from that goddamn thing!" But the boy was curious. He found the hem of the black sheet and lifted it, exposing the creature's pale, naked buttocks to the campground. A cheer went up. The creature grunted and turned in a low, hunched-over circle; the boy circled with him. Then he reached down and picked up a handful of gravel and, holding the sheet up with one hand, prepared to fire. "Gunnar!" his mother screeched. But the boy didn't listen. He whipped the gravel point-blank at the creature's tender buns, making it howl in pain. It jackknifed upright and turned on the boy. But Gunnar was too fast. He picked up his little dirt bike, mounted it on the run, and sped away.

The black thing hunched down again, groaning. It turned to the group and spoke in a low, mournful croak: "Hey, brother, gimme back my clothes."

Ruth gasped. "That's—"

"You oughta know, missy," Susie said. "Your name's right on his lips."

"Whose lips?" Larry said. He didn't like the way that sounded. He looked at his watch. "I'd like to stick around, folks, but—"

"Hold your horses, hippie," Susie said. "I think your brother's got somethin' to tell you."

"Okay," he said, "but I'll tell you right now: He thinks I'm Larry, too."

"That's absurd," said Ruth. "He knows who you are."

Susie turned. She put her fists on her hips and scowled. "Just who in hell are you, anyway?" she snapped.

Larry chuckled. He held out his arms to her. "That's right," he smiled, "it's me."

Susie's chin snapped up. She spun around to face the plodding black creature just as Zippy stuck his head out of the sheet.

"Oh, man," he breathed. "That tequila must have been bad. I just had the most fearsome nightmare. I mean, talk about vivid, man—this boy is in serious pain."

It seemed that the entire campground had fallen to a sudden hush—campers nearby stopped whatever they were doing to study the curious group. Carl himself looked from cowboy to bedsheet to cowboy, not understanding. Larry toed the grass with a cowboy boot. Ruth's eyes darted guiltily. A slight breeze blew and ruffled Zippy's black sheet. At last Susie looked up at Larry. "Then," she said hopefully, "that wasn't you before?"

He shrugged his shoulders. "What before?"

She sighed happily and smiled, moving toward him. But then, eyeing Ruth, she stopped.

Larry said, "Oh, Ruth was just helping me look for you when you—so where've you been, anyway?"

Susie looked over at their new house, then at Zippy. She froze in secret embarrassment. And then her embarrassment turned to anger. "You know I been in town all day, Larry," she snapped.

"Larry?" Carl said. He studied the cowboy and chewed on the name.

Larry spun away from Susie. "Gotta go now," he said. "Important business."

"Wait, where you going?" she said. "Don't forget about tonight."

"Hey," Zippy said, "I want my clothes."

"Yeah," Carl said. "Hold on a second."

But Larry was already going, skipping backward away from the group, looking at his watch. "Gotta run, really. I'm late." He pointed to Susie. "Later. Promise. I won't be long." He turned and jogged to his Mercedes.

All the while Harvey studied Zippy's face. Finally he turned to

Susie and said, "What was you sayin' before about her name bein' on his lips? I don't see nothin' on his lips."

"Tsk!" Susie spat, wheeling to escape the group—and the question. "I'm sure it's none of your business, Einstein!"

Carl said, "C'mon, Harvey, we've got work to do."

Harvey hesitated. He rolled his sleeve back and studied his watch. Then, with a sigh, he said, "Okay. But just one more hour. I'm havin' supper over to the store with Jean tonight, at six o'clock."

Ruth and Zippy were left alone in the breeze. Ruth was emaciated. Her stomach felt like newspaper. Her eyes were dry and burning, and her mind was racked with confusion.

Zippy said to her, "Let's go home, babe. We've gotta get rested for tomorrow."

Ruth looked at her husband, all hunched over inside the black silk sheet, his left eye swollen, yellow, and blue. She said, "Huh?"

"The moon, babe. The moon! It isn't every day you go to the moon, you know."

Ruth's eyes opened wide. "Christ!" she cried, looking to the sky in her frustration. "Listen to me, Zippy." She doubled her fists and spat out each word with loud, staccato clarity: "I don't want the moon. I . . . want . . . appliances!" And she marched straight up the side of Lookout Hill.

35

Rip Rider

Larry was gone longer than he had planned. When he got to the hospital, it took over an hour—and fifty dollars—to get into Weasel's room, and when he finally did, it took him another half hour to tell his story.

He told Weasel he was Rip Rider, a rodeo cowboy from Santa Cruz, New Mexico. "Well, pard'nr," he said, "it's like this. I was in this dinin' car on a Chicago-bound train one evenin', and this tall Swedish feller named Hanson comes in and sits hisself right down at mah table. Well, this 'ere Swede commences to actin' all jitterylike, like a hoss with a burr under his saddle. Now I figgured somethin' fishy was blowin' in the wind. And sure as shootin', it turns out he's a-bein' follered by the FBI, 'cause all of a sudden a man in a dark suit hightails it into the dinin' car, flashin' a badge. And just like that the Swede ups and dives clean out the train window—but not until he takes the time to stuff this old paper bag under mah seat. So then ol' Rip's stuck with this confounded paper bag, see? And when Ah looks inside, there, starin' me right in th' eye, is this god-awful mess of money and little bags of white powder, and a little note that says, 'Camp Wind In The Pines.' Now, to make a long story short, Ah gots this cousin in Portland that Ah ain't seed in years, and Ah got a powerful hankerin' to come east and pay 'er a visit. And while Ah was there Ah figured, why not swing by Camp Wind In The Pines and return all this mess, whatever in tarnation it is? But somebody there by the name of Mason says the rightful owner is laid up in the hospital. So here Ah am, and here's your goods. A reward ain't necessary."

Rip Rider's accent was not honed particularly well. He sounded like he was part Downeaster, part Carolina plantation owner, and part Swede, with a heavy dose of Jethro Bodine from the old "Beverly Hillbillies" show.

Weasel looked up and said, "Nnyw fngng nd mng, ahoo!" ("You're fucking dead meat, asshole!")

To which Larry—Rip Rider—replied, "You're more'n welcome, pard'nr. Just take care of yerself, maybe use some of that money to take yerself a little vacation. I hear Hawaii's a fahn place to visit this tahm of year."

After Larry boarded the elevator, it dawned on him that he had neglected an important detail in his story, so he returned to Weasel's room and woke him up. "About that bag there," he said. "I plum fergot to tell you, but that Swedish feller said he shared the stuff in the bag with a Russian gentleman, whose name escapes me, uh, Ivan somethin' or other. Well, now, wait a cotton-pickin' minute. I got mah facts messed up again. It weren't the Swede that actually done the talkin', 'cause he had already jumped out the window and didn't have tahm for pleasantries, but the FBI told me later—that is, I overheard 'em talkin' about the case. So that's why the bag's a little short. If it is short. Is it? Well, Ah kin see that's none uh mah concern. Y'all take care now."

Wind In The Pines was a bedlam. The Camp Road, from the office all the way back to the River Road, was lined with idling vehicles towing boats or campers—or both. Cars and vans, pickup trucks, boats, motorcycles, touring bikes, tents, teepees, and campers were everywhere in the campground, illuminated by hundreds of small fires and lanterns. And the campers all displayed their various musical tastes with blaring cassette players and radios—or they gathered around guitars singing folk songs. Somebody up on Lookout Hill brought an electric guitar and a battery-powered amplifier which he aimed down at those below. By eight o'clock the store had run out of beer, ice, mixers, cigarette papers, and firewood, and Carl had grudgingly paid Harvey ten dollars to take the Big Truck to Atlas Grocers for replenishment.

While up on the ridge, in a sweeping haze of woodsmoke and the cacophony of musics below, Nighthawk sat with bow and arrow poised, aiming from camper to camper, thinking: Is now *our* moment of purity? Is now *our* moment of purity? Is now *our* moment of purity?

Susie sat dourly in her new chiffon dress on her father's porch. She had sat on the same milk case for over two hours, watching the campers roll in, hoping each car that turned out of the woods onto the Camp Road would be Larry's forest-green Mercedes. But it never came.

She began to resent the campers who pressed onto the porch to register, imagining they all knew that she had been stood up. She began scolding them for various infractions, such as talking ("Hey—somebody lives here, you know"); or scuffing their shoes on the steps ("Lift up your feet"); or laughing ("Split a gut, why don't you?").

Larry remembered their dinner date as he passed the Yankee Fifer Inn in Bluffton. He went into the restaurant and ordered dinner, then called her on the telephone. He said, "What are you doing, honey? I've been waiting and waiting for you here. I can't believe you stood me up the night before our wedding." To the string of obscenities that followed, he replied, "But I thought we agreed that you'd meet me here. Oh, well, my mistake. Anyway, as soon as I finish eating and do one more errand, I'll be home. And then we'll have our celebration in private—if you know what I mean."

Susie blew off the porch in a rage and stormed across the Camp Road to expend her wrath on her new house. She flew into the kitchen and hurled her new china and crystal against the walls. She tore off her chiffon dress and whipped it into the corner of her bedroom; then climbed into her tight white jeans and purple sweater. She jumped onto her bed and screamed into her pillow. She ranted and cried. Then she marched outside and pushed through a crowd of people to the side of the office, where she picked up a rock and flung it at Angel's house. "You filthy slut!" she screamed. "Slut! Slut! Slut!" She turned for the porch, but the sea of hopeful campers there refused to part for her.

Carl stood before them, like a sheriff protecting his prisoner from a lynch mob, pleading with them to turn back. "Go on home," he said. "There's just no more room. Honest, folks, We can't squeeze another person in."

But the mob wouldn't listen. "There's plenty of room!" they hollered back. "Up on the hill, in the woods! We'll sleep in our cars! We'll sleep anywhere."

"Sorry," Carl repeated again. "Try us next weekend."

"Just ten more!" the tenth person in line begged. "You can do it."

Susie could listen to no more. She grabbed the man and threw him aside, then pushed into the press, shoving people off the porch on both sides. "No!" she shouted. "Are you pigs deaf? He said we're all filled up! There's—no—more—room!" And with that, she threw her head back and strode majestically to the front door, losing a pair of pink panties from the leg of her white jeans as she passed. She turned again and shot her right thumb up over her shoulder. "Now, get out!" she shouted.

36

Quiet Time

At ten o'clock Carl locked up the store and sent Jean Duckoff home. He pulled down the shades and counted the money in the cash drawer, and when he was through, a warm, red smile crossed his face. The store had taken in over four thousand dollars—a thousand-dollar profit—on only the first night! Added to over three thousand dollars in camper fees, it looked like he had seriously underestimated the Camp's earning potential. An image crossed his mind that made him chuckle: the faces of Rutus and Tiffany Sny.

Rutus Sny opened his door and chuckled. "Now, isn't that the darndest thing? I had a feeling I'd be hearing from you today." He stepped back and Larry Jones walked into the vestibule, tipping his hat as he passed through the doorway. "So what brings a young cowboy like yourself out to this neck of the woods tonight? Let me guess. You're tired of losing your hard-earned money over there in Little Appalachia. Eh? Ready to start making some real dough for a change?" He motioned Larry to a high-backed, red velvet chair.

"Love to," Larry said, sitting. "Yep." He rubbed his hands together, waiting for Sny to pick up the conversation. But the older man was silently unwrapping a thick, dark brown cigar. "Money. That's what it's all about, isn't it, Rutus? At least that's what they say." Sny studied him, wetting his cigar in his mouth. Larry continued: "Funny thing, us talking about money. That's just why I stopped over to see you. Little cash-flow problem."

Sny lit the cigar, took three short puffs, then sat down opposite

Larry. He said, "Tell me something, Larry. Do you know how many owners control Camp Wind In The Pines?"

"Yeah," Larry said. "Two. Me and Mason."

Sny chuckled. He blew a cloud of smoke toward the ceiling. "Wrong," he said. "Camp Wind In The Pines had two owners before you ever heard of the place. Now there are three owners: you, Carl Mason, and Mason's daughter, Susie—whom I understand is soon to be your wife."

"Right," Larry said. "We're tying the knot tomorrow afternoon. To tell you the truth, Rutus, I haven't chosen a best man yet. I was wondering if you—"

"Do you know who'll have the controlling interest in the campground as soon as you're married, Mr. Jones?"

Larry thought. "What do you mean?"

"I mean, do you know who'll own two of the three shares of that property, who'll be able to do any damn thing they please with that dump, including selling one of those shares to a partner with real business intelligence, a partner who might have plans—and the capital—to turn that place into a gold mine?"

Larry's eyes searched the ceiling.

"Hello?" said Sny.

"Yeah, I'm just thinking about something else. But I think we're on the same wavelength here."

"Larry, I'm prepared to pay you handsomely for one of those shares."

Larry sat back and folded his arms. That's the kind of talk he came to hear: a little Wheelin' and Dealin'. "Oh, yeah?" he said coyly.

Sny rose and flicked his cigar ash into a standing brass ashtray. "Do you hear me, Larry? Do you know what I'm saying to you? I'm proposing a partnership. I'm talking about a corporate team—you and me—a team that will exercise the power of the vote. Democracy, Mr. Jones. America. And that little team will vote Carl Mason clear into the next county." He saluted.

"I hear you loud and clear, Rutus. And I'm thinking team here, just like you. All the way. I just don't know how my, er, other half will feel about it, if you get my drift."

"I see." Sny scowled.

Larry drummed on the chair arm. Then he pointed a finger at Sny. "Rutus, let's talk turkey. What would you figure this share in Wind In The Pines is worth to you? In terms of money."

Sny took a deep breath and blew it out. He sat down again, on the edge of his chair so that his knees touched Larry's. He said softly, "You've never met my wife, have you, Larry?" Larry shook his head. "And do you know why I haven't introduced you to my wife? I'll tell you why: Because she's just not in our league, Larry. She just doesn't have that good ol' business sense. God's honest truth: That woman wants your property so bad, she talks about it in her sleep." He chuckled. He coughed. Smoke came from between his teeth. He took another puff on his cigar. "But, you see, I make all the business decisions in my house, just as, I suppose, you do."

Larry nodded in agreement. "I'm thinking a hundred-twenty thou', Rutus. Cash money."

Sny smiled at him. "I like to keep the wife out of my business dealings, Larry, if you know what I mean." He puffed cigar smoke thoughtfully. "Let's face it, Larry, these women—just between you and me—they just don't have that savvy. You hear me? They don't have that business sense." He tapped on the top of his head.

Larry pointed at him. "Right. Course, since this is between friends, I'd probably settle for a bit less—say, an even hundred grand."

"Larry," Sny said, stroking his chin, "let's get right to the point. Can you get control of your wife's share? I mean, have you got that savvy?"

Larry gave him the thumbs-up sign. "No sweat," he said.

"Atta boy!" He reached out and clapped the cowboy on the shoulder. "Tell me, Larry, what have you got for a title?"

Larry shrugged his shoulders. "Manager, I guess."

Sny laughed. "No, no, no. I mean, what sort of document do you have? When you bought your share from the Masons, they must have given you a bill of sale, no?"

Larry laughed along, as if his mistake had been intentional. He stood and took a folded sheet of notepad paper from his back pocket. He opened it and handed it to Sny.

"And this is the title that you'd transfer to me," Sny said, standing, "for, what did you say, sixty thousand dollars?"

Larry snorted. "Not quite, Rutus. I was thinking more in the range of, oh, ninety to a hundred."

Sny raised his eyebrows. "Ninety thousand, you say." He chuckled to himself, shaking his head. "Oh, boy, I think we're in two different leagues here, Larry. This is America, man! I mean, we're talking about a piece of property that's all but condemned, for heaven's sake. We're talking about pond water I wouldn't wash my tires in. I hate to say this, Larry, but you're not showing your usual business sense. Nobody, I mean nobody, is ever going to pay you that kind of money for what you've got to offer."

Larry drew a breath, ran his fingers through his hair. He looked down at his cowboy boots. "Okay," he said. "Final offer. Seventy-five grand. And that's rock bottom."

"Sixty-five."

"Seventy."

Sny appeared thoughtful. He turned and blew a puff of cigar smoke at the ceiling. Then he turned back to Larry and smiled. "What the hell? Between partners. Seventy grand it is." He took a checkbook and pen from his bathrobe pocket and sat down to write.

"Whoops," Larry said. "Can't take a check, Rutus. No, no. I said cash. It's got to be cash."

Sny let out a long sigh. He shook his head. "Can't do it, then. Not for seventy. Sorry." He stood and walked to the end of the vestibule, then said, "If we're talking cash, I'm afraid sixty is my top dollar."

Larry said, "Sixty thousand dollars?"

"Right."

"Cash on the barrelhead?"

"Right."

"But you don't have that kind of cash handy, do you? I mean, just layin' around?"

Sny took a long puff on his cigar. He raised an eyebrow. "Final offer," he warned.

"I'll take it," Larry said. He stood to shake Sny's hand.

But Sny turned away, holding Larry's title over his shoulder.

"Ah, but you see, it's still not yours to sell, is it, Mr. Jones? Your title states clearly that you don't come into possession of the property until you're married. Until tomorrow. Remember?"

Larry smacked his forehead. "That's right," he hissed. He looked at Sny and shrugged. "What can I say, Rutus? It's as good as mine. I mean the relatives are on their way for the wedding. No problem."

Sny shook his head. "That, my friend, would be what I call bad business sense, you know what I mean? No sir, you come back here tomorrow when you're legal, so to speak, and I'll pay you your cash—fifty thousand, wasn't it?"

"Sixty," Larry said.

"Sixty." Sny laughed. "My mistake. You know, you're quite a horse trader, Larry. Quite a businessman." He went to a small mahogany end table beside a wicker couch; he opened a drawer and took out a piece of paper. He handed the paper to Larry. It read:

> I, Susan S. Mason, on this date _____, do hereby transfer my interest in the property known as Camp Wind In The Pines, on the River Road, in Norwood, Maine, to Lawrence A. Jones.

Sny said, "Take this with you. It's a title transfer, Larry. Get the little woman to sign her share over to you, see? Then you'll have her share, I'll have your share, and it's goodbye, Carl Mason. Sky's the limit, partner, hear me?"

Larry nodded. But he was distracted. The document was already prepared. Had Sny really known he was coming?

Sny chuckled again. "I can read your mind, Larry. Believe me, it was just a matter of time before you came to me." He opened the door for Larry and handed him his cowboy hat. "Now I can't stress enough how important it is that she turn that share over to you. And right away, too."

"Right," Larry said, stepping outside.

"Let me put it this way. I can't have Carl Mason and his daughter as business partners, can I, Larry? I need a man that thinks like I do. I need a man with this." He pointed to his head. "Good old American Business Sense. Capisce?"

Larry put his cowboy hat on his head. He pointed a finger at Sny and said, "Consider it done."

. . .

Susie and Larry celebrated on their new king-size vibrating water-bed, and when they were through, Larry said, reflectively, "I've been having second thoughts about this wedding—"

Susie jumped up. "Oh, sure!" she said. "Everyone's gonna be here tomorrow, that's all. My cousin Amy from Fort Lauderdale, and my aunt and uncle, and my grandparents—"

"But—"

"Hey!" she snapped, kneeling over him so that her breasts swung like sandbags above his face. "Don't you mess this up!"

Larry got off the bed. "It's just that, well, maybe you're not ready for the responsibilities of marriage," he said. Her lower jaw dropped and protruded viciously, but he went on before she could speak. "Look," he said, "you don't even trust me." His voice filled with hurt. "I mean, you actually thought I was fooling around with, uh . . . what's-her-name."

"Ruth?"

"No, the other one . . . uh, Angel. You thought I was fooling around with her. You know, love and marriage are built on trust—not suspicion. Trust and faith."

She glared at him. "I trust you," she shot back defensively, although she wondered why she had said it at all.

"You call that trust?" He was indignant now, whining.

"I said I was sorry."

"You did? Funny, I didn't hear you."

"Well, I am."

"What?"

She sighed. "I'm sorry, okay?"

"You're sorry? Does that mean it won't happen all over again? You think sorry fixes the hurt I feel? The pain?" He walked ponderously across the room. "I think we should have some way of really proving our trust in each other. You know, something on paper."

"We're getting a marriage license," she offered.

"No, no," he said. "I mean something more. Something that would really prove your love for me. Like in the old days, when a woman's family would give the groom farm animals, money, property. Ever hear of that? Now that's what I'd call trust." Susie looked at him suspiciously. He continued. "Let's take an example here.

What if you were to, say, sign over your share of Wind In The Pines to me? I mean, just as a gesture."

Susie was dumbfounded. She picked up her clothes and slowly began putting them on. But as she dressed, her confusion turned to rage. "That's it, huh? You want my share of the campground."

"Well, only as a gesture—"

She went to the door, wheeled around, and shot him the finger. "There's your gesture," she spat. "You friggin' best not frig this wedding up or I'll be down in Fort Lauderdale sellin' hot dogs so fast it'll make your friggin' head spin!"

Carl walked down into the campground, moving from site to site, cordially announcing, "Quiet time, folks. Let's keep it down now." When he got the last radio turned off, he walked down to the shore where a group of older folks were gathered by a fire singing World War II songs in drunken harmony: "There'll be bluebirds over the white cliffs of Dover . . ." Their campfire was raging, its flames leaping above the nearby tents and trailers, while silhouetted men and women, moving as if in a jungle line, fed the fire with brush, branches, and deadwood foraged from along the ridge-path. Carl said, "Excuse me, folks, but it's after eleven-thirty—quiet time here at Wind In the Pines. Kids have got to get their sleep, you know."

A familiar figure rose. It was Mr. Rogers. "Ladies and gentlemen," he began, "I would like to introduce you to our host for this evening, the proprietor of Camp Wind In The Pines, the venerable Mr. Carl Mason."

"Quiet time," Carl said again. "Let's just hold it down, okay?"

One of the men took Carl's hand and pumped it. Then another, and another, all introducing themselves and their hometowns, saying things like, "Great job here, Carl," and, "Best of luck to you, Carl," and, "Never thought it was possible."

Then a pink-cheeked man rose unsteadily from the group. He had white Thomas Edison hair and a smile of such intensity that his eyes became glistening black slits behind his bifocals. He sang out, "What do you say, you old farts? Let's hear it for this guy!" The small crowd began applauding.

"Quiet time," Carl repeated. "Let's hold it down, folks."

"Toast to Mr. Mason," the pink-cheeked man said. "Hip, hip—"

"No, don't."

"Hooray!" they all yelled.

"Quiet time," Carl said more firmly. "That's enough now."

"Hip, hip—"

"Hooray!"

"Hip, hip—"

"Shut the hell up, I said!"

They all stopped and stared, each one wobbling a bit, no one knowing quite what to say. Meanwhile, the wood line continued so that the fire roared behind Carl like a blast furnace, licking the stars with flames.

"Look," he said, "it's after eleven-thirty now, and we've really got to keep it down."

"No problem, Carl."

"Will do."

Carl smiled. "Good. Thanks a lot, folks. Good to see you all here, by the way." He turned to leave and then turned back again, speaking to the man feeding the fire. "Oh, and about that fire—" The man stood wide-legged, unsteadily draining a glass which contained nearly a dozen lime wedges. "Why not let it burn down now? There are buildings around, you know what I mean?"

"I hear you, friend," the man said, tossing on another log.

"Excuse me," someone said.

Carl turned around. A young couple stood behind him, illuminated orange in the blaze of the fire. They were dressed in khaki. The man wore round glasses. They looked to Carl like environmentalists. Nevertheless he remained polite. "What," he said neutrally.

"There's a poodle running around here, dragging a half-eaten raccoon by a leather leash. We think the raccoon was somebody's pet because of the leash. Anyway, we tried to get it away from the dog, but he wouldn't let us near it."

The girl said, "We think the dog's wild."

"A wild poodle," Carl said thoughtfully, knowing full well it was Maurice—he had broken his chain again. "Okay, thank you," he said. "I'll call *National Geographic.*"

He went back to the store and found a heavy, ten-foot tow chain in the back, and he brought it to Angel. "Your dog's loose again," he said to her. "Get him back here and put this around his neck. 'Cause if he gets loose again, I'm gonna have Root take care of him."

"You wouldn't dare," she said.

He fashioned his hand into a pistol and pointed it at the ground. "Bang," he said. "Get that dog back here in five minutes or it's au revoir, Maurice. Good night now," he said lightly, walking away.

The volume of the campground was rising again. As Carl walked back through his backyard, he cupped his hands around his mouth and hollered angrily, "Quiet time!" His own volume brought him relief.

"Quiet!" someone else yelled. There followed a dark, scattered cheer.

"My gosh, where have you been?" Shirley said when Carl came in. She was in her pink robe, watching Johnny Carson and polishing her nails. Her hair was in curlers.

"How is she?" Carl asked.

"The same. She told me to drop dead."

He walked down the hall, saw the line of light from under Susie's door. He wanted to talk to her. He felt it was his fatherly privilege on the night before her wedding. But he didn't know what to say. So he went back to the kitchen and poured himself two shots of bourbon and drank them down. Then he returned to Susie's room and knocked softly.

"What." It was more a statement than an invitation to enter.

"Can I come in?" he asked.

"Knock yourself out," she answered, meaning, "Yes."

He walked in and found her lying on her bed, staring at the ceiling. "They're some noisy out there tonight," he said, trying to ease the tension, but her eyes never left the ceiling.

"Sons-uh-bitches," she said dreamily.

He had never heard her curse before, and in a way he felt proud at how naturally the words flowed from her mouth. Even so, he told her, "Don't let your mother hear you talking that way."

He sat down next to her and rubbed the back of his neck, wondering how to begin. He wanted to tell her how much he loved her and how much he regretted her growing up so fast. But there was something else. What he really wanted to tell her was that he didn't want her marrying this fortune hunter, Larry Jones. That the very idea of having him as a partner and son-in-law for the rest of his life was sheer torture. But he would not say that. No, he would not say that to her. Because she loved Larry Jones. And he would do nothing to mar her happiness.

He could tell by the redness around her eyes and the shards of glass in the corner that something had made her unhappy. "Did you see Larry tonight?" he asked.

"Mm."

"Everything okay?"

"I guess." Susie wanted to tell her father how much she loved him, and how she was frightened to leave his care. She wanted to tell him that she would go through with the wedding only so he wouldn't lose Wind In The Pines. But she knew if she said that, he'd call the wedding off right then and there—and then he would lose the Camp.

"Daddy?" she said finally.

"Mmm?"

"When did you first know that you loved Ma?"

Carl paused. "What do you mean, honey?"

"I mean, how are you supposed to know if it's the real thing?"

"I don't know," he said. "I guess it just feels right. When I married your mother, well, that was it for me. There was just nothing else I wanted to do. I still had my friends—Bert and Jimmy and the guys—but I just couldn't see any other life for myself other than with Shirl—your mother."

"Yeah, but what about love?"

"I don't know." He squeezed the bridge of his nose. "I think I probably love your mother more now than I ever did." Just for an instant he pictured Shirley as she was years ago, standing naked one morning in the gritty sunlight of their third-floor attic apartment, her body slender and taut. "I guess the years do that," he said softly.

She moved her head onto his lap. "But did you know you loved her when you married her? I mean, did you love her the same way you love your car, or the Camp, or the way you love me?"

"I never," he began, then cleared his throat and continued in a low, hollow voice, the kind of voice that used to put her to sleep, "I never loved . . . or dreamed it was possible to love anybody as much as I've loved you." He coughed and wiped his nose. "I love you so much," he said, "sometimes it kills me." He thought again of Larry Jones.

"Daddy," she said, "I'm scared."

He felt a tear on his hand. He looked down at her. "You want me to call it off?"

"No . . . not unless you want to call it off. Do you?"

"Not if you love him, honey. I'd never interfere. Do you? Do you love him?"

She closed her eyes in thought now, seeing her future as a large, clumsy, formless hulk balancing on the question, and she knew his own future was poised on the same question. In the silence of the moment they could hear the strains of The Marines' Hymn coming from the shore. "Yes," she said with a sigh of relief, feeling suddenly like she really did love Larry. She pulled herself up and kissed Carl on the cheek. "But not as much as I love you," she said.

Now the singing came through her window louder: ". . . First to fight our country's battles, On the land and on the sea. . . ." Carl's stomach contracted like a fist. "Everything'll turn out fine," he said, rising and turning out her light. "Now get a good night's sleep."

He went back to the kitchen and looked out the window at his campground. The bonfire at the shore had mushroomed so it filled the entire window, and he could see the long line of wood gatherers now marching as they sang: ". . . Over hill, over dale, we will hit the dusty trail. . . ."

He took three full swallows of bourbon and then grabbed his megaphone from under the sink. He stepped onto his porch and shouted through it: "Quiet time! Now shut up down there and put that fire out!"

"Shut up yourself, you goddamn jerk!" a woman shouted drunkenly from the shore. Carl recognized her voice—Gunnar's mother. She was in line with the wood gatherers. He started down there, watching four elderly men in underwear march the length of the dock and then goose-step off the broken diving board into the water.

"Whoooop!" they cried upon surfacing.

"Get outta there!" Carl yelled on the run. "Get out of that pond!"

Others were marching in place on the picnic table—Mr. Rogers among them: ". . . For it's hi, hi, hee, in the field artillery, Shout out your numbers loud and strong—"

"Shut up!" Carl roared. "It's quiet time!"

Now others in the campground joined in the song—"Two, three, four . . ."

"Whooo!" Gunnar's mother yelled. She was belly-dancing on the dock.

Carl stepped onto the dock and walked past her. "Hey!" He shouted at the four men in the water. "Out of the pond, all of you. Now!"

"Oh, booo!" Gunnar's mother said. "Ya fuckin' party pooper."

"And you—watch your mouth!"

"C'mon, Carl," one of the swimmers said. "We're just blowin' off a little steam."

The pink-faced older man hoisted himself up on the dock, his bifocals dripping pond water. He stood wobbly, grinning so hard his eyes squinted fire. He crouched, wide-legged like a wrestler, and moved toward Carl. "C'mon, you old fart," he laughed. "You're going in, too." He wrapped his arms around Carl.

"The hell I am," Carl said, dropping out of the man's grasp and throwing a right uppercut to the man's jaw, snapping his head back so that his glasses flew in the air. The man staggered back to the edge of the dock, still holding his arms as if they were wrapped around something, and dropped into the pond.

Now Gunnar's mother became more vocal. "You fuckin' bully," she snarled, wobbling toward Carl. "Who the Christ do you think you are, King Shit on Turd Island? You got no goddamn right punchin' an old man." She came so close to Carl that her beery breath blew in his face.

He reached out and covered her mouth with his hand and shoved her backward into the water.

She came up sputtering: "I'll fix your friggin' ass, mister," she promised. "You'll regret the goddamned day you ever touched this woman!"

Carl was not intimidated. He looked down at her and smiled warmly. "Nice talk," he said.

Part
Four

37

Opening Day

Carl folded his arms and squinted out his kitchen window into the rising sun. The morning was bright, blue, and already warm. Wind In The Pines was overfull—it looked to Carl like pictures he'd seen of refugee camps. By the crowd of people milling aimlessly along the shore, and the pack of boats wedged together there, it appeared these were refugees from somewhere across the pond. There were two long lines of them at each side of the lavatory, holding towels, toothbrushes, and soap. Some rocked anxiously from leg to leg. They didn't look happy about having to wait. Screw 'em.

Then Larry marched past, heading for the pavilion area, dressed in his red Camp Uniform. He was carrying the megaphone, looking businesslike. "Busy day," he called, seeing Carl in the window.

Carl stepped out onto his porch and followed Larry skeptically with his eyes. He flexed the stiffness from his right hand, dimly recalling the two people he had punched the day before, dimly wishing one of them had been Larry Jones. Morning sounds rose from all around—the bright clanging of metal coffeepots and breakfast utensils, the chattering of birds and children, the easy laughter of men and women, the mechanics of fishing reels. . . .

A sudden metallic cry pierced the air: "Good morning, fishermen!" At once the mob of campers began pouring into the pavilion area from every corner of the campground, overrunning its boundaries, crushing Carl's neat rectangle of sapling hedges. "Attention campers," Larry announced to the pitching sea of heads— but his words were drowned out by the excited din of the mob.

"Attention!" He turned the volume knob up and the horn squealed horribly, silencing them. "Thank you."

"As you know, today is the first annual Wind In The Pines Fishing Contest, sponsored by yours truly, your host, L.A. Jones."

Applause.

"Thank you. We hope your stay at Camp Wind In The Pines is a pleasant one, and we hope you will take advantage of our fine Camp Store and new bathroom facilities. And don't forget, tomorrow— especially for the kids—we're going to have a wild animal show up there in our all-new Indian Village, with an animal you just won't believe. And also, in the near future—"

"Let's fish!" someone shouted.

"—adult entertainment.

"Okay. Now for the fishing contest. The official fishing will get under way at eight o'clock and end at five o'clock. And the man that catches—"

"Ahem," a woman coughed pointedly.

Larry smiled. ". . . or girl—that catches the biggest fish will win first prize—five thousand Wind In The Pines dollars."

"What's the biggest?," someone yelled from the back. "The longest or the heaviest?"

Larry chuckled as if to say, What's the difference, you're not gonna catch anything anyway. "Whatever," he answered.

"Well, what is it?" the crowd demanded.

"Heaviest," Larry said. He reached into his pocket and withdrew a hundred-dollar bill. "Here it is, folks. Who's gonna be the lucky son-of-a-gun that takes fifty of these home?"

The crowd cheered.

"Okay," he said, throwing his fist into the air. "Go get 'em!"

In minutes the pond was crawling with boats, and the shore buzzing with anglers. Lines crossed, bobbers and worms caught overhanging tree limbs, and angry words filled the air. A motorboat carrying four men from the cotton plant struck the ridge outcropping and sank, motor first. Undeterred, the men climbed onto the outcropping and continued to fish from there. By ten o'clock the store was once again depleted of its beer and wine, and Harvey was sent to Bluffton in the Big Truck to get more.

Meanwhile, up on the ridge, Larry made a desperate appeal to Nighthawk.

"C'mon, man, we're brothers," he beseeched, holding up a large, motley Indian headdress, replete with brightly dyed gull feathers, turquoise beads, and leather straps. A pale suede tunic and trousers lined with fringe lay on a stone at his feet. "You've been a brave too long, man. It's time someone called you 'Chief.' I mean, how can you refuse? Just try it on. I guarantee you'll love it. Just think of those chicks, those squaws. Huh? When they see you in that cage snapping your whip at that monster, I mean, hey, talk about your horny Indian maids, man. What do you say, baby?"

Nighthawk turned a dour eye on Larry, then headed for the woods.

"Okay, we won't turn your wigwam into a gift shop. Not this weekend anyway. But there's one hell of a profit potential here. Think about it."

Nighthawk kept walking.

"Hey, Kimosabe, White Man need help, you know what I'm sayin' to you?"

Nighthawk spun around, an arrow notched in his bow. He pulled the bowstring back and aimed at Larry's stomach.

"Okay, okay. Let's talk money then. Wampum. A thousand dollars for the wigwam and fifty bucks a performance for you."

Nighthawk stretched the bow further.

"All right, you name it. What do you want?"

The Indian said two words. "You. Leave."

"Leave?" Larry said. "What about the kids? What are they gonna think?"

Nighthawk fired the arrow into a birch tree beside Larry. But the entrepreneur was not intimidated. He raised his hands in mock surrender and continued walking toward the Indian. "Just one day, then; Chief. Just tomorrow. All I'm asking you to do is just step into that cage for five minutes. That's all. Two hundred bucks for five minutes."

Nighthawk stared at him. He tried to incinerate Larry with his eyes. Then he dropped his bow and reached for Larry's throat.

"Okayokayokay," Larry said, dancing back. "No show, right? Is that what you're trying to tell me? No show? Okay. All you have to do is tell me, you know? I'm not a mind reader." He walked away, calling over his shoulder, "I'll tell the kids—no show."

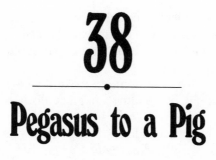

38

Pegasus to a Pig

Susie looked through her veil at the mirror. "This really eats," she said. "I'm so fat."

Shirley disagreed with a maternal smile. "That's not fatness, dear," she said. "That's fullness. The Mason women are all wide in the hip."

"Oh, bull. And this neckline," Susie complained. "It's way too high." She tugged at it until her breasts bulged half out of the gown.

Shirley put her hands on her hips, mock scolding: "Well, you're not a movie star, you know. You're a bride."

"Oh, stuff it."

"Stuff it yourself."

Meanwhile, outside in the pavilion area, Carl and Harvey were silently arranging chairs for the ceremony, and Shirley's sister Grace, just in from Illinois, was surrounding the area with long, sagging lines of pink crepe paper stapled from tree to tree. Her daughters Bethany and Clara Belle were stapling baby-blue paper tablecloths to a dozen tables borrowed from the Lions Club.

Shirley opened the front door and said, "Oh, girls, it looks so nice."

"Thank you," Carl teased.

"Honey," Shirley said to him, "shouldn't you have Jean start on the sandwiches?"

"Good idea," he said. "She just has to fill the rolls with ham salad, right?"

"And she has to make the punch."

"I'll make the punch," he said.

"I don't know if I trust you," Shirley said good-naturedly. "Please, Carl, don't make it too strong. My mother's going to be here."

And that's just why I'm going to make it strong, he thought to himself. He'd stashed three quarts of grain alcohol for just such an occasion.

Susie called out the window, "Is Amy here yet?" Amy was her favorite cousin. Until adolescence, when her family abruptly moved to Fort Lauderdale, she had been Susie's closest friend and confidante. And though they hadn't seen one another since, Amy, in her letters, had promised Susie a job whenever she wanted, peddling hot dogs from a cart on the beach.

"I haven't seen her," Shirley said. "But I'm sure she's on her way."

"What about the band?"

"Who's that, now," Carl asked, "Wop and the Guineas?"

"Tony and the Hitmen!" Susie yelled. "And don't make fun of them. They're great."

"Oh, yeah. Tony and the—no, wait," he teased. "I canceled them. Bobby Lee Lewis and the Truetones are coming instead."

"Daddy!"

"They all love Bobby Lee down at the lodge, dear," Shirley said to her. "Everybody says—"

"Oh, bite," Susie said. "It's *my* wedding."

Zippy awoke at noon from a troubling nightmare. He had dreamed he was a contestant on the old TV show "Beat the Clock," and had been given sixty seconds to put four objects into a nylon mesh crib. But there was one stipulation. (The audience groaned.) The objects were all weightless! (The audience howled.) Bud Collier wound the large time-clock, and the second indicators lit up along its rim—sixty of them. Bud Collier said, "Ready . . . begin!"

The curtain opened, and Zippy began. The first object was Jimi Hendrix. He was floating in air, playing "Purple Haze" on a Day-Glo Stratocaster. Zippy easily snatched him out of the air by his boot and set him inside the crib, wrapping his guitar cord around the crib so he wouldn't float away. The audience applauded. Then he turned and ran for the next object, a stereo system—the sleekest, most powerful, most state-of-the-art system ever invented. It eluded him at first, but he deftly cornered it and brought that, too, back to the crib. But something had happened to Jimi Hendrix—he had turned into a toaster-oven. And suddenly the stereo system turned into a washing machine in his arms, pitted and rusty. The audience roared with delight.

Only twenty seconds to go—no time to ponder. The third object was Ruth, who floated gracefully above his head, teasing. He reached up for her and missed on her first pass, but he stood on the crib and snared her the second time around. Tick. Tick. Tick . . .

The last object was a pegasus, a glowing white stallion that was shrouded by its own brilliance. The winged horse swooped down, and Zippy leaped for it, but the pegasus whinnied and easily soared away. Five seconds. Zippy ran to the side of the stage. He climbed the curtain rope and crossed hand over hand along the bank of lights above the stage. Two seconds. Then, just as the pegasus flew by, Zippy dropped down onto its back and steered it into the crib. The audience rose and cheered as one. The buzzer sounded. And suddenly the audience fell into raucous laughter. Because the glowing white pegasus had changed into a pig—a squealing, mud-caked hog—and the Ruth he had captured had become a slouched, coffee-stained, pregnant woman with tired eyes and children hanging on her legs.

Zippy popped awake with an overbearing feeling that life on Earth was homely and mundane and worse, that there was no escape ever. He tried to will away the ominous feeling—he jumped up and splashed cold water on his face, hoping to wash it away. But it lingered. He rolled a joint, then went to the medicine cabinet for aspirin. Or something stronger.

Down on the pond tempers were rising. But the fish weren't. There had been a double capsizing earlier in the day, and an ensuing oar fight, in which one laughing teenager with a dark, bloody gash on the side of his head was helped ashore, and another was driven to the hospital with a broken finger. A small gang of teenagers from Bluffton came in retaliation for their friend with the broken finger and pelted a boatload of Norwood teenagers with rocks. When one of the rocks strayed and struck a boat full of older men, both boatloads came ashore to do battle. It was a rollicking donnybrook that lasted nearly a half hour, with three other boatloads of drunken anglers taking a break from the contest to join in.

Carl's brother Don arrived during the melee, with his wife Marilyn and their daughter—Susie's favorite cousin—Amy. Amy ran inside to help Susie with her hair, while Marilyn got the family luggage squared away in the guest room. Don helped Carl prepare the wedding drink: Waterloo Punch—a communal potion Carl had discovered in the army—a deadly mixture of squeezed citrus fruits, juices, gin, vodka, and grain alcohol. Testing its bite, they both got tipsy.

Larry remembered his best man a half hour before the ceremony. He ran over to Zippy's dressed in his blue swirled tuxedo and found his twin brother semiconscious, adorned in his cowboy finery, sitting in a lotus position on the kitchen floor.

"Hey, brother," Larry said, wiping perspiration from his forehead, "I want you to be my best man. I rented a tux for you."

Zippy looked up slowly. His left eye was a purple, puffy slit. "Oh, man, I can't do that. I've got to contact the cowboys."

Larry ignored him. "Just hurry up. Put the tux on and come on." When Zippy still didn't move, Larry became excited. "Move, brother, move!"

Zippy looked annoyed. "I am moving," he said, believing that he was.

Larry looked suspiciously at him. "What's with you?"

"I dropped acid an hour ago, and I'm just getting off," Zippy said. "Wanna hit?"

"You know I don't take that stuff," Larry said, pacing. "Where's Ruth?"

"Changing," Zippy answered. Then he laughed weakly. "Her corporeal body is off in her secret place, where her spiritual body is

searching for her true . . . changing . . . true . . . changing . . .
true . . . changing—infinite identity. Now, can you dig that?"

"Yeah, real deep, brother. Now listen, I mean it, try to understand me—"

"I understand. But I'm going to be detained. I've got to contact
the cowboys. I have to find out if they use guns up there. Because if
they do, then this boy's staying put."

"Yeah, swell. Here—put this tuxedo on."

"It's on, man. I'm in my tuxedo."

"No, you're not. You're in your cowboy outfit," Larry said. "*I'm*
in my tuxedo."

"Well." Zippy took a deep, deep breath. He watched his chest
with amazement as it expanded. "Wow!" he breathed, releasing the
air. "Okay, man, I'll come with you, but I'm going to wear my own
skin. 'Cause I don't want to be mistaken for you. Dig? Imagine if
they picked you up instead of me? Matter and anti-matter, dig? . . .
and they're cousins," he sang, "and they're two of a kind." He
laughed slyly then, somehow keeping his teeth tightly clenched as
he did.

Larry pulled him to his feet and walked him into the sunlight.
"Brother, you've got to straighten up for this wedding."

"Listen, I can be as straight as a circle." It was a statement fraught
with meaning. And to prove his point, Zippy stood and stiffly led his
brother to the ceremony. As they approached the pavilion area,
Zippy searched the sky. "Any one of those could be the ship," he
said.

Larry looked up. There wasn't a cloud to be seen. The sky was as
empty as Norwood Pond.

39

The Wedding

Larry stood beside the young minister, arms folded, his head tilted in a semicasual pose, looking more like an *Esquire* model than a groom. Zippy, beside him, was no less dapper in his cowboy duds, though his downcast eyes and slouching posture suggested mourning. He was breathing loudly through his mouth, lost in the swirls of his sharkskin boots. Larry hoped he wouldn't speak.

Then the band started. Larry had told them it was a hip wedding, to crank it, so they attacked the wedding march with a vengeance—in this case, a Tony and the Hitmen original entitled "Love Rockets." The introduction was a riveting rimshot on the snare drum, with Tony leaping into a visceral crouch, shouting, "Five, four, three, two, one . . ."

Carl and Susie walked arm in arm out the kitchen door and down the porch steps. She had lowered the top of her gown with safety pins, and now her breasts shone voluptuously in the hot sunlight. She looked ahead at Larry. He was fine and handsome, and she was proud that her relatives, particularly Amy, could see the man who had fallen in love with her. She squeezed her father's arm, and he squeezed back. Then he let go and did a two-step to the loud music, his good-natured way of mocking it. Susie's face flushed. She grabbed his arm and locked it with her elbow.

The ceremony was short and understated as Larry had requested, and it went smoothly until the minister asked Zippy for the rings. At that point Zippy just stared vacantly at him and repeated the word: "Riiings." Larry remembered that he hadn't given the rings to

Zippy—they were still in his pocket. He took them out and handed them to his brother, who put them up to his eyes and peered through them at the sky, laughing, sharing his good humor.

Carl elbowed Larry. "Take the rings," he said in a low voice.

But Larry was distracted. A small, yellow-haired boy was standing just outside the pavilion area, holding up a fishing rod. Carl saw the boy, too. Gunnar. From the end of his fishing rod a yellow perch dangled, no more than four inches long, pale and frosty-eyed. Gunnar's mother stood behind her son in a pink, sleeveless tee-shirt and flowered orange shorts, a satisfied, vengeful smile on her face.

Larry's lungs sucked air. In his imagination, it was the scant remains of his fortune dangling from the line. Carl nudged him and whispered, "Another brainstorm bites the dust, huh?"

"No way," Larry whispered back. "They caught that fish somewhere else. I saw 'em drive in just a while ago."

"So what are you gonna do about it? Disqualify 'em? You gonna announce that all the fish in the pond are dead?" He shook his head in disgust.

The minister cleared his throat for attention. Larry glared at Gunnar. Carl glared at Gunnar's mother. The ceremony continued without further incident, and when the bride and groom were finally wed, Susie kissed Larry a long tongue kiss, grinding her pelvis slowly against him.

"It's party time!" Tony and the Hitmen shrieked, winding into another of their hits. "We're Gonna Rock, Rock, Rock." The guests, all friends and relatives of the Masons, gathered around Susie with hugs, kisses, and wishes of good fortune, while Larry walked over to Gunnar and patted his head.

"Nope," he said to the boy, "too small. You might as well throw that little guy back. Or just give it to me and I'll take care of it for you."

"Too small, my ass!" his mother barked.

Larry shrugged. "Well, I just figured there'll be lots bigger—"

She stuck a finger in Larry's face. "I ain't seen a fish caught in this pond in over a week—includin' today. Exceptin' this one that little Gunnar caught, of course." She poked her finger into her son's back. "You got the winner so far, sunshine, and ain't nobody's takin'

it away from you." She leered at Larry. She twisted the hook out of
the perch's lip and dropped the dead fish into her shorts pocket.
"We'll be back in an hour for our prize money," she announced,
turning on her heel and leading the boy away.

Larry retreated quietly to the tub of Waterloo Punch. The color
was gone from his face. He dipped a glass in and took a long drink.
Must think. Must concentrate.

Just then Harvey and Jean Duckoff appeared beside him. "So,
L.A.," Harvey said, "how's married life? Did you open our present
yet?"

"Did you?" Jean asked.

"Nope, he didn't," said Harvey, "'cause I kin still see it on the
table. Go get it, tubby."

Jean brought the gift to Larry and put it in his arms. "Open it
now," she said, clapping her hands.

Larry wanted to tell them he was too busy, but he knew they
would simply stand around pestering him, so he tore the wrapping
paper off and opened the box. And then he stared at the gift perplex-
edly. It was an avocado-green rubber bucket with a digital watchface
on its lid. "What is it?" he asked.

"You tell him," Jean said.

"It's a Garbage Remind-all, just like it says," Harvey said.

"Garbage Remind-all?"

"Yeah," Jean said. "A pig bucket."

"With a digital thing on it—like my watch."

"It tells you what day it is."

"Yeah, so's you don't forget to empty the garbage. You set the
alarm and it beeps."

"Yeah, then the swill don't get rotten."

"And stink."

"Yeah."

Larry looked up. His eyes shone. "That's it!" he said. He set his
glass down and grabbed Harvey by the arm. "Come on, Harvey,
let's find some shovels. We've got work to do."

After a few more Tony and the Hitmen songs, once everybody
had taken time to mingle and have a drink or two of Waterloo

Punch, Tony asked everybody to rise. He said into the microphone: "Now it's time for the best man, Mr. Zippy Jones, to toast the happy newlyweds." He looked at Zippy and shook his head. "Folks, it's tough to tell who's the groom and who's the best man here—watch out tonight, Susie." The guests laughed and applauded their delight. "Okay, my friend Zippy Jones. What have you got to say?"

Zippy stood dumbly, still considering the implications of Tony's opening remarks: "Now it's time . . ."

Time.

Time, he thought, is only relative, as Einstein had proved. Time and distance: the fourth dimension. Everything that had ever happened in the past, and everything that was bound to happen in the future, was going on at this very instant, only on different planes. A revelation hit him: That explains déjà vu! It's just a split second when you jump planes and glimpse what is about to happen, so when it actually does happen, it seems like you've experienced it already. Yeah. "Far fucking out," he breathed.

A moment of silence passed. The guests looked at each other, buzzing. What did he say? I think he said, Far effing out. Far effing out? That's what I heard.

"Okay," Tony said into the PA system. "'Far out.' Thank you, Zippy Jones. Short and sweet, ladies and gentlemen, and to the point. So now, to the bride and groom, folks, in the words of the immortal Zippy Jones, 'Far out.'" The guests raised their cups of Waterloo Punch and drank. "But," Tony announced, seeing Susie standing alone, "where is the groom?"

The stench of the pit was so strong, so overwhelmingly rank, that Harvey had to stop digging repeatedly and run upwind to get some good air. Once he didn't make it to the good air. He vomited, and Larry compensated him with a ten-dollar bill, with the promise of another ten dollars on completion of his duties. Even the wedding guests, upwind and a hundred yards away, began complaining of the sickening wafts and suggested to Carl that a septic line had probably ruptured. Carl promised to check it out, but he was becoming too drunk to care. He'd smelled worse things, he told them.

The thousands of fish in the pit had, for the most part, melded together into a sickening, glistening black ooze.

"Pick through 'em," Larry said. "There's gotta be a good one in there somewhere."

"Aww," Harvey complained. "You pick through 'em."

"C'mon, Harve, look at me. I'm in a rented tuxedo here. Look at my shoes. Look at my pants."

"So? You pick through 'em. I ain't gettin' in there no more."

Larry put his hands on his hips. "Oh, you're not, huh? Okay, but I'll tell you one thing. That's the attitude that's ruinin' this country, Harvey. Guys like you, sayin', 'Let the other guy do it.' That's what's driving America to her knees. Guys like you."

Harvey stared at him. He wiped his lip on his sleeve.

Larry continued. "You don't like America, do you, Harvey?"

Harvey scowled. He brooded. Then he said, "You're talkin' America, and I'm talkin' stinkin' fish: two different things."

"I'm sorry, but that's where you're wrong," Larry said, but Harvey had already dropped his shovel and begun walking away. "Okay, okay, thanks for nothin', Harve. God bless America, right?" Larry waded into the quagmire and sank to his knees. "But it'll be your fish."

"What do you mean, 'my fish'?"

"That's right."

Susie lifted her wedding gown up to her waist and flapped her eyes. "Come here, handsome," she said seductively, even as Larry's rank odor reached her nose. He pulled off his tuxedo trousers, but turned away from her to put on his red Wind In The Pines shorts.

"Can't right now," he said, wagging a finger at her. "Business before pleasure." He snatched a folded-up piece of notepad paper from the top of his bureau and hurried out the door. Then, just as quickly, he returned, saying, "Honey, did you get a chance to look at that little title-transfer business we talked about last night? I left the paper right there on your vanity." He picked it up and showed it to her. "I think it would be, well, a beautiful thing if you'd sign it for me." He kissed her and pressed the paper into her hand. "Think about it," he said, hurrying out. He drove to Rutus Sny's house in his blue swirled tuxedo top and his red Wind In The Pines shorts, reeking.

Sny conducted their brief business outside by the pool, so that he was at once upwind from Larry and concealed from Tiffany by a well-placed hedgerow. He said to his junior partner, "So you're finally legal—did you get her to sign?"

"Not yet, Rutus, but she will tonight—guaran-goddamn-teed." He made a fist and grinned slyly. "Or no honeymoon."

"Atta boy," Sny said. "I'm counting on you, now." He reached into the pocket of his golf bag and handed Larry two stacks of bills: sixty thousand dollars in twenties, fifties, and hundreds. In return, Larry gave him the notepad paper he had gotten two weeks earlier from Carl Mason.

As Larry counted the money, Sny wrote on the title with a ball-point pen. "Short and sweet, just the way I like it," Sny said when they were done.

"Short and sweet," Larry agreed.

Sny pointed to the notepad paper. "You sign there," he said. "It's a standard title transfer, Larry. You're just transferring your share of Wind In The Pines to me for X amount of money—I've altered the figure, Larry, to save you some tax dollars. And I've also dated the agreement—that is, if you don't mind—for the twenty-seventh— day after tomorrow—the day when we drop the bomb on Mason. I think it will be an appropriate day to officially begin our partnership. Don't you?"

"I couldn't agree more, Rutus," Larry said, signing the paper.

The partners walked down the sidewalk to the Mercedes, where Larry opened his trunk and slipped the wads of money into his suitcase.

"You're a cash man, right after my own heart," Sny said. "The less the banks make, the less Uncle Sam'll take. Right?"

Larry climbed into the car and started it. "Tricks of the trade," he said with a wink. Rutus Sny laughed at that. He laughed so hard and so long, he was still chuckling when Larry drove down the long, straight, canopied road and out of sight.

Fifteen minutes later Larry strode onto the dock, smiling confidently. He lifted the megaphone to his lips and announced: "Attention! Attention! Worms up! All fishermen to the dock. The contest is officially over!"

The ensuing crush of anglers that swarmed into the pavilion area wasn't happy. By now, word of the pond's fishlessness had spread. "Attention, please," Larry said into the megaphone, stepping up onto a folding chair. But the angry murmur only swelled. "Wait, wait," Larry said finally. "What's this I hear? Somebody said a word I don't like. I heard somebody say the word 'fix.'"

"Yeah!" the mob yelled at once. "Fix!"

Larry held up his hand. "Not so fast," he said confidently. "Not so fast. There's something here I think you should all see." He announced: "Would all the lucky anglers please step forward?"

The mob parted and heads turned as Gunnar pushed through, greedily clutching his four-inch perch.

"Okay!" Larry announced, holding the tiny fish high in the air with a finger and thumb through its gill and mouth. "Does this look like a fix to you?"

"Is that it?" someone cried incredulously.

"Gotta be shittin' me, mac," someone else said. "That's a friggin' goldfish!"

"Wait, now, wait," Larry said, holding a hand up. He put the megaphone to his lips and said with a metallic squeal, "Any other entries? Are there any other entries today?" He looked directly at Harvey.

"Yo!" Harvey said. "Got one here. Bass, I think." The crowd quieted as he approached the truck, his fish hanging heavily from his fishing line, hooked through the lip. It was a big fish, twelve inches long, and fat. Its eye sockets, however, were vacant and dark. And the fish itself was black and misshapen. And it reeked. A black, oozing hole had been gnawed in its belly.

"Well, well," Larry said into the megaphone. "Looks like a winner here." He took the fishing line from Harvey and held the fish in the air. "And what's your name, sir?" he said.

"Harvey," Harvey said.

The murmur rose again. A man in front reached up to touch the fish, but Larry swung it jealously away from him.

And then the fish on the line did something peculiar. At first those in back thought they saw the fish jump with one last flutter of life. Those closer thought Larry had dropped the line. But then everybody realized that the fish's flesh, in sickening slow motion,

had separated just below the gills. Its heavy lower half pulled
away—thread by black thread—and finally dropped in a stinking
heap on Harvey's shoe, while Larry remained stupidly displaying its
head, from which excited worms and maggots evacuated.

"Fix!" the crowd shouted at once.

Larry pointed at Harvey. "You're disqualified!" From out of nowhere, a pair of hands pulled Harvey back into the mob. An anony-
mous fist caught him on the back of the head, knocking him
forward into another fist, which caught him high on the cheekbone.
Then someone else grabbed him from behind.

"Let the little kid hit him!" someone yelled, and Gunnar's face
sparkled at the prospect. He searched the ground for a rock.

"Okay," Larry cried. "Okay. Let's calm down here." His knees
trembled visibly, and he had to sit down on the chair. He pulled a
wad of bills—five thousand dollars—from his tuxedo pocket and
held it aloft. The money felt like granite, but the sight of it calmed
the crowd. They released Harvey, satisfied with their bloodletting.
But the boy remained facedown, covering up, crying, "Mr. Mason!
Mr. Mason!"—cries that were drowned out by the cheers of the
mob as Larry handed over the prize money to Gunnar's beaming
mother.

Zippy leaped out of bed from a late-afternoon half dream in
which he was a department store clerk—for life. It was the waning
effects of the acid he had taken, he told himself. He was crashing.

He went to the refrigerator. He opened the freezer and took out a
small aluminum-foil wedge and carefully unwrapped the wedge
until a tiny purple pill no bigger than a peppercorn fell onto the
floor. He found it in the lint under the refrigerator. He put it into
his mouth, lint and all, and swallowed it, then washed it down with
a handful of tap water: Purple Haze, his favorite LSD. He glanced
at the clock. Only hours until the exact full of the moon. And then
they'd be here for him. And whatever happened then . . . would
happen. He was grateful for his clearness of vision. He tipped his
ten-gallon hat back on his head.

He would tell them before he got into the spacecraft: "I'll come
with you on one condition: no gunfighting." Or maybe he'd simply

tell them that he's decided not to go, that he'd rather stay with his wife. Or maybe he will just jump in and go. Or maybe he'll wake up in the morning and still be sitting here—maybe it was all a hoax. Maybe the CIA was behind the whole thing. Suddenly he became very confused, and he wished Ruth were back from her secret place, back beside him, with an answer.

40

Firewater

Nobody noticed when evening came. Even though the sun had fallen and the tip of a big orange moon was peeking above the pinetops, the air was still overwarm and static, the campground buoyant and raucous. A party was mushrooming down by the dock, with campers, visitors, and leftover party guests.

Larry downed his fourth glass of Waterloo Punch. Then, with renewed courage, feeling nearly weightless, he climbed the ridgepath, dressed in suede and fringe, his head adorned with the full Indian headdress. Under his arm was a pitcherful of Waterloo Punch bobbing with ice cubes. He found Nighthawk inside the wigwam supping on a dark rabbit stew.

"How," Larry said, holding his hand up to the window.

The Indian ignored him.

"Don't get up," Larry said. "I just brought you a little peace offering." He held the jar up to the window. "Just a little fresh fruit juice and ice. Thought we might bury the hatchet, you know?"

Nighthawk grunted. Larry took it as an invitation, and he entered the dark hut.

"I just wanted to let you know that I won't be coming around with these Indian clothes anymore. Course, I liked 'em so much myself, I just had to try them on, you know? They don't look half bad either, I'd say. What do you think?" He turned slowly for Nighthawk. "Anyway, I'll just leave this juice here for you as a token of my friendship. Wow, these clothes are comfortable. And warm, too. Well, not too warm, but just right, if you stop and think about it."

Nighthawk scowled at him.

"Yeah. Well, so here's the juice. All natural fruits. And ice cubes. Be sure and tell me how you like it."

The nipple holes just weren't right. Cheap, stupid thing. Susie adjusted the straps and shifted the black lace corset, but still her nipples would not line up in the holes. So she reached into the holes and pulled her nipples out. And for the moment, they stayed. For no particular reason then she puffed a circle of steam onto the mirror and drew a line through it.

She heard the front door open. "Larry?" she called.

He rushed into the room in a chieftain's headdress, suede fringe from shoulder to foot, and started changing into his street clothes. He glanced at Susie and said, "I'll be right back. I'm onto something big."

"Larry—" She had wanted to sound seductive, not nagging, but her voice split the difference.

"Ten minutes," he promised, hurrying from the room. "This can't wait."

"Hey!" she called, waving a piece of paper. But he was gone. "Yeah, sure," she said to herself.

The only remnant of the former Root estate was the sign: UN-WaNTed PeTS LaiD AWay. It was nailed to a pine tree beside a smaller, whiter sign which was driven into the ground. The new sign said, simply, THE ROOTS. A short plastic garden gnome stood beside the sign. A twelve-foot satellite dish stood beside the garden gnome. A brand new seventy-foot luxury house-trailer stood behind that—a Detroiter—fifty thousand dollars' worth, counting the furnishings—and the satellite dish. Dolly had stuck twenty-four oversized plastic butterflies to the trailer's side.

Larry shook his head at his own indiscretion. He should never have given the Roots all that money. It was his brother's fault. Zippy had forced his hand by humiliating him in public, by questioning his status in front of his tenants. At the time, it seemed the only way to redeem himself. At the time he had felt rich. He knocked on the door. The outside light came on.

"Larry!" Earl said. "Come on in, Larry. Can I buy you a drink? Scotch? Rum? Whiskey and Coke? You name it. The liquor cabinet's full."

Ten minutes later Larry left, carrying a stack of pornographic magazines. But they had not come easily. He'd been forced to bargain away Carl's bullet ban, giving Earl permission once again to lay away unwanted pets with a handgun.

He climbed the ridge-path quietly, his arms full of the magazines and Indian clothes. He considered himself a good judge of character, highly perceptive of nuance and innuendo, a trait he'd developed as a child—a trait which told him Nighthawk had tired of his appeals. He watched the ridge ahead of him, warily.

But his caution proved unnecessary. He found the Indian facedown beside his fire, his leather loincloth halfway up his back, the empty punch jar on its side beside him. Larry laid the buckskin and magazines on the ground. He shook Nighthawk gently.

"C'mon, Chief," he said. Nighthawk snored loudly. "I didn't mean for you to guzzle the whole thing." Larry was struck by how much the Indian looked like a black man. "Hey, slick. C'mon, muh-fuh, what's happ'nin', man?"

"Mmm," Nighthawk growled. He rolled his head and smacked his dry lips apart.

"C'mon," Larry said. "White Man back. Let's talk-um turkey." He pulled Nighthawk upright.

The Indian's eyes rolled in his head. "Sick," he moaned.

"No, no, it's okay. Snort some of this." Larry held out an open perfume bottle full of white powder. A sawed-off drinking straw stuck out of the top.

Nighthawk looked at it with confusion. He put his lips to the straw.

"No, no," Larry said. "Like this." He pinched the straw and sniffed a bit of coke into one nostril, then into the other. "Oh, that hits the spot," he said. "Wakes you right up." Nighthawk took the bottle and put the straw to his own nose. "Not too much, though," Larry said.

Nighthawk ignored his advice. He dipped the straw to the bottom of the bottle, and a visible lump climbed like an elevator car into his nose. Nighthawk's head jerked back.

"That was a little too much, Chief. Here, do the other side, too."

Nighthawk obliged, and his eyes snapped open as if with great insight. "Mmmm," he smiled. His eyebrows pushed furrows into his forehead, and they stayed that way. In one motion he rocked back and somehow rose to his feet.

"Brought some stuff for you," Larry said. He indicated with a sweeping hand gesture the magazines and the Indian clothes.

Nighthawk bent and snatched up the headdress. The feathers had lost their garishness with the setting of the sun. Now they were subdued—earthy and noble. He fitted the headdress on his head and stumbled to the edge of the ridge to look down, as if into a mirror. Then he reeled and faced Larry, his eyebrows still raised in a look of surprise, a look of wonder.

"Great," Larry said. "You know who you look like?"

Nighthawk rocked.

"Sitting Bull. And that's no lie." Nighthawk smiled. He bent for the rest of the garments and clumsily put them on, while Larry lit a pipeful of pot. "Let's smoke-um peace pipe," the white man said.

"Smoke-um!" Nighthawk mimicked, laughing so hard that he stumbled through the fire and fell to his hands and knees.

Laughing along, Larry clinched his sales pitch: "Hey, Chief," he said, holding up a copy of *Milking Maids*, "ever see anything like this?" Nighthawk grabbed the magazine and laid it open on the ground. "Here," Larry said, "lemme put a couple of logs on your fire, give you some light." When he had done that, he rose and said, "Get a good night's sleep, now, 'cause tomorrow you've got a show to do with Bullwinkle there. And don't forget, there's twenty bucks in it for you. And there's more of this stuff whenever you want it."

41

The Honeymoon

The wedding guests in Carl and Shirley Mason's house were drunk
and loud. As Mason tradition dictated, the men sang together (har-
monizing on "Sweet Adeline"), while the women sat in the den
sipping Waterloo Punch and laughing uproariously at off-color
jokes.

At eleven-thirty Shirley called to Carl, "Quiet time."

Carl rose and hunted up his megaphone. "Be right back," he
said, heading out. "Keep those voices warm."

"I'll come with you," said his brother Don.

Outside, Wind In The Pines resounded like three carnivals in the
fluorescence of the full moon. Carl thought of the Korean War
fought with musical instruments, and he laughed at the idea. The
center of the commotion was a circle of cars and vans down by the
dock, where a congregation of teenagers from town was clapping
and chanting, "Everybody rock, rock, rock, Everybody roll, roll,
roll . . ."

"Look at that," Carl said, grabbing Don's arm. A girl had
climbed, dancing, onto a van roof. She was naked except for a pair
of black bikini bottoms, and she threatened—to the cheers of those
below—to drop them. Then another figure rose to the roof, aided
by a small forest of arms—a whitehaired man, paunchy and
stooped, also naked except for a towel wrapped around his waist.
Carl recognized him immediately. "That's old man Rogers, the guy
I bought the camp from. Look at him up there. You'd think he was
sixteen years old."

Bending, the girl dropped her bikini bottoms. Carl grabbed at Don's arm. "Look, look," he said. But Don was wobbly. He pushed off Carl to keep his balance, and Carl reeled to keep from falling. "Steady as she goes there, matey."

Then Mr. Rogers threw off his towel. He put his hands behind his head and did a bump and grind to the cheers and handclapping of those below.

"That's not right," said Carl with drunken sanctimony. He raised the megaphone to his mouth and turned the volume full blast. The megaphone screamed. "Quiet time!" he shouted, his thin metallic voice cutting through the riot. He exchanged a swaying look with his brother, waiting for the noise to cease. But it didn't. So he tried again, this time in his "proper" voice: "Oh, say there, it's quiet time. What say we all retire now, ladies and gentlemen, so that the youngsters can go ni-ni."

Carl and Don looked at each other, giggling, and Don grabbed the megaphone. Carl tried to take it back, but Don swung away from him, fumbling with the trigger. "Quiet time, everybody!" he shouted into it. "Time to go ni-ni!" He howled then, without releasing the trigger, and his laughter echoed across the pond. Then suddenly he grew serious. He looked at Carl with boyish daring.

Carl knew that look. He remembered seeing it on his brother's face forty years ago, just before the kid pitched a bag of shit through old man Swenson's workshop window. Carl made a move for the megaphone, but his brother dodged him.

"*Sex time!*" Don shouted with a wicked metallic squeal, laughing so hard he doubled over and sank to his knees. Down at the shore the teenagers cheered. Carl knelt with his brother and wrestled the megaphone away, but only after Don had managed to squeeze the trigger once more and yell, "Time to screw!"

"Hey!" Carl said, pulling the horn away from him. He stood and weaved. "This is serious."

"Carl." It was Shirley, standing on the porch.

"Yeah, yeah, yeah," he said, waving her away. "Ev'ythin's unner control." He put the megaphone to his mouth, to demonstrate. "Seriously, folks," he announced, "fun time's over. I mean it now. Why? 'Cause I said so, that's why. Don't get smart. It's eleven-thirty around here, and that means one thing—quiet time. Time for quiet. Quiet time. Thank you."

But all around him, the din seemed only to increase.

"Quiet time, beginning right now," he announced.

". . . Everybody rock, rock, rock, Everybody roll, roll, roll . . ."

"Last warning!"

". . . Everybody rock, rock, rock, Everybody roll, roll, roll . . ."

"Awright, fuck ya's!"

"Carl!" Shirley scolded.

"Hey, Carl," Don said, putting his arm around his brother. He bent for the megaphone and sang loudly:

"Walkin' up Canal Street,
knock on every door . . ."

Carl raised the megaphone and joined in, aiming directly at the teenage party:

"I'll be a son-of-a-bitch,
if I can find a whore."

His front door slammed and the porch light went out, but Carl didn't care. "Don, come here," he said. "I want you to meet my man Harvey. Harvey's a good boy—not the brightest light on the circuit—but he's a good boy." They staggered over to the Duckoff trailershack and banged on the door.

"Oh, Harvey," Carl yelled. "It's party time. Come on out." Carl nudged Don. "Watch this," he said.

Harvey opened the door, humorless in his red pajamas. His upper lip was puffy and split. Carl and Don stepped inside, and Don lost his balance on the slanted floor. He fell slowly and rolled over onto his hands and knees. Whoops, he said. Slow down, Carl said to him.

"Kids, I want you to come over the house and join our celebration. We got lots of food—sandwiches, chips, and plenty of my famous, delicious, mouth-watering . . ."

"Effervescent," Don added.

". . . Waterloo Punch."

Jean became excited. But Harvey remained dour.

Carl said, "You kids are gonna have something to celebrate too, you know. Because I have decided today to promote you, Harvey Duckoff." He clapped his employee on the shoulder, and the boy's knees gave in. "I'm gonna make you foreman of Camp Wind In The Pines."

Jean thought he said "I'm gonna make you four men," and she scowled puzzledly at her husband. But then he smiled, and she clapped her hands excitedly. She said to Don, "I'm pregnant."

Larry tiptoed into his new house, hoping Susie was asleep. He was much later than he'd planned, having climbed Lookout Hill in hopes of finding Ruth—but he had gotten lost in the woods and come out on the River Road a mile away.

"Nice of you to drop by," Susie said. She stood in the doorway with her hands on her hips. Her breasts had shifted in the corset so that the nipple holes revealed only pale flesh. "Just where the hell have you been, if you don't mind my asking?"

"Business," he said with finality.

"Business, huh? What kind of friggin' business?"

"I had a little business, all right?"

"No, it's not all right! This is our honeymoon, in case you've forgotten."

"So now I'm back. Big deal." Then suddenly, and with terrible impact, Larry realized that he was married, and this was home, and this was his wife. He hadn't considered it until now. His third wife! As if by habit, he went into the living room and turned on the television.

Susie called after him, "Larry!" She followed him as far as the living room doorway, where she stood and hollered, "You turn off that friggin' TV right now and get into the bedroom." She folded her arms and glared at him. "Or I swear to God I'll walk out that door and I won't come back!"

Larry didn't respond at first. But then he rose from his chair, turned off the television, and headed, not for the bedroom, but for the kitchen. Susie followed him. He turned and studied her. His eyes darted, searching. She could see the brainstorm as it happened.

"Suppose you tell me what there is to think about, mister!" she demanded.

He appeared thoughtful. "If you leave me, then I'll have your share of the campground, right?"

Susie's eyes narrowed, her lips tightened, her whole body coiled. She scaled an ashtray at his head, but he ducked, and it bounced off the screen. "If that's all I ever meant to you . . ." she cried, storming out of the kitchen, toward the bedroom. A moment later she returned and slammed the document on the kitchen table—signed. ". . . then you take it!"

Larry picked it up and examined it. His heart surged. He wanted to call Rutus Sny right away—but, of course, not so Susie would hear the conversation. He started out the door to call him from Angel's cabin.

"Where the hell do you think you're going now?" she barked.

"Just a little more business," he answered. "But I'll be right back—really."

"Oh, business, huh?" she yelled. "Then that's it! That's it!" She started for the bedroom, then stopped and came back. "I really mean it, Larry. If you leave this house now, then I'm leaving, too. For good!"

Larry stood in the doorway for a second, pondering. Then he sighed and came back into the kitchen toward her.

Susie felt her tear ducts open, felt a surge of heat sweep over her. She opened her arms to him.

But he walked right past her and tossed a set of keys on the table. "Take the Camaro," he said. "You can keep it." He kissed her on the forehead and said, "Sorry it didn't work out."

And then he left.

42

The Backup

Larry knocked on Angel's door, but she wouldn't get up to answer it. She knew who it was. "Go away," she called from her bed. "I don't play with boys that are married." It was a lie, of course. The truth was he had nothing else that she wanted. She had wrested both secrets and wealth from him before he managed to lose it all. Now he was just another married man with nothing to offer.

"You don't understand," he called softly through her front window. "Just let me in."

"No. You're on your honeymoon, for godsake. Just go away." For a minute there was silence. She listened for his departing footsteps.

But then he was at her bedroom window. "Susie and I split up," he whispered.

"What? Am I on 'Candid Camera'? Piss off. Please? You're brain damaged."

"Okay, I'll level with you. I'm on the verge of making a deal. A big one. But it's extremely sensitive. All I can tell you is that it involves a new partnership and a lot of money. And I want you with me all the way on this one. But I've got to call this guy tonight—right now. Let me come in and use your phone."

Angel sighed.

"Trust me on this."

"All right," she said. And she got up and let him in, not because she trusted him, but because of her insatiable curiosity. "But make it fast."

Once inside, Larry walked directly to the telephone. He got the man out of bed—but Sny was happy to hear from him just the same. "Hello, partner," Larry said. "She's leaving—I've got her share."

Angel was confused by what she heard. After Larry hung up she said, "Would you mind telling me why you couldn't use your own telephone?"

Of course the real reason was that he didn't want Susie hearing the conversation. But he said, "Because I want you with me in this operation. You're my secretary, right? Well, these are things you ought to know. Angel, a man in my position needs somebody he can talk to, someone he can share his secrets and his dreams with— let's go into the bedroom."

She led him in, saying, "Do you really think I believe you—that you've got some secret operation, as you call it? Wait, let me guess—you got yourself a paper route, right? No, it's seeds, isn't it? You're selling flower seeds. Christmas cards?"

"No, really," Larry said, taking off his shoes. "I'll tell you all about it—"

Chief Nighthawk tried to make the *Carwash Bimbos* centerfold adhere to the walls of his wigwam, but no matter what he used— saliva, pine pitch, rabbit stew stock—it kept falling. So he gave up. He took the centerfold back outside and tossed it into the fire with an overhead hook shot, tripping on his suede fringe cuffs as he pivoted and landing on his knees in front of the cage. The moose stared balefully down at him. He adjusted his headdress and pulled himself to his feet. He pondered the caged beast; he searched the animal's mind—it seemed to have knowledge over him. But Nighthawk couldn't understand why. He became self-conscious and bent for his jar of punch. He put the jar to his lips, but it was empty.

Why do you disgrace me? he asked the moose.

Suddenly he knew. And the knowledge made him tremble with rage. He swung the jar against the corner of his wigwam, felt the breaking glass sink painlessly into his wrists and hands. But his rage did not subside. He ripped off the headdress and pushed it onto the fire. He pulled off his shirt and threw that into the fire. Then, stumbling, he took off his pants and did the same with them. The fire devoured all of it greedily.

Yes, mighty beast, we disgrace ourselves.

He opened the cage door and stepped inside. The blazing fire flickered his shadow against the moose, as if joining their spirits. He placed his hand on the moose's muzzle and the moose pushed against his hand. He stripped the papier-mâché horn off the yellow arrow stub and dropped it to the ground. And then he moistened the dried blood of the animal's wound with the fresh flowing blood of his hand.

Yes, my friend, and we have disgraced each other. But tonight we shall both be free. He stepped aside and the moose walked calmly out of the cage into the dark of the woods.

Maurice was sullen. The chain around his neck was thick and heavy. And it was far too short. But there was nothing he could do about it. He had pulled on it; he had bitten into it until his teeth chipped; and he had thrashed until he dropped from exhaustion. But there was no escape. He resisted the urge to bolt again. Instead he sulked and gnawed angrily on a squirrel's back.

Then suddenly, without will, his back leg twitched and his foot scratched at his side. His ears perked. He lifted his nose into the air and sniffed deeply the steady northern breeze. The scent grew stronger. He leaped to his feet and charged, without thinking, to the limit of his chain. "Kiiipe!" he cried as it snapped him back. But he foolishly charged again. "Kiiipe!"

He stopped and collected himself, panting. *Patience is the hunter.* He rose again and stalked the perimeter of his tether, but finding no escape, he returned to the center, to the stake itself.

He saw the chain linked through a rusted metal loop stuck into the ground. He closed his teeth on the loop and pulled back, growling. But it didn't budge. So he tried it from the other side, pulling, pulling with all his might. Again it held fast. He walked round the stake, then turned and circled it the other way. Then he dived on it, growling and shaking the loop with his teeth. And, suddenly, the stake gave. The scent grew stronger. Maurice bent his head sideways to the earth, closed his teeth like a vise around the exposed iron stake, and pulled with all his might.

Zippy had fallen deep within himself inside his unlit cabin. He hunched under the kitchen table, his ten-gallon hat squashed down over his forehead to fit, watching glowing orbs spin like firewheels in his inner vision.

They were coming, Hallelujah, they were coming to get him. Yes, they were coming—he could even see their vessel in his imagination. Visual contact verified, a voice said. And the message became a song, not unlike "Joshua Fit the Battle of Jericho": *Visual contact verified, verified, verified; Visual contact verified, verrrr-i-fied . . .* and so on, with a chanting urgency.

Then suddenly his senses became alert. He imagined antennae rising from his cowboy hat. He imagined himself a lobster. He pinched himself. Then he heard stray radio waves: an announcer chanting, "Sunday! Sunday! Sunday!" He heard the shifting of gravel outside on the Camp Road. He slowly opened his eyes, and the room danced into focus, full of rhythm. And there on the opposite wall, where the moonlight cast a pale image of the window, colored lights appeared—red, yellow, blue, and green.

His heart jumped. They were here!

ZippyZippyZippyZippyZippyZippyZippy, said the spaceship's engine.

He slid to the door like a spirit, his guitar and travel bag slung over one shoulder. He opened the door and saw the ship, saw it actually touch down on the Camp Road, saw the smoke from its burners and its brightly colored lights. A bright white light suddenly came on from the ship's dome and shone in his eyes. "Ohhh," he gasped. It was a gorgeous, radiant light—more beautiful than he could imagine.

Harvey and Jean Duckoff were the life of the party at Carl and Shirley Mason's house—whatever life there was left. Almost everyone had retired for the night. Even Shirley had gone to bed after playing five rounds of Harvey's favorite game, Guess What I'm Thinking About. Only Clara Belle and Bethany remained in the living room, and that was because they were waiting to unfold the studio couch and go to sleep. Clara Belle had earlier gotten sick to her stomach, and now she sat beside Harvey in a pale, frightening trance, facing Jean Duckoff. Jean was into her fifth glass of Waterloo Punch, eagerly holding forth on the relative merits of her favorite color, red: ". . . red balloons and balls, red bowls, red boxes,

berries . . . lots of red things start with C, too—cars, kites, cranber-
ries . . ."

Then, mercifully, the telephone rang.

"Shouldn't you get that?" Clara Belle asked Harvey. He stood up,
and she quickly unfolded the couch.

Harvey picked up the phone, and as he listened, his neutral red
face went white. The voice on the other end said: "I can't tell you
my name, but listen—I hope I'm not too late. There's a guy coming
to your campground tonight—right now. He busted out of the
hospital, he's got a gun, and he's crazy. He's nuts. He's gonna kill
Larry Jones. Got that?"

"Yup," Harvey said.

Click.

Harvey stood like a statue. Someone was coming to kill Larry
Jones!

"Jeezum!" he said, doubling his fists. Jean didn't notice him
running out the door (". . . dishes, deck of cards; skip the E ones
. . . skip the F ones, too . . .").

Zippy took his sunglasses from his shirt pocket and put them on.
He gazed into the glare of the searchlight but could see only a vague
outline of the commander's head through the porthole. The commander seemed to be speaking. "Nnguh, pngkukuh, nhuh nn
nhoh, kun hnn uhn nih mnn nuh babuh bng (Okay, pigfucker,
nice and slow, come here and give me that paper bag)."

Zippy shrugged his shoulders and opened his mouth in a wide,
cosmic grin. "Ning-ning," he said, pointing to his ear and shaking
his head.

The commander shot a finger out the porthole and pointed at
Zippy's grocery bag. "Nnuu!" he snapped.

Zippy understood—the commander wanted the bag. Protocol.
He strode, squinting, into the brilliance of the searchlight, right up
to the purring ship, and offered his grocery bag with two hands. The
pale hand snatched the bag and withdrew it into the murky, swirling
darkness inside.

Then Zippy saw something clearly—much too clearly—something that was not at all right. He saw the commander push his

hand back out the porthole. There was a six-shooter in his hand. It pressed against Zippy's shoulder, just above his breast. "Hnun mn hh nnh hfin (Tell me how this feels)," the commander said with a chuckle. Zippy started to tell him: No gunfighting, but even as he opened his mouth, he saw the commander's index finger flex, the stringy pink finger muscles contract; he heard the moon-white phalanx bone slide smoothly in its socket. *Trigger finger!* The moment stretched on. He thought to pull off his cowboy hat, to show the commander his haircut, but he knew there was no time. There was not even time to duck. No gunfighting, he thought, just as the hammer snapped down.

The pistol exploded. The guitar on Zippy's back snapped and doubled upon itself with a sick, tuneless *twaaang*. Zippy's shoulder flared; he wondered at first if he had only been branded, but when he touched the burning spot just above his breast he found it warm and sopping. Another spot, on his back, began to itch fiercely; he contorted his shoulders to stop the itch. Now he could feel wetness on his back, too. The commander laughed. "Lit nt, hnbn? Wa, nen, nih uhunnuh (Like that, cowboy? Well, then, here's another)."

"No gunplay," Zippy muttered, holding a hand in front of his face, backing away. But again the gun fired. The bullet came out of the lights like a wasp, and Zippy tried to dodge it. But it tore flesh from his side and drove him, spinning, to the ground. He rolled to his back, holding his new wound tightly, hoping to keep the blood from running out of his body. But he could hear its relentless flow through his veins. He could hear the pump-pumping of his heart with every warm spurt through his fingers. He listened and could hear the electronic crackle of his excited nerve endings. He heard his food digesting. He heard the paperlike crumple of his lungs working. Or was it the paperlike crumple of his brain? He listened deeper. No, it was a rustling from outside his body—the rustling of crisp paper, of his grocery bag, from inside the ship. He rolled his head to the side and gazed at the ship. It seemed to float, to dance gingerly in the air. Then suddenly he heard a brutal cry— "NNNG!"—and his brown grocery bag flew out the porthole, spilling toothbrush and apples, playing cards and loose Oreo cookies.

The hatch flung open. The commander stepped out stiff-legged and crossed into the beam of searchlight, suddenly becoming a silhouette—the frail, black shadow of death.

Zippy yawned. His body was leaden and numb. The shadow came and stood over him. It held its pistol at arm's length and took aim directly at his face. "Ny, pngkukuh (Die, pigfucker)," it snarled, and its thin white finger squeezed the trigger.

When the shot was fired, a sudden gray blur passed before Zippy's eyes, which he first took for the parading past of his own bleak life. Upon focusing, however, he realized that the gray blur had not been his life passing, but a fleecy gray poodle that had flown into the spaceship's lights and taken the cowboy leader to the ground in a vicious, snarling tangle of teeth and chain. "Oh, good," Zippy breathed, glad to be alive, even as the ship came toward him and rolled over his foot, thump-thump, on its steady, quiet descent down the gravel Camp Road and into the marsh.

Maurice, despite his frenzy, could not penetrate Weasel's thick bandages. So he scanned the body with piranha teeth, *snap-snap-snap*, until he found an area of softness and warmth. And then he ripped savagely at the clothes, pulling Weasel's shirt apart at the sleeves and tearing a pants leg away.

Cowboy leader in trouble, Zippy thought frantically. *Cowboy leader in trouble.* Send help!

The poodle next lunged for the bare thigh and successfully sank his teeth into Weasel's flesh. He pulled away a dark hunk of gore and shook it triumphantly over his horror-struck victim, jangling his heavy chain merrily. He was poised to lunge again at the same wound, when suddenly he froze and stared up into the moonlight— *bum-didda, bum-didda*—his jaw dropped helplessly—*bum-didda, bum-didda*—his eyes glazed with terror—*bum-didda, bum-didda*. "Kiipe!" he screamed, and then he was gone. Weasel saw only the shadow of the great beast pass over him before he drifted off.

But Zippy saw the whole thing, saw the great black moose attack, saw the gray poodle skewered neatly on the arrow stub between its antlers, and then watched the monster trot away, wearing the slack poodle on its head like a crown, ten feet of heavy chain dragging a two-foot stake behind. The alien king, Zippy thought. *Thank you, Your Majesty.*

"Get out! Get out!" Harvey shouted, galloping through the newlyweds' kitchen. "L.A.—Hide! Somebody's coming to kill you!"

Susie came out of her bedroom with two full suitcases. She looked at Harvey and bristled. She dropped her suitcases and covered up her nipple holes. "He's not here."

"Somebody's coming to kill him!" Harvey gasped.

She passed him, snatched the Camaro keys from the table, and threw them down the kitchen drain, into the garbage disposal. She flicked on the unit. It whirred, then a crunching sound, and finally hummed deeply, seized up. She pulled a chair to a cupboard, she climbed on the chair, opened the cupboard, and withdrew a different set of keys—the spare Mercedes keys that she'd had made in Bluffton. *A girl needs to go in style,* she thought with a half smile.

"I ain't kiddin'," Harvey said. "Somebody's comin' to kill him!"

"Good," Susie said, pushing past him to open the screened door. "They'll be doing the world a favor. Good-bye."

She walked out the door, and Harvey followed. "But where is he?" he persisted. "I gotta warn him."

Susie glanced over at Angel's shack, saw candlelight flickering behind her bedroom curtain. "I haven't the slightest," she said, climbing into the Mercedes.

Harvey ran ahead through the moonlight, calling, "L.A.! L.A.!," passing Weasel as he staggered down the Camp Road toward the lights of his slowly sinking truck; overtaking Ruth, who was at last returning from her secret place, returning to her husband, famished yet finally reborn; and then tripping over Zippy, who had struggled gallantly to his hands and knees. They tumbled together on the rough gravel road, and when Harvey sat up he found a ten-gallon hat in his hand. "L.A.," he cried, shaking the moaning cowboy. "Hey, L.A."

Zippy heard the voice and looked up quizzically, wondering if he was flying over Los Angeles. Then he recognized Harvey. "They captured you, too?" he exclaimed.

Harvey jumped back. His hand had found the bullet wound on Zippy's shoulder. It was sticky and warm. "Hey," he said. "You been shot already!"

Zippy sat up. "I think so," he said. His shoulder throbbed; his side burned; his foot ached. "Something's wrong."

Harvey tried to lift Zippy to his feet, but the cowboy was moist and slippery, and Harvey lost his grip. "You got blood all over you, L.A. I can't get a grip. Can you walk?"

"No, my foot's asleep. Spaceship ran over it."

"Oh," Harvey said. He cocked his head curiously and said, "I better go in and wake up Zippy."

"What?" Zippy asked fearfully, wondering if somehow the aliens had transferred his consciousness into another body. Matter. Anti-matter.

"What?" Harvey said.

Then Ruth came upon them. She bent to look at the couple. Harvey explained, "He got shot."

Ruth gasped. She peered into Zippy's eyes and asked with trep-idation, "Which one are you?"

"Harvey," Harvey said.

"Not you. Which one is he?"

"Oh, babe," Zippy said, reaching for her with his one good arm, "no moon tonight."

She took him into her weak arms and held him tightly. She kissed his cheek and said, "I know why I was born now. I'm back, babe, and I'll never leave you again."

She turned to Harvey. "Harvey, help me bring Harold into the house."

"Harold? Aw, jeez," he said, shaking his head in confusion. But he helped just the same. They hoisted Zippy to his feet, led him into the house, and sat him in a chair. Ruth removed his shirt and squeezed aloe juice onto his wounds, while Harvey gawked at him, picking at his ear. "L.A.?" he asked. Zippy gawked back at him, grimacing, just as confused.

Ruth saw Harvey's bewilderment and said, "Harvey, this is Zippy."

"Naw," the boy said, still staring at Zippy. But Zippy nodded his
head emphatically. Harvey told him: "Don't look much like you."
"He got his hair cut," Ruth explained as she bandaged Zippy's
wounds. "And his beard."
Harvey stepped closer. There was a thick gray mantle of confusion over him, clouding his thoughts. "But . . . them cowboy
clothes . . . you look just like . . ." His fists clenched. "Jeezum!"
he cried, wheeling for the door, "I almost forgot, I gotta find L.A.
before it's too late. Somebody's comin' to kill him!" He ran out the
door.
Ruth turned to follow him, saying, "I'll run over to Masons' and
call an ambulance for you." But Zippy caught her with his good
arm and pulled her close. He kissed her on the mouth. "That can
wait a few minutes, babe," he said, pulling her onto his lap.

Susie turned on the ignition and put the transmission into Drive.
But just as she lifted her foot from the brake and started to roll, she
struck something solid and watched in horror as the shadow of a
man went down in front of the car. She turned on the headlights
and jumped out. And there, like a vision, was Weasel, lying on his
back in a bright cloud of gravel dust.
She knelt by his head and gently lifted it in her hands. "Oh,
Weasel," she cried. "Don't die." She climbed onto him, straddled
his middle, and began massaging his chest, thinking to revive his
heart. His chest was warm and hairy, and she found herself stroking
harder, pushing with her legs, feeling his hot, moist thigh against
her own nakedness.
When he came to, her mouth was pressed against his and she was
humping him gently. He feebly swung his bandaged arms.
"Oh, thank God you're alive," she said, sitting up, fixing her
hair.
He gazed at her in the stark lights of the Mercedes, sitting atop
him with her buoyant breasts peeking down through their black lace
peepholes. He reached up to touch them, then lost consciousness
again.
"You're coming with me," she said, and she dragged him into the

passenger seat. She threw the Mercedes into Drive, then steered the car across her father's lawn into the backyard, weaving between tents and trailers as she went. She stopped just outside Angel's bedroom window and gently slapped Weasel's face.

"Wake up," she said, "and look over there." She honked the horn three times, watching the bedroom window. When the curtains parted, she turned on the car's interior light and held Weasel's head upright by the hair. Suddenly the curtains were yanked back, revealing the startled, gaping faces of Angel and Larry. Susie waved, blew the horn three more times, then drove the forest-green Mercedes out of Camp Wind In The Pines, straight for Fort Lauderdale.

Larry chased after his car, but it was gone even as he ran out the front door. And then, with sickening impact, he realized what was in the trunk of that car: all his money—even the cash that Rutus Sny had given him. All his cocaine. All his power. Gone. His mind raced; adrenalin streamed through his body. He turned two circles, panting, not knowing where to go. He felt dizzy and faint. He felt sick. He sat on the doorsill and laid his head in his hands. "Ladies and gentlemen," he blurted, then stopped and wondered why he had said it. What went wrong? he thought. Yesterday he was a rich man—today he had nothing.

Then a ray of hope pierced his stormy thoughts. He reached into his pocket and withdrew the piece of paper Susie had signed—the paper that transferred her share of the campground over to him. Yes, he thought, at least he still had Wind In The Pines. And on Monday he and his new partner, Rutus Sny, would take over the entire operation. And they would nurture it and make it grow. "I have not yet begun to fight," he said with gritty resolve. Behind him, Angel's door swung shut and locked.

Then he saw the lights, the odd arch of colored lights in the lily pads by his new house. The arch reflected off the water and formed a rectangle. It was a truck. Weasel's truck, he guessed. But why was it in the pond? He wondered, and then he hoped, and then he was certain, that Weasel's bag of money and coke would still be in it. He rose to his feet. When the going gets tough . . .

The campground was quiet now. Just a few soft conversations and the crackle of dying campfires drifted in a growing wind. Larry crossed the Camp Road and walked down to the bog, dodging tent lines and lawn chairs as he went. When he got to the shore he slogged through the muck and weeds until he was knee-high in the icy water, and then he waded the rest of the way to the truck. Luckily the window was open—he crawled through. The truck shifted under his added weight, and he feared for a second that it would sink into the muck as if in quicksand. But the truck settled. He crawled belly-down into the cold water on the front seat and shuddered. He found the interior light switch and turned it on. He opened the glove compartment and, just as he'd hoped, the brown paper bag was in there, all balled up, safe and dry.

His heart pounded. He snatched the bag and carefully worked it open so as not to spill its precious contents. He angled the opening to the light and peered inside. The small plastic bag of coke was there. "Awright," he said. He pushed his hand into the paper bag and felt under the cocaine for the wonderful touch of legal tender. But the money was gone. He drew a long breath and blew it out. No money. He was broke. He shook his head sadly. He took the rolled bag of cocaine and worked it gratefully in his fingers, thinking, Well, at least I've still got this. He felt the need for some now. He rolled the bag open, stuck a wet finger into the granular white powder, and pushed the finger into his nostril. Not enough. He opened the bag fully, rolled down the flaps, and stuck his nose right into the thick of it. He sniffed, and his nostrils burned with the bitter drug. He felt better at once, suddenly sharp and vital. Yes, he thought, with growing confidence, just a minor setback. On Monday an Empire would be born. And he would be on its throne. And someday, inevitably, he would be called upon to face the rigors of political life. "Ladies and gentlemen," he said aloud, "the President of the United States." Rolling up the bag, he backed out the window into the pond and headed for shore, holding the cocaine like a torch high above his head. He imagined he looked like the Statue of Liberty. He tried to.

Suddenly someone jumped out from behind a tree and came splashing toward him, a short board raised above his head, attacking. But in the moonlight Larry could see it was only Harvey.

"Cool it, Harve. It's only me," he said.

.   .   .

Nighthawk stood tall and naked by his fire. He ripped up another magazine and dropped it into the blaze. The stupefying effect of drugs and alcohol had all but subsided now, and he felt ashamed for having been tricked by Larry Jones. He stepped to the edge of the ridge and looked out onto the campground. The fires that had blazed there during the evening were dying out, now just orange dots scattered about, like the scattering of stars at dawn. A cool wind was blowing out of the north, and there were voices on the wind— soft, nearly imperceptible voices. He closed his eyes to listen: *Huh-yuh-yuh-yuh, Huh-yuh-yuh-yuh, Huh-yuh-yuh-yuh.*

Depart, the voices sang. Depart into the highlands, deep into the forest, and return no more. He watched the car's taillights disappear from the campground below. Yes, he said, I will go. I will leave the side of the White Man forever, and return to the forest of my ancestors. *Huh-yuh-yuh-yuh, Huh-yuh-yuh-yuh, Huh-yuh-yuh-yuh.*

He looked to the sky and settled his gaze on the pale planting moon and the glowing white ring around it. The moon was alive, dancing behind the blowing, thickening clouds. He raised his arms in praise, and sang, "Huh-yuh-yuh-yuh, Huh-yuh-yuh-yuh, Huh-yuh-yuh-yuh." His feet picked up the rhythm—he danced on his tiptoes. Then slowly—very slowly—his spirit once again ascended. (This is not a dream, he told himself.) He rose freely, willingly, until he was able to look down upon himself: the naked, dancing Indian on the ridgetop. And he smiled, hearing the ancient beat of tom-toms on the wind: *bum-didda, bum-didda, bum-didda, bum-didda.* And then his grandfather, Running Bird, was there in the air with him. The old Indian blessed him with a sprinkling of rain and then disappeared, as Nighthawk eased back down onto the ridge, back into his naked body. Fulfilled.

But there was something lingering in the sky where he had been—like a shadow of himself left behind, a dark and imperfect shadow against the dancing moon. He had thrown off a skin—he was cleansed. But as he watched, the shadow grew. He willed the circle of light around it to become a wheel of fire, to consume the tainted thing. And the wheel of fire grew. *Bum-didda, bum-didda, bum-didda, bum-didda.* And as it grew, so did Nighthawk's own knowledge grow.

His moment of purity was at hand:

It was the beast—the great, mocking beast—inside that circle of fire. *Bum-didda, bum-didda, bum-didda, bum-didda.* But the animal was vain. It wore a talisman on its head, thinking the charm would gain it knowledge over Nighthawk.

But it would not. For Nighthawk stood pure and noble, his senses grown perfect: All-seeing. Even without turning he knew the demon was behind him, breaking through the brush, foolishly attacking from the rear. Nighthawk watched the sky. *Bum-didda, bum-didda, bum-didda, bum-didda.* Yes, Nighthawk thought, our moment is at hand.

The beast broke through the campfire, scattering flame into the night sky. *Bum-didda, bum-didda, bum-didda, bum-didda.* The Indian leaped aside, and the moose flew, bellowing, off the ridgetop. And in the supreme moment that followed, Nighthawk watched the circle of flame burst over him and scatter upon the earth: The chain and stake that hung from the dead poodle's neck caught between the Indian's legs and swept him, from the ridge:

Moment of purity.

Harvey pulled a short one-by-six board from a pile of picnic table stock. He held it tightly in his right hand, tested its heft, and went down into the campground. Somebody's comin' to kill Larry, he thought, trembling. (He wished the board were a gun.) He skulked from tent to tent, watching, listening for anything suspicious. Each whisper, each rustle of cloth, was suspect. He noticed the colored lights down in the marshy end of the pond. They made him think of Christmas, and he smiled. He thought of ribbon candy. He thought of the time his family got lost in the woods hunting for a Christmas tree. He tripped over a tent stake and dislodged the guy line so the tent folded and collapsed. Confused voices erupted inside. Heads bobbed. "Shhh!" Harvey hissed, but the noise only increased. He was tempted to quiet the canvas with a swing of his board, but he thought better of the idea and hurried away from the commotion instead.

He stepped into a close stand of birches and scanned the campground with narrow, detective eyes. It was too quiet, he thought, much too quiet. It struck him that there seemed something fishy about the colored lights in the pond. Deciding to investigate, he went dodging from shadow to shadow until he reached the shore. There he hid behind a pine and stared at the lights good and hard, chewing his bottom lip. He nodded his head. Yessir. It was the back of a truck cab stickin' outta the pond. "Chevy," he whispered.

He stared and thought: New Chevy truck in the pond. Lights on. Somebody comin' to shoot Larry. He drove his little finger into his ear, desperately trying to sort out his confusion. But every time he assembled a couple of facts, when he reached for a third, the first and second would fall away again: Zippy was gunshot. And he had been dressed like a cowboy. But where was Larry? And why was someone coming to shoot him? It just wouldn't add up. He cursed his stupidity.

Then he heard a noise from the truck. A voice. A familiar voice. It said, "Ladies and gentlemen . . . the President of the United States." He ducked behind the tree. President? It meant something, he was sure. He watched a dark figure slide out of the truck and start toward shore. President . . . President . . . He thumped his head with his fist, but all he could come up with was, George Washington Father of Our Country. The figure was wading closer. President . . . President . . . Roy Rogers? Was that right? President Roy Rogers? He held his board with both hands. Yes! Roy Rogers! Harvey jumped out, raising the board above his head.

"Cool it, Harve," Larry said. "It's only me." But the board came down just the same—*crack*—on the top of his head, driving the entrepreneur to his knees in the greasy muck, where he helplessly watched his bag of cocaine float on the pond inches from his grasp, and then roll onto its side and sink without a sound.

"Stupid!" Larry snarled, rocking in the slime, rubbing his starry head. "I told you—'It's me!'"

"I ain't stupid," Harvey said. "I knew it was you."

Larry glared up at him.

"I just figured things out, that's all," Harvey said. "You was the cowboy yesterday. Remember, President Roy Rogers? And you musta done somethin' wrong. 'Cause somebody was huntin' for you. But tonight Zippy was the cowboy. And he got shot—instead of you. And you did that on purpose. You fooled the guy that shot him. And you fooled your own brother, too. Just like you fool everybody. But you don't fool me. I ain't no dang *Eye-sty*, but I figured you out, chummy."

"What are you talking about, Harve?" Larry attempted to rise on his trembling legs. "It was all just a big mistake. An accident."

"Aw, there ain't no accidents," Harvey said, hitting Larry again with the board to keep him down. "Everythin' happens cuzza somethin' else. Just like I got all stave up today cuzza you. That weren't no accident. And like I just hit you 'cause you tried to make me think I was stupid. Well, I ain't."

They heard a moose's long bellow across the pond, followed by two hearty, faraway splashes. A pine tree burst into flame high on the ridge. Again Harvey swung the board down onto Larry's head— *crack*—as a second and then a third pine went up in flames. "Just like them trees there. Even though you're right here with me, I'll betcha dollars to doughnuts it's cuzza somethin' you done."

43

·

Wheelin' . . .

Carl stood in the morning rain. He lifted his face against the downpour, rubbed the cold water from his cheeks onto the back of his neck. Nearly twenty acres of pine had burned to the ground before the clouds had mercifully opened and extinguished the fire. Today the ridgetop looked like a gray jawbone of rotted teeth stubs.

Fire rangers had evacuated Wind In The Pines during the night, so the campground was desolate now, looking like pictures Carl had seen of Woodstock after the hippies had ravaged it. The ground was covered with water and trash. The trim green lawn had been worn red with muck; a few tents had been left behind by people scrambling to escape the fire, and now the campers were soberly returning in the deluge to pack them up.

Firefighters had found Nighthawk's naked body still clutching the chain that was attached to the poodle that was impaled on the yellow arrow stub in the drowned moose's skull. They had asked Carl for a statement. I don't know a thing, he had said. The police had naturally been called in to investigate, and they had found Weasel's truck in the lily pads. They, too, had asked for a statement. I don't know a thing, Carl had said. Reporters from the *Bluffton Daily Journal* had shown up after learning that Zippy had checked into the hospital with a .22-caliber hole through his shoulder, a flesh wound on his side, and a bruised left foot. They had asked Carl for a statement. I don't know a thing, he had said.

And Susie had called from Baltimore to say good-bye to her parents. She was gone. Carl shut his eyes and raised his face again to the rain. He shook his head to clear it, but it did no good. He thought he was going to cry.

He didn't hear Angel's footsteps over the slapping of rain on the dock. She came up behind him and said, "Portrait of the Yankee . . ." He jumped. A tremor rolled in his stomach. ". . . Rugged individual to the end . . ."

"Get the hell away from me—"

". . . He stands—and he falls—alone."

Carl inhaled deeply. He turned to leave, but she reached out to stop him. "Don't touch me," he warned.

"Wait a minute, Yankee," she said. "I've got something to tell you."

He pushed by, knocking her arm down as he passed. "You got nothin' I wanna hear."

She said two words then, very softly: "Rutus Sny"—and he stopped . . .

By suppertime the rain had ended and the pale sky had softly torn apart, marbled with dark, peach-edged clouds. Carl sat high on the ridge, on a rounded stump, panting, wiping the grimy wetness off his brow with his forearm. With only a splitting maul he had chopped nearly two cords of charred firewood out of the desolate pine on the ridge. He was barechested, streaked with charcoal slurry, and his dungarees hung black and heavy on his hips. He was exhausted. His heart pounded as he sat, his knees trembled, and the muscles of his back contracted and relaxed at will. But he needed to chop more (he had chopped wood this way the afternoon his mother had died), so he stood and stalked another green-bottomed pine, all black and bony at the top. He swung the maul with an abrupt, satisfying chunk low into its side, and the brittle black branches at the top rained down all around him.

There was no logic to his chopping wood—the campground was lost. Larry and Rutus Sny had beaten him. That's all there was to it. He had figured Larry all wrong. He'd thought the kid green, lazy, maybe ambitious—crafty at best. But never treasonous.

Gather wisdom slowly, an inner voice said to him. *Wisdom from pain.*

"It's too goddamn late for that," he said aloud, with a savage chop into the dead pine. The tree groaned. Carl leaned into it with the maul, and with a sudden crack it gave and fell across the ridge, scattering its black, spidery top down into the water below. He went to the black, stubbled end to start chopping when he spotted a lone figure coming across the pavilion area toward the ridge—Larry Jones!

"Son-of-a-bitch," he said. If I had my twenty-two, I'd shoot the bastard; wing him, anyway. He lifted the maul to his shoulder and sighted down its handle. He squeezed the imaginary trigger. "Pkew," he said. But Larry kept coming. So he picked up a plum-sized stone and flung it sidearm down into the campground. The rock wasn't far off the mark—it careened off a birch just in front of Larry and bounced across his pathway.

"Whoa!" Larry called, waving his hands. "Somebody's walking down here."

Carl turned and began chopping furiously at the fallen pine, hoping the kid wasn't stupid enough to climb the ridge—yet also wishing he would. And of course he did.

He came up behind Carl, folded his arms, and shook his head. "Tsk, tsk, tsk," he said. "What a mess."

Carl's muscles tensed. He said, "I'm not gonna hit you. I'm gonna give you ten seconds to get away from me. But if I turn around and you're still there, I'm gonna punch you so hard, you'll starve to death before you stop rolling."

"Yeah, okay, you're a little peeved because of Susie and me. That's cool. But these things happen, Carl, to the best of marriages—"

". . . One, two, three—"

"Actually, the reason I came up to see you is, I'm a little short in the money department today—a little cash-flow problem. I was figuring maybe I'd skim a couple hundred off the weekend's profits—"

". . . Four, five, six, seven . . ."

"Hey, Carl, no kiddin'. I need a little bread to tide me over. Just a couple of hundred."

". . . eight, nine, ten!" Carl let the maul drop from his hand. He turned, doublefisted, and faced Larry, who slowly assumed the defensive posture of a martial artist. But the thought of punching the kid wasn't enough. Carl wanted to destroy him. His temples throbbed; his face heated; he felt his heart suddenly kick his rib cage. Fearing his own fury, he brushed past Larry and began his descent down the ridge-path for the cool waters of the pond. Larry followed.

"Hey, man, that bread's mine, as much as it is yours—more, even, if you think about it."

When Carl reached the shore he dipped his hands into the water, beyond the froth, and rubbed them onto the back of his neck. He lifted another handful to splash against his face—

"You're not going to drink that shit, are you?" Larry said.

Carl turned. He glared. He spotted a flattened wax paper cup by his feet and bent to pick it up. He worked the cup whole in his hand and then scooped it full of shore water, froth and all. And then, staring hard at Larry, he slowly drank it down. His stare took on a queer, distant gleam.

Larry raised an eyebrow.

"So you want money, do you?" Carl said, crumpling the cup and snapping it at Larry's chest. "I'll tell you what, then—you're a wheeler-dealer, right? I'm gonna make you an offer—let's see if you take it." There was more gravity in his voice than he had ever mustered. "Because if you don't grab it, son, you're gonna be in Deep Shit."

"Hey," Larry said, "I need some bread. That's all."

"Pay attention," Carl said evenly. "This is it: I'm gonna give you twenty grand right now, right this minute—twenty thousand dollars—to dissolve our partnership. Twenty thousand, cash money. And then I don't ever want to see your face around here again. Ever."

Larry sneered. "Hey, man," he said, "just give me the bread— two hundred bucks. And a little word of advice: Don't lock horns with me, because when it comes to wheelin' and dealin', there's two leagues around here." He pointed at Carl. "Think about it."

Carl smiled at him. It was a warm, sincere, red-faced smile such as Larry had never seen on the man. "Are you sure now? You've thought it over, and you want the two hundred—not the twenty thousand. Right?"

Larry nodded smugly. "Damn straight," he said, tapping his outstretched palm with his index finger.

Carl reached into his pocket and pulled out a roll of twenties. "Somehow I thought you'd say that," he said.

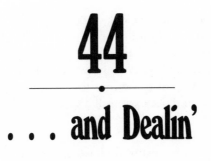

44

. . . and Dealin'

LOCAL BLACK IN BIZARRE
ALCOHOL-AND-DRUG-CRAZED
SACRIFICE/SUICIDE/FOREST FIRE

NORWOOD—The naked body of a black resident of Camp Wind In The Pines in Norwood was found early Sunday morning, chained to a poodle which he had ritualistically impaled on a broken arrow embedded in the skull of a twelve-hundred-pound bull moose. Luthor P. Ellis, 35, was found in three feet of water by forest rangers Sunday, after they successfully extinguished a blaze that flattened nearly twenty acres of prime Norwood forest land. Fire officials say they are reasonably certain that the black man started the blaze after ingesting a substantial quantity of alcohol, marijuana, and cocaine.

The reasons for his actions remain unclear. However, remains of a substantial amount of pornographic literature were found in a pile of ashes where the blaze is thought to have started. Investigators say that tests are being performed on the dead animals to determine if there was any foul play.

The dead black's estranged wife, Trudy Parker Ellis, of Bluffton, said that her husband had been despondent over his lack of employment. Norwood police said the investigation into the incident is continuing.

Carl looked up from Monday's newspaper and stared out the window to the ridge. He took his last bite of fried egg, then wiped the yoke off his plate with a crust of toast and ate that. He finished his coffee. He looked at the clock, then walked out onto the porch. It was a sharp, sunny morning—one puffy white cloud lazed high in the sky. A white station wagon was parked down at the pond, where two men in white smocks walked along the shore with stainless steel pails. Carl came into the house again.

"Maybe you should pour yourself a short drink," Shirley said, "to take the edge off."

"Nah, I'm all right."

He checked the clock again, then paced once around the kitchen. He looked out the window and saw Larry come out his front door in a three-piece gray tweed suit, carrying a clipboard under his arm. "Here he comes," Carl said.

But just as Larry got to the corner of the store, he was distracted. "Psst."

It was Angel, stepping out from behind a tall Scotch pine. Despite the chill in the air, she was barely dressed in an embroidered silk haltertop; its color was beige, a shade lighter than her own soft skin. The outline of her nipples showed through darkly. She said in a soft, tantalizing voice, "Boy, you look good enough to eat."

Larry took his shades from his breast pocket and put them on. "I don't look half bad, do I?" He turned to look at his reflection in one of the store windows and chuckled.

She said, "Got time for a quickie, mister?" She brushed hair back over one ear and nodded toward her shack. "My place?"

"Later," he said. "We'll really celebrate then. But I don't want to be late for this meeting."

"Come on," she pouted. "Just for a minute—nobody else is at the meeting yet."

He swallowed. He checked his watch. "Well, I guess I can spare a minute or so. But I want you at that meeting, too. You're my personal secretary, remember."

She shot him a quick, determined look. She blinked her lashes. She took him by the hand and led him away, saying, "I never could resist a successful man."

Rutus and Tiffany Sny rolled into Wind In The Pines in haughty splendor at ten A.M., followed closely by their attorneys, Mr. Marks and Mr. Roberts. Mr. Marks was a dour man, large and egg-shaped, dressed in a light blue tailored suit. Mr. Roberts, of similar stature and attitude, was dressed in gray. They arrived in separate automobiles and remained inside them while Sny danced up the wooden steps and rapped on the screen door. "Hello?" he called in a neighborly voice.

"What the hell do you want?" Carl said, not opening the door. Shirley stood at his side. Her hands crawled up to rest on his shoulders.

"We thought your partner Mr. Jones might have explained that already," Sny said.

"Explained what?" Carl said.

"May we come in?"

"No. We can sit out there," Carl said, going out. "Now, what's going on?"

Rutus smiled imperiously and signaled for Tiffany and his attorneys. Tiffany swung out of the car with a heavy sigh and climbed the porch steps with a doubtful scowl for her husband. She sighed again as she lowered herself cautiously into an aluminum frame lawn chair.

Sny said, with a mocking bow, his fingertips pressed together and spreading, "Well, Mr. Mason, I have a dandy proposition to discuss with you. I only wish Mr. Jones were here, too." He looked at his watch and said. "It is ten o'clock, is it not?"

"No," Carl said. "It is."

"Oh, there," Shirley said, pointing. "Here he comes, late as usual." Her comment was good-natured. She smiled at Tiffany Sny.

Tiffany turned her head away to look down the Camp Road at her husband's new partner. She grunted. He was dressed in red shorts and a red tee-shirt which, on closer inspection, said, MANAGER in green letters along the breast. And, worse, he was wearing dark sunglasses. He walked slowly, as if time were eternal, with one arm draped around a young woman's shoulder. At least the woman was dressed smartly, even if she did seem to be supporting the man. "Nouveau riche," Tiffany muttered.

"Well, Mr. Jones," said Rutus Sny with a broad smile, as the couple mounted the steps. "Glad you could make it." They shook hands. "I guess it's time we dropped the bomb, so to speak, on Mr. Mason." He looked over at his wife and winked. She looked away. "So, Larry, would you like the honors, or should I?"

"You do it."

Sny walked a small circle on the porch as he spoke. "Well, Carl, to make a long story short, it seems Mr. Jones has sold me his share in your little operation here."

Carl made a grunting sound deep in his throat. He shot an angry glance at his partner.

Rutus Sny grinned, clasped his hands. "But that's only the beginning, folks. It also seems that Larry still owns the third share in the family business, the share his bride left to him when she so abruptly departed." He studied Carl's face again. "Oh, yes, Mr. Mason. Think about it. Three partners. And two of them have already had a business meeting. And do you know what the outcome of that meeting was?"

Carl looked away, suddenly more interested in the goings-on down at the shore. Two more cars had parked down there, a dark blue official-looking sedan and a town police car.

Sny cut through the distraction. "Well, the upshot of that meeting was this: We at Wind In The Pines have decided by a majority decision that this property would be better served in other ways than as is presently, uh, being served. Isn't that right, Mr. Jones?" Sny shot another glance at Tiffany. She raised an eyebrow at him that expressed surprise and a certain grudging hopefulness. Her chin lifted. She seemed to grow in her chair.

Carl interrupted them. He stood and cupped his hands around his mouth and hollered down to the shore, "How is it?"

One of the men in the white smocks held his nose and shook his head emphatically. Another, a tall, balding man in a dark blue sport coat, seemed to be questioning the other man.

Sny peered down at the man. "Say," he said, "isn't that Jim Gardiner, the county D.A.?"

"That's him," Carl said.

"Nice fellow, nice fellow," Sny said. "Looks like you got yourself into a little hot water this weekend, eh, Mason?" He let out a laugh that sounded to Carl like a fart.

"So, back to business," he continued. "The bottom line is this: You will no longer operate this campground, Mr. Mason. Plain and simple. Furthermore, we want to buy you out." He watched Carl's face again and saw it redden. "Now Larry here suggested that twenty thousand dollars would be a fair price, but I'm not a man to hold a grudge. I think we can go to forty."

Tiffany Sny leaned forward in her chair and addressed Carl. "Just let me savor this moment," she said. "I believe those were your words not too, too long ago." With her lips together she gave him a broad smile, and then turned her head majestically away.

Just then the district attorney crossed the Camp Road, approaching the porch with long, deliberate strides. "Whoops," Sny said. "More company for Mr. Mason."

The D.A. shook his head as he mounted the steps. "No, sir, actually, we're here to see you."

Sny smiled playfully and held out his hand. "How goes the battle, Jim?" he said.

The D.A.'s face remained sober. He said, "Those men down there, Mr. Sny—they're from the state lab. Carl Mason called them this morning to come test his pond water. And they say the water is unfit."

Sny looked at Carl. He said, "*You* called them?"

Carl smiled. "I think he wants to know how much my partner paid you for the phony license."

Sny pointed a threatening finger. "You're playing with a libel suit, mister."

The policeman, Sgt. Pauley Johnson, climbed the steps. Sgt. Johnson was an old friend and bowling partner of Carl's. He turned to the handsome young man in shades and said, "Suppose you tell us, Larry."

"I didn't know it was against the law," the young man stammered. "Mr. Sny said the license cost five thousand bucks, so that's what I paid him."

Rutus Sny sprang to his feet. "What are you saying?" he shouted.

"Don't be preposterous!" Then he appealed to the D.A. "Come on, Jim, you know me better than that." Suddenly Sny's attorneys were leaning forward in their chairs, silencing their client.

But they couldn't silence his new partner.

"Yeah, I paid him five thousand dollars in cash, just last Saturday. But I didn't think we'd get into trouble."

"He's lying!" Sny blurted.

Then the smart-looking young woman by his side shook her head. "No, sir. He's telling the truth. I was there. He offered Mr. Sny two thousand dollars to falsify the permit, but Mr. Sny said he wanted five thousand." She turned and said, "Now, don't lie, Larry. You knew what you were doing. Take your punishment like a man."

The D.A. gestured to the officers. "Read them their rights, fellas," he said.

"No!" shouted Sny. "You can't pin this on me! This is entrapment! Entrapment!" He turned to leave the porch, but the big young deputy blocked his way.

Ruth continued: "Larry had to pay him four hundred dollars just to come out and do the test."

"Oh?" said the D.A., jotting the information down in a notepad. "And your name, please, ma'am?"

"I'm Mrs. June Jones," she said, "Larry's sister-in-law."

"I see. Is there anything else you'd like to add, Larry?"

"Yeah. Are we being arrested?"

"I'm afraid so," said the D.A.

"Then do you mind if I change out of these clothes? I promise I'll only be a minute." He shot a secret smile at Carl, a smile that revealed his missing tooth. Carl scowled at him and furtively shook off the smile.

"Okay," the D.A. agreed. "You've got one minute."

Officer Johnson escorted his limping prisoner to Angel's house. When they went inside, Angel winked at the policeman and pointed to a door. "In there."

Zippy opened the bedroom door and found Larry gagged and spread-eagled, each limb tied to a corner of the bed frame. Zippy took off his shades and said, "Hey, man, what happened to you?

They're all waiting for you out there." He untied his brother with one hand—the other hung limply by his side.

Larry stood and brushed off his suit. He looked at Zippy and shook his head. "That," he said with pride, "is one kinky lady." When he had examined himself in her full-length mirror, he opened the door to find Angel and Sgt. Johnson waiting for him. He said to Angel, "Hey, so where'd you go, anyway?" He greeted the policeman casually. "More questions about the other night, Pauley?" he said.

"Nope," the policeman said. "Actually, we've got a little surprise for you." He took Larry by the arm and walked him through Carl's backyard, around the store to the Camp Road, where Sny was already sitting in the back of the police car.

Larry looked at him, gave him the thumbs-up sign. "Travelin' in style these days, eh, Rutus? Hey, sorry I'm late, but I was . . . tied up." He shot Angel a crafty smile.

Sgt. Johnson said to his deputy, "You'd better read this one his rights again. He seems to have forgotten." He slapped Larry on the shoulder.

"Hey—" Larry protested.

"Bribing a public official," the deputy said, leading Larry to the police car. "That's bad news."

"What?" Larry demanded. "What's happenin' here?" He turned for an answer to Carl Mason, who was nonchalantly digging in his ear with his index finger. "Hey. Wait a minute," Larry said.

One of the men in white smocks stepped between them and said to Carl, "You realize, Mr. Mason, that we can't allow any public swimming in the pond until such time—"

"Yeah, yeah," Carl said, walking to the police car. "Thanks, fellas." As the deputy sat Larry in the back seat of the police car next to Rutus Sny, Carl strolled over to the car. He put his hands on the roof and bent to look in at the fuming, confused pair.

"Should've taken the twenty grand," he said to Larry. "Should of listened to me." He shook his head. "But I knew you wouldn't."

Shirley came off the porch and stood at Carl's side. She wrapped an arm around his waist. Angel came and stood at his other side. She put a hand on Carl's shoulder—he reached up and gave it a squeeze.

Harvey and Jean Duckoff joined them. Jean cupped her hands around her eyes and peered through the driver's window at the dashboard. Harvey pulled roughly at her ear, trying to dislodge a blackfly from its rim. Carl tousled Harvey's hair.

"My new partners," Carl said to Larry, as Zippy hobbled around the house with his arm over Ruth's shoulder for support.

Sny did a double take—he looked first at Larry, then at Zippy, and then back at Larry.

Carl smiled. "Quite a brainstorm I had, huh, fellas?"

Larry looked away. He caught his reflection in the rearview mirror and fixed his hair. A drop of perspiration rolled down his cheek.

Carl continued. "Now I don't suppose we'll be seeing you around here any more, Mr. L.A. Jones. I imagine you'll be taking to the long, high road. So I'd like to leave you with one last piece of advice."

Larry looked ahead, disinterested. "I'll be back," he sneered.

"I know you'll agree with me that this is real good advice, so pay attention, 'cause here it is: Larry, if you ever decide to buy into a business—let's say a campground, for example—just make darn sure that your money is clean." Carl smiled warmly. He pointed at Larry. "Think about it," he said.

Larry became indignant. "And what's that supposed to mean?"

"It means I know where your money came from." He pointed a thumb toward Angel. "But we won't discuss it in mixed company," Angel said, nodding to the policemen. "That is, if you'd rather not."

Larry glared at Angel; then, turning to Carl, his glare grew cocky. "Hey, pal, you can discuss anything you want. The joke's on you. So what if I did buy a share in your campground with dirty money? The money's in your pocket, now, and I don't even own that share anymore. I sold it to Rutus Sny—and you know his money is clean." He withdrew a folded paper from his pocket and held it up for Carl to see. "See? This is the share I own now—the one that Susie gave me Saturday night."

"Slight correction," Sny said, snatching the paper from Larry. "You sold both shares to me." He nudged Larry. "Didn't you, Mr. Jones?" He withdrew a piece of folded paper from his own shirt pocket and snapped it so it unfolded. It was the piece of notepad paper on which Carl had signed over a share of Wind In The Pines to Larry, and on which Larry had transferred the share to Sny. "This document says, quote, 'I hereby transfer my interest in Camp Wind In The Pines to Rutus Sny, effective May twenty-seventh.' That's today, isn't it?" He held up the paper for Larry, and then Carl, to inspect. "Well?" he said to Larry, waiting for a reaction.

But Larry only scowled in thought.

"C'mon, Larry, where's that business sense of yours? Look, you got Susie's share two days ago—on May twenty-fifth. And today your interest in the property transfers to me—both shares. See? You signed it." Sny held up both documents. "Am I right, Mr. Jones? Mr. Mason? All fair and square?"

Larry gazed upon the documents with disbelief.

Sny turned haughtily to Carl, a slow, mean smile developing on his face. "And as our former partner said, Mr. Mason, my money is clean—clean as the driven snow." He winked at Carl and laughed loudly.

Carl registered no expression. He raised his head and stared blankly over the car roof at the pond. His throat closed. He breathed deeply, as if the wind had been knocked out of him.

Sny smiled. "So, my friend and partner—my suddenly very silent partner—and soon-to-be very ex-partner—what more can I say? You should have taken the sixty thousand when I offered it to you. But I knew you wouldn't." He flashed a triumphant smile at Carl, then at Larry, and then he laughed again.

"Sixty thousand?" Angel mumbled to herself.

Sny continued: "I'll be back momentarily, as soon as this little misunderstanding is cleared up. And then we'll sit down together and discuss the dissolution of Camp Dump In The Pines—"

"That's it!" Angel blurted. "The silent partner." She turned in a circle, ruminating, nodding her head. She let out a small, self-deprecating laugh and cuffed her own forehead. "I can't believe I didn't see it," she said. She squeezed Carl's arm, nudging him aside, and said into the car window, "Slight correction, Rutie. I wouldn't say your money was clean as the driven snow—though I must admit it is an apt choice of words." She reflected for a moment, then whistled softly. "In fact," she said, now addressing the policemen, "boys, could you give us a minute to ourselves here?" They turned doubtfully, but Angel coaxed them out of the cruiser with a wink of her eye.

Then she said to Sny, "Rutie, I have this boyfriend—a business associate of Mr. L.A. Jones—and I'll bet he's a business associate of yours, too." Sny looked doubtfully at Larry, scowled in puzzlement, and shrugged his shoulders. "Seems he did quite the little business deal with Mr. Jones a couple of weeks ago—more than two hundred thousand dollars, isn't that right, Larry?"

Larry looked away. "You can't prove anything," he said.

"You know my friend. His name is Pinky."

"Never heard of him," said Larry.

"No? How about you, Rutie? He wears a pink suit, pink-tinted glasses, drives a brand-new pink Trans-Am. You know him, don't you?"

Sny's lips tightened; his eyes grew fixed and grim. "Never saw him before."

Harvey interrupted. "I seen that car," he said. "Spoke wheels, right?"

Angel nodded. "That's the one."

Harvey said, "L.A., you remember that pink Trans-Am. I seen you talkin' to a guy in it right over there. Just a couple weeks ago." Sny shot a startled glance at Larry Jones. Angel continued: "And right after Pinky's visit to Wind In The Pines, Mr. High Roller Jones here went out and bought a new Mercedes, a diamond ring, and a share in this campground—not what I'd call real discreet, Larry. Coincidentally, on that same day, our friend Pinky started flooding the entire county in cocaine."

Larry and Sny shifted in the back seat. Larry crossed his legs. Sny uncrossed his. They both kept their eyes on the policemen.

"Naturally," Angel continued, "when I heard about Pinky's acquisition, I felt compelled to pay him a visit."

"Naturally," said Larry and Rutus in low, humorless voices.

"Now, boys, I was curious, that's all. But Pinky was pretty tight-lipped—I couldn't get much out of him, except that he had what he called a silent partner—somebody who bankrolled him two hundred and forty thousand dollars for the weekend—for a sizable profit."

Sny watched out the window, still pretending disinterest, but sweat was rolling down his red face in rivulets. He cleared his throat. "Are you quite finished with this nonsense?"

Angel smiled. "I have another boyfriend, Rutie, a relative of yours—a Mr. Ed Stevens, president of the Bluffton County Savings Institution. He told me that he made you a very large, very unreported, very illegal cash loan a couple of weeks ago—two hundred and forty thousand dollars—just a weekend loan, mind you. You told him you needed cash to flash under Mason's nose, to get Wind In The Pines from him. Funny thing is, you never offered Carl Mason that much money. You only offered him sixty thousand, like you just said. Makes me wonder what you really needed two hundred and forty grand for, you know?"

Sny bristled. "I've listened to about enough of your kangaroo-court shenanigans—"

"Gentlemen of the jury," she interrupted, folding her hands, "I rest my case."

Jean Duckoff began applauding, but cut it short.

Carl came to the window and leaned in. "Let's save ourselves a lot of needless trouble, Sny. Why don't you just give those papers to me." He held out his hand.

Rutus looked wan. He turned a threatening stare at Angel, but the expression quickly wilted. He rubbed his mouth roughly with the back of his hand. "Not on your life," he croaked. "It's all circumstantial—there's not a thread of solid evidence here. And there's not a single witness who would testify against me—they'd incriminate themselves if they did."

"I would," Harvey said.

Sny scoffed, dismissing the boy with the back of his hand.

"So would I," said Larry.

Sny glared at him. And then his business-wise, bankrupt gaze settled on Angel.

She smiled. "You know I will."

Carl snapped his fingers. "Come on, Rute, let's have 'em."

Rutus Sny clutched the documents.

Carl said, loud enough for the policemen to hear, "Or maybe you'd rather let these guys in on our little secret?" He waved to the policemen. "Hey, fellas," he called, "I think Mr. Sny has something to say to you."

They walked back to their car and looked in at the first selectman. "Mr. Sny?" the sergeant said.

Sny fidgeted. His moist upper lip quivered. He began breathing heavily through his nose. His eyes grew distant and pained.

Carl reached into the back seat and gently pried the papers from his fingers. "Mum's the word," he said with a wink. Then to the policemen: "I guess he doesn't have anything to say after all." Sgt. Johnson got in and started the car. "Take 'er easy, boys," Carl said, as the cruiser pulled slowly up the Camp Road and drove out of Wind In The Pines.

"Who's got a match?" Carl asked. Harvey pulled a pack from his pants pocket. "Thank you, my good man," Carl said, preparing to torch the documents in his hand.

"Excuse me," a voice called. Carl turned around. A man and a boy were standing on the office porch; dressed in high rubber fishing boots and tan canvas fishing vests. The man's fishing hat was lined with trout hooks and spinners. A woman waited in their idling car beside the office. "We'd like a campsite for a couple of days," the man called. "You open for business?"

Carl snorted, suppressing a bitter laugh. He turned away from them, shaking his head. "Christ," he muttered. "Now you can't keep 'em away."

He looked out at his pond, at the sunlight flickering off it. He recalled how it had seemed covered in fire a couple of nights ago, reflecting the blaze on the ridge, and gazed up at the blackened ridge and at the charred wigwam there. He thought sadly of Nighthawk. He thought of his daughter Susie on her way to Fort Lauderdale; thought of Larry Jones and Rutus Sny on their way to the county jail; he recalled the night Hammer, pinned to the wall by an arrow, blasted his own foot away with a shotgun; he remembered Angel's trailer exploding and the Jones cabin burning; he remembered the way his pond had looked covered with silvery, dead fish; he thought of

Dolly Root cemented at the shore; of Harvey Duckoff getting beaten up by an angry, fishless mob; the rampaging moose; Gunnar. . . . He spat on the ground.

But then he recalled the look on Shirley's face when they had first driven into Wind In The Pines. It was the same look she had worn when they were first married: daring and independent. And proud. And that's how he had felt, too. Now she was behind him again, massaging his shoulders, her thumbs kneading the back of his neck.

He lit the match. He turned back to the campers, papers aflame in his hand. "Yeah," he called. "We're open. And the fish are biting."

Epilogue

Spring again. Harold Jones opened the front door for his wife, and she pecked his lips as she went out. He spotted a dandelion poking through the daffodil patch beside the front door and pulled it.

"See you tonight," June said with a smile. She got into her car with difficulty—her tight skirt and high heels didn't help. "If you need me," she said, "I'll be in town all morning. We've got a sales meeting." She turned on the ignition and the Cadillac purred out of their driveway.

Nearly four years had passed since she'd come down off the mountain—that's how they referred to her metamorphosis on Lookout Hill—when she had found her new direction: cosmetics. She had become a door-to-door cosmetics saleslady, and in just three years had set a company sales record.

Yes, a lot had changed since then. For one thing, Zippy had finally agreed to go by his birth name, Harold; and to wear "nice" clothes; and to swear off LSD; and space travel. They weren't diffi-cult concessions—except the part about the clothes—he loosened the necktie knot at his throat and unbuttoned his collar button. (He would remember to fix them before she came home.) But he hadn't agreed to keep his hair cut. In fact, after he'd been shot he vowed never again to cut his hair—or shave his face—so his beard was full and gray-streaked, and his thinning black hair, pulled back in a ponytail, hung down past his shoulder blades.

And that was June's concession to him. In addition, she agreed to wear no makeup or high heels around the house. But he didn't hold her to it all the time. Because she worked hard. And she came home tired lots of times. And she banked every spare dime she made—six thousand dollars now—in the hopes of someday putting a down payment on a house of their own.

Yes, a lot had changed. He followed her trail of dust up the Camp Road, while inside their cabin, deep in the corner of the bedroom closet, inside a cardboard box, four little red lights blinked silently on a black, zinc-lined box. A thin dark wire came out of the back of the cardboard box and disappeared through a hole low in the wall, emerging outside the cabin at ground level and snaking its way under a thin cover of earth and pine needles all the way to the Camp Road, where it burrowed under five inches of gravel and headed for the Root estate.

The Roots were still the same, basically. The UNWaNTed PeTS LaiD AWay sign still adorned their front lawn, the home business just as slow as ever. But Slug and Junior were out of the state pen, and so the family fencing operation was prospering. Earl and Dolly could afford dinner at Bonanza twice a week these days.

Earl was just coming outside now in boxer shorts and a torn, grayed tee-shirt, stalking his satellite dish with an adjustable wrench when Zippy walked away.

"Careful," Zippy called. "You don't want to damage it."

"Friggin' piece of junk," Earl muttered. "She's slippin' some awful on me lately. Every mornin' I come out here and she's pointin' straight up in the sky. And all you get up there is jibbuh-jabbuh."

"You never know," Zippy said.

Yes, things had changed. The ridgetop had grown back thick and motley green in sapling birch, spruce, and pine. The old wigwam had been made an ivy-covered shrine. Carl had chosen to build no campsites up there.

Carl and Shirley Mason wintered every year with Susie and her little girl in a Fort Lauderdale trailer park—they were due back shortly. Weasel, their granddaughter's natural father, was dead—executed shortly before her birth in a Miami cocaine war.

Harvey and Jean Duckoff were the off-season managers of Camp Wind In The Pines now. They had five children already, and another on the way. When the floor had fallen through their trailershack, Carl let them move into the big log cabin by the marsh—the one that had been built for Larry and Susie.

Harold hadn't heard from Larry since the arrest, but he had learned from his parents that, following a suspended-sentence judgment in his bribery charge, his brother had gone to Dallas and bought into a bootleg videotape company which failed. The last they had heard, he was a male stripper in Los Angeles by the name of "L.A. Lancelot."

Rutus Sny had also been given a suspended sentence in the case, and of course relieved of his duties in town government. His wife Tiffany had made him third-shift supervisor at Stevens' Cotton Mill and then kicked him out of the house.

Mr. Rogers was recuperating from a liver operation, but, as always, he remained in high, optimistic spirits.

Angel moved to Saint-Tropez after delivering Jean Duckoff's first set of twins, where she lived for a while in a tent. A couple of months later she was involved in a minor scandal with a Greek and a Soviet ambassador. The last anybody had heard, she was living in splendor in a spacious beachfront villa.

Harold reached the end of the Camp Road. He looked up and down the River Road, then swiped the SWIMMING PROHIBITED. WATER UNFIT poster from the Camp Billboard. He stuffed it in his pocket.

Then he checked the mailbox. As always, bills, bills, bills, bills. And, as always, nothing from Johnny Cash, nothing from Merle Travis, nothing from Dolly Parton (he was into country music these days), nothing from Carl Sagan. But then he came across a strange letter addressed to "Mr. Zippy Jones." Hmm. He scratched behind his ear. Nobody called him Zippy these days. He tore open the envelope and read:

SAMCO NOVELTY, INC.
319 Hollywood Blvd.
Suite 3001
Albany, NY 12204

Dear Mr. Zippy Jones:

I certainly hope this letter finds its way to you. Please forgive us for the long delay, but patent searches, product compatibility, product feasibility, and test marketing all take more time than any of us seem to expect. And you neglected to include your address in your query letter to us, so locating you also took some time.

We are referring, as you know, to your "Bug Shaver" design. We certainly hope you haven't become frustrated and sold the patent to another manufacturer.

If you are still interested in our company, Mr. Jones, please accept the enclosed advance check for five thousand dollars, and be assured that our royalty rates are second to none. Be assured also that if you accept our offer, production of the "Bug Shaver" will start immediately.

We would very much like to have you on our "team," Mr. Jones, and we sincerely hope you feel the same way about us.

Please contact us toll-free, 1-800-555-4342, with your decision, at your earliest convenience.

Sincerely,

Bud

Buddy Samuels
President
SAMCO NOVELTY, INC.

Zippy's heart raced. He read the letter twice. And he studied the check to make sure it wasn't one of those contest gimmicks. Then he put his head back, buttoned his collar button, and tightened the knot on his necktie. He stuffed the letter and check into his back pocket and looked south down the River Road. A car was coming up, heading for town. He stuck out his thumb.